The Second Coming of Eve

Volume 1

The Long Road Home

By A.P. Cruickshank

New Generation Publishing

Also Published by A.P. CRUICKSHANK

No Turning Back
The Betrayal of Innocence
From the Smallest of Beginnings

For further information please go to:

www.apcruickshank.co.uk
www.apcruickshank.com

'As the pre-eminent species on the planet, we have spent millennia destroying the very thing that sustains our lives and safeguards our futures, so is there little wonder the Gods have washed their hands of the human race and all its overindulgences?

By ridding Earth of such a self-destructive, egoistic yet indifferent influence, Mother Nature will be offered the time and opportunity to make good the colossal damage inflicted by humans, and although it will probably take tens, if not hundreds of thousands of years, this awe-inspiring world will one day be healed and returned to its former glory.'

Part 1

The Boy

Chapter 1

Horatio Mott was considered a loner. As one of the few young people of his generation who had no affinity with the multitude of social media outlets on offer, or for that matter, with any other part of what he viewed as the juvenile behaviour of his peers, it was hardly surprising he had few friends.

When aged twelve, he was eventually told to leave St. Indract's, an Independent School not far from the Somerset town of Glastonbury, no one who knew him was the least bit surprised. If truth be known, the final act by the headmaster could easily have taken place appreciably earlier.

The problem was that unlike his older siblings, twins Rachael and Thomas, Horatio was simply not cut out for living twenty-four seven, in a residential institution. After many discussions and much soul-searching, he may have come to understand his parents' decision to send him away, but that didn't make it any easier to accept.

As with his brother and sister, Horatio was innately bright with enormous potential, however, that is where any similarity ended. Unlike Thomas and Rachael, Horatio was disruptive, wilful and morose and from almost the moment he dropped his trunk on his bed in the dormitory, it was clear he rejected all the codes of behaviour demanded or attitude to work expected by the school authorities.

Even though he cruised through the entrance exam, scoring higher than any of the other candidates, the pattern of his primary school reports describing him as disinterested in the extreme, persisted at his new school. It was abundantly clear Horatio was only prepared to study when he was interested and felt like it, resulting in him simply opting out of subjects he found tedious or undemanding.

On his arrival at St. Indract's aged eleven, it took little time for the majority of his teachers to come to the opinion that what was being asked of Horatio was beyond him, not necessarily in terms of the rigours of learning, simply his commitment to do so. Plus, to make matters worse, his siblings, who were four years older, had established strong friendships with other pupils and were popular with just about the entire school community.

There were though, a few teachers who attempted to excuse Horatio's apparent indifference by putting forward the argument that it was only to be expected, especially early on, when he was living in the shadow of his brother and sister. Unfortunately, at least for Horatio, it was a belief that almost certainly delayed the inevitable.

In the end, whatever the reasons, Horatio was a child who refused to conform or make any genuine effort to become part of school life. From the word go, he decided boarding school was not for him and that really was an end to it.

The difficulty for his parents, and to a lesser extent his new school, was that prior to joining St. Indract's, Horatio had appeared to be a relatively contented child. He had always lived in Somerset in the village of Berrow and their house was just a five minute walk from open countryside and a two minute walk from a sandy beach, which ran for over ten kilometres from Burnham-on-Sea to Brean Down.

Except for the fact he was made to attend the local primary school, his childhood was just about perfect. Whatever the weather, Horatio would spend his free time swimming in the sea, if he could get his parents to watch over him, playing in the sand dunes that ran adjacent to the beach, or just roaming the local area searching for species of birds, insects and animals he had not come across before.

Horatio was fascinated by all forms of wildlife, sea life and plant life, always returning home with a list of questions for his parents or to look up on the internet. When something caught his imagination, Horatio's desire to learn more was limitless and his search for answers insatiable.

*   *   *

Horatio's parents, Peter and Jessica Mott, were both specialists in the study of endangered birds and worked in the David Attenborough complex at Bristol University. Peter was a senior lecturer, Jessica a Research Reader and although they usually travelled to work together, they saw little of each other during the day.

Both accepted that their lives could be so much easier if they moved closer to the university and got rid of the time-consuming and tedious commute, however, that was not their priority. Even allowing for the fact that some of their research, especially in Jessica's case, could be done from home, the decision not to move closer to work was for their children.

From the outset, it was expected that Rachael and Thomas would flourish at school and this proved to be the case; leaving their parents determined not to do anything which might disrupt their education.

However, when it came to their youngest, the situation was the exact opposite. Unlike the twins, who were happy and positive, Jessica and Peter had genuine concerns about Horatio; especially his inability to interact positively with children of his own age. A revealing instance of this was at the local swimming club. Even though Horatio proved to be an extremely capable swimmer and enjoyed attending twice a week, he still made no close friend, girl or boy, from those of his age who attended.

Certainly his refusal to be involved in any opportunity, either curricular or extra-curricular at his primary school, a fact repeatedly commented on in his teachers' reports, didn't help.

And, just to add to his parents' quandary, Horatio appeared a happy child; never more so than when he was following his own interests.

At the end of the day, most had to agree with the twins when they explained candidly that it was best not to interfere and to leave him be; it was just 'Horatio being Horatio'.

Nevertheless, on a more official level, it was agreed by his teachers and parents that Horatio's issues were not due to some deep-rooted problem, rather the result of him being immature, something he would grow out of, eventually.

*   *   *

During the Easter holiday, just after Horatio had celebrated his eleventh birthday on the twenty-second of March and just before the twins celebrated their fifteenth birthday on May the third, the three siblings were confronted with the most unexpected news possible.

Whilst they were eating their Sunday lunch, their father told them that he had been offered a unique opportunity by the university. The twins were immediately interested, especially when he added that part of the offer included being able to work alongside their mother on a permanent basis.

Horatio's response however, was markedly less than enthusiastic.

"So what's the catch?" he asked.

Peter smiled as he had anticipated a moody reaction from his youngest.

"Well... if we accept," he replied, "it will mean some fairly major changes in our lives."

"Like what?" Horatio demanded.

"You two," Peter said, turning to the twins, "will have to switch from weekly to full boarding and you Horatio will have to join your brother and sister at St. Indract's."

"No way!" Horatio stated petulantly. "I don't care where you're going so why can't I come with you?"

"Well… that would be difficult. You see, we'll be living and working on an uninhabited island in the Cape Verde Islands.

"Where on Earth is that?" Thomas asked and Horatio answered dismissively,

"Don't you know anything? It's in the Atlantic Ocean, off the west coast of Africa."

"Uninhabited?" Rachael said, and when her father nodded, she added, "How cool is that?"

"But they must have schools on the larger islands, especially Santiago Island, which is where the capital Praia is?"

The twins looked at their brother with their usual mix of irritation and disbelief, Horatio was clearly not giving up on his idea of moving with his parents.

"They do," his father replied. "But, unfortunately it would not be practical for you as we will be based on the isolated island of Ilhéu de Cima."

*   *   *

That evening, the twins were clearly thrilled with the news and talked incessantly, not only about boarding full time, but also about visiting the island during the long summer holidays and even began planning their first trip.

Rachael wanted to know whether there would be running water and electricity, plus what they would eat and a thousand other things, leaving her parents laughing at her enthusiasm.

Horatio though, was inconsolable. He remained in his room, struggling to believe that his parents would actually make him leave the house that had always been his home.

7

Not only that, but he would also be taken away from the sea, the beach, the fields and all the other things he loved; and, to make it far, far worse, they were replacing all these things with a boarding school.

*   *   *

The following day over breakfast, all the chat between the twins and their parents again revolved around the island, the work they would be doing and what life-style they would have.

Horatio sat silently, looking miserable.

After the kitchen table had been cleared and the plates washed, Peter and Jessica asked their children to remain at the table.

"We know how unhappy you are about what's happening," their father began, looking at Horatio. "So we need to talk. But, it's only fair your brother and sister hear what we have to say."

Horatio just shrugged his shoulders and remained silent.

"We have never for a moment considered leaving this house," his mother began gently, "and…, well, we never applied for this or any other job. In fact, over the last few years there have been opportunities for us to say no, or to move on, but we always turned them down and the reason was you three. This time though, we're sorry but… the offer is really too important for us to turn down."

"How come?" Horatio asked with slightly less venom than earlier. Unknown to the rest of the family, he had spent the previous evening researching the Cape Verde Islands and was struggling to hide his interest in the possibility that his parents might actually move there.

"Well… your father and I are being given a joint contract, meaning we can work together, and, that work includes research that is extremely important to both of us."

The three siblings sat attentively, even Horatio was desperate to know more.

"Your father has been working with a team of colleagues on the planning and logistics of this project for over two years but we... well he, never thought he would be offered the overall leadership of the programme. If we do accept, there is a good chance it could lead to a professorship for your father." She reached across and took hold of her husband's hand and smiled.

"The research will be vital," their father quickly added, clearly uncomfortable at the mention of promotion, "As you already know, too many species of birds face possible extinction and sadly for some, their chances of survival are almost non-existent, their situation is at a critical point.

So... we'll be leading a team of scientists, all rare bird specialists and will be living and working just metres from some of the most endangered birds on the entire planet."

The twins mouthed 'wow' together and even Horatio was obviously fascinated.

"However, and here's the problem," their mother explained, "The location of the project is this uninhabited island of Ilhéu de Cima."

"I know of it," Horatio said, as he opened up his tablet and went on line. His parents smiled, whilst his brother and sister both looked at the ceiling with an expression of 'here we go again', on their faces.

"Look, here it is," Horatio said eagerly and began quoting from the site, "Ilhéu de Cima forms part of the Cape Verde Islands. It's located four kilometres east of Ilhéu Grande and eight kilometres northeast of the island of Brava. Also..." he looked at his parents, managing a smile as he read, "it is west of, and quite close to, the larger island of Fogo. Its capital is Sao Filipe and it has an airport."

Not finished by any means he then explained for the benefit of his uninformed siblings,

"Ilhéu de Cima is tiny." then again looking at his parents, added, "It's just a kilometre long and only six hundred metres across and... there are no communication links."

Both parents complimented Horatio, **realising their youngest was showing serious interest in where they would be living, even if they knew he resented being left behind.**

"At the island's south east," Horatio pressed on, much to the growing irritation of the twins, "is the only bay and at the opposite end, eighty metres above sea level, is a lighthouse. Now... this is really interesting. The island is well known for its unique seabird colonies and was made a Nature Reserve in 1990."

"And that's when many of the problems began," his father said. "You see, it's all very well creating Nature Reserves but they will make little difference to the survival of wildlife if there is no way of enforcing the law. For Ilhéu de Cima, the problem has been local fishermen. For as long as anyone can remember, they have raided the seabird colonies to steal the eggs and kill larger birds for food."

Chapter 2

Horatio arrived at St Indract's to begin his boarding school education on the second of September, the same day the twins also became full boarders and Peter and Jessica Mott finally had the time and opportunity to prepare for their move to Ilhéu de Cima.

The date for them to leave the UK was the seventh of January, only four months away, so having the house to themselves for just about the first time ever, was a real treat.

They visited the school every weekend to take the three children out for the day, or to watch one of the numerous sporting or musical events in which the twins were invariably involved.

Initially, Horatio appeared to settle in reasonably well, however, little did the rest of his family know that within just the first twenty four hours, he had managed to upset most of the boys in his dormitory. It wasn't that he was aggressive, a bully or loud, it was quite the opposite; Horatio was simply not willing to talk to anyone, leaving those around him with the impression the new boy was seriously odd. This view was reinforced whenever he was in the dorm, when he sat on his bed with his back turned away from the room and surfed the internet on his phone or tablet. He was seen as deliberately ignoring the other boys.

Up to arriving at St Indract's, Horatio had rarely been attracted to social media or the multitude of devices and apps available, that is unless it helped answer any of his endless list of queries on one of his pet subjects. However, all that changed when he realised by using headphones with his mobile or tablet, he could have the privacy and solitude he craved.

*   *   *

The October half-term break came and went with the twins continuing to be painfully enthusiastic about everything to do with St. Indract's and their future holidays on the island. However, with Peter and Jessica Mott being so worried about Horatio's uncertain start at his new school, their short time together was not that enjoyable.

At one moment, when alone with the twins, they had tried to talk about their concerns but were told in no uncertain terms by Rachael that her brother had quickly gained a reputation for being an oddball. Thomas then explained that unlike some of the other 'problem kids', who caused trouble to prove themselves and get accepted by the other pupils, with Horatio it was quite the opposite; he never misbehaved, never upset people and never got involved in anything, let alone troublemaking.

With no attempt to understand what might be going on inside Horatio's head, the twins went on to describe how they had tried to warn him, but along with everyone else, he ignored them. He was behaving like he didn't care, rejecting all attempts to include him in the life of the school and appeared determined to cut himself off from everyone and everything on offer.

*   *   *

A couple of days before returning to school, Horatio and his parents went for a walk on Berrow beach. When his father asked him how things were going Horatio told them gruffly he was fine, and, from then on, every attempt either parent made to encourage him to talk about school, ended with the same answer; 'he was just fine'.

In the end, his exasperated mother said,

"You know we're worried about you?"

"Why?" Horatio answered guardedly.

"Well, we've been told…"

"By Thomas and Rachael, I suppose."

"They did mention a few things," his mother answered honestly. "But also, when we picked you up, a couple of your teachers including Mr. Young, your housemaster, mentioned that there were a few concerns."

Both parents could see tears growing in their son's eyes and both moved at the same time towards him. As they did, Horatio stepped backwards, wiped his face and sounding far older than his eleven years, said,

"Look… everything's fine. Don't worry. Soon you'll move to the island and start something that's incredibly important to both of you and… and… I would never do anything to stop that happening."

Without waiting, Horatio then ran back to his bedroom where he proceeded to rip up the homework he had been working on during the break.

*   *   *

Over Christmas and New Year, the last school holiday before Jessica and Peter left the UK, the three weeks at home proved a disaster for everyone. The twins were clearly ignoring their younger brother, explaining with little sentiment that he deserved whatever he got; they had tried to help him at school, but he disregarded any advice they gave him.

Extremely anxious and unsure what to do, Peter and Jessica endeavoured to moderate any excitement about the move to Cape Verde, instead focusing all their time on the children, but even in this, they failed.

As team leaders for the research camp being set up, every day one or the other was required to resolve any last minute questions or glitches that arose.

Rachael and Thomas were quite happy, spending most of their time ignoring their brother and his moods, working for up and coming exams or just talking to their friends.

13

Horatio, on the other hand, seemed determined to snub everyone, spending virtually the entire holiday in his room reading or on line. When he did eventually emerge, usually for meals, he was morose and withdrawn.

Sadly, Christmas day proved no better, leaving Peter and Jessica Mott wondering if they were about to make the biggest mistake of their entire lives.

*   *   *

The children returned to school in the first week of January and the concerns surrounding Horatio persisted. If his teachers tried to talk to him he was disinterested to the point of being rude, however, early in the term, a bright spot began to appear on the horizon.

At primary school, when he'd first been introduced to French, Horatio had proved innately gifted at both learning and retaining the language; in fact, it was one of the few subjects where the teacher was able to write something positive in his final report.

It stated that he had a promising aptitude for foreign languages, and, if his interest endured at his new school, Horatio might become a more than capable linguist.

Having discovered from his parents that Portuguese was the main language spoken on the Cape Verde Islands, once he was at St. Indract's with all the resources available to him, he began researching the origins of both French and Portuguese; quickly becoming enthralled by the shear brilliance of the Romans.

Horatio being Horatio, once he got started he was hooked and his admiration for the Romans grew as he unearthed a link between French, Portuguese and ancient Rome. He learnt that both languages were part of the Romance Languages which had originated from Vulgar Latin, a term discovered in writings from the ninth century. Horatio especially loved the fact a language could be called 'vulgar'.

However, it was at this stage, he began to struggle and knew if he wanted to continue to widen his understanding, especially of Portuguese, he needed help.

* * *

Miss Stanley was one of the language specialists at St. Indract's and she quickly saw that for an eleven year old, Horatio had a voracious appetite for searching out facts, as well as a rare desire to learn about the origins of languages.

After discussing this with her Head of Department the two of them agreed Horatio's curiosity for their subject might just be the making of him. As a result, she gave him a number of books from the department library, plus various apps and websites to research, telling him that in return she expected him to document all his discoveries.

A delighted Horatio went back to work determined to find out as much as he could about the Portuguese spoken in his parents' new home, and, to Miss Stanley's surprise, he recorded all his findings and results.

* * *

Peter and Jessica Mott finally left England on the seventh of January and Horatio was beside himself. It certainly didn't help that the twins seemed to be just getting on with their lives as normal, which merely added to Horatio's hatred of the world around him.

At night he would lie in bed imagining his parents in Cape Verde beginning their new lives and was happy for them. But, no matter how much he tried to be positive, no matter how much he pretended everything was just fine, he simply could not break the endless cycle of misery and loneliness that overwhelmed him.

Horatio knew the only solution was to be back living with his parents, but he also understood it was not going to happen.

On one evening a week, all three children spoke to their parents via a satellite link and those moments were wonderful. Yet, for Horatio, as soon as the call ended and the twins had disappeared back to their friends, he was left feeling abandoned and his weekly contact with his parents merely added to his loneliness.

*   *   *

As January moved into February, Horatio spent most of his time in the library continuing to ignore all attempts by his brother and sister, or other pupils, to involve him in the numerous school activities on offer.

There was though one person with whom he was spending more and more time talking to, his language teacher Miss Stanley and inevitably, this led to more jokes and even more low level bullying at his expense. But Horatio really didn't care, he ignored the taunting, accepting that whatever the negatives in his life, he had found a way to survive under what he saw as the most punishing of conditions.

By mid-February, his fascination with Latin based languages had grown to such an extent that he was attempting to teach himself Portuguese, in addition to refining his timetabled French. He had also begun to look into Spanish, another of the Romance Languages originating from the time the Romans ruled Western Europe, and he was frequently in need of Miss Stanley's guidance.

One morning break, when she was on playground duty, he told her he'd found an article explaining that as far back as the beginning of the third century B.C., ancient Latin had been introduced to the whole of the Iberian Peninsula by Roman soldiers. Miss Stanley listened to Horatio's findings and seeing his need to delve deeper, decided to play devil's advocate. She suggested that if his assertions were correct, then how did he manage to explain the significant differences between Portuguese and other Romance languages such as French and Spanish? She argued that if they had all originated from the same source, as he claimed, then they should sound more similar.

And, of course, Horatio took the bait.

The following day, he sought out Miss Stanley and clearly thrilled, explained to her that Portuguese had only developed as a separate language when the Romans had lost the Western Empire to German invaders. He described how once the barbarian invasion, as it was known, had been completed, the languages under the control of the new rulers began to move away from traditional Latin. He went on to describe how that resulted in some modern day languages evolving from a combination of the original Latin dialects, mixed with strong influences such as German; this he added, partly explained the guttural emphasis of spoken Portuguese.

Miss Stanley was impressed and told Horatio to see her in the main language lab after school. He duly turned up to find her with Mr Henshaw, the Head of Languages. Without any warning, he was asked to describe what he had discovered about Modern Western European Languages and for the next fifteen minute he did just that, not only surprising himself, but confounding both adults.

*   *   *

The February half-term holiday proved just as wonderful for Horatio as he had hoped, even the twins clearly loving having their parents' home. Though just a short break, the family spent the entire week doing things together and Horatio, to his parents' joy and siblings' disbelief, joined in everything.

However, when the time came to return to school, Horatio felt crushed; his dark mood becoming noticeably worse when the children were told by their mother that the plan for the family to be together on the island for the Easter holidays had to be put on hold.

It seemed Peter and Jessica had encountered a series of unforeseen problems with the local authorities over the constructing of buildings and both had to accept that by the March school holiday the new accommodation would not be ready to receive visitors.

None of this helped the fact that the trip was to be part of a delayed twelfth birthday present for Horatio and it merely deepened his hatred of the school.

*   *   *

For the first two weeks back after the few days break in February, Horatio spoke to no one; his entire time was spent on his phone or tablet, listening to an eclectic mix of both contemporary and classical music, being angry or crying.

Every attempt by Miss Stanley to reignite Horatio's enthusiasm for languages fell on deaf ears and so serious was her concern that she spoke to Mr Young, his housemaster; but as with everyone else, he had no answers. Worryingly, Horatio's determination to withdraw from school life came over as a permanent state of affairs.

Music was perfect for him; it needed no one else's involvement and at least gave him a little solace from his misery. Uncharacteristically though, at no time did Horatio feel like researching facts or information on the subject; only genuinely concentrating on the summer holiday when at last he would join his parents on the Island of Ilhéu de Cima.

*   *   *

In the end, the Easter holiday was spent at the house in Berrow. His mother flew home to be with the three children and although Horatio adored being with her, he found it difficult not to feel bitter about the fact that not only was their trip to the island postponed but he would have to celebrate his twelfth birthday without his parents.

For Jessica, through no fault of her own, the three weeks at home proved emotionally unbearable. The twins, who were fifteen, nearly sixteen years old, wanted to spend most of their time with friends from St. Indract's who lived close by which resulted in Horatio being on his own unless she was at home; but even in this Jessica felt she had failed.

Most days Jessica was in the UK, she was expected to travel to the university in Bristol. She knew, and was frequently reminded by her bosses, how critical it was she make the most of every opportunity to promote the project.

From its inception, all connected with the Ilhéu de Cima proposal accepted finance would be a constant issue. Long-term research projects invariably depended on benefactors, therefore each and every occasion to update existing or new sponsors had to be grasped and being in the UK gave Jessica a chance to speak in person rather than by satellite link, to these crucial supporters.

*   *   *

It was hardly surprising therefore that as Horatio was driven back to St. Indract's for the summer term, he felt robbed. So many of his hopes and expectations had been dashed and once again his parents were a very, very long way away from him.

And his return to school was as people had come to expect from him; Horatio was antisocial in the extreme, communicated voluntarily with no one, and spent most of his free time on his phone or tablet.

Yet, for Horatio, it was not that simple. As the term got underway, he immediately knew he couldn't go on; somehow he had to get away.

That didn't mean he was not at fault and he was gracious enough to acknowledge that it was more than likely of his own making. Just maybe, if from the word go he had been friendlier, even participated in clubs and other school activities, his life might have been happier.

But it was far too late. Even if he had wanted to, which he didn't, Horatio had no idea how to take the first step to joining in; becoming part of the school community.

* * *

Quite unusually for Horatio, he remembered the twin's birthday on May the third and had written a card for each of them. When he eventually found Rachael, she was sat with a group of her friends in the courtyard, causing him to hesitate before approaching her. After a few moments though, Horatio decided he was being childish. However, as he walked towards his sister the group spotted him and began to snigger leaving him feeling utterly humiliated. Even though Rachael told her friends to be quiet, Horatio turned and quickly walked away, ripping up the birthday cards before dumping them in the nearest bin.

* * *

During that summer term, the majority of Horatio's teachers came to the conclusion that as his attitude had not improved a single jot since his first day, and the effort he was putting into his studies remained negligible, a recommendation should be made to the headmaster that his parents remove him from the school.

Mr. Young, Horatio's housemaster, whilst taking on board the views of his teachers, felt a pupil as innately bright as Horatio should be given additional time, allowing him to eventually see sense; he therefore chose not to pass staff reservations on to the Headmaster.

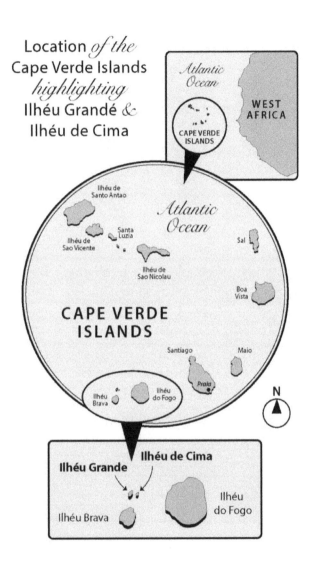

Location *of the*
Cape Verde Islands
highlighting
Ilhéu Grandé &
Ilhéu de Cima

Atlantic Ocean

WEST AFRICA

CAPE VERDE ISLANDS

Ilhéu de Santo Antao

Atlantic Ocean

Santa Luzia

Ilhéu de Sao Vicente

Sal

Ilhéu de Sao Nicolau

Boa Vista

CAPE VERDE ISLANDS

Santiago

Maio

Praia

Ilhéu Brava

Ilhéu do Fogo

N

Ilhéu de Cima

Ilhéu Grande

Ilhéu do Fogo

Ilhéu Brava

Chapter 3

At last, the moment Horatio had longed for arrived. Their mother picked them up from St Indract's front gate and after spending two nights in the Berrow house, sorting out the things to take with them, they headed for London Heathrow.

The flight to Portugal left on time and after a one hour wait in Lisbon they boarded a second plane to Praia, the capital of the Cape Verde Islands and principal city of Santiago Island.

Arriving just after midnight at the Nelson Mandela International Airport, they found their father waiting at the arrivals gate. At last the Mott family were all together and Horatio could not have been happier.

They spent that night in a hotel close to the town centre, shopped for supplies requested by the team on the Ilhéu de Cima in the morning and following lunch, caught a local flight to Sao Filipe on the Island of Fogo.

*   *   *

The flight lasted thirty minutes, with memorable views over the Atlantic Ocean and on arrival the Mott family passed through the airport with no hold ups to find their bags waiting for them by the exit.

The taxi drove them the three kilometres to the town centre and then on to the harbour which was old and run down. Horatio spotted a rusty, dilapidated car ferry about to leave for the island of Brava and he wondered whether they would be taking a similar boat for the last leg of their journey, however, they boarded a small motorboat instead.

Setting sail in conditions that were less than perfect, after a couple of hours Peter Mott pointed out two small dark shapes on the horizon and said enthusiastically,

"There... that's our new home."

Their mother then spoke over the sound of the engine,

"The one nearest us, see... that's Ilhéu de Cima; our island. The one further away... the larger one, that's Ilhéu Grande. The two are quite close together and although we live and work on the smaller one, we are hoping in the future to carry out research on Ilhéu Grande.

Our island, although very small and barren, is perfect for our needs."

Their father again pointed and said,

"If you look carefully you can see the lighthouse, and look, those small dark shapes next to it are the cottage and our base. That's where we live."

The nearer they sailed to the islands, the clearer the views became and it was quickly apparent Ilhéu de Cima was not going to be the paradise island the twins had envisaged. Interestingly though, as their enthusiasm faded, Horatio's excitement grew and rather unsteadily, he moved to the very front of the boat saying he wanted the best possible view as they docked.

As the motorboat swung away from Ilhéu Grande, Horatio decided it looked like half a large, roughed edged pebble, jutting out of the sea; whereas Ilhéu de Cima looked uncannily like a baseball cap with two flat peaks sticking out at opposite sides of a high mid-section. Those two ends were only just above sea-level and Horatio thought they might be swamped by the waves at any moment.

Pulling into a small bay, they grounded the boat on a small sandy beach and apart from the crew who tied ropes to secure the vessel, Horatio was first to jump off. As he walked up the beach he saw another craft tied up further out in the bay and he then sprinted up a steep path that led to the camp and lighthouse. As Horatio arrived at the top, his parents and even Thomas and Rachael, laughed at his impatience and followed him at a far more leisurely pace.

*   *   *

In total the three siblings spent two and a half weeks on the island, and the family all had very different opinions of how the holiday went.

Without question, Peter and Jessica loved having all three children with them, nevertheless it was impossible for them not to be especially overjoyed with the transformation of their youngest.

Just as unexpected though, was the way the twins struggled to adapt. As their parents looked on in disappointment, almost hourly the two eldest found something to moan about, even the simplest of chores.

Within a couple of days, Rachael and Thomas had made it apparent they were already fed up, and as a consequence, instead of mucking in with the team, spent as much time as they were allowed, chatting to friends on the satellite phone or on one of the computers.

Predictably, their attitude embarrassed Peter and Jessica and they knew they had to act. Telling Horatio to run some errands, they sat down with the twins.

Struggling to excuse their behaviour, Thomas and Rachael claimed they were no longer children, and all their hopes of a relaxing break from school and exams, had evaporated the instant they arrived.

Thomas, bordering on the disrespectful, added candidly that from their perspective, rather than visiting an idyllic island retreat, what they actually faced was an exceedingly uncomfortable, primitive 'resort'.

After some discussion, most of it constructive, the four decided the twins had failed to think through the reality of their parents' work, leaving them with unrealistic expectations and unprepared for life on the island.

*　　*　　*

In contrast to the twins, Horatio was in his element. From the second day onwards, early each morning, he would set off with either Libby, Simon or Francis, the researchers, and spend hours helping in any way he could. On the days he was with Simon, as he was a French national completing his Masters at Bath University, there was the added bonus of practising his French.

By the end of the first week, such was the impression he had made on the team, they renamed him 'H', much to his parent's delight and siblings' antipathy, but without doubt, the highlight of the holiday for Horatio was when Libby asked if he wanted to observe one of the rarest birds in the world.

Seizing the opportunity, the two of them then spent the day watching a narrow, rock ledge half way up a steep cliff.

"This is a breeding site of the Cape Verde Peregrine Falcon," Libby explained as they settled down to photograph a pair she wanted to study.

"If we are lucky, you will see not only one of the rarest land birds in the entire world, but one that you can only find on Ilhéu de Cima. You see, because they are non-migratory, they are, in effect stuck on the island and sadly at the mercy of the greatest of all predators, man. For our Falcons, it's the local fishermen."

Horatio vaguely remembered his father mentioning the local fishermen at home and was surprised when Libby described how it wasn't until the nineteen-sixties the existence of the Cape Verde Peregrine Falcon was formally accepted as a distinct species. She then added dishearteningly, that at that time there were thought to be only fifteen to twenty pairs left on the island, and therefore in the world.

"But, by nineteen ninety- four," she went on to explain, "Just a couple of decades later, the number had fallen to between six and eight pairs, and today, well... current estimates are that there may be as few as two pairs still around, and it's one of those pairs I'm interested in researching.

Leaning over the high cliff edge, roped on for safety, whilst in the most uncomfortable position he had ever experienced, Horatio was in heaven and though they never spotted a Peregrine Falcon, to him it just didn't matter; he was out in the open and helping the team study endangered birds; surely nothing could be better?

That evening, Horatio began researching the Cape Verde Peregrine Falcon and became both intrigued and dismayed by the difficulties facing such a stunning creature. Reading everything he could find, he learnt that all falcons, including their own kind, hatch their eggs on a ledge, high up amongst the cliffs. This confirmed Libby's explanation that over time they had hit upon the ingenious tactic to keep their eggs and chicks out of harm's way.

Finding endless related sites, Horatio kept researching, becoming ever more captivated by what he had come to realise was an amazing bird.

Falcons were not only a lethal assassin but the only bird to take most of its prey whilst in the air, and gruesome as this was, Horatio was riveted when one article described how all falcons used a similar method to kill. Setting out to hunt, they would fly high up in the sky before plunging down whilst constantly increasing their speed until they were travelling in excess of two hundred kilometres an hour. Pursuing a target, they would use their long, 'elasticated' hind toe to strike their prey, killing it outright.

Horatio also learnt that there were rare cases when falcons had been observed taking prey from the ground, even from water, which to him seemed somewhat logical. To survive on islands, surrounded by the sea, fish would have to form part of their diet.

*   *   *

Horatio's life-long interest in the Cape Verde Peregrine Falcons began that day, and it never faltered. That night, as he lay in bed unable to sleep from all the excitement, he challenged himself to become an expert on the birds. He decided if he worked really hard at gaining a thorough understanding of their lives and the difficulties they faced, when he was older, he might play a part in helping their survival.

Still unable to sleep, his next decision was to commit himself to recording his time on the island especially when observing the nest so the following day, feeling rather tired Horatio began to ask questions.

All five adults quickly realised his appetite for answers was insatiable and as with Miss Stanley they struggled to keep up. Nevertheless, none were willing to show any sign of annoyance and this was especially true of Libby, who after hearing about Horatio's problems at school, was genuinely pleased he had become so absorbed in his wish to support such an endangered species.

*　　　*　　　*

Sadly though, for Horatio, nothing was to last forever and it seemed he had only just begun exploring the island, when it was time to return to England.

Before leaving however, to his astonishment, Libby, Simon and Francis sat Horatio down and told him how much they had enjoyed his company. They thanked him for his work and quite unexpectedly presented him with a series of photos of the Cape Verde Peregrine Falcon; a gift he would always treasure.

As he boarded the boat to take him back to Praia and the airport, Horatio had to hold back the tears. He was leaving not only the camp where his parents lived but new friends and he was left wondering how it was possible he was being forced to replace a place he already adored with somewhere he loathed.

It was then, as he watched Ilhéu de Cima disappear from view that Horatio made a promise; whatever he needed to do, whatever the personal cost, under no circumstances would he remain at St. Indract's, and what a huge undertaking that proved to be.

Chapter 4

Within minutes of landing at Heathrow and for the first time since leaving the UK, Horatio was on his phone ignoring everyone. Just a couple of hours after arriving back at school, he had finalised the specifics of how he would get away, permanently.

Horatio knew it would be unfair to involve the twins in his plan, and also decided to avoid any behaviour that might adversely affect their happiness at the school or their friendships; no matter how things went for him, he would never risk their futures at St. Indract's.

This had resulted in Horatio rejecting any criminal actions, e.g. theft, damage to property, or anything similar that might lead to people or animals getting hurt; what he was left with was quite simple; he would run away.

*   *   *

A month into the new term, Horatio made his first bid to escape, managing to get as far as Glastonbury before being found at nine o'clock in the evening by one of the teachers who happened to be driving by.

Two weeks later, and following yet another wretched half-term break, Horatio walked out of school again. Neither of his parents could fly home for the short holiday due to some important work on the island, so, the three siblings spent the week with their aunt and uncle who made it quite obvious they had only agreed to have them under extreme duress.

Horatio's second attempt to flee, also ended in abject failure. Frustratingly though, he actually made it as far as Bristol before running out of money and was eventually found by the police sleeping rough at Temple Meads Station.

Accepting he would never succeed without significant funds, Horatio saved his weekly pocket money for a month, and then convinced Rachael to lend him some of her savings on for a book to do some important research.

Mid-November, his third 'break out' ended before it had hardly begun. Having gathered all the things he needed together in a rucksack, with money in his pocket, Horatio set off. However, just fifty metres from the school gate, he walked into Mr. Young, his housemaster.

*　　　*　　　*

Horatio was immediately marched to the headmaster's study by his housemaster and deciding he needed to be honest, told an infuriated Mr. Roger Bartholomew-Smith, that he did not wish to remain at the school.

Unfortunately, Mr Bartholomew-Smith was not impressed and informed Horatio that whether he liked it or not, twelve year old boys did not decide on their futures, adding in no uncertain terms that Horatio should grow up, accept his situation and get on with school life in a far more constructive way.

As a punishment, Horatio was told he would be 'gated' and a block placed on his weekly pocket money until he could convince the Headmaster he could be trusted. In reality though, even after everything that had happened, Horatio remained determined to escape. As far as he was concerned, he would not remain at St. Indract's any longer, and no punishment, however severe, would make him change his mind.

Early the following morning Horatio was called to Mr Young's office, where he was informed his parents were online waiting to speak to him. He was then left alone as Peter and Jessica Mott appeared on the screen and it was abundantly clear his mother had been tearful whilst his father was extremely cross.

"Oh, Horatio, what have you been up to?" his mother asked him quietly.

As he was about to respond, his father interrupted,

"For crying out loud, what the hell possessed you to run away?"

Again, before Horatio could answer, the next question was delivered.

"Are you really so thoughtless; can't you see the worry you're causing us?"

This time, whilst there was a short break in his father's verbal assault, Horatio managed a reply,

"I'm truly sorry. I don't want to cause you problems, but I won't stay here, I hate it."

As his mother asked why, his father, ignoring her completely, stated tersely,

"Right… I will fly home and find you another school. You're going somewhere and that's all there is to it."

"It's not…" Horatio replied, surprising even himself by his determination, however, before he could continue, his father said,

"I will be there tomorrow evening."

And the connection was broken.

*　　*　　*

Early the following morning, Horatio was told to be at the school office immediately lessons ended and when he arrived, he was again shown into the headmaster's office. Facing Mr. Bartholomew-Smith, Mr. Young and his father, Horatio was told to stand silently whilst the three men continued what had obviously been a considered debate.

From what he could make out, because of his serial truanting, neither the headmaster nor his housemaster trusted Horatio sufficiently to let him continue at the school.

"You see, he is so wilful, if we decided to let him stay, he would just carry on running away," Mr. Young explained to Peter Mott. "If there is an accident, which in my opinion is certainly not out of the question, we, as the school, could be held liable."

Mr. Bartholomew-Smith turned to Horatio and asked,

"Young man, will you repeat to your father what you said to me."

Horatio took a short amount of time before deciding that, again, honesty was the best course to pursue.

"I said I do not want to be at this school."

Horatio saw such bitter disappointment on his father's face that for a second he regretted his words, but it quickly passed and he was certain if he remained resolute, he would eventually be taken out of the school.

After a long pause, Peter Mott asked to speak to Mr Bartholomew-Smith on his own and following that meeting, Horatio was told to pack all his things and return to the school office.

With the clothes and few belongings he had accumulated, he found the twins waiting with his father outside the Headmaster's office. His first thought was that because of him, Rachael and Thomas were also being asked to leave, but he discovered that was not the case.

As the four walked outside, nothing was said, that was until Thomas told Horatio he was selfish, and immature, and giving their parents nightmares on what to do with him. Horatio took great hope in what was said.

As it was evident nothing positive could be gained by delaying their departure, Peter Mott told his youngest to get in the car. Without saying a word, Horatio climbed into the front seat and watched as his brother and sister gave their father a hug, and prayed his relationship with his parents, especially his father, would quickly return to how it had been.

As the car pulled away from the school gate, Horatio was euphoric and struggled to hide his pleasure at saying goodbye to St. Indract's.

*   *   *

As soon as they arrived at the house in Berrow, Horatio was sent straight to his bedroom without any of his devices. Nothing had been said between father and son on the journey home, but it was evident their once close relationship had been seriously compromised.

The following morning, with Horatio sat in silence next to him, Peter Mott began to ring every school located within a reasonable distance of St. Indract's. He had spoken to Jessica the previous evening and agreed that any new school for their youngest, would have to be reasonably close to Rachael and Thomas; under no circumstances would they create complications for the twins' education because of Horatio's selfish behaviour.

Peter and Jessica Mott were determined the twins would not miss out on their support and attendance at events, because of their younger brother and accepted that coordinating holidays, parent's evenings, sporting events and musical activities would all become unmanageable if Horatio's new school was any distance from St. Indract's.

Horatio had manipulated his departure from St. Indract's so he could not expect to be their priority, and he would have to accept whatever school they found.

*   *   *

Peter Mott identified a number of boarding schools in Bristol and throughout Somerset, some of which were considered to be the best in the country. The problem was that headmasters evidently spoke to each other and finding a place in a new school for Horatio was going to be a good deal more difficult than he had estimated.

Horatio's parents agreed they should be as honest as possible when contacting new schools, however, as Peter attempted to explain Horatio's recent behaviour, any interest in him quickly evaporated. Quite understandably, all headmasters appeared unwilling to take a chance on him; something no one could blame them for.

There was a solitary occasion when a secretary suggested they might be able to help, but after looking at their prospectus online, it was clear to Peter they were prepared to accept just about any child whose parents were willing to pay the fees up front. It wasn't difficult to conclude the school in question had financial worries, quite possibly the result of falling pupil numbers, and, no matter how angry he was with his youngest, he was not prepared to send him just anywhere that would take him.

Early that afternoon, an exceedingly frustrated Peter Mott sent Horatio to his room and called Jessica to explain what was happening. After a protracted, and at times tetchy exchange it was finally agreed that at least in the short term, they had no alternative but to move Horatio to the Ilhéu de Cima, where he would be home tutored.

Peter called his son from his bedroom and explained their decision. Horatio was of course thrilled and he promised to do everything and anything he was asked to do, and much, much more.

Nevertheless, this euphoria was short lived as his father told him that the next day they would be returning to St. Indract's to meet with Mr. Young his housemaster.

*   *   *

The following morning, they returned to the school and a confused Horatio was left waiting outside the office as his father described to the housemaster the many complications he had encountered attempting to find a new school for his son.

"Unable to find any acceptable alternative school for Horatio, I spoke to my wife last night," he explained. "and basically, we feel we have little choice but to take Horatio back to Cape Verde with me, but, and it's an enormous but, it can only be on the understanding he can continue with his education by being home tutored."

Peter went on to ask Mr. Young whether St. Indract's would be prepared to supply him with all the necessary study material, including the syllabi, text books and computer programmes that a boy of Horatio's age would need to continue his schooling.

Rather unexpectedly, a relieved Mr. Young agreed. He had assumed Horatio's father would ask the school to rescind the decision to expel the boy, which, if the case, would have proved extremely problematic.

Previous experience had taught both Mr. Young and the headmaster, Mr. Bartholomew-Smith that concessions would inevitably lead to considerably more misery and distress for all concerned; this was particularly true for parents.

Another consideration was also the twins. By assisting the family at such a challenging time the school would definitely help keep relations positive, something Mr. Young knew was important to the headmaster. Mr. Bartholomew-Smith had continually stressed to him that any thought of Rachael and Thomas leaving St. Indract's, should be rejected out of hand.

Whatever the reasons, Peter Mott was delighted and before leaving it was decided they would return the next day to pick up materials for home tutoring which Mr. Young would organise with Horatio's teachers.

*   *   *

Early the following morning, Peter and Horatio returned to St. Indract's where Mr. Young went through the study material required for home tuition.

He explained for both their benefits that on the whole Horatio's teachers felt the demands of the syllabi were well within his ability, however, all agreed that the only possible barrier to him completing the courses successfully, was in his lack of interest in studying any set work.

When the meeting finally closed, Peter Mott asked the housemaster how much he owed the school only to be told that as he had already paid the school fees for all three children, and as there were no discounts for pupils leaving mid-year, it had been decided no payment would be required.

Driving home to Berrow, Horatio was dismayed at the large bundle of resources passed on by Mr. Young, and to make matters worse, as they left the school his father had told him his mother had already drawn up a daily timetable for his home tuition.

He added, in no uncertain terms, that Horatio would study five mornings a week, beginning the first day following his arrival.

Finally, just to clarify any possible confusion, Peter stated definitively that the subject of home tuition was not open for debate, either then or at any time in the future.

<u>Chapter 5</u>

So, twelve year old Horatio returned to Ilhéu de Cima towards the end of November and his parents had to accept he would remain there for as long as it took to find an alternative boarding school. In truth though, both knew the prospect of that ever working out for their extremely wilful youngest, was nigh on impossible.

Horatio began the steep walk up to his new home from the beach and half way up, he stopped to look around. Clearly visible was Ilhéu Grande, so close he thought he could touch it, and as he stared out over the sea, the only sounds were coming from the colonies of birds scattered across the island.

Spreading his arms wide, feeling the sunshine on his face Horatio couldn't stop himself laughing; it may have been very different from his home in Berrow with its beach, sand dunes and magnificent countryside; but even though the island was barren, rocky and exposed to the worst of the elements, it still had a charm and beauty of its own.

*   *   *

Approaching the camp, he thought it looked very much the same, although there were a few add-ons and alterations.

He saw the eight Porta cabin style buildings; six of which were positioned close to each other in a circle and the scene reminded him of the old wild west films where the wagons were placed in a ring for protection.

The unmanned lighthouse and derelict keeper's cottage were to one side, between the camp and the cliffs.

Of the five cabins, one was for Horatio's family to live in and another housed the researchers. Of the remainder, the largest was open-planned and contained a kitchen and dining area with a social area for the team to meet when they were not working. At the rear of the building, Horatio was told there was a small living space where Filomena da Silva, a widow from another of the islands and her sixteen year old daughter Sofia lived.

Filomena had been employed as the camp 'housekeeper' and together with Sofia she undertook many of the daily chores including cleaning, cooking, washing and generally making sure the researchers could concentrate on their work.

A further cabin, the second largest, contained a fully equipped science laboratory and research areas. This building was critical to the effectiveness of those involved in the project; everyone understanding that its accomplishments or otherwise would clarify the viability of the group's research in the long term.

A fifth cabin had been set aside for the use of guests. The Cape Verde Government had generously granted a tourist license for an initial seven year period and it was hoped visitors would holiday on the island. The importance of these wildlife tourists could not be underestimated as they would ultimately underwrite much of the business and commercial side of the entire project.

Finally, a smaller sixth hut was at the far end of the camp, set apart from the main living areas and Horatio knew this building housed the communal toilet, showers and washing block.

*   *   *

As his father had stated so explicitly before they had left the UK, at nine the following morning, his first full day on the island, Horatio began his studies. After being shown the work for that day by both his mother and father, he was left in his bedroom to study. There was little discussion, and by his parents' firmness Horatio knew that he must not let them down.

He was allowed only one short break before class ended at one o'clock, when Peter and Jessica returned to check his efforts; the three then joined Libby and Simon for lunch.

Horatio was hoping that as on his first visit, when he was alone with Simon they would speak French, however, Simon spoke almost perfect English and would never use French with the others in the team.

As the meal got under way, Horatio asked where Francis, the fifth member of the team was. His mother explained that he had left the project because the support from his university had come to an end.

"In certain subjects," she added, "University students are offered sabbaticals, or time out of their course to undertake research projects. The length of that time depends on the generosity of their University and degree they were undertaking.

For someone like Libby," his mother smiled at the young student sat across the table from her, "because she is studying for a Ph.D., she has been offered an eighteen month sabbatical to work with us. This is so she can complete her thesis. Simon, on the other hand, has only been offered a twelve month assignment and Joshua, Francis's replacement who will be arriving next week, will be here for nine months."

Following lunch, much to Horatio's disbelief and annoyance, his father produced a roster detailing the chores that everyone was involved in including the emptying and cleaning of the communal chemical toilets.

The cleaning of the cabins, showers and other facilities were undertaken by Filomena and Sofia who were also responsible for all the communal washing and ironing.

What was not on the list was the cleaning of the labs. This was not to be undertaken by Filomena, Sofia or Horatio as there were chemicals and other potentially dangerous substances alongside vital research that should not be touched.

*   *   *

Following the list of chores, Peter told Horatio they were going for a walk and he would be given the same tour as new researchers were given on their arrival.

With his father talking to him as though he was a member of the research team, not for the first time Horatio promised himself that he would do everything possible to live up to his parents' faith in him; any other course and he knew they would have to send him back to England and another boarding school.

Whilst pointing out different features of the camp, rather surprisingly, considering his son's age, Peter described how those responsible for the project in the UK were adamant it must be cost effective. He went on to explain that this meant they had to build a community which was as self-sufficient as possible. He added that by living wisely and prudently on a day to day basis, they would create comfortable lives for all those on the island.

It was becoming ever more evident to Horatio that he was not going to be presented with a relaxing life compared to that at St. Indract's; any thoughts he might have had that his stay on the island would be a stress-free substitute to living back home was clearly way off the mark.

*   *   *

As his father then led him away from the camp towards the far side of the derelict cottage, he explained that the three most important elements to self-sufficiency were water, electricity and waste.

Horatio saw they were heading for a large prefabricated hut, which he had failed to notice on his earlier visit.

"We may be surrounded by the sea," his father said, "but without access to drinking water, we would survive for only a few days on the island."

Pushing open the door leading into the hut he added, having to raise his voice above the noise,

"And this is the reason we can stay here for the foreseeable future."

They stood before what to Horatio looked like four giant versions of the central heating boiler in their Berrow house.

"But how do you get drinking water out of these?" he asked, puzzled.

"Well, in simple terms, these machines take seawater and heat it until it turns into water vapour... you know, steam. That vapour rises and when it does, all the impurities including the salt are left behind. It then cools and as it does, we collect it as fresh water."

"That's really clever."

"Yes, but..." his father continued, "there were two problems we had to solve if we were to use the system for our camp. Firstly, getting seawater up to this height; secondly, producing energy to create heat."

"So how does seawater get up here?"

"That's the easy bit. We pump it from the sea. Look, just over there."

His father pointed through the rear window to a large plastic pipe that ran away from the back of the hut.

"But how; we're so high up?"

Peter Mott smiled as he heard the bewilderment in his son's voice and pointed out two large containers at the far end of the hut. By the sound coming from them, it was obvious they were working flat out.

"Those are the pumps. One feeds the desalination units, the other provides us with seawater for showering, toilets, washing, laundry; in fact everything that does not use fresh water."

"How cool is that," Horatio said, clearly astounded.

42

"It is, isn't it?" his father answered, before carrying on.

"Distilling seawater is an excellent illustration of how ingeniously the project site has been planned by the experts back in Bristol. Now, tell me, what's missing?"

"The energy source," Horatio answered without hesitation and his father smiled; he was impressed.

"Okay, now, follow me."

As they left the hut, Peter pointed out the pipe running from the back of the building to where it disappeared over the cliff.

"Whenever you're outside, especially on your own, never go near the cliff edge. Many of the rocks are unstable from the battering they get by the weather and it can be dangerous, okay?"

As Horatio agreed, they passed the cottage to the other side of the lighthouse where hidden from view and on a remarkably flat part of the landmass, were three banks of solar panels.

"An issue we had in the planning of the camp," his father explained, "was the shortage of rainfall; the island only has rain in August, September and October and then not very much. That's why it is so barren, but... what we do have is sunshine. On average we have six to nine hours a day, throughout the whole year and these solar panels supply us with all our energy needs. These ..." then indicating yet another hut to the far side of the panel, Peter said, "In there we have a series of rechargeable, long-life batteries for storing the energy. That means we can have electricity night and day."

Horatio stood staring at the solar panels, and after a few moments, said,

"So what happens if they break, or anything else that's important, can we stay here?"

"Well... it was one of our most important concerns when we looked at the practicalities of a project in such a challenging environment, a project that we want to last for years."

Without waiting, Peter set off towards the lighthouse and approached the only door in the building. Pushing it open, they entered what appeared to be the only space on the ground floor and Horatio saw it was stacked full of cases and crates.

"Along with most of the cottage," his father said, "this is the only part of the original lighthouse keeper's accommodation that survived. You can't quite see them, but at the back of the room there are steps leading up to the machinery and solar panels which keeps the lighthouse operating. It's all automated and although we are allowed to climb to the top to observe the island and surrounding sea, we have been asked not to touch anything to do with the actual light.

Everything in this room is for the project, the boxes mostly contain spare parts for every conceivable difficulty we may have."

"But why so much?" Horatio asked.

"Well, think about it. If for some reason we get stuck here, er... seriously bad weather for example with the island cut-off and satellite phones down, we can live here safely for some considerable time. It might look like more than we could ever need, but by investing in spares, in the long term it will be more cost effective. You see, transporting anything to the island is expensive and some of these spares are not only large but heavy, it cost a huge amount to get them here."

As they walked on, Horatio continued with his questions,

"How do the phones and the internet work?"

"Well, we're fortunate to have access to a satellite communication system which gives us three phones in the social hut and six computers, four in the lab and two in the social hut.

If you think about it, there would be little point in us being here if we couldn't do our research because of

problems with internet access. But... and it's a big but...
it's expensive."

*　　　*　　　*

As father and son returned to the camp, Horatio realised
how incredibly carefully everything had been planned.
Even to his young and inexperienced eyes every
eventuality had been covered, which not only reinforced
his already high opinion of his parents, but clearly
illustrated how vital the work being done on the island was
to important people in the UK.

It was only after walking with his father that Horatio
realised how, on his first visit with the twins, they had all
taken so much for granted; fresh water, electricity, food,
hot showers, toilets, computers and phones.

The twins might have complained endlessly, and he
accepted some things on Ilhéu de Cima were rather
primitive; to him, it was not that much different from St.
Indract's.

Rachael and Thomas would never hear a bad word said
against the school, but it could never be described as
comfy or attractive and Horatio knew how lucky he was to
live on an island in such an isolated and inaccessible place,
yet still have everything he needed.

*　　　*　　　*

The following day, after his studies and lunch, Libby asked
Horatio if he wanted to see something rather special. When
he enthusiastically agreed, she walked towards the
research hut.

Up to that moment, Horatio had been told to stay away
from the lab and adult work areas, but when he realised
that's where they were headed, he began to speed up.

"Hey, slow down," Libby called out, and as she caught
up with him, said,

"Your parents have allowed me to show you this; they've also said you can help with some of my work, that's if you want to?"

"But what is it?"

As they entered the hut, she told Horatio to follow her and they skirted the benches, computers and work areas and headed towards the rear of the building.

"Now, you must be very quiet and whatever you do, do not make a sudden move."

Libby opened the door to a small back room and as Horatio followed he noticed on a desk in the far corner, a plastic container with bright lights shining over it. Staring into the box, he saw nothing except some straw, but then something moved; just a miniscule twitch, but enough and Horatio spied a tiny… well… he was not sure what.

"Oh my golly gosh. How incredible is that. But, what is it?" he whispered, breathlessly.

"You may not believe this, but it's the chick of a Cape Verde Peregrine Falcon; the bird we were keeping an eye on during your last visit."

"But why is it here?"

"Well, I was observing one of the breeding sites we have identified as possibly being in use, even having eggs, and as I filmed; this little fella fell off the edge. I have no idea how it happened, but it was a chance in a million that I was there when it happened.

I got Francis and Simon to help me and I climbed down the cliff to retrieve him. Originally, we were going to put him back on the ledge but I realised that he was really shaken up and most unlikely to survive the rest of that day.

Although it's agreed that whenever possible we must let nature take its course, I decided to talk it through with your parents and in the end, because it is such an incredibly rare and endangered bird, they felt like I did that we should help."

"How old is it?" Horatio asked, excited almost beyond words.

"We're not sure, but probably just a few days old."

"It's... it's... incredible. I don't think I have ever seen anything so small and vulnerable, yet it will grow up to be one of the planet's most effective killers. I read somewhere it's the ultimate assassin."

"It is, but as I told you last time, this species is running out of time."

"So what are you going to do?"

"We have to accept that in the next day or two, it will die. If it doesn't, then we will have to care for it. You see, once we help it, it can never go back to its parents; they will almost definitely reject it.

So, it will have to live with us until it is an adult; if by then it can fend for itself we will release it, if not, we'll find it a home in a zoo or bird sanctuary."

"Can I help you raise it?" It was obvious Horatio was having serious trouble keeping his impatience under control.

"Why do you think I wanted to introduce you to it?" Libby replied laughing.

She led Horatio back in to the main lab where there were four chairs in one corner and told him to sit.

"Okay. I'll explain what's needed to help the falcon, then you can tell me if you still want to be involved."

Without hesitation, Horatio, almost shouting answered,

"I do! I really do."

"Well… let's see shall we."

Libby then detailed what was needed to give the chick even the smallest chance of survival, and unusually for Horatio, he sat in complete silence taking it all in.

"We will take turns in feeding him during the day. He must have food every three hours and that means we must catch, kill and cut up the meat whilst it is still fresh. If you agree to help, Simon, we'll work in shifts…. and, young man, your parents told me to tell you that the time you spend helping, will not replace your chores or morning school work, okay?"

47

Libby grinned as Horatio pulled a disappointed face, however, she could see he was absolutely thrilled.

*   *   *

The rest of that afternoon and early evening, Horatio was on one of the computers looking up everything he could find on the Cape Verde Peregrine Falcon, before widening his search to include all falcons. After downloading the material, he went in search of Libby; eventually finding her in the lab with Simon.

When he was invited to join them, Horatio said coyly,

"I've found some information on looking after falcon chicks."

Libby and Simon looked at each other, clearly surprised. They had hoped Horatio would take helping with the chick seriously, and it was obvious he had already made a promising start.

"Although you probably know most of it," he continued, "I wondered whether you would like me to go through a few facts."

"Absolutely. You see… because this particular falcon has not been one of our research priorities up to now, we know very little," Simon answered and asked Horatio to carry on. However, before he could begin, the door opened and Jessica joined them.

"Horatio is about to go through some data on falcon chicks." Libby told her.

"Can I stay?" his mother asked, looking at her son, who was clearly torn between being uncomfortable and delighted,

"Okay," he answered, timidly.

Jessica sat next to Libby as Horatio explained,

"I thought the most important thing was their diet and discovered much of their food is other birds. They will eat small reptiles and mammals, even insects, but they prefer birds." He looked down at his tablet before continuing,

"Next, I wanted to find out which of those birds are around here and which would be the best for the chick to eat. I hope that's okay?"

"That's really good," Simon answered, impressed. "We've no idea what to feed it on. Till now we've been giving it small pieces of raw meat."

"Okay, but I think we should use a bird called the White-Faced Storm-Petrel."

"Why that one?" his mother asked just a bit too formally.

"Firstly, they're not endangered and secondly, they are in their breeding season and must come ashore to build nests and tend their young."

"Okay," Libby said, delighted with the confidence Horatio was revealing, and then added, "We'll have to reduce any unnecessary harm and avoid birds with their own young."

Jessica and Simon nodded in agreement as Libby continued,

"Simon, if you're okay with it, let's try catching one tomorrow morning. I think we will need to catch one bird every two or three days."

Simon agreed and then asked Horatio to continue.

"Yes, well... I then decided to look at falcons in general, and it's amazing." Jessica smiled, delighted with her son's enthusiasm. "There are nineteen species of falcons and they exist across the entire world, except in rainforests and very cold areas such as the Arctic.

Females tend to be about a third bigger than the males and they mate for life."

All three adults were struggling to hide their smiles at this point, Horatio, oblivious to them, ploughed on, "Usually, they nest on cliff edges or in crevices to prevent predators getting to their young.

Many types of falcon do not migrate and this includes those here on Ilhéu de Cima, so those we have, will never leave."

Horatio stopped, looked up from the screen and realising he had been talking nonstop said, just a touch embarrassed,

"Sorry, but is it helpful?"

Libby, Simon and his mother nodded their heads in unison and a relieved Horatio went back to his screen and didn't notice Libby turn to his mother and mouth silently, 'this is really good'.

"A pair of falcons will raise one clutch a year, and it takes about thirty-five days for the eggs to hatch. Chicks remain in the nest for around forty days before taking their first flight; called fledging. It then takes approximately six weeks for the chicks to become fully independent, which means we will have to have our chick ready to leave the incubators in thirty-five days, plus six weeks."

Again, Horatio looked up and asked if everything was still okay and got a repeat nod from all three adults, although this time Simon said,

"Horatio, this is excellent."

"That's good. Okay, half of all peregrine falcons' chicks do not survive the first year, those that do, should live to thirteen and in exceptional circumstance, twenty.

Now, something very important," Again Horatio didn't see the smile on his mother's face or the reaction of both Libby and Simon who found it hard not to laugh. Incredibly, the twelve year old addressing them sounded just like their old school teachers.

"When a young chick wants food their call is; 'screea, screea, screea'; I listened to it on line. Anyway, we'll know when our chick is hungry. Now, if our bird's call is a 'cack' sound, this means, alarm; actually, it's more like 'kaa-a-aack, kaa-a-ack'.

I found a whole load more calls; but these two are the most important."

"Good. Now what happen if our chick survives?" Libby asked.

"I'm not sure," Horatio turned to her, "but we are going to have to raise it ourselves. After that I don't know; maybe a zoo or sanctuary will give it a good life."

"So, what about keeping it here on the island?" Simon asked.

"I suppose if it can fend for itself, maybe, but we would have to teach it to hunt?"

"Is that possible?" his mother asked.

"I saw a couple of sites about raising falcons for sport, and it's possible. Shall I go through a few of the things I found?"

"Well… yes… it might give us an idea of the practicalities of keeping it," it was Libby who answered, genuinely fascinated by the prospect.

"So… there are a few does and don'ts. You should talk to the chick at all times, it needs to get used to you and your voice. Always treat it with respect and give it a lot of love and affection. Offering it small pieces of meat will be a sign of your affection, oh… and never take food away from your bird.

Let it hear unfamiliar noises and have contact with different people and animals. Never shout or get angry with it and never forget they are extremely dangerous creatures.

Finally, if we follow these guidelines, our chick would never be independent of us."

"That's a lot to take in," Simon said thoughtfully, "Whatever, the chick is going to take up a lot of hours and I can't afford to lose time from my research."

"But, I'll do it! I will, I'll do it all." Horatio stated impulsively.

"You won't have time," his mother countered, slightly fretful. "Your st…"

"I know, I know; Libby told me. But I promise I'll do all my lessons… and I'll work really hard."

"If Simon and I share the mornings…" Libby proposed calmly; genuinely believing that if Horatio looked after the chick, both would benefit, "Do you really think from lunch onwards you can look after the chick until you go to bed?"

"Horatio?" His mother asked.

"Yes, please. Let me try, and I promise I'll do all my studies and chores."

"Well... okay, let's see how it goes."

*   *   *

Later, once Horatio was in bed, as Libby and Jessica were talking, the young researcher said,

"You know, that was quite incredible for a kid his age, he sounded like a college student."

"I know," Jessica replied uneasily, "and it just adds to my worry about him being here. Peter and I cannot provide him with the education he needs and I'm starting to think he's in entirely the wrong place for a twelve year old boy with his potential."

Chapter 6

Within just a couple of days, Horatio had taken over all the duties for the chick outside of his mealtimes and when he was working on his studies and chores. His parents were astonished with the way he organized his routine, while Libby and Simon were so impressed, they spent less and less time checking up on Horatio or the chick.

Apart from the catching and slaughter of the birds for food, Horatio undertook all other tasks for the chick and it was clear he was utterly devoted to this new responsibility.

Spending every spare moment he had with the falcon, always chatting to it, Horatio began to relentlessly repeat a few simple sounds, and, to his astonishment, within just a couple of weeks, he heard the chick attempting to copy him.

To Horatio his method of teaching the chick was relatively straight forward; if he could communicate basic commands to it, then training it to fend for itself should be a good deal simpler.

Initially, working on two calls; one to 'come' to him, the other, to 'move away' from him, an initially disinterested chick began to recognize the sounds especially when there was fresh meat on offer.

*   *   *

On the Monday of the following week Joshua, the new researcher, arrived. The next morning whilst Horatio was completing his studies for the day, the rest of the team dragged and carried a pile of crates up the hill from the bay.

That afternoon, before Horatio could begin his duties with the chick, Peter Mott gathered everyone including

Filomena and Sofia together in the centre of the camp where the crates had been dropped and began to prise open one of the largest.

"The final hurdle we've got to remaining here in the long term is food," he explained whilst working. "Of course, we have an abundant quantity of fish from local fishermen and that will continue to be our staple diet; also, the supply boat will bring meat, which we can freeze, but fresh food will not keep, so, why not grow our own?"

The incredulous look on the faces of all three researchers made Jessica Mott laugh, so she attempted to appease the team.

"Think about it. What does this island have in abundance?" She waited a few second before saying, "Oh… come on."

The students were clearly baffled; whilst Horatio didn't have a clue what was going on, all he wanted to do was get to the chick.

"Okay, this place is a barren, rocky island, lacking virtually any fertile soil, but …"

"Guano!" Libby stated, almost shouting the answer.

"Exactly!" Peter said. "Guano; one of the world's richest natural fertilizers and we have hundreds of tons of the stuff. Look around; the island is literally covered in it. So, if we are creative, it can be collected and used to help grow the majority of our fresh food."

"What's guano?" Horatio asked, as his father continued to open the first crate.

"Bird droppings," his mother answered, to which her son pulled a face of disgust.

"It's all the whitish stuff that covers the rocks," she explained. "and it's used as a compost. Just think about it. It has extremely high levels of nitrogen, phosphate and potassium; all essential for growing plants."

After finally opening the crate, Peter Mott pulled out what appeared to be long planks of thick plastic. Then, with screws that had been provided, he began to fit together an elongated, rectangular shape, leaving all watching absolutely confounded.

"Okay," he said continuing to construct the box which was about fifteen metres by four and one metre high. "These will be our growing beds. They are simple, durable with no top and no bottom and in total there are eight. We've found a good place for them and we'll need to secure them to the ground before we fill them up with soil and guano."

Again Jessica laughed at the disbelieving look on the other's faces and she pointed and said,

"The crates over there are full of bags of soil and fertilizer,"

"God... no wonder they were so heavy to carry," Simon said smiling.

Everyone, including Horatio, was then asked to help screw the plastic planks together before they placed them on a flat piece of ground close to the solar panels.

*   *   *

That evening before supper, as everyone gathered in the social area, the talk was of the new planters. Although the three students felt the idea of growing their own food was pretty crazy, they had to concede that Peter and Jessica had got just about everything right in the design and setting up of the camp. They also knew without the Motts input and extraordinary commitment, the camp and their lives would be far less comfortable.

Sat around the table, after finishing an unfamiliar meal Filomena had cooked for their supper, Jessica asked what they thought of it. Without exception, all agreed it was delicious and filling.

"It's a local stew called Catchupa," she told them, "and it's made out of fish or meat, plus other ingredients which all come from the islands. It's just an example, but I'm convinced if we experiment with what is eaten locally, then we can grow the vegetables to recreate our own variations of those local recipes."

"You see, it's really just common sense," Peter went on to explain. "Grow the crops we need and it will help persuade the bosses and backers at home that the project is sustainable. I'm also convinced the more we can show how self-sufficient we are, the more likely the Cape Verde Government will continue to support us, extending our licence for the foreseeable future.

"Oh, and by the way, before you decide all this will interfere with your research, Jessica will have responsibility for the crops, but, she will need help from us collecting guano."

And that is exactly what happened. The beds were filled with the soil and compost; Peter and Horatio dug a storage pit for the guano that everyone had helped collect, and Jessica, with Filomena and Sofia's help began experimenting with the crops that could flourish in the conditions on Ilhéu de Cima.

*   *   *

Towards the middle of December, Jessica returned to the UK to spend Christmas with the twins, flying home with Libby, Simon and Joshua, who were also returning to their families.

The twins had been offered the opportunity to fly out to the island but due to the short holiday, both said they would prefer to concentrate on revising for their exams and wait until the longer summer break when the weather should be warmer.

Jessica and Peter had agreed from the outset, that whenever possible, one of them should be on the island to ensure the camp was secure from trespassers. This was especially important for research being undertaken; months of work could be ruined in the wrong hands.

When Horatio's mother asked him what he preferred to do, he replied definitively that he had to stay behind as the following few weeks were crucial to the chick's development and he could not expect his father, with all his other duties, to take responsibility for the young bird.

What he didn't add though, was that not only did he prefer to keep his father company, but he was beginning to make real progress in teaching the falcon to respond to his simple calls.

Filomena and Sofia also remained for most of the festive season, but it was agreed they could travel home over Christmas to celebrate with their family. Filomena's village, Sao Francisco, was not that far from Praia, on the island of Santiago so if they flew they would only be gone for a couple of days.

* * *

In the end, Christmas Day proved extremely quiet for father and son; that is except for a long phone call with Jessica and the twins. Following breakfast, they opened their presents and as research, studying and chores were off the agenda, Horatio intended to spend most of the day with the falcon chick and on the computer. After lunch, however, as it was such a lovely day, Peter suggested they went for a walk and they circled the entire island, before swimming in the wonderfully warm waters of the bay.

That evening Horatio told his father that although he was missing his mother, he had had a fun day, describing it as one of the most enjoyable Christmases he could remember. Peter Mott found it difficult to disagree.

* * *

At the beginning of January, all who had travelled home returned safely to the island, and their lives returned to the established day-to-day routine.

Horatio continued to work diligently on his morning studies and during the afternoons, spent as much time as he could with the falcon. When they were together, he would chat to it ceaselessly, sometimes using different languages, or he might spend time practising the calls he was teaching the chick. However, without fail, on every occasion he was in the bird's presence, Horatio was affectionate and gentle.

By regularly hand feeding it small pieces of meat, he came to realise that physical contact was underpinning the growing closeness of their friendship, and that is how Horatio saw it, a friendship.

Never bored with the commitment, never regretting the promise to his mother, as the bond between 'keeper' and chick grew stronger, Horatio had to ensure he remained fully up to date on best practices. He knew by continually improving his knowledge, not only would the chick have a far better chance of surviving, but he would be confident about being involved in crucial decisions for the bird's future.

'Don't ever take the easy option when caring for your bird. If you do, you will make mistakes, and there will always be consequences. This internet advice, became Horatio's mantra.

*   *   *

However, as the weeks passed, the chick became the focus for his entire life outside of the classroom; except when he was undertaking his chores, eating or sleeping, he was completely wrapped up in the tiny, defenceless, but breathtaking hatchling.

It was therefore no surprise that Horatio decided to give it a name.

When he discussed this with his parents and Libby, they had agreed that no harm could come from it and it took just seconds for him to decide; he was Horatio, his bird would be Nelson.

*   *   *

Horatio had been cataloguing the progress made by Nelson from when he was just a few days old. He noted how he had swiftly grown to almost an adult's weight and size and how he had been a smidgeon upset when the gorgeous downy white feathers were replaced by quite ugly juvenile feathers. He was pleased though that they were quickly replaced by new adult colouring including a black moustache and hood, white neck and contrasting bright yellow eye-rings, feet and cere, the fleshy covering at the base of the upper beak.

At four weeks he had worked out that Nelson was a male, which was fortuitous considering the name he had chosen. To Horatio's relief, he found a site on the computer that helped him identify Nelson's sex through his size, facial markings, colouration and wing shape - he was definitely a male!

Nevertheless, even with all these encouraging changes and developments, nothing could compare to Horatio's excitement at Nelson's first flight.

He had read that once falcons were airborne, it still took at least four weeks for them to learn to hunt for themselves, meaning he would need to return for food, and following that, there was a real possibility Nelson would fly off and they would never see each other again.

*   *   *

Strapping the thick rubber sleeve his father had made onto his lower right arm, after just one week's practice and with little persuasion, Nelson jumped straight onto the arm protector.

That done, the next stage was more demanding as the falcon was required to enter the unknown. With Nelson completely reliant on Horatio, the two of them then moved tentatively towards the office door.

Rotating the door handle, Horatio felt the bird tense and immediately stopped. He then stroked the top of Nelson's head and calmed him by whispering gently.

Moments later, Horatio crept agonizingly slowly through the laboratory, aware that Nelson was eyeing up the new world enveloping him. For the fledgling, every step revealed something unfamiliar, something momentous, yet to his credit, he never cowered.

Approaching the outside door, Horatio again petted the falcon, talking nonstop, gentle and supportive until finally they stepped into the big, wide world. Fresh air immediately engulfed them, the wind blowing Nelson's feathers and he squawked contentedly.

*   *   *

Watching from the social hut window, the five adults were desperate for the experiment to work, whilst Filomena and Sofia, who were next to the hut used for showering, stared in awe as they saw the falcon for the first time.

Horatio called 'away' and gently raised his arm to encourage Nelson to leave the safety of his protection; however, although he spread his wings and flapped them, he hung on resolutely.

It took a number of attempts before he worked his wings, left the arm protector, and instantly plummeted to the ground landing on his head with an almighty thump.

Moving unhurriedly, Horatio approached Nelson, gently reassuring him before bending down to allow him to return to his arm.

Again and again they tried, until finally it happened and it may have been a flight of only a few metres but those watching realised it was just a matter of time before Nelson flew high into the sky.

Determined not to push the young falcon too much on their first outing and undermine his excellent achievement, Horatio carried him to the office, though, unknown to Nelson, it would be the last time he would return to the incubator.

*   *   *

As Nelson's chances of surviving improved, all agreed he needed to get used to living outdoors and having the independence to come and go as he pleased. As a result, Peter Mott built and then attached a weather proof hutch with a perch to a tall post, directly outside Horatio's bedroom window.

The following afternoon the flying exercise was repeated and it was immediately noticeable Nelson was calmer. He was more confident and after about an hour of practice, when Horatio saw he was tiring, Nelson was introduced to his new home. Not surprisingly for everyone except Horatio, it took just a few seconds for Nelson to check out his new lodgings, before he jumped on the perch and relaxed.

*   *   *

What none of the adults realised and Horatio certainly wasn't going to admit to was that on the first night, whilst there was a truly spectacular electrical storm out to sea, an overwrought Nelson tapped on Horatio's bedroom window with his beak to be let in. To Horatio's delight, not only did the falcon spend the rest of that night, but every subsequent night perched on the end of his bed.

*   *   *

In total it took five weeks before Nelson was flying confidently and also hunting down and killing his own food. However, it had been anything but easy. Horatio was incredibly tolerant repeating every task, time and time again, until the bird eventually became proficient at the skills he would need to survive in the wild if that is where he chose to go.

At first Horatio had thrown meat ever higher into the air, shouting, 'attack' and Nelson caught it on the fly. He followed this by standing unnervingly close to the cliff edge, tied to a security rope held by his father and Simon, before pitching pieces of meat over the edge and watching proudly as Nelson swooped down at amazing speed to seize the food mid-air.

The next day, Horatio had just collected fresh meat for the day's practice when he heard Nelson calling from high above. Initially not seeing him, he suddenly spotted the bird dropping rapidly before hammering into a live target. Feathers flew in all direction, before the falcon disappeared behind high rocks. As proud as he was, Horatio knew it was not only the moment when all his work had come to fruition but illustrated how his usefulness to the falcon had come to an end.

Nevertheless, Nelson's first kill was quite extraordinary and the sight would stay with Horatio for the rest of his days.

*   *   *

Later that evening, with still no sign of Nelson, Libby found Horatio sitting by the bird's hutch, just outside his bedroom window and asked if he was okay.

"I suppose," he replied gloomily.

She sat down next to him and said gently,

"If Nelson leaves for good, it will be a wonderful achievement. You would have taken a chick that had little or no chance of surviving and given him a life. Not only that, and never forget this, he is one of the rarest and most endangered birds on the entire planet."

That night, Horatio couldn't sleep. He kept waiting for the tap, tap, tap on his window but it never came and the next day, after his studies and chores, he went walking the island, searching. As it became dark, he returned for his evening meal to tell everyone that there had still been no sign of Nelson.

Later, as he climbed into bed, Horatio was brokenhearted and desperately lonely. For weeks, every spare moment he'd had was given over to Nelson and he absolutely knew it was right he had given the falcon every opportunity to become independent and free. Of course Libby was right; he should be pleased, proud of what he'd done, and he was, but Horatio had never expected the success to come at such a cost, and because of that he felt terribly let down.

*   *   *

Four evenings later, with still no sign of Nelson, another powerful storm was brewing out to sea. The wind had increased until it was difficult to stand up outside and when the rain, thunder and lightning arrived, Horatio decided that after they'd eaten he would go out and search for him.

During the meal, all five adults tried to convince him the falcon would be safe and that he would fly away from the storm only returning when it had calmed down. Even Libby, who Horatio knew was hiding her worry, tried to explain that as Nelson was native to the island, he would be unfazed by the weather, no matter how loud and violent.

After clearing the plates, Horatio took his anorak off the peg by the door. Both his parents told him he was not going out. As he began to argue, Libby told him that as anxious as she was about the falcon, she completely agreed with Jessica and Peter.

"Horatio, stop being so difficult," she told him, "You cannot go out in this; it would be dangerous and thoughtless."

Looking out of the window at the wind and lashing rain, Horatio knew they were right.

*   *   *

Lying in bed unable to sleep, Horatio prayed that Nelson had left the island to escape the dreadful weather, but he knew that was doubtful. One of the unique features of the Cape Verde Peregrine Falcon was that it was non-migratory and never left its territory. If he was to survive, Nelson would have had to find shelter on the island and he'd never been shown how to do that.

An exhausted Horatio eventually fell asleep but woke with a start when he heard a tap, tap, tapping on his window. Initially, he thought he was dreaming but lay awake listening, just in case.

As the rain continued to pound his window, with the gale tearing at the roof of their cabin, it came again, faintly, indistinctly, but he definitely heard it; tap, tap, tap.

Leaping out of bed, Horatio ran to the window. As he pulled the sliding frame open, water poured in and within seconds he was saturated but he didn't care; there was Nelson, waiting.

Horatio gathered him up, not caring about the razor-sharp talons, and carried him into the warmth and calm of his bedroom before wiping him with a dry towel.

From that moment onwards, the two of them were literally inseparable.

—Ж—

Chapter 7

A week before his thirteenth birthday, Horatio accompanied his father and Simon on a trip to the Ilhéu Grande. His father had only travelled to the largest of the island group once before, so when Simon said he was interested in looking at why the vast colonies of seabirds that had once inhabited the oversized rock had been wiped out, it was decided to make a visit.

Simon explained that if they could discover the root causes of the disappearance of birds on Ilhéu Grande, they may be able to counter the same thing happening on Ilhéu de Cima.

As they walked down to the small bay, Horatio was surprised when he spotted a motor boat moored a little way out. He had never seen the craft before and when he asked where it had come from his father told him,

"It was only delivered by the sellers last night. They were supposed to arrive earlier in the day but got delayed, so when they got here you were in bed."

Approaching the water's edge, Peter continued,

"We bought it in case we have an emergency which traps us on the island. Today's trip though, gives us a chance to find out how it sails."

Horatio stared at a rather old and battered boat and wondered whether it would make it all the way to Ilhéu Grande and back again.

After swimming out and boarding and whilst Simon prepared for the journey, Peter proudly pointed out to his son a few of the main features.

"It's named Defender," his father explained, "was built in nineteen seventy-five and is a Hatteras 38 Double Cabin. In its former life, it had been chartered to tourists for deep sea fishing and we were told it was extremely dependable, and, it was cheap."

Quite clearly enjoying himself, Peter continued in far greater detail than Horatio needed or wanted, but he listened patiently.

"The craft is twelve metres long, three and a half metres wide, it has two Cummins diesel engines to power it, two rooms, toilet, a GPS, depth sounder and VHF radio. Now... if you look there," Peter then pointed to the rear of the boat, "you'll see it also has an inflatable dinghy. You know, all in all, it's perfect for what we need."

Horatio spotted a dirty orange boat on a thick line as his father took him down into the cabin and laughing said,

"Now, can you believe this?" And he slid open a concealed wooden panel at the far end of the cabin.

"We were shown this when we were first interested in buying it. Apparently, at one time the boat was used for smuggling and this secret compartment can conceal our valuables if we have to leave the boat unattended. Great isn't it?"

To Horatio's relief, his father led him back to the deck and told him there were just three points to remember before they got started.

"Firstly, it runs on diesel fuel, which is easy and cheap to buy in Praia, but difficult to transport here and store; we therefore have to use it sparingly. Secondly, no matter how little we use the boat, it is essential it is properly maintained and running efficiently, just in case we face an emergency. Finally, over the next few days, Joshua and I will show the others, you included, how the boat should be looked after and how to navigate with or without the GPS."

Horatio found that rather extreme as he could never envisage being alone and lost at sea with a broken GPS. Nevertheless, he couldn't disagree when he was allowed to take control of the boat once they were clear of the bay and in open water.

As Horatio worked the wheel, his father taught him not only how to steer, but also how to be aware of different currents, how the wind affects the sea, and how to control the correct speed for the conditions.

"How do you know all this?" he asked surprised by his father's knowledge.

"When I was at school and university I loved being on the water, but since your mother detested sailing, and once we had you kids, there was never enough time, but it's just like riding a bike, you never forget how to do it."

"Maybe if you stay here you can buy a small sailing boat and go out every day."

"That would certainly be nice, but I doubt there will be the time."

*   *   *

Throughout the journey, Nelson flew above them, constantly calling; it was as if he was guiding them; however, by mid-journey he appeared uneasy. Horatio wondered whether it was because they were moving further away from his territory, so he called him back. Perching on the bow of the boat for the rest of the voyage, Nelson was more relaxed, but remained watchful.

After dropping anchor in the deepest bay and negotiating a difficult climb to the higher parts of Ilhéu Grande, it became quickly evident that it would prove impractical to live there without investing a good deal of money in the venture, something the Ilhéu de Cima project could not afford.

After a couple of hours, during which Simon walked most of the island searching for signs of the once heavily populated bird colonies, he had to accept there was no clear evidence as to why the island had been abandoned by the birds but he still felt the trip was useful for their own research.

*   *   *

The return journey proved uneventful. With clear blue skies, beautifully warm temperature and calm sea it couldn't have been better.

Whilst Simon skippered the boat, Peter showed Horatio some charts for the seas around the islands and explained, in the simplest of terms, how to read where they were and where they were headed. He pointed out the many small but treacherous groups of rocks, some almost totally submerged, that they needed to avoid.

As they headed for home, Nelson took to the sky, always staying ahead of the boat. Interestingly Horatio noticed that every few minutes he returned to the boat, then swooping down he would call out; it was as if he was talking to them, letting them know that everything ahead was safe.

*   *   *

Horatio's already busy routine needed revising after the arrival of Joshua. He had only been with the team for a couple of weeks, when noticing the majority of their food was fish, delivered by locals, he told Peter that he was an experienced deep water fisherman.

He explained,

"For the last five years, I've spent as much time as I could spear fishing in the Caribbean and the Maldives. I really love it as a break from work and thought I might be able to do some in my free time here.

I don't know whether you would be interested, but I could try to add to the seafood and fish we're already having delivered."

Peter instantly understood the potential of catching fish themselves and knew it would certainly improve the self-sufficiency of the project, increasing the arguments about the camps sustainability.

As part of the next requisition to the project coordinator in Bristol, Peter included two spear guns recommended by Joshua and spare parts for them.

The order arrived three weeks later on the supply boat and, being watched with interest by the team, Joshua spent that first afternoon out in the bay fishing.

Noticing his parents on the beach and wondering what was going on, Horatio went to join them and it took no time for him to become fascinated with the whole idea of fishing with a spear gun. Over dinner, and later in the social hut he asked Joshua dozens of questions including how the gun worked and how it was maintained.

Then before going to bed he asked if he could try fishing with the spear gun the following afternoon, but the newly arrived researcher refused, saying the guns were dangerous weapons and he was too young.

*   *   *

Next morning, a frustrated Horatio woke determined to help Joshua on his fishing trips. Even though he had only done a little supervised swimming since arriving on the island, he knew he could help provide food for the camp.

After being brow beaten by Horatio for just about the whole of that Saturday morning, when he was supposed to be free to do his own thing, Joshua eventually gave in and said,

"Look, I have no problem with you coming with me, but you will have to talk to your parents."

Within minutes, Horatio had hunted down his father, knowing he was more likely to agree than his mother.

"Talk to your mother," was the only reply he received.

Refusing to give up, Horatio again found Joshua and begged him to persuade his mother to let him fish. As expected, Jessica said she felt someone as young as Horatio should not be taught to handle such a lethal weapon.

A week later, following incessant badgering from Horatio and support from his father and Joshua, who agreed to teach him, Jessica conceded. However, all had to agree to a number of non-negotiable conditions, the most important being that under no circumstance should Horatio go near any spear gun without Joshua or his father being with him.

*   *   *

After some initial training and a number of practice sessions, virtually every afternoon after his studies, chores and lunch, Horatio fished in the bay with Joshua whilst Nelson circled overhead. A few hours later, tired but happy, he would deliver the day's catch to Filomena and Sofia.

Understandably, when he saw how much fun his son was having, Peter ordered a further three spear guns, plus spares; then, along with Simon and even on occasions Jessica and Libby, they helped catch that evening's meal.

*   *   *

On March 22nd, Horatio celebrated his thirteenth birthday and just a week later, Sofia her seventeenth. Becoming a teenager was not a big deal; even so, he did enjoy opening his presents from the twins, his parents and others on the island.

When he thought about it, which was not that often, even allowing for the fact he had to study every weekday morning, Horatio had to admit his life was close to perfect.

And he wasn't the only one who was content. His parents were delighted with the progress he was making in his studies, an opinion supported by his results in external exams. These were set and marked by his former teachers at St. Indract's and it was clear Horatio was ahead of his peers at the school.

Nelson of course, was ever-present and for Horatio, his companionship only made each day that much more enjoyable. During his morning lessons the falcon would wait patiently, perching somewhere close until Horatio completed his studies. At meal times he was always around, unless he was also hungry, in which case he would fly off to hunt down his own food.

During the fishing parties, once Horatio had swum out into the bay, Nelson would fly overhead before swooping down and skimming over the water. It was as if he was constantly checking that everything was safe.

If Horatio walked the island during any spare time, Nelson would be with him, either flying above or sitting on the arm protector; and if he met up with one of the researchers to help with their work, the falcon would always be nearby.

In fact, although Horatio hated to admit it, at times having Nelson on his arm protector could become a burden. He needed to free up both hands, and on those occasions would have preferred the bird on his shoulder rather than his arm.

After discussing it with his father, after Horatio had gone to bed, Peter cut a leather pad so that it could be tied under the armpits and spread across the shoulders.

*　　　*　　　*

It was on one of their daily walks that Nelson unintentionally found a secret hideaway; something Horatio would never have expected on such a small island. They were making their way towards the bay, when Nelson flew off, leaving Horatio walking on the path. Just a few minutes later, he heard the falcon calling loudly. It was an unusual sound, so he headed towards the noise thinking he might be in trouble. Fifty metres from the path and towards the cliff edge, he found Nelson perched on top of a large boulder, preening himself. As he reached the spot, Horatio saw the bird was on the edge of a cluster of large rocks, in an area he had noticed but not explored and as he searched around he found a hidden cave.

Initially Horatio thought it was nothing special, but when he crawled in, he found a small space that was dry and snug. Over the next couple of days, he transferred a few things from his room, to what was to become his sanctuary; a place he could always go when he needed to be alone.

*   *   *

Most evenings, Horatio would more often than not be on one of the computers in the social hut searching for answers or looking up information on some obscure thought he'd had during the day. Much to the amusement of the adults, Nelson would always be there, sitting patiently next to him, and he would invariably end up being the centre of attention; especially with Sofia, who from originally being terrified, had come to adore him.

It was quite obvious Horatio's relationship with the falcon grew ever stronger and as the months passed they were rarely seen apart; to the others it seemed, somewhat anthropomorphically, that Nelson had taken on the role of Horatio's companion and guardian.

Part II

Sanctuary

Chapter 8

When the slayer of the human race emerged, any thought of an end to civilization, was, as usual, rejected as scaremongering and all things considered, this was hardly surprising. Historically there had been so many examples of media exaggeration and doomsday predictions, that when a new risk hit the headlines, it was simply disregarded by the majority. The public, especially those in developed countries, had become immune to the prospect of an uncontrollable natural assassin wreaking havoc.

Time and time again research had highlighted the adverse effect of the excessive use of anti-viral, antibiotics and other critical medicines, whilst scientific experts endlessly stressed that some of the most effective weapons in man's armoury against a pandemic, were being dished out like candy. But did anyone listen?

Many experienced health workers strongly counselled an immediate end to this irresponsible practice, many others alleging that crucial medicines were thrown at trivial complaints just to get patients off medical practitioners' backs; but did anyone really listen?

The world had been told; but still, predictably, advice and recommendation were sidestepped or deliberately ignored.

*   *   *

For men, women, even children, there was an assumption that the world they lived in was far too advanced and far, far, too adept for a real life catastrophe.

But surely, it didn't take a genius to take notice of the blatantly obvious?

Every year for decades, somewhere on the planet, an outbreak of a deadly illness had occurred, so why did humankind fail to grasp the potential for a cataclysmic disaster?

With hindsight, the answer is obvious. In the hustle and bustle of their hectic lives, the so called well educated believed that solutions to acute danger were somebody else's problem, and if that failed, well... it was the government, the health services, or the doctors' and nurses' obligation to sort it all out.

As long as people had someone or something to blame, rather than looking at themselves, as long as they didn't have to ask themselves whether they were contributing to an ever-growing menace, then personal accountability could be ducked.

Finally though, and what was so ludicrous was that all the world's most powerful leaders had to do was, stop, reflect and then cooperatively finance a deterrent to the ubiquitous threat of unidentified viruses seeking out the weakest point in humanity's leaking dam of wellbeing.

If that had been agreed, the global priority would have been to find solutions, rather than mitigating the capriciousness of indecision.

Or, maybe not.

More than likely, modern mankind had become so self-interested and arrogant it was simply incapable of being that selfless?

Chapter 9

At the beginning of November of Horatio's thirteenth year, the work on the island was progressing so well that Peter Mott had been able to tell the team their sponsors were so encouraged by the initial findings, they were prepared to extend their support of the project.

Interestingly, only the researchers on Ilhéu de Cima knew of the nearly two years of Herculean effort that had gone in to the papers Peter had submitted.

And that was not the only success. Following a number of attempts with a variety of crops, Jessica, Filomena and Sofia were able to provide fresh fruit and vegetables from the growing beds to supplement their meals and as the boys investigated the sea around the island, the seafood they uncovered was limitless. In fact they became so adept at spear fishing there was no longer a need to buy food from local fisherman.

As Peter and Jessica had predicted, although the supply boat continued to dock sporadically to deliver extras they required, overall the community had managed to become mostly self-sufficient.

*   *   *

During July, at the end of his sabbatical Simon departed, leaving with promises to return once he had graduated; whilst Joshua, Libby, Filomena and Sofia, along with the Mott family had become virtual fixtures on the island.

Simon's replacement, Andrea who was a PhD student and, like the Motts, from the University of Bristol, arrived with Rachael and Thomas for their two week summer break.

At seventeen, going on thirty, not only were the twins extremely mature, but they had grown up in so many other ways, even embracing life on the island with a good deal more eagerness than on previous visits.

Horatio was thrilled to see them and when both appeared genuinely captivated by Nelson, whilst being seriously impressed with the way their little brother had kept him alive and raised him, Horatio was in his element.

He was also just as delighted by the fact the twins were utterly disbelieving that their younger brother was allowed to go spear fishing with Joshua, helping to catch a good proportion of the food cooked in the camp kitchen.

When Jessica and Peter noticed in the first few days of their visit the number of occasions Rachael and or Thomas, asked to join Horatio and Nelson on one of their walks around the island, they realised that at long last the siblings were beginning to understand and value each other's company.

It was also intriguing, as well as sad, for their parents when the time came for the twins to return to St. Indract's. For the first time, Rachael and Thomas were clearly unhappy at the thought of leaving their parents and even their younger brother, and the quite extraordinary lives they had built for themselves on the island.

*   *   *

Over time, it had become an evening routine for one or more of the team to be found in the social area watching the international and/or UK news on the monitor. Late one Saturday in the second week of November, Libby was following the BBC World New and heard a short report about an outbreak of an unidentified illness on the border of three South East Asian countries, Laos, Myanmar and Thailand. The report claimed it had resulted in five deaths.

Because her parents worked for the British Red Cross, Libby was troubled as both were part of the team of health workers sent to the 'front line' in an evolving crisis.

At breakfast the following day she mentioned the story and asked if anyone had heard details of the incident.

"I saw something earlier in the week," Joshua answered, "but it was only a short piece. I remember them saying that countries, including the UK, immediately sent in teams of specialist health workers and that contained the illness. I think most of those involved have already returned home."

That was the last time it was mentioned until a few weeks later when, with the exception of Horatio who was in bed, the team members were all in the social area.

Peter Mott was at the monitor and called to the others.

"Hey, take a look at this."

He turned up the volume and they all pulled up chairs. The screen showed a link to a young female reporter with a microphone, standing in what was clearly a desperately deprived village surrounded by jungle.

"It is quite apparent the health agencies," the correspondent was staring directly at the camera, "originally sent here, but which left more than two weeks ago, have misjudged the seriousness of this outbreak."

The woman then turned, whilst the camera swung round with her to film people in all-body protective suits and helmets moving between large military style tents.

"As you can see, a skeleton team of nurses has remained and I'm told they will monitor the recovery of those infected. Local doctors though, are bewildered saying it is premature in the extreme to withdraw specialist health workers at such an early stage of what has proved a lethal infection."

The camera then returned to focus on the reporter.

"Quite rightly, questions are being asked. Who for instance felt sufficiently confident the source of the infection had burnt itself out, that they stood down the majority of the international medical staff? It is obvious standing here, that whoever they were, that decision was based on flawed data."

The camera then zoomed in on the reporter's troubled expression,

"I have been unable to speak to any senior member of the health agencies. When I ask for information, the reply is always the same; refer to the official statement we are releasing.

I quote from the last of these statements; 'until we have updated information on what is a rapidly evolving situation, we will be making no further comment'.

By chance, just a few minutes ago, I managed to speak to a health worker but only if it was off the record."

The camera turned back to the tented village, scanning the jungle as it did so.

"These are her words," the reporter continued. 'There are elements in the behaviour of this virus which are certainly causing concern'. When I asked her whether the number of deaths had risen over the last three days, she declined to answer.

I have been told from another source however, that the death rate is rising, causing serious distress throughout the teams working in the contamination zone.

Finally…"

The camera returned to focus back on the reporter's face,

"I have been informed by a local government representative that although the situation continues to be handled effectively, international health agencies are planning to return in the next few days.

Witnessing firsthand what is happening, 'a few days', appears a derisory, even irresponsible reaction."

The screen returned to the studio and Peter muted the volume. He then turned to Libby,

"Are your parents there?"

"Not that I know of, but there again, they'd never tell me if they were."

*   *   *

Midday the following day, as they were about to have lunch, an agitated Libby arrived and asked if she could turn the monitor on. With the agreement of the others, she switched on the BBC world news to see a U.N. Health spokesman standing on a raised platform.

"I can categorically deny," the man was asserting authoritatively, "the irresponsible rumours currently circulating which claim health workers who returned to their home counties from South East Asia, did so having been infected.

As always, every possible precaution was taken prior to the medical teams travelling out of the contamination zone and we have no reason to believe any of these people could be infectious.

However, I can confirm that the expert help being given to the local community by the remaining health workers is being seriously hindered by the remote location, whilst their ability to work effectively has been compromised by the area of the infection overlapping the borders of three countries. I want to stress though that the local authorities are doing their utmost to support the medical personnel on the ground, as I say… in what is an inhospitable and extremely challenging location.

Finally, as of today, we have not as yet, identified the exact nature of the infection and its source; we have though established that the virus appears to have a longer incubation period than similar ones we've encountered in the past."

The man left the platform, answering no questions.

*   *   *

The following two weeks, leading up to the beginning of December, the story was on the minds of everyone in the camp except Horatio and Sofia.

Libby had been unable to contact her parents and although she wasn't panicking, she had told the others it was unusual for them not to speak to her at least once a fortnight.

Plans for Peter to fly home to be with the twins for Christmas, had been finalised, as had the travel arrangement for the three researchers, Libby, Joshua and Andrea; who were travelling home for the festive season.

Rachael and Thomas had considered spending their holiday on the island however, needing to revise for mock exams which were held immediately the school restarted, it was agreed their father should travel to them. It was the second year running the family was to be separated for Christmas and, although Jessica and Peter were saddened, they accepted the twin's exams had to come first.

*   *   *

The various flights for those travelling were booked for the fifteenth of December, but along with hundreds of thousands of other people wanting to fly over the holiday period, there was increasing unease in the camp over rumours that the sickness in South East Asia was being spread by air travel.

These stories originated on the internet and claimed the infection had finally been identified as an airborne virus, inferring it could be passed from one person to another with little difficulty, particularly within the confines of an aircraft.

Predictably, with no 'official' clarification to help calm public concern, this uncertainty strengthened creating greater anxiety, all of which was not aided by stories alleging news channels were being censored.

This further assertion, and that is all it was, appeared to be supported by blogs describing how news correspondents and journalists, based close to the original region of infection had been instructed to leave.

Apparently, local government representatives endeavored to explain the decision by declaring the directive was simply precautionary; for the protection of only those working for the media, not medical personnel.

As momentum in social media panic became overwhelming, the ongoing absence of information on actual deaths resulting from the virus, merely added fuel to the rapidly intensifying flames. These figures had not been released in over a fortnight, yet all queries were simply dismissed as irrelevant and unhelpful.

It was scarcely unexpected therefore, when gossip, theory or conjecture, voiced over social media took on a life of its own. In the blink of an eye, internet 'experts' predicted global chaos; these extreme views declaring that if the incubation period for the sickness was weeks rather than days, containing an airborne virus with the number of air passengers travelling each and every day throughout the world, would be impossible.

These alarmists, empowered by their hordes of sycophants, screamed loudly that questions must be asked and answered, whilst checks on the hundreds of thousands of people who had flown since the initial outbreak, must be undertaken. The doomsayers were only just getting started as they told the world it would only take a handful of infected air passengers travelling to a variety of different countries for the sickness to envelop the planet.

As night follows day, everything came to a head as someone, somewhere returned to the question of the original health workers. The general public were quick to recall that the local authorities of the three original countries involved, had admitted the international health workers had been withdrawn before the virus had been fully contained. The resulting question on the world's lips was whether those people were still healthy, posing no threat in the countries they had returned to.

*   *   *

The night of the fourteenth of December, Jessica, Filomena and Sofia cooked a special Christmas dinner for the team. Photos were taken, presents were swapped, even carols sung with Andrea accompanying them on a mini-keyboard she had brought with her.

Before heading off to bed, Peter Mott again tried to find updates on the troubles in S.E. Asia and for virtually the first time since they had been on Ilhéu de Cima, the internet connection was unresponsive. Rather confused, he tried the phones, finding all links with the satellite down.

Early on the morning of the fifteenth, the four adults boarded the boat to the Island of Praia and the Nelson Mandela International Airport. As he left Jessica and Horatio at the bay, Peter promised to contact them as soon as he landed at Heathrow, hopefully that same evening.

Chapter 10

Jessica allowed Horatio to stay up until ten-thirty as the flight was due to land in London at nine-thirty. However, throughout the evening there had been problems with the phone and computers, leaving them unaware that Peter and the three researchers had encountered delays with the flights. After a lengthy stopover in Lisbon, they were finally due to arrive in the UK at seven-thirty am, Cape Verde time, the following day.

*   *   *

Before breakfast next morning Horatio again tried and failed to get connected. When he told his mother, he saw that she was becoming increasingly concerned, but didn't really know how to help.

At nine o'clock when there had still been no call, Jessica told Horatio to begin his daily studies, saying there were still two days before the official school holidays began, so he had to do his lessons. To his credit, without so much as a moan, Horatio, with Nelson in tow, made his way to his bedroom.

Although he was not overly concerned, as he had rarely been part of any discussion about any sickness, Horatio was no fool and of course knew something out of the ordinary was going on.

Over the previous few weeks, when he had logged on, it was almost impossible to avoid information about the events in S.E. Asia, however, as with so many other, what he considered petty diversions in his life, he wasn't interested so he simply ignored it.

At eleven fifteen, Horatio heard the outside bell ringing, followed by his mother calling, and he ran across to the social hut and sat down next her.

"I can't hear you," she was yelling into the receiver and Horatio could see tears in her eyes.

The call then ended. His mother tried to dial the number back but couldn't get a signal.

"What's wrong?" he asked.

"I can't hear. I'm sure it was Rachael, but we were cut-off."

Horatio moved across to the computer to try to get online, but found it was the same, no satellite connection.

*   *   *

At lunchtime, Jessica asked Filomena and Sofia to sit with them to eat. It seemed ludicrous with everyone away and with far more room at the table then the two of them needed, for the housekeeper and her daughter to continue to eat in their small kitchen.

Whilst they ate, with Horatio translating for Filomena and Sofia where necessary, Jessica explained her impression of what was happening but admitted she had very few details. It was indisputable though, that like Jessica, Filomena had encountered serious difficulties trying to make contact with her family.

That evening, and the next day, there was still no news from Peter, or contact from anyone, leaving even Horatio uneasy.

*   *   *

Finally, on the twenty-first of December, six days after they had left, and just as his mother was about to send Horatio to bed, the phone rang.

"Hello," Jessica said impatiently. When she realised it was Peter she switched on the speaker for Horatio to listen.

"Thank God," Peter Mott's voice was shaky and indistinct; the quality of the connection was abysmal.

"How are…?" Jessica asked urgently, but, Peter instantly interrupted,

"Please, listen. Can you hear?"

"Yes, but…"

"Okay." There was some crackling and Horatio thought they had lost the signal, but his father spoke again,

"Do not leave the island. Whatever news you hear, do not leave the island. Do you understand?"

"Yes, but…"

"No buts. Under no circumstances must you and Horatio leave the island."

"But… what's going on, are you okay?" Jessica said forcibly, however, before Peter could answer there was more interference and crackling on the line.

"I'm fine." He finally answered, but it was so difficult to catch everything, "The twins are with me and we are at…" crackling, then a long continuous whine, finally back to Peter, "… the UK and probably most of the world have gone down with the virus. We've been told it quickly spreads and there is no antidote, so we must stay at…" More crackling, more frustration and so much more heartache, "… airports, railway stations; everything is shut; the country has come to a standstill… don't worry if I can't contact you, all the systems are overloaded and crashing. Christ, Jessica, I don't know what the hell to do."

He sounded exhausted as he said,

"We'll speak again, but if you don't hear…"

There was suddenly a loud crack and the connection failed.

Horatio again went to the computer to log on and found a message across the screen, 'due to unprecedented demand, we are unable to connect you. We apologise and ask you to try again later'.

As he looked across at his mother, she was sat motionless, except for her hands which were trembling.

"Mum," he said, but Jessica appeared not to hear him.

Ignoring his concern for his mother, Horatio tried again to get connected. Hearing his father's voice left him determined to speak to one of the twins or just anybody on the outside.

Eventually, his mother stood and crossed over to Horatio. She held him tightly and with little conviction whispered tearfully,

"At least we've spoken to them and they're together. If they're at home, they'll be safe."

Horatio hugged his mother.

"What did Dad mean; you know… about a virus? Is it that thing in Asia?"

"Probably, but whatever, Dad says we must stay here until we know more, so we must."

Over the next twenty four hours the phone rang three times, twice it was Peter and once Rachael but on each occasion the connection only lasted a few brief seconds.

And… those miniscule rays of hope, proved to be the final contact between Peter, or the twins and Ilhéu de Cima.

*   *   *

The next day, the twenty third of December, Filomena asked if she could leave; she explained she had elderly parents and wanted to make sure they, plus the rest of her family were safe. Jessica of course readily agreed, as she did for Filomena's additional request that Sofia remain behind; and of course it didn't occur to any of them that returning might prove impossible.

Mother and daughter then tried in vain to reach their family by mobile and camp phone. Their village was on the island of Santiago, only a few miles outside Praia and Filomena needed her nephew's fishing boat to pick her up. However, it was becoming clear that making contact with the outside world, was virtually impossible.

Late on the afternoon of the twenty-fourth, a fishing boat entered the bay. It was Horatio who spotted it first on one of his walks with Nelson and he ran to the camp. When Jessica heard the news, she called Filomena and with Nelson soaring above, the four walked down to the bay.

Horatio and Sofia were told to stay back, and Jessica warned all of them they must not touch, even get close to any visitors.

As the boat dropped anchor, just short of the beach, Filomena recognised her brother-in-law on board. Jessica relaxed... slightly, but still didn't allow any of them to approach the water's edge.

Peter's terrifying warning was engraved on her thinking and Jessica knew, certainly in the short term, she would have to be able to guarantee visitors did not carry the sickness, before inviting them ashore.

There were three men onboard and as they began to call out to Filomena and Sofia, Horatio translated for his mother,

"They've come to get Filomena and Sofia."

Filomena began to call back and again Horatio translated,

"She's asking about the village and the men are saying the island is safe; no one has the sickness."

Two of the men then jumped out of the boat and waded ashore.

"Horatio, tell Filomena she must not get close," Horatio translated his mother's message into Portuguese and the reply from Filomena.

"She's told them to stay on the boat and the men are saying they're healthy. Filomena's getting upset because that man," he pointed to the one speaking, "is saying that we are foreigners and it is not safe to stay with us. He just said it is us that caused the sickness."

The same man dropped into the water and waded towards Jessica and Filomena. As he got closer, Jessica pulled Filomena backwards, away from the beach.

"He's angry, Mum; he's saying if they don't go, he'll make them."

As Jessica watched an angry exchange developing, she knew they could not defend themselves against three men. In fact, she was quickly coming to the realization that they could not prevent the men doing whatever they wanted to.

Asking Horatio what was going on, he had to admit he was struggling to understand as things were becoming heated. Realising his difficulty, Sofia said to him in simple Portuguese,

"He's warning us, saying what he'll do if we refuse to go with him."

As the man closed in on Filomena, she turned to Jessica, and with Horatio translating, she said sadly,

"I'll go to my parents. It is the right thing to do, but please, can Sofia stay here? I know she will be safe with you." There were tears building in her eyes.

"Of course," Jessica replied, hugging Filomena and Horatio saw his mother welling up.

After further angry exchanges, which Horatio explained were about Sofia not leaving, Filomena hugged Horatio before holding her daughter, kissing her and whispering in her ear; she then embraced Jessica a final time. With her brother-in-law gripping her arm, she waded to the boat and climbed aboard.

As the small vessel moved slowly towards the open sea, Jessica held Sofia, and together they cried.

*   *   *

Christmas Day dawned and it proved extremely challenging for Jessica and Sofia. Of course they attempted to celebrate, but in different ways both believed that whilst they were safe, their families were anything but and their ever-increasing guilt was becoming intolerable.

For Horatio, well… it was just like any other day, except for the few presents he received and the fact he didn't have to do his studies. Watching his mother though as she tried to be cheerful, he knew she was missing his father and the twins dreadfully. On a couple of occasions during the day he had looked for her to find she was in her bedroom crying, but as desperate as Horatio was to comfort her, he just didn't know how.

*　　　*　　　*

There was no further communication with the outside world until December the twenty-ninth, when another fishing boat was spotted.

Again it had been Horatio who first saw it, well actually, it had been Nelson. They had been on the highest point of Ilhéu de Cima when the falcon had flown straight at Horatio squawking loudly before swooping down in the direction of the bay.

Running back to camp, Horatio called his mother who in turn called Sofia, and much to his astonishment, Jessica joined him carrying a shotgun. As they walked down the path towards the bay, she loaded cartridges into the twin barrels and told Sofia and Horatio to stay behind her.

As the boat sailed towards them, they could see someone standing at the front and after a few moments recognised Filomena. Sofia was overjoyed and they all waved and shouted to her.

When it was just off the beach, however, the skipper changed direction and one of the men dropped anchor. Jessica placed the gun behind the nearest rock, out of sight and walked towards the beach.

Filomena began shouting and with Nelson on Horatio's shoulder, he translated for his mother.

"She says we must not get close, terrible things are happening in the village."

Sofia, visibly desperate to get to the boat, began to cry and as he held her back, Horatio carried on translating for his mother.

"When she first got home, her family were okay, but the very next day three people in the village fell ill and one died within hours. The next day two more got sick, and seeing what was happening, she had to see Sofia one more time before it was too late."

Filomena told them they would all stay on the boat; seeing Sofia, even from a distance would be more than enough.

Jessica asked about her parents and Filomena answered that up to when she had left, they were fine, but added wretchedly that it really was only a matter of time for all of them.

Sofia was beside herself and kept asking her mother why she wasn't coming back.

A tearful Filomena described how the television was still working, but only on and off, and the news she'd heard said the illness was highly contagious and an unidentified strain of measles. People were being advised that even if they felt fine, they might be carrying the virus, so must be extremely cautious. Apparently, every country was affected and most cities were virtually out of control; everyone was being told to stay indoors and wait.

Filomena went on to say that there were so many rumours, but one seemed likely to be true. It was said that because of the number of international flights in and out of Praia's main airport, there was no way the island could avoid being infected.

Continuing to translate, whilst Sofia held Jessica, Horatio said,

"She says she has some things for us."

Clearly attempting to sound positive Filomena described what she had brought with her.

"This is for you Sofia; just a few special things my darling."

Powerless to stop her tears, she said,

"This one is full of English newspapers for the tourists, all the local and Portuguese papers had been taken. They're all out of date but might give you some idea of what's been happening.

Lastly, this one has a few medicines. I collected everything I could find but the pharmacies have all been looted."

As brave as she was being, Filomena was undoubtedly overwhelmed with hopelessness, and as her tears flowed, so did Sofia's and Jessica's.

Slightly regaining her poise, Filomena described how her nephew Juan, would swim to the beach with the bags before immediately returning to the boat. She told them they must move well back, away from the water's edge.

Jessica, Sofia and Horatio grudgingly began to climb the steep path towards the camp. Half way up, they saw a young boy wade ashore and place the bags on the beach before returning to the boat.

Jessica could see he was a defenceless, innocent child who would probably be dead within days and she despised what was happening to the world.

Once he was back on board, Jessica, Sofia and Horatio walked back to the beach, but before they'd reached the water's edge, the boat's anchor had been raised and with Filomena nowhere to be seen, they sailed out of the bay towards the open sea.

Sofia screamed at her mother to come back, begging her not to go. She ran out into the water, trying to catch her up and as Horatio moved to follow, Jessica held him back,

"Let her be," she said gently.

After a few heartbreaking moments, Sofia gave up the chase and as she stood with the water up to her neck, she shouted and waved at the fading silhouette of her mother, never taking her eyes of the boat as it melted into the sunset,

Jessica shivered, knowing it might well be the last contact with human beings for weeks, months, even years.

Chapter 11

Back in camp, Jessica went directly to the lab to see what information they had on measles. She remembered from when she had been involved in an avian research project aligned to contagions, that measles was an airborne infection passed from person to person principally through coughs and sneezes,

The books and papers she found in the lab were of little help as most of the scientific material needed for their research was done through the internet, a source that had come to an abrupt end.

$$* \qquad * \qquad *$$

Following their evening meal, when the new team of only three, were sat together in the social area Horatio asked his mother about the shotgun.

"Before we left England," she answered guardedly, realising where the question might lead, "your father told me as we were coming to a very different place to the one we were used to, we should make sure we were protected. He spoke to the university, our sponsors and even the Cape Verde Government and they all agreed it was a sensible precaution."

"But you knew how to load it?"

"Well… once you had gone back to school after your last summer holidays at St. Indract's, a local farmer showed us how shotguns work. We then shot clay pigeons… I think four times; it was at the range. I practised loading and firing it."

"So, how many guns do we have?"

"Just the one, and we only have a small number of cartridges, so we must be careful about wasting ammunition."

"Cool," was the only thing Horatio said, as he moved to the computer.

Relieved the subject was closed, Jessica opened the bag from Filomena containing the newspapers and spread them out on the low coffee table; she counted eight before placing them in chronological order.

She then asked Horatio and Sofia if they were interested and wanted to help; neither was as they had just started playing a game that Horatio had downloaded before Christmas.

Jessica began with the oldest newspaper dated the tenth of December and found the broadsheet contained little of interest, which surprised her considering the difficulties Peter had encountered travelling home just a few days later.

The next paper was dated the fourteenth of December; again it was a broadsheet, and she found one article at the bottom of the front page relating to problems in S.E. Asia. It again contained little useful information and when she searched through the rest of the pages, found no other references to the sickness.

The next three papers were all dated the fifteenth, which was the day Peter had flown out. Two were broadsheets and one tabloid, and all three had headlines referring to the infection. Scanning the pages, she saw a number of articles referring to previous health scares in poorer parts of the world, specifics about the response or rather lack of response from the international community to the S.E. Asia sickness, and quite comprehensive information on measles.

Jessica placed them to one side and browsed through the last of the newspapers which were dated the sixteenth of December. All three were tabloid and all had their entire front pages devoted to the virus.

After moving to one of the desks and finding a pad and pen, Jessica reread the articles from the fifteenth and sixteenth of December. She was acutely aware that any useful information, especially evidence or substantiated facts associated with the outbreak might prove crucial in the future so she took notes as she read.

It was clear that by the fifteenth of December, the blame game had begun and the editorial fingers were being pointed at the World Health Organisation. Many of the pieces claimed that when the virus had first raised its ugly head in S.E. Asia, the health workers had done everything possible to control the spread of the sickness, but their efforts had proved fruitless. An opportunity to contain the sickness had clearly been missed.

As she read on, Jessica found an article which contained irrefutable verification that the problem was caused by an, as yet unidentified, exceptionally virulent strain of measles; a claim Filomena had said she heard on the television news.

Jessica was then amazed that she only found one headline which highlighted what no one other newspaper had been prepared to admit.

'People around the world must accept without further accusations that no matter what precautions may or may not have been put in place, no medicines or drugs are currently available which combat or even slow down the spread of this deadly virus'.

Jessica then found a lengthy report which described how as it was a measles strain, an illness no longer considered uncontrollable, the international health agencies placed little importance on the outbreak. Adding that these same organizations did accept that with hindsight their initial findings were significantly flawed and attempted to justify their complacency by saying these were based on previous comparable epidemics, all of which had been quickly contained.

Only one health organization actually admitted their response to the S.E. Asia crisis had been too little too late, and yet another article went on to say that all things considered, it was relatively easy to appreciate why the response time had been so pitiful. It clarified this surprising comment by describing how in a world of never ending demands, when as a result of the decades long UN mass-inoculation efforts tens of millions are immunised against measles; when the validity of that programme had been endorsed by data revealing a number of nations, including the likes of the U.S.A., were measles free, indecision at the top of the health agencies was understandable.

It then concluded critically though, that as commendable as these worldwide achievements were, they led directly to the regulatory authorities failing to act upon annual data which clearly revealed measles as remaining highly active.

'Far too many countries continue to suffer deadly outbreaks of measles resulting in tens of thousands of deaths, each and every year. Surely not acting upon the well documented death of innocent people, was irresponsible in the extreme.'

*   *   *

As she read, Jessica wrote down a list of significant facts about measles in the hope that she might be better prepared, if God forbid any of them became infected.

Once she had finished all the newspaper articles she then tore her notes from the notepad, spread them across the desk and began to study them:

- Measles is also known as morbilli, rubeola, or red measles.
- It is a highly contagious infection.

- The symptoms include red eyes, runny nose and a high fever.
- Small white spots may form on the inside of the mouth after a few days.
- After three to five days, a rash will appear on the face which then spreads to the rest of the body.

Also included were the things she remembered from her earlier research:

- Measles is an airborne disease.
- It is spread through the coughs and sneezes of infected people.

What she had forgotten however, was that in a minority of cases, the virus could also spread through contact with an infected person's saliva or secretions.

This made Jessica ask whether she'd been in too much of a hurry to retrieve Filomena's bags from the beach and prayed that none of the items had been contaminated. On reflection she wished she had worn gloves and mask before making a search of the contents, but it was too late; she would just have to monitor the three of them to make sure they remained in the clear.

Attempting to ignore her unease, she went back to her notes:

- Ninety percent of people, not immune to measles, who share a living space with an infected person, will catch it.
- Infected people are a danger to others for eight days; four days before the rash appears to four days after.

There followed details which exposed the enormity of the crisis mankind was facing:

- Twenty million people a year are affected by the virus, primarily in poorer countries of Africa and Asia.
- Death rates have fallen dramatically since the nineteen nineties, however, it is estimated that as many as one hundred and fifty thousand people lose their lives annually to measles.
- Some people will develop pneumonia as a consequence of being infected. Other complications include diarrhoea, blindness, ear infections, bronchitis (viral or secondary bacterial) and, or, brain inflammation, known as encephalitis.
- Most people survive measles, but, the report emphasized, this refers only to known strains where treatment or immunisation has been administered.

Rechecking the newspapers, wanting to be aware of anything that might prove important, Jessica noticed an editorial she'd missed. It was from the sixteenth of December and as she read, her unease grew.

The piece began by quoting a virologist in America, who suggested the new, unidentified type of measles had characteristics unlike any known strain.

It continued by explaining that research into common forms of measles, undertaken over many years had discovered that infected people reacted in a variety of ways; for an extremely small minority, it could be life-threatening or life-changing, but for most, it was far less severe.

However, studies into the characteristics of the new strain, especially the results gained from autopsies undertaken on those who had died in the initial contagion in S.E. Asia, revealed that all those infected displayed clear signs of suffering from the most severe complications.

Jessica was dismayed. If every case of the new strain of measles resulted in pan-encephalitis and/or acute measles encephalitis, then what hope was there? Any infected person would end up dead or with irreparable brain damage.

Struggling to ignore her growing horror, Jessica returned to her notes.

- It was reported that well into the new millennium, there had still been almost ten-thousand cases of measles in Europe and of those, ninety percent occurred in just five countries including the UK.

Replacing her pen on the desk, Jessica sat feeling numb; if countries such as the UK were not measles free, then what chance was there for the rest of the world?

Turning again to the last newspaper, she saw an article she had initially disregarded. It was printed on the inside back page and looked as if it had been rushed out in time for that edition. The headline screamed 'The Second Coming of Eve'. When she had first scanned the paper Jessica had assumed it had nothing to do with the pandemic, however, taking a second look, something caught her eye.

The writer claimed to have been given access to highly sensitive data, collected from both the original site of the outbreak, and from the countries where fatalities from the virus had occurred.

In any other context, the conclusion reached by the writer bordered on science fiction, but as Jessica read, the evidence appeared indisputable. It stated that the virus was killing over ninety-nine percent of infected males, compared to only seventy-five percent of infected females.

Jessica was astounded by the word 'only', but knew if the article was accurate, the implications for the future were beyond understanding.

Rapidly doing her own calculation, she realised that with the world's population approaching nine billion:

- If ninety-nine percent of the four-point seven billion males were wiped out, there would be just four and half million left.
- If seventy-five percent of the four-point three billion women died out, there would be over one hundred and seven million survivors.

Staring at her figures, she whispered,

"There will be nearly twenty-five females for every male… and what about those men and boys who may die before the virus finally burns itself out?"

Jessica looked towards Horatio, who sat next to Sofia playing on the computer and asked herself what sort of life a male survivor would have? And…, God forbid, if the few finally succumbed to the virus, leaving no males, the human race would disappear in just a few decades.

Returning to the article, Jessica then understood: 'The Second Coming of Eve'.

The figures revealed women would be the future; the decision makers, the leaders. They would oversee the next chapter of human development; something Jessica saw fraught with unintended consequences.

Again, returning to Horatio, she realised if the death rate for males came to fruition, the odds of him surviving away from the island were next to nothing.

Two thoughts then came to her; firstly, the probability of them being rescued by non-infected people was practically zero and secondly, any healthy survivors would more than likely be living in remote areas, similar to themselves where they were cut-off from exposure to those carrying the virus.

Staring at her notes and calculations, Jessica knew that under no circumstances could they leave the island, and no one, neither friend or stranger could be allowed to come ashore, unless she was unequivocally convinced they were still healthy.

*   *   *

Even allowing for her understanding of the facts, Jessica could never have predicted they would remain on Ilhéu de Cima for more than six years. Six very long, lost years, and at the end of that self-inflicted exile, it would not be three but only two, who finally escaped.

Chapter 12

For Jessica, Sofia and Horatio, the island became their sanctuary and each in their own way knew they must come to terms with an immediate future cut off from all other people.

As the months passed, Jessica saw that in the longer term Horatio would have little trouble accepting their circumstances. Apart from clearly missing his father and the twins, the island undoubtedly suited him; he had Nelson and was surrounded by the things he loved most; also, rather reassuringly, he rarely appeared downhearted.

Sofia, on the other hand, who on March the twenty-second had celebrated her eighteenth birthday, just a week after Horatio celebrated his fourteenth, concerned Jessica. It was quite apparent she had led a sheltered life; no doubt one of the reasons why her mother brought her to the island in the first place, and Jessica's worry stemmed from not knowing how she would react to a life devoid of male company.

Sofia had reached an age where normally she would be searching for greater independence and she would be deprived of those episodes when you choose to push your luck or not. Of course she'd want to experiment, and hopefully learn, especially from her mistakes.

Without her mother, Jessica felt Sofia would need a confidante in the months, even years, that lay ahead and decided to offer herself as the aunt that would always be there if and when she was needed.

*   *   *

Whilst acknowledging that to all intents and purposes Sofia was legally an adult, Jessica felt she had little choice but to accept it would have to be she, and she alone, who took responsibility for making key decisions.

Jessica also knew though, that however difficult the choices she had to make, her focus must always be on creating a life that was happy and secure for all three of them. Without that, any chance of Sofia choosing to remain on the island to outlive the infection would disappear and she would have failed in Filomena's final request to her.

*   *   *

Early in May, six months after Peter had left, with life on the island settling into an agreeable routine, Jessica said she needed to speak to Sofia and Horatio.

She began by explaining as sympathetically as she could, that to stay safe they would have to remain on the island for quite possibly many years and they needed to make the most of it.

Jessica told them she'd made a list of the things it would be good to discuss and as she spoke, was pleasantly surprised. The habitually restless Horatio sat still, listened, and whenever Sofia struggled to understand, translated the words and meanings in a most mature manner.

Originally, his mother had decided they should discuss the virus. She believed with no internet, neither of them would have any understanding of the illness, its rapid spread or the cataclysmic impact it was having on countries around the world. However, as it turned out, before she had hardly got started she saw that Sofia was simply not ready to discuss the ghastly details of a virus that had probably killed her entire family.

Deciding to move on, she said to Horatio,

"Since your father and Joshua left, I know I have stopped you fishing." Horatio pulled a face that clearly revealed he was not overly happy with the decision. "You see, I've been worried about you getting into trouble in the water, but things have changed. Our supply of frozen fish has almost gone and from now on, we will have to catch it." Horatio's frown turned into a grin; that was until his mother added, "There are though, conditions!" Jessica smiled as Horatio groaned. "You may only fish when one of us is on the beach. Although we're not strong swimmers like you, we should be able to help if anything were to go wrong."

Although Jessica was anxious about her change of mind, she had to admit that there was no simple way of protecting either of them from danger; for the next few years they would all have to play their part in solving problems that arose, no matter how dangerous.

The fishing having been decided, Jessica looked at her list.

"Okay, we've also used up all the frozen meat, so you and I Sofia, are going to grow all the food we can, okay?" Sofia nodded with a willing smile.

There followed a short discussion before it was decided that each of them would be responsible for their own bedrooms. Sofia would prepare all the food, whilst Jessica and Horatio would clear up after meals. Sofia would also undertake the general cleaning except for the lab, which Jessica would do. Although she saw little chance of continuing her research, the lab still contained hazardous items.

Moving rapidly through the list, next it was agreed that whenever things required maintenance or repairs, they would work together, allowing each of them to learn how to keep essential machinery going. Jessica reinforced the need for this by saying that if one of them became sick, they must not have become dependent on that person to keep equipment working, especially anything critical to their survival. She then emphasised the crucial importance of the fresh water system, solar panels and energy storage; without these, she stressed, they could not remain on the island.

Horatio and Sofia seemed happy to agree with Jessica's plans; that was until she made the suggestion that they should speak English on a Tuesday, Thursday and Saturday, and Portuguese on a Monday, Wednesday and Friday. She finished saying on a Sunday they could choose whatever language they wanted. Sofia looked disappointed until Jessica explained,

"Your English has improved so much but, when we are together without Horatio, we sometimes have a few problems understanding each other. We can usually make each other aware of what we want to say, but it can get confusing."

When Horatio saw Sofia looking edgy, and knowing how important the matter was to his mother, he began to translate.

"You see, even if all three of us are together," Jessica carried on explaining, "I'm nervous that if there's an emergency and we need to react quickly, if we cannot understand each other and misunderstand what needs to be done, a problem could become far more dangerous."

After a short discussion, Sofia agreed with Jessica that rotating their languages was a sensible precaution. For Horatio, well he thought the whole idea quite amusing.

*   *   *

Jessica was delighted Horatio and Sofia had quickly adopted the agreed routine, but she knew in the back of both their minds, they questioned whether she was making a huge mistake. She could just imagine them talking about whether the virus had really been as devastating as claimed and because they were so cut-off, they might never know? Just maybe everything on the outside had returned to normal.

At the beginning of June, whilst eating their evening meal, Horatio raised the uncertainty. Jessica thought about it for a few moments and decided to answer, with a number of other questions,

"Well… if that's the case; if everything has returned to normal, where are Peter and the twins? Why haven't they come back to us? And… where's Filomena and the rest of Sofia's family? Surely, living so close to us, don't you think they might have been in touch or even come to take her home?"

Of course… neither had answers and sat there slightly embarrassed.

"You see, "Jessica continued generously, "The problem is the only way to find out what is happening, is to leave the island and travel."

Knowing the discussion was moving into areas she was keen to avoid, especially as it would raise the possibility of Sofia wanting to go home, Jessica needed to end their uncertainties.

"The way I look at it, if we were ever to agree the gamble of leaving the island is worth the risk, you both have to accept we may never find the same level of protection we have here, or even somewhere remotely safe."

Primarily for Sofia's benefit, Jessica then continued.

"Look, whatever you are missing in your lives, whatever your frustrations, at least we have a home that is safe and secure. You see, I believe we are truly blessed; we're being spared the unimaginable horror of witnessing everything we've ever known, falling apart.

So… please, tell me why would you want to waste the incredible good fortune we three were given when the virus struck?

You know, you really couldn't make it up. Just as the human race was being slaughtered in its millions by some lethal bug, we were safe on what until just recently had been an uninhabited island in the middle of the Atlantic Ocean? Would anyone really believe that we could have been that lucky?"

Sofia and Horatio, who had never heard his mother speaking so forcefully, sat quietly, avoiding eye contact with Jessica or each other.

* * *

As the weeks moved into months and then into years, Jessica's and Sofia's lives changed little, apart that is from how they dealt with their darker moments. There were no intimate friends or close relations to share their worries, hopes and expectation. No one to hug in those moments of despair, especially when memories of lost loved-ones enveloped them. No one to lean on when the pain of knowing there was a whole world just around the corner that could not be visited or contacted, became intolerable.

For Jessica, she told herself daily that taking into consideration the unprecedented turmoil that had entered their lives, they had created a home which couldn't be bettered. However, she understood, it would never be as simple as that.

Her life had been turned upside down in the most harrowing of ways; two of her children along with her husband were missing and she had no idea if they were alive or dead.

The reality was, Jessica had no choice but to accept things as they were and how they would continue to be.

Everything she had ever worked for throughout her whole life, all she had achieved, professionally and personally, was no longer relevant. There could only be the here and now; whilst the leftovers... well... they were just unhelpful memories.

By not looking back, by discarding so many things that had once mattered; the way she looked, the clothes she wore, her desires, even her happiness; she was left to concentrate on the only purpose she still had; keeping Sofia and Horatio alive.

*   *   *

For Sofia, remarkably for someone of her age, after a shaky start she settled into the demands of her new life with few difficulties. She cherished the time spent in the garden, cooking; even the cleaning, though it was when she was cleaning she missed her mother the most.

Nonetheless, following the firm talk from Jessica, Sofia knew she was indeed blessed and couldn't imagine how her life would be if she had not been allowed to stay on the island.

Sofia had no idea what had happened to the people in her village, but at least she was alive and healthy. Destiny, or maybe God, had decided she should be protected when the rest of mankind was being annihilated by some great act of nature, and, she knew there would never be answers as to why she had been in the right place at the right time.

Of course there were frustrations, sometimes daily. Sofia was a healthy young woman with the needs and desires of any other healthy young woman and she was desperate for contact with men of her own age. Unfortunately, the only male she was likely to see for a very long time was Horatio, and in so many ways he was still a little boy who routinely drove her up the wall with his juvenile behaviour. Nevertheless, she did have to admit that most of the time he was fun and she readily conceded her genuine admiration for the way someone so young was dealing with the loss of his father and siblings.

Sofia knew no one could replace her mother, but it took just a short time for her to come to value and adore Jessica. Her 'new' aunt, would always talk to her. When she needed support Jessica was always willing; she was constantly there to give her a huge hug when Sofia felt miserable, and because of her resilient, positive attitude, Jessica was nearly always a joy to be around.

All in all Sofia decided Jessica may have been her adopted aunt, but under the circumstances, she couldn't have wanted or needed anyone more.

*   *   *

For Horatio, well… it was very different. At the beginning, he found everything about the island amazing. He seldom got bored and was never restless or lonely, which was mostly down to the fact that Nelson rarely left his side.

However, losing his father and the twins had been awful and Horatio still missed them dreadfully. He understood though, if he could bury the feeling of sadness, whilst never forgetting them, living on Ilhéu de Cima could go back to being truly remarkable.

On the very rare occasions Horatio did become upset, he'd go to his secret hideaway and sit on his own, recalling better times; Nelson was always outside, perched on his favourite boulder, patiently waiting for him.

As he passed his fifteenth and sixteenth birthdays, physically Horatio continued to grow and grow, and grow. His mother was somewhat surprised as she knew of no other members of either Peter's or her family who were tall. It seemed that almost overnight Horatio had shot up and filled out and by the time he had finished growing, he stood well over six-feet.

Looking up at her son, Jessica realised he had become a handsome young man and she began to muse over what Sofia thought of him, and, just as importantly, what he thought about the only girl in town.

As she considered the situation, Jessica burst into a fit of giggles, deciding Horatio probably hadn't even noticed that Sofia was anything other than a big sister.

Chapter 13

Two years and five months APD, or After Peter's Disappearance, for that was how Jessica measured time; the island received its first visitors since Filomena had sailed away.

The boat's arrival had not been spotted by anyone and Jessica only realised they had uninvited guests as she looked out of her bedroom window and saw two men, both holding machetes, reaching the top of the steep climb from the beach.

Jessica knew Sofia was in the kitchen preparing their evening meal and assumed Horatio was out and about with Nelson. Taking the shotgun she kept next to her bed, she loaded both barrels and opened the cabin door.

"Stop! Do not come any closer," she called out.

The men stopped and stared in obvious interest, as Jessica moved out of the hut, though their expressions swiftly altered when they saw she was carrying a gun.

Sofia, hearing Jessica call out, opened the door of the social hut to see what was happening; the men were undoubtedly delighted to see not one, but two women.

"No understand," the older of the men called back in pigeon English.

"I said, do not move closer!" Although there was menace in the way Jessica spoke, the men laughed at her.

"No understand," the older man repeated, still amused.

Without warning, Horatio, who had been out walking with Nelson, appeared from behind the lab hut and loudly translated his mother's warning in Portuguese.

The older man turned, appearing less assured at the arrival of a large, healthy young man with an enormous, evil looking bird on his arm. After a few moments he then answered Horatio, who relayed the message to his mother.

"It seems they only want to make sure we are okay. They were told about us and were concerned for our safety."

"Tell him we're fine and they must leave, now."

As Horatio passed on his mother's demand, smirking distastefully the man said something quietly to his friend and the younger one moved towards Sofia, the elder towards Jessica.

"I'm sure he said you won't fire," Horatio yelled to her.

As they walked in to the centre of the camp, the two men reached under their jackets and Nelson instantly took off, screeching loudly before flying directly at the men.

Both men ducked but ignored the falcon and moved quickly towards the two women, leaving Jessica with no option but to fire both barrels.

The first shot hit the older man in the chest and he went down with a howl, the second caught the younger man in the midriff.

Horatio ran towards the two bodies but hesitated when he heard his mother scream.

"Horatio, stay back!"

Jessica reloaded the gun as she ran to the lab, returning with gloves and masks and made Horatio put them on before dressing herself in protective gear. Taking her son by the arm, with Nelson flying overhead screeching and Sofia staring in disbelief, Jessica pointed the shotgun at the men and walked slowly towards them.

It was clear the older of the two seemed lifeless so they approached him first. Jessica bent down, checked for a pulse and found no sign of life; there was though a pistol in his right hand and she took it along with the machete, and threw them out of reach.

With Horatio in tow she moved towards the younger man who was still alive, but bleeding profusely.

With no apparent interest in his discomfort or injury, Jessica told Horatio to ask him what was happening on the other islands.

"Mum, he's dying."

"Just do it," she answered indifferently, and reluctantly he asked.

In severe pain the man tried to answer. Eventually, after coughing up copious amounts of blood, he whispered and Horatio translated his words.

"The other islands are deserted. There are dead bodies though, still lying everywhere."

"Ask him what the chances are of finding people alive?"

"None." Horatio said as the man continued coughing up blood.

Suddenly Jessica pulled Horatio further away,

"Don't touch the blood!" she said as the man tried to move.

Looking at Horatio, he begged him.

"I'm dying, please help me."

Ignoring him, his mother told Horatio to ask where they had sailed from.

"They've been sailing around the islands for months."

"Ask him why they came here."

"Mum, we must do something for him."

"Just ask!"

"He says his father wanted to find women."

The man began to choke as large globules of thick blood spurted from his mouth. He tried to speak but only muttered a few words before choking.

"Mum!" Horatio implored his mother.

"No. He will die, soon. What did he just say?"

"That they had to make children."

Moments later, a horrified Horatio looked on as the young man died. Jessica told him to help her search the body, avoiding any blood and they found yet another pistol; it confirmed both men were reaching for their guns when Jessica fired.

With great difficulty Sofia, Jessica and Horatio dragged the corpses to the cliff edge before rolling them over the drop, into the churning waves below.

*   *   *

That evening, their meal was eaten in virtual silence and Jessica knew her son was extremely upset about the earlier events. After the plates had been cleared and washed, she asked Sofia and Horatio to sit with her.

"What happened today is something I will never forget, but never regret."

"But you killed two men, how can't you regret that?" an incensed Horatio asked.

"Yes, I did, and you know what, I will do exactly the same again if our lives are ever threatened. Try to understand, you two are my responsibility, there is no one else to look after you and I will do absolutely everything I can to make sure you stay safe, and that includes killing anyone who wants to hurt us."

"But I don't understand how you could just let the young one die."

"If it's any help, I now realise I should never have told them they could leave. If they had gone, you know, they would have come back, most probably at night, and done God knows what to us."

Horatio looked unconvinced as Jessica said,

"They would never have helped us. They were here to steal, and that by the way, includes Sofia."

She stared at her son and before he could disagree, she added candidly,

"Firstly, as their main threat, they would have killed you. Next they would have raped me, then killed me. Finally, they would have taken what they wanted including Sofia, probably after having raped her. So, thinking through what happened, I was extremely stupid to have offered them the chance to leave and then return." Jessica

115

took hold of one of Horatio's and one of Sofia's hands, and said calmly,

"I'm sorry, but you must understand that if anything similar happens again, I will kill whoever it is; I just won't wait so long to do it."

"Can I say something, please?"

It was the first time Sofia had spoken.

"Of course," Jessica answered gently.

Looking at Horatio and speaking in heavily accented English, Sofia said tentatively,

"Your mother is right... I know men like these; they are very, very bad people. They would come back, kill you and take us." Sofia moved to Jessica and hugged her. "Thank you for saving me. You are so very brave."

Lost for words, Horatio realised he had been too quick to judge his mother and after a few moments of thoughtful silence, he whispered,

"You're right, I'm sorry, I didn't think."

His mother looked at her son, smiled and said warmly,

"Okay, let's learn from it. Oh... don't forget by the way, Nelson's bravery. If he hadn't flown at them, I really don't know what might have happened."

Horatio didn't need reminding, it was just another example of how extraordinary the falcon was. It was as if he had a sixth sense for danger and somehow knew he had to react to it.

"Didn't you find it interesting what the man said about the sickness killing everyone?" Jessica asked, and when she got little response, added, "Think about it, that's the first time we've been told what's happening away from our island and worryingly, it probably means the virus is still active."

The inference was clear to all of them, they had to remain where they were and Jessica understood the frustration and resentment Sofia and Horatio must have been feeling.

The following morning, nothing could have prepared them for what they found on the fishing boat the men had used. The two cabins had been stripped away converting them into a large storage area which were full of boxes, crates, packages and most bizarrely of all, seven live chickens in a wire cage.

Jessica told Horatio to unload the chickens first and asked Sofia to take them up to the camp and make sure they were fed. If, and it was a big if, the chickens were healthy, and if there was a cockerel, they would have an endless supply of eggs and fresh meat for the first time in years.

Once Sofia had gone, Jessica and Horatio began to unload the boat. Everything was placed on the beach and when they had finished, Horatio was told to take the boat out in to the sea and sink it before swimming back. Horatio was horrified until his mother explained that they already had a boat, which was reasonably well hidden but if seen could encourage passing vessels to investigate, two boats and they would almost certainly get visitors.

The rest of that day was taken up with transferring the items from the beach up to the social hut and during the evening, they went through each box. Sifting through the items, it became obvious that they had discovered a treasure trove of useful as well as some valuable objects.

In one box they discovered dozens of tins of food, all out of date but useable so Jessica asked Sofia to store them in the kitchen. There were half a dozen suitcases full of clothes and she spread the garments on the floor before the three of them sorted out what they wanted and what they thought might be useful later on.

Sofia then opened a large cardboard box to find it full of jewellery and trinkets, which merely confirmed the two men had raided the islands, stealing the objects that took their fancy or could be profitable.

Jessica opened another large cardboard box to find it full of knives, followed by another which contained dozens of watches, some of which must have cost a fortune when originally bought. Shockingly, Jessica realised that the only way the men could have collected so many watches was off dead bodies, but she decided to say nothing.

Horatio opened a heavy wooden crate to find an assortment of guns and as they went through them, Jessica said,

"Unless we can find bullets, they're all useless."

Horatio and Sofia began to search other boxes but found nothing that looked remotely like ammunition.

"I wonder how many people they murdered to get this stuff?" Horatio said thoughtfully, "You know, I don't believe what he said about no one being alive on the other islands. They probably killed everyone who got in their way, just like they would've killed us."

Chapter 14

One year after the shooting of the two men, simply put, Horatio and Sofia had sex.

Jessica had been aware for some time the two of them were becoming ever closer and if she was honest, she was just astonished it had taken them quite so long. Horatio had celebrated his seventeenth birthday a couple of months earlier and one week after that, Sofia her twenty-first. It was therefore, hardly surprising that having spent three and a half years being forced together on an isolated island, with no other people of their respective ages to mix with, the temptation to push the limits with each other had obviously become irresistible.

*   *   *

When he thought about it, which he did, habitually, Horatio realised how nerve-racking the whole thing had been. He accepted, with some discomfort, that initially it had all been a bit of a disaster; in fact, if he was honest, it had been a complete disaster. Neither of them had any idea of what they were doing, and even though they both knew the mechanics of sex, they ended up groping around each other trying to figure out how and where various parts of their bodies were supposed to go.

Six weeks later, and after a good deal of experimentation, the two of them had settled into a physical relationship that seemed assured and fulfilling.

Early on they had agreed to do nothing which might embarrass or disappoint Jessica and therefore only enjoyed each other down by the bay, usually after Horatio had finished fishing.

And that was how it had all started.

Following the agreement with his mother, most days, Sofia watched over Horatio when he fished, then on one occasion she asked Jessica if she could join him.

There had been many months of 'accidently' touching; discussing the intimacies of young people's relationships, joking suggestively in Portuguese so that Jessica would not be offended, contriving to be as close to each other as they could without drawing attention to themselves. However, Sofia in a bikini had probably been the final shove Horatio needed. As they lay drying off in the warm sun, being watched over by Nelson who was perched on a rock nearby, out of the blue, Horatio asked Sofia whether she had even been with a man.

"What a question," she replied, but happily answered with a meaningful smile, saying she hadn't.

"But didn't you ever want to?" he probed, surprised at his candour.

Sofia rolled over on to her front and looked at him.

"So, would you like to... you know... with me?" she replied.

"Well, I..., oh, I... oh God, of course I would, yes."

She then stretched towards him and kissed him. His immediate reaction was to pull away in shock, but then felt an irresistible need, and returned the kiss. In no time, both of them had managed to remove each other's swimwear and when Sofia saw Horatio's arousal, she laughed,

"My God, look at that!"

Mortified, Horatio made a grab for his trunks, but Sofia took his hand and placed it on her breast. She then pulled him towards her. He urgently rolled on top of her, having absolutely no idea what he was supposed to do. Sofia opened her legs to make him welcome, but he didn't know where to put himself and it was all over before it had even got started.

Again, feeling completely hopeless, Horatio reached for his trunks and without saying anything, he began to get up.

"Don't go," Sofia said gently and took his arm to stop him leaving.

Horatio lay back down and as Sofia lay naked next to him, he looked at her and realised what a wonderful body she had. With light copper skin, to go with her jet-black hair and deep brown eyes, he couldn't believe that she would be interested in him.

Plucking up courage, with his fingers he traced an imaginary line from her lips to her breasts, then down to her midriff and as he discovered her most private parts, he realised he was getting aroused once again. Sofia, noticing what was happening said,

"This time let me help you." She again drew him on to her, made herself available, took his manhood and manoeuvred it to where he could enter her. As soon as he did, Sofia cried out and Horatio thought he had hurt her, not realising the pain was not unusual the first time for a woman.

Sofia then began to moan and Horatio lay completely still, again thinking he was hurting her, but when she told him how incredible it was, as much as he tried, he couldn't hold himself back.

Horatio rolled away and as they lay next to each other hand in hand, he at last understood why there had always been such a fuss made about sex.

"How did you know what to do if you've never been with a man?" he asked a few moments later.

"Well, girls talk about it, quite a lot." She laughed as she rolled over on to her front, faced Horatio and kissed him again.

"Before I came here with my mother," she said, "quite a few times I had wanted to do it with a boy I knew, and a couple of times we got very close but I always stopped him because I wasn't really ready."

"And now?"

"Now, we are stuck on this island and only have each other. I'm twenty-one and normally in my family, I would be married and pregnant with my third or fourth child."

"Good God," Horatio stuttered, quickly sitting up. "Does that mean you'll be pregnant now?"

"I have no idea, but what happens, happens, I really don't care. We may never get away from this place and... Well, I really like you." Sofia answered and gently kissed Horatio again.

"But what about my mother?" he asked, concerned.

"If it happens, we'll have to talk to her."

Before he could say anything else, Sofia's hands began to explore his body and all thoughts of the possible consequences quickly vanished.

Chapter 15

Eighteen months later in early November, the final chapter of their lives on Ilhéu de Cima began.

No matter how often they made love, for some reason Sofia never fell pregnant and they never needed to talk to Jessica. She on the other hand knew exactly what was going on and was happy for the two of them.

Jessica was, nonetheless, acutely aware of Horatio's and Sofia's ever growing antipathy towards being trapped. On the surface, Sofia appeared content; enjoying her work in the garden and kitchen, whilst Horatio had Nelson, his fishing and his walks across the island, but as the months passed, their frustration at being cooped up on the island became more and more noticeable.

Even Jessica had to admit she found it hard to accept they had been together for over five years APD and though she was enormously proud of the lives they had managed to make for themselves, it really was anything but simple.

Being organised helped. This led to them having plenty of food, even if their diet was somewhat predictable and their accommodation far more extensive than they would ever need, but the big plus was they lived on an island where the weather was pretty perfect all year round.

Even with all the positives, Jessica accepted their lives were never going to be plain sailing, and this was especially true whenever any of them fell sick. Over the years they had all been poorly, but it was rare and when Jessica began to feel run down and constantly cold, regardless of the temperature outside, it was obvious something was not right. She then began not sleeping well at night which resulted in her catnapping during the afternoons but most worrying of all, she was losing weight and her clothes began to hang loosely off her.

Initially Jessica said nothing. After all, there was no doctor to consult, no one to discuss problems with but as the weeks passed Horatio and Sofia realised something serious was going on. One night as they were sat together playing cards, Horatio said,

"You're not well are you?"

"I'm fine," Jessica answered as casually as she could manage.

"What is it?" he asked.

"Nothing, really, I'm a bit tired that's all."

"Please stop it. We know you've not been well for weeks and that you've been trying to hide whatever it is."

"Please… I'm okay, really; it's just a bug and in a few days I'll be back to normal."

But that never happened.

*   *   *

A few nights later, as Jessica was struggling to sleep, she began to feel disorientated. She had nodded off but woken almost immediately covered in sweat and aching all over.

Feeling the areas of her body where the pain was most severe, trying to locate exactly where the problem was, Jessica realised that she had lost the use of her legs.

In a state of frenzied panic, she ordered herself to calm down and strong-armed her feet over the side of the bed, before attempting to stand. Rapidly losing her balance, she collapsed onto the mattress.

Pulling the quilt over her body, to try to stop the shivering, Jessica scolded herself for being scared and then lay completely still attempting to sort out what was actually happening to her.

The more she considered her symptoms, the more Jessica knew how serious things were and understood that without specialist medical help, the likelihood was, she would die.

Taking deep breaths, trying her best to relax, with tears beginning, Jessica told herself placidly and rationally that her only task was to ensure absolutely everything was in place and ready for the time she would no longer be with Horatio and Sofia.

Emotionally exhausted, Jessica finally fell asleep, waking sometime later to find it was still dark. Feeling dreadful, she forced herself to stand again and although light headed and wobbly on her feet, she managed a few steps, followed by a few more.

Little by little she dressed, constantly reminding herself that she had work that must be completed, then staggered across the camp to the social hut. Once in the kitchen she made herself a mug of hot water with mint from the garden, and then sat at the table making a list that she hoped would help Horatio and Sofia stay alive and safe once she was gone.

*   *   *

An hour later, Jessica heard Sofia on the move and hid her notebook. For the rest of the day, Horatio with Sofia's support, forced her to rest. The two of them then prepared the meals, fed the chickens and collected the eggs, and undertook all the jobs that Jessica would normally have done. Twice during the afternoon she fell asleep and after struggling to eat the evening meal of hot, thick soup, went off to bed; it was food that should have been perfect for her but Jessica had no appetite.

During the night, she managed to fall into a light sleep, but woke soon afterwards again covered in sweat and aching, mimicking the pattern from the previous night. Lying still to reduce the discomfort, Jessica was frantic with worry, not for herself but for Horatio and Sofia.

Praying the pain would go away, it merely intensified, becoming intolerable and Jessica assumed things were coming to a head.

Knowing time was short, she forced herself to get dressed and somehow managed to negotiate her way to the kitchen. With hot water and mint, Jessica sat down with her lists. As she was writing, her vision became suddenly blurred and a pounding headache exploded deep inside her head.

Writing as fast as she could, determined to complete the final part of the list, including what to do with her remains, Jessica leant back, wrapped her cardigan tightly around her body for warmth, and closed her eyes.

The very last words on her lips were a silent prayer to God to protect Sofia and Horatio, and if by some miracle they were still alive, Rachael, Thomas and her beloved Peter.

Chapter 16

Horatio woke early. With the worry over his mother's health playing on his mind, he'd slept restlessly. Climbing out of bed, he said good morning and petted Nelson, before opening the window for him to fly off in search of breakfast.

As he dressed, Horatio thought about what he could do for his mother. He had often spoken to Sofia about his concerns and like him she was desperate to help, but also like him, she had no idea how.

As he was about to leave the family cabin, he heard Sofia shouting,

"Horatio, come, please, hurry."

Sprinting across the camp as fast as his legs would carry him, Horatio begged God to save his mother, but knew it was too late.

*　　　*　　　*

For the following three days Horatio felt a mixture of utter despair, alongside a deep-rooted belief that he could not survive without his mother.

For Sofia, there was just a feeling of emptiness; first she had lost her mother, now it was the person who had saved her.

That first morning, as they stared at the cold, drawn, colourless skin on Jessica's face; the two of them sat silently fighting a sense of abandonment.

"What do we do?" Sofia asked tearfully, but Horatio ignored her.

"Horatio!"

"What!"

"Please… what do we do now?"

Horatio looked at the weeping Sofia and realised it was not her fault, or anyone else's; it was just the way it was and he moved over. As he held her tightly he noticed a notebook and pen on the table.

Opening the front cover he saw his mother's writing and it was at that moment, that exact moment that it struck him, his life would never be the same again. His mother was gone, truly gone and with her all the love, guidance, friendship and strength; all the irreplaceable qualities he'd always taken for granted.

*   *   *

But how had he missed it?

How on earth could he have missed something so obvious? She was dying and he hadn't even noticed the everyday deterioration in her condition?

How, had he not seen it? She'd been unwell for so long, and he had missed the signs, HOW?

And... stupid, stupid him, for God's sake, even his beloved mother had been so certain she was dying, she'd written a list of instructions for him.

So how! How! How!

Horatio couldn't bear the pain, the shattering guilt of not grasping the obvious.

*   *   *

Staring at her precise handwriting, Horatio was determined not to give in to his desolation. The rage he felt at his inadequacies was clearly palpable, but he had to be strong for Sofia. There could be no crying.

'My darling Son, you cannot imagine how proud I am of you. When I remember those difficult years before you came to the island, and all the worry and heartache you

caused your father and me. But, from the day you arrived, I couldn't have wanted more from you.

For so many years now we have been without your father and the twins, but you have kept me going. Your willingness to help out, your love for Nelson and of course, your fascination for all things here on the island has made the last few years not only bearable but a great joy.

From now on though, your life will change. You are now the one who will have to make the decisions.

I have come to love Sofia like a daughter, but she will struggle when things become difficult; I'm afraid, it'll be up to you. Before you commit though, consider all the options wisely and please, don't rush any final decisions on what the two of you should do.

Remember though, you cannot stay on the island forever and if I was still with you, it is a conversation we would have had in the very near future.'

Before reading on, Horatio explained to Sofia what the notebook was and asked if she wanted him to translate. When she nodded, Horatio reread the first section, choosing to omit the section about her; the first of many occasions he showed a maturity beyond his years.

He then continued translating his mother's words,

Accept that nothing could have prepared us for what we've had to face, and crucially, what now lies in wait for you.

At times you will feel utterly lost; and bitter at how unfair life is, and you'll probably loathe how complicated everything has become. I know I've been there on so many occasions.

But please, take your time and think before acting, consider your options before deciding on what to do, and never, ever, take anything for granted. From the moment the virus struck, we lost any rights from our previous lives.

It is a new world out there and if you decide to leave the island, expect the unexpected.

I know that sounds crazy, but the more prepared you are, the safer you'll be. Don't ever think though, that you will find your old lives away from the island. That world has gone, nothing will be as it was.

So, should you stay or go? It's a decision you must make. But remember, it is inevitable the vital equipment that has sustained our lives, will begin to break down. You already know we've been having issues with the pumps and solar panels, not insurmountable problems, but worrying all the same; and we're virtually out of spare parts.

How silly. I'm writing as if I'm still with you! But, you know what? I am. Whatever has happened, I'm still watching over you, and doing my very best to help.

Now, when the time does come for you and Sofia to move on, you have two choices; go to Sofia's village and find out what's happening, or sail east.

Whichever you decide, my advice is that eventually you should try to get home to England. We don't know whether your father or the twins are still alive, but if they are, then at least you have a family to return to.

Horatio, there are no guarantees the virus has burnt itself out, but after nearly six years I am as sure as I can be that it will be safe to travel. I know if the decision was mine, I would leave the island, especially if it meant we would eventually find your father and the twins.

If you do decide to attempt to travel to Berrow and you find no one at the house, then we had a safe in the study. It's behind the settee, in the wall. If you look hard enough you will find it behind a hidden door.

If your father is not there, he will have left a message in the safe telling us where they've gone, and probably what has happened to them. I know it's a long shot, but I cannot think of how else he could let us know where they are.

Now, the combination of the safe is not complicated, but you must remember it.

Take the five members of our family, place their names in alphabetical order; Horatio, Jessica, Peter, Rachael and

Thomas. Take the first letter of each name; H, J, P, R, T and work out the corresponding number of that letter in the alphabet, H therefore is 8, J 10, P 16, R 18 and T 20. That's the combination:

810161820.

Please try to remember, because if you do make it home, it may be the only way you can find the others.

Turning the page, tears immediately came to Horatio. Sofia held his hand firmly.

Now, I am so sorry to talk about this, but, I have not died as a result of the virus so I am not infected. Will you therefore lay me to rest overlooking the bay. If you completely cover me with quite large stones and boulders, that would be perfect. I cannot imagine how you must feel, being left with the responsibility for burying your own mother, but my darling if it were possible, I would do anything to ease the pain I am causing you and Sofia.

As Horatio read on he saw that his mother's writing suddenly became uneven and increasingly difficult to understand.

Do you remember the newspapers that Filomena gave us? I never discussed any of the articles with you, but there are things you need to know, things important for your future.

I stored those papers with a notebook in my bedroom cupboard. Please read my notes. I made a list of all the important information I could find. Please...

The next three paragraphs were impossible to read and Horatio realised his mother must have begun to lose her vision. However, implausibly, her last few words were immaculately neat and perfectly legible.

It's time for me to go. God bless you both.

Take care and stay safe,

All my love,
Mum xxxxx

—Ж—

Part III

The Journey Begins

Chapter 17

As Jessica had requested, they buried her at the highest point of the island overlooking the bay and that night, for the first time, they slept together in Horatio's bed. It wasn't sexual but emotional; neither wanting to be alone, whilst Nelson as always, sat on the end of the bed watching over them.

The following day Sofia and Horatio got up late and once breakfast was cleared away, they spent what was left of the morning walking. With the falcon flying overhead, little was said, so after a while, Sofia suggested she return to the camp to make some lunch.

That afternoon they swam, not to fish but simply to enjoy the warm water and try to relax, but Horatio continued to be withdrawn and morose, so again, Sofia left him alone and walked back to the camp.

By the evening, she was becoming extremely nervous. Nothing seemed to help, especially as Horatio was avoiding any conversation and it left her wondering if a dark, destructive depression was brewing within him.

Horatio not to be working on his latest project, discovering new things or just exploring the island or sea, was unheard of, and with Nelson the only company he wanted, Sofia felt miserable and hurt.

Ominously, there appeared no discernible improvement over the next few days, although Horatio and Sofia grudgingly fulfilled their daily chores, adding Jessica's jobs to their lists. Both evidently understood that to survive they had to get back into a routine, accepting if they didn't, their lives would slide irreversibly into a merry-go-round of indecision. The good-life Jessica had worked so hard to create, would then be needlessly lost.

But time dragged heavily, and without admitting it to each other, they felt an overwhelming urge to run away. Without Jessica there to encourage them, being trapped on the island was wearing them down and curiously, they reached the same conclusion independently of the other. Their lives had to change. Things could not remain as they were. Jessica was gone. Sofia and Horatio were desperate for something different, something challenging and inspiring.

*   *   *

Following breakfast on the sixth day after Jessica's death, Horatio told Sofia he wanted some time alone. Although initially disappointed, she understood it might finally help him come to terms with the loss of his mother, never realising the severe turmoil and endless, exhausting struggles he was experiencing.

The two most extreme examples of these were that firstly, Horatio had begun to hate Ilhéu de Cima. The island had robbed him of his mother and he could never, ever forgive it. The second was his recognition that in the not too distant future they would have to sail away leaving his beloved Nelson behind to fend for himself.

Horatio felt helpless as he attempted to come to terms with such heartache, on top of the devastating loss of his mother, and he was no fool; he recognized the extreme despair he was experiencing was stripping away his ability to make rational decisions.

God bless her. Jessica knew and had warned him in her letter that decisions made when emotions ran high could place them in danger.

He didn't deny he was desperate to leave the island, to find a new life where he could remember his mother joyously; but then, what about Nelson? Horatio knew himself well enough to know that if he chose to remain with the falcon, the persistent feeling of his mother's presence and her grave so close by, would lead to him despising his life, including Sofia, and that was something he could never accept.

*   *   *

With Nelson on his arm, Horatio walked to his secret hideaway, telling himself that he had to sort himself out, and quickly or something pretty awful might well follow. Surprisingly, for one so innately naïve, he understood that without his mother he would take the easy option and remain on the island indefinitely

Leaving Nelson on the boulder outside, he entered the cave, lay on a blanket, closed his eyes and remembered.

Contentment, the first he'd felt for so long, swept over him as vivid images of his brother and sister, his father and of course, his mother, liberated him from his hurt. In his mind's eye, he saw the seven miles of stunning, golden sand next to their house in Berrow and the glorious Somerset countryside which surrounded them. He caught a glimpse of the swimming club, his days exploring, witnessing nature at its best and smiled as he remembered spending days out in the fresh air.

With his heart crushed, Horatio knew he must get home. Inexplicably, at that precise moment, and for the first time ever, Nelson joined him in the cave. His best friend jumped on the arm protector and tenderly pushed the smooth, feathered crown of his head into Horatio's neck and cooed.

"I know," Horatio whispered, determined again not to give in to tears, "but what do I do with you?" Caressing the top of Nelson's head, he tried to explain. "I'm going where it's cold and wet, but… oh, God… you see, I miss my home so much… but your home is here, it's the only place you can make friends with others like you, and…" then with a sad smile, he said gently, "You'd hate England

and wish you'd stayed here, and so... that's what I have to do, I have to leave you behind."

*   *   *

After all the soul searching though, unexpected events became the decision maker; and as Horatio looked back months later, it seemed fate intervened to prevent him avoiding the appallingly difficult choices he faced.

As they were sitting down to their midday meal, there was the sound of a huge explosion. With Nelson squawking overhead, Horatio raced out of the hut towards the noise and found flames and smoke coming through the roof of the pump house.

Two things immediately struck him; firstly, they must prevent the fire being seen from the sea and secondly, they had to quickly douse the flames or the pump house would be destroyed and with it, their fresh water.

The irony was however, that to put the flames out they needed water and the pumps were on fire.

Sofia ran to the showers to see if there was any salt water to use, but the little she found had no effect. Horatio knew he must do something worthwhile and attempted to enter the hut; if he could flood the flames it might slow the fire down, but as he moved to the door, the heat forced him back.

The blaze lasted less than an hour, destroying most of the building. A downcast Horatio knew they would have to wait until the heat had died to discover the full extent of the damage. Looking at the destruction though, he already knew the answer.

Together with Sofia he searched for all the drinking water left; it came to three large bottles in the fridge and a small amount in the washroom for cleaning teeth.

*   *   *

Horatio saw little point in returning to the pump house until the following day but during the evening and again before he went to bed, he checked to make sure the fire had not spread. On each occasion there was little to see apart from smouldering ashes and black smoke spiralling up into the night sky and Horatio thanked God that as darkness fell, the flames had died keeping them hidden from passing ships.

Next morning, as he approached the wreckage, Horatio knew the damage was so severe nothing could be saved. The pumps that supplied their drinking water; the single most important requirement for remaining on the island, had been destroyed.

Returning to the kitchen where Sofia was clearing away breakfast, Horatio said as calmly as possible under the circumstances,

"I'm afraid the pump hut has gone,"

After a thoughtful silence, Sofia asked,

"Is there nothing we can do?"

"Nothing," he replied irritably, then realising how he had spoken, added gently, "Sorry… but, we must sort out what we're going to do."

Horatio was remembering his mother's advice as he walked across to the table and sat where she'd sat. Her pen and paper were in the same place and he felt it was a timely reminder that to survive, they needed to follow his mother's words very carefully.

Revealing huge restraint, a seriously troubled Horatio said,

"Okay, Mum told us we are naïve, that we have little understanding of the world outside or the things we will need to deal with. I now know how right she was."

*   *   *

Horatio asked Sofia to wait whilst he went to his mother's bedroom; it was the first time he had been in the room

139

since she had died and with unsteady fingers, he opened the cupboard to retrieve the newspapers and notebooks.

As he was leaving he spotted her mobile on the bookshelf and decided he ought to take all the phones, tablets and solar charging packs with him. Before the internet had crashed, like himself, his mother had regularly downloaded information which might prove useful to them.

Returning to Sofia, he took a seat at the table and said,

"These are the newspapers your mother gave us, and in this..." he pointed to the notebook, "are notes from the articles." Sofia nodded and he continued,

"Before I start, I remember my father saying to me when I first arrived to live here, that we may be surrounded by seawater but without drinking water, we could not survive for more than a couple of days.

So... with the pumps gone, we must leave."

Sofia again nodded her agreement.

"I'm hoping if we are careful," Horatio continued, "the fresh water we've got should last a few days; it'll give us time to sort things out."

"So, what should we do?" Sofia asked.

"I'm really not sure except we must decide where we're going."

"What choices do we have?"

"Well... my mother told me there were two possibilities; travel to your family on Santiago."

"Or...?"

"We sail east to Africa and from there travel north to Europe."

"So, which one do you prefer?"

"I'm not sure. If we survive, and I feel that's a big if, at some stage I want to get home to England."

"I'm the same; I want to know about my family," Sofia moved across to Horatio and held him tightly, "but I don't want to be alone."

"Me neither."

*   *   *

With the falcon perched on the top bar of the nearest chair, Horatio began looking at his mother's notes and it took no time for him to realise how dreadful the sickness had been.

Clearly, if the virus was still active their chances of surviving after leaving, were slim; and it didn't help Horatio's confidence when he read how boys and men died at a far greater rate than women and girls.

Reading the alarming details of the infection, Horatio decided not to mention any information on the measles virus to Sofia. In her letter, his mother advised him not to place pressure on Sofia, so he would keep the facts to himself and do his best to remain confident.

*   *   *

Finishing his mother's notes, Horatio felt shattered and needing to talk to Sofia, he went in search of her. Having discovered her staring at the burnt out shell of the pump hut, as they walked back to the social hut, he said,

"We'll go to your village, but on the way I want to go to Fargo; we must find out how bad things are."

"If you're sure, I would like that, but what about Nelson?" Sofia asked, concerned.

"There's nothing to be done."

"Can't we take him with us?"

"No. This is the only place on earth his kind are found. To take him with me would be selfish and far worse for him than leaving him behind."

Ending any more talk of Nelson and with a great deal more confidence than he felt, Horatio then said,

"We need to gather all the things we want to take. If we put them on the floor here, I can see whether they will fit in the boat."

*   *   *

That afternoon, whilst Sofia sorted out their belongings, Horatio worked on Defender. He assumed the diesel engine and the inflatable dinghy would prove vital to their survival once they had left the protection of the island, and as so often, he silently thanked his mother. After his father had left, she had insisted the crafts fortnightly maintenance checks were always completed, and not for the first time, Horatio marvelled at her insight into their future.

As he worked on the boat, even as he dragged the store of fuel down to the beach, Nelson hardly left Horatio's side. The bird knew something was going on.

Feeling guilt-ridden, Horatio chatted constantly to the falcon, reassuring him that everything was for the best; time and again explaining that by remaining on the island he would be able to live safely, and in the company of other Cape Verde Falcons.

Nonetheless, for all his attempts at staying positive, Horatio's emotions were being shredded. Nelson was not going with them. He argued that to do otherwise would be cruel and selfish and under no circumstances would he put his own needs before his feathered friend's wellbeing. But none of the arguments helped his desperate feeling of despair. First his mother, then Nelson.

*   *   *

With Defender as sea-worthy as possible and with Nelson perched on his shoulder, Horatio made his way to his bedroom where he collected the things he wanted to take.

Carrying them to the social hut, he found Sofia sorting through, not only clothes, but what looked like a thousand pieces of needless junk.

"Do we really need all this?" he asked.

"Well if we have room, why not?"

In the end Horatio agreed, however, he insisted they could not compromise on packing the essentials first. This list included: food, especially anything fresh such as eggs, chicken meat and vegetables; the shotgun with the few remaining cartridges; the four spear guns and all spares alongside the thick rubber bands still wrapped in protective bags; essential clothing, including footwear for all conditions.

Over the previous few years Horatio's feet had grown considerably and he had ended up making use of his father's and Joshua's spare boots and trainers; although not a perfect fit, he knew the boots would be vital for when they arrived in colder countries.

Finally, all the mobile devices, books, maps, atlases, or any other documentation which might aid them as they travelled.

After the 'essentials' were packed, they spent the rest of that evening going through every room of every hut to make sure they were not leaving something important behind.

It was then Horatio discovered the photos.

*   *   *

He and Sofia had just finished looking around the Mott's hut when he saw his mother's briefcase pushed under her bed. Initially reluctant to pry, Sofia persuaded him there may be something important inside, so he opened the case.

It was so like his mother. Organised, tidy and full of important items including passports, a good deal of money, mostly UK pounds, but also Cape Verdean Escudos and the much maligned and virtually worthless Euros. There were scientific reports and papers and at the bottom, buried deep, were a collection of family photos.

Up to that point, with Sofia's considerable support, Horatio had managed to hold back the tears. However, as he stared at pictures of his father, the twins, him as a young boy, his mother and so many of the whole family, he curled up on the bed and wept away all the bottled-up sadness, the remorse and his fury at the death of his loving, incomparable mother.

*   *   *

Later, once they had completed the search of the camp, Sofia and Horatio noticed Nelson was becoming restless.

That evening before going to bed, the falcon sat on the shoulder pad the entire time, never once allowing Horatio to place him on a different perch.

Following breakfast the next morning, wanting to study his father's charts of the waters around Ilhéu de Cima, the Cape Verde Islands and further afield, Horatio had to work the entire time with Nelson on his arm. But it was not the falcon being left behind which caused him a stomach-churning sense of dread; it was the thought of what would happen if he ended up lost in the middle of the ocean with absolutely no idea where he was?

Chapter 18

The build-up to their leaving had been physically and emotionally exhausting for both Horatio and Sofia. With their drinking water running out, Horatio felt under pressure to leave, but he was determined to set sail when the weather was at its best.

After taking his father's advice to go online immediately following their trip to Ilhéu Grande, Horatio had learnt the rudiments of navigation, such as using charts, the sun and the stars, but he was no fool, he knew he was inexperienced in the extreme and would not gamble with Sofia's life.

*   *   *

After almost six years on Ilhéu de Cima, the final decision to leave was made early in the morning on a day with almost perfect conditions. Looking out of the bedroom window at first light, Horatio had seen a beautiful sunrise, little wind, a cloudless sky and a calm sea. There was no reason for remaining on Ilhéu de Cima.

Leaving his mother's resting place proved as difficult as he believed it would be; however, the thought of never seeing Nelson again was utterly heart-breaking. In the end Horatio allowed himself one concession; he would take the arm and shoulder protectors as reminders of an almost perfect friend and companion.

He had initially waited for Nelson to leave for breakfast, then watched disconsolately as the falcon rose effortlessly up into the clear blue sky. Horatio then walked away refusing to look back.

*   *   *

It took little time for Horatio to realise he had been right to be nervous. Only an hour out from Ilhéu de Cima and approximately half way to the island of Fogo, a thick sea mist appeared and visibility dropped to just a couple of dozen metres.

He slowed the boat and studied the chart. Without the GPS, which had probably stopped operating years before, Horatio accepted that unless things improved, and swiftly, there was no way of knowing where they would end up.

He had planned to arrive at Sao Felipe harbour at around midday, but feeling so disorientated by the poor visibility, he wondered whether they were even on the right course.

Looking around at the disquieting scene, Horatio was furious with himself. He had been so determined to wait for perfect conditions, he had forgotten that the safest weather for sailing was also ideal for the arrival of sea mist.

Reducing their speed further, but trusting they had sufficient momentum to avoid 'Defender' being driven too far off course by the currents, Horatio prayed the good visibility would return. If they were close to Fogo, wonderful, if not, then he really had no idea where they might be.

After an hour of thinking the worst and losing all sense of perspective, without warning the mist lifted leaving them with a beautifully clear sky and calm sea.

Horatio immediately spotted all four islands he knew; directly behind were Ilhéu de Cima and Ilhéu Grande, to their right and slightly behind them was Brava and straight ahead, Fogo.

He smiled uncomfortably as Sofia congratulated him; knowing only a sizeable chunk of good luck had kept Defender on the course he had planned.

*   *   *

Sofia applauded when she spotted the blue and white twin towers of the Catholic Cathedral of San Felipe whilst a much happier Horatio couldn't resist the temptation to look back at Ilhéu de Cima. Seeing no sign of Nelson following them, he tried to be happy; reason told him that if his much-loved friend had stayed behind, he should be safe.

* * *

As they approached the black volcanic sand of the San Felipe beach, Horatio thought the town looked the same as on his last visit, so many years earlier. Everything certainly appeared normal and he wondered, not for the first time, whether his mother had made the most enormous blunder by keeping them on Ilhéu de Cima for so long.

Turning north towards the harbour, Sofia called to him and pointed.

"There's a man over there."

Horatio spotted a boat bobbing gently on the waves and reduced their speed. As he steered

Defender closer, he knew he should keep a sensible distance. Thinking Sofia, as a local should speak to him, he said,

"Ask what's happening, but don't tell him where we're from."

Sofia nodded and when they were within about thirty metres of the fisherman, she called out,

"Hello,"

Before they could move any closer, the man shouted angrily.

"Stay away!" He picked up a long pole holding it as a spear and Horatio could see there was a lethal looking knife strapped to the end.

Sofia persevered,

"Please, we've been away. Can you tell us what's been happening on the islands?"

"Away, have you? Well you must have been gone for a hell of a long time if you don't know what's been going on."

"We have, please... tell us?"

"Do not get any closer, or I will hurt you."

As slowly as possible without drawing attention to himself, Horatio slowed the boat to a stop and went down to the cabin. He picked up both the shotgun and a spear gun, making sure they were both loaded, before returning to the deck.

"What do you want to know?" the man asked.

"What happened when the sickness arrived?" Sofia asked.

"What do you think? Nearly everyone died." There was still anger in his voice.

"But not you," Horatio said, unable to stop himself.

"No, not me."

"How many people survived?" Again it was Horatio asking.

"Very few. A couple of dozen on this island, but today, there are children to share our lives."

"Did both men and women live?"

"Mostly the women; only a handful of men and boys made it."

Horatio was stunned. His mother had been right; but he was nowhere near as shaken as Sofia, who had little prior warning of the virus and its victims. Noticing her reaction Horatio asked,

"And food, is it a problem?"

"We have plenty of fish and some of the others grow vegetables and tend animals."

"Can we put ashore?" Horatio asked.

"We don't know whether you've got the sickness. My advice is you'll keeping sailing to some other place."

"Well... thank you," Horatio said as politely as his disappointment would allow. "You have been a great help, good luck."

"And to you."

With that, Horatio restarted the engine and they continued northwards.

As he considered what the fisherman had told them, Horatio was incredulous. His internet searches from before the virus, indicated Fogo had a population of over forty-five thousand, half of who lived in San Felipe; if the fisherman was being truthful, then tens of thousands must have died.

He then recalled that Praia, capital of Sofia's home island, Santiago, had close to one hundred and fifty thousand residents and the island approaching a quarter of a million. Abruptly, Horatio told himself to stop. The probable impact of the virus on Sofia's village didn't bear thinking about, and he was extremely uneasy at what they would find if they made it that far.

*   *   *

"What do we do now?" Sofia asked, as she joined Horatio at the wheel.

"I want to have a look at the harbour, see if there's anyone around," he answered trying to sound positive. "We might be able to land, but after what the fisherman said I'm not hopeful."

Steering Defender to within thirty metres of the black sandy beach, still travelling northwards, what they witnessed was startling. All the buildings appeared derelict ruins, the town abandoned. It was just like a war zone with a menacing feel to it.

Ten minutes later, they arrived at the harbour. It had an 'L' shaped concrete pier jutting out in to the sea and Horatio could see a number of small boats anchored alongside the old Brava ferry. Horatio remembered the ferryboat from his previous visit, but it had become just a half-sunken rusted shell.

As he moved Defender closer, people began to appear on the harbour wall and Horatio noticed all except two were women. He also saw they were armed with an assortment of weapons, two being shotguns.

"What do you want?" one of the men called out.

"We were passing and wanted to stop for supplies," Horatio answered pleasantly in his slightly accented Portuguese.

"You can't. We have nothing to give you."

As their boat moved closer, one of the women shouted, angrily,

"Stay away!"

Horatio put the engine into reverse for a moment and then Defender came to a stop.

"We'll stay here, but please tell us what has happened; we were cut-off from the sickness and we've had no news for a very long time."

"Where have you been?" another of the women asked.

"Trapped... on one of the islands," Horatio replied, attempting to avoid being more precise.

"So, you're the English from Ilhéu de Cima?"

Horatio realised lying could be dangerous. If the locals had a faster boat than Defender, it could leave them in serious trouble.

"Yes," he answered, "my mother died recently. We are the only ones left and had to leave."

"Well, you're not coming here." Again it was the man who spoke.

"We heard you the first time," Sofia answered impatiently, before adding, "I am from just outside Praia. I am a local but you don't care."

"We don't," the insensitive reply came, "we have our own problems. We've had years of going without, so why would we want to share the little we have?"

"Fine," Horatio answered, frustrated. He started up the engine and headed towards the northern tip of the island.

*   *   *

From the northern most tip of Fogo, Horatio had calculated Praia was one hundred kilometres, due east. Given the choice, following the unpleasant talk with the locals, he wanted to get started on the journey without delay, however, there were only a couple of hours of daylight left and he didn't want to be navigating the crossing at night.

As they rounded the northern coast of the island, Horatio decided it would be better if they found a safe bay and waited until first light before heading out.

Sailing as close to the shore as was sensible, they passed a built up area that Horatio thought was the town of Queimada Guincho. He then spotted a number of bays that might provide them with a safe haven for the night, but for varying reasons, was not sure about any of them. Eventually, arriving at the most easterly point of Fogo, much to his relief, Horatio saw a bay which looked perfect. It was enclosed, like the letter 'U', the two legs jutting out into the sea. It looked well protected and deserted, with no building close by and no other ships in the vicinity.

Horatio piloted Defender into the calmer waters and when they were about one hundred metres off the beach, he dropped anchor.

With an hours daylight left, they had something to eat and as both were exhausted and Horatio wanted to make a start at first light, they made up their bed on the deck and settled down for an early night.

*   *   *

Having only just fallen asleep, a strange sound quite close by woke them with a start. Horatio looked across the starlit bay and then inland but saw nothing to concern them. As they lay down again there was a piercing scream from the direction of the beach; it sounded as if someone was in trouble so Horatio quickly moved to start the engine.

Another scream followed and Horatio spotted movement on the shore. As he struggled to see exactly what was happening, people on the beach began calling out to each other.

Much to Sofia's surprise, Horatio then swore at himself.

"What is it?" she asked anxiously.

"I can't understand why locals are on the beach? If they came to find us and I start the engine, they'll know for sure."

"It might just be a coincidence, maybe whatever's going on has nothing to do with us."

Hesitant about what to do next, Horatio thought for a few moments before saying,

"You may be right, but what if they already know we're here? I think we should get going or we could have serious problems." He didn't add, 'including losing our lives', something he acknowledged was a genuine possibility.

Horatio then went to the cabin and collected the shotgun, all three spear guns and flares. He returned to the deck and told Sofia to go down to the cabin.

She refused, saying,

"Whatever happens, we deal with it together."

Horatio nodded at her with a grateful smile.

Moving once more towards the wheelhouse, again he hesitated.

"What's wrong?" Sofia asked tensely.

"We should leave, but... well... if we do I might get lost. If the clouds come and I lose the stars and light of the moon, we could sail in completely the wrong direction and end up God knows where."

"Then let's wait; see what happens."

Suddenly hearing loud, extremely agitated shouts, Horatio prepared one of the flares.

"What are they doing?" Sofia asked, fear in her voice.

"I really have no idea but it sounds as if whoever they are, they're being attacked."

Aiming a flare upwards he fired, and with Sofia holding his arm tightly, they watched the streak of orange soar high, illuminating the night sky.

Then, staring at the beach to discover what was happening, neither could believe their eyes. A group of people were cowering, whilst flapping their arms around their heads. Two others from the group were in the water, holding onto a small boat.

Something dark and sinister then appeared in the sky, directly over the people and whatever it was, it was moving at an astonishing speed.

In the last of the bright light from the flare, Horatio saw a black shape swoop down, heading for those on the beach.

"Nelson!" Sofia shrieked.

Just before the flare finally died, they watched as the group skulked inland, dragging someone who was seriously injured with them. The two people by the boat just abandoned it and tried to catch up with the others.

*　　*　　*

Nelson carried on patrolling overhead, clearly waiting until the group had left whilst Horatio rowed the dinghy to check their boat and finding nothing useful, rocked it back and forth until it sank.

Only when Horatio had finally returned to Defender, did Nelson fly to him and land on his shoulder. Their brave little rescuer then snuggled his head into Horatio's neck, making a sound that was almost identical to the purring of a contented cat.

—Ж—

Chapter 19

Next morning, after Horatio and Sofia had taken shifts during the night in the unlikely case the locals returned, they set a course due east in calm and sunny conditions.

From the moment they left the bay, Nelson alternated between perching on the ledge next to the wheel watching Horatio and taking off before circling Defender.

On one occasion he hurriedly left the boat. A number of birds had appeared overhead and as Horatio watched him bombing and scattering the panicking flock, he once again marvelled at not only the speed Nelson could generate, but his astonishing ability to kill on the wing.

Horatio thought the one hundred kilometres to Praia should take around three hours at Defender's top speed of twenty knots but knew at that speed their fuel would quickly disappear. Hoping it would only add an extra hour to the journey time, he set the speed at a more leisurely fifteen knot.

At midday they ate lunch, finishing the chicken from Ilhéu de Cima, aware that it was unlikely to last for another day. Even though they were both hungry, they did resist the temptation to start on their store of fruit and vegetables as it would stay fresh longer.

*　　　*　　　*

Early afternoon after an uneventful journey, they saw the hazy outline of the island of Santiago.

"I don't want to stop in Praia," Horatio said to Sofia who had joined him and Nelson at the wheel.

"Why?" she asked,

"Well, after what happened last night, I don't want to chance it."

"But that's silly; this is my home. My family and friends will be here."

"And if they aren't? What if the only survivors are like those on Fogo?"

"You don't really think that do you?"

"I do, because they are the only ones we've come across."

Trying to change the subject Horatio asked,

"Is there anywhere close to your village we can drop anchor. You know, a bay where we might not be noticed?"

"The village is quite close to the end of the runway of the main airport," Sofia answered moodily, clearly irritated by Horatio's pessimism, "and not that far from the sea. Our nearest beach is Praia de Sao Francisco, but I'm not sure how well hidden we would be." After a few moments thought, she then said with slightly more enthusiasm,

"I know... between the city and our beach, about one kilometre from the runway, there is a bay called Praia de Sao Tome. It's lovely and hidden; it should be safe if we stopped there."

"Okay, so how do we get there?"

"We have to pass the harbour at Praia and continue around the coast; it's not that far."

"That's it then."

*   *   *

Horatio decided to remain well out to sea, hoping to avoid the capital and only a few minutes later, he had to concede Sofia was right; the bay at Sao Tome was stunning and sheltered.

It was similar to the one on Fogo in that it had two fingers each side of the bay jutting out into the sea; however, what made the Praia de Sao Tome perfect was that it had a lovely beach and a narrow entrance into the bay which meant they could not be seen from the open sea.

After dropping anchor, they placed as many of the valuable items as they could fit into the concealed compartment previously used by smugglers, the same one his father had shown him on his very first sailing trip to Ilhéu Grande. The shotgun, three spear guns, his mother's notebooks and family photos, the mobiles and pad, plus food were all safely hidden away. It was then that Horatio appreciated how fortunate they were to have the hidey-hole.

Sofia then tied any other items that might be stolen by unwelcome visitors in a double plastic bag and after attaching it to the anchor chain, Horatio pushed it underwater.

Horatio told Sofia that he did not want to take the inflatable dinghy. Left unattended on the beach, it would be ideal for someone to use it to steal Defender, so they swam ashore carrying dry clothes in bags above their heads.

*   *   *

They first set foot on the island of Santiago mid-afternoon and Sofia was clearly thrilled to be home.

After changing out of their swimming costumes which they buried with their towels behind a large rock on the beach, Sofia took the lead and headed inland up a narrow valley. Ahead to their right, were a few houses and further on, to the left, a small hamlet.

Carrying the fourth spear gun and keeping it ready to fire, Horatio's first impressions were that the island was similar to Fogo, barren and stony.

Sofia then turned right and began climbing. At the highest point, the view was impressive. Looking back the way they had come, Horatio could see the beach and bay with Defender. Ahead, the panorama revealed a greener landscape than on Fogo or Ilhéu de Cima.

A hundred metres to their left there was a large herd of wild goats which Horatio had read about, and as they eyeballed him, he decided they weren't domesticated.

Further to his right, he saw another beach, which Sofia said was Praia de Sao Francisco. She then pointed inland and towards a valley and asked,

"Can you see those buildings?" When Horatio nodded, she said, "That's my village, Sao Francisco."

As he studied the houses, becoming ever more anxious about the reception they might receive, he said,

"It looks bigger than just a village."

*   *   *

With Nelson flying overhead, Sofia led them down to the road and then inland towards the buildings.

Increasing their speed to a swift jog, Horatio, who stayed close behind, smiled at her understandable elation. It took them just minutes to reach the outskirts of the village.

As he followed, Horatio tried to remember what he knew about Ilhéu de Santiago and its capital Praia. Bizarrely, he actually recalled some pretty irrelevant facts, including: the island was about thirty kilometres wide and fifty long; that fishing, coffee, sugar, bananas, and most importantly corn were the main crops grown, but then his knowledge dried up.

Arriving at what was undoubtedly the main street, Horatio saw the buildings were mostly square and colourless, with adjacent fields that appeared to be in use. To him, the village looked alive.

On the left there were two tennis courts that were covered with weeds and a broken, rusted metal gate. On their right a little further on, there was a church and Horatio noticed its grounds and cemetery were unquestionably being looked after.

As they walked on, two things occurred to Horatio: one, people were definitely living in the houses, and two, religion still mattered.

Approaching the centre of the village, with Nelson still flying in close proximity, Horatio saw a crossroads directly ahead. Sofia explained,

"That street splits the village in two; I live just the other side of the junction."

"Where does that road go?" Horatio asked pointing,

"From a roundabout over there," she pointed to the left, "it goes into the hills. There," this time she looked to her right, "Can you see?"

Horatio thought they were more than just hills.

Pressing on, Sofia then said,

"People are still here."

"I know; we must be on our guard."

*   *   *

Thirty metres from the crossroads, an agitated Nelson suddenly landed on Horatio's shoulder and shrieked. Horatio and Sofia stopped, aware of how threateningly exposed they were.

"Wait," he said, but Sofia ignored him and carried on.

Suddenly a group of people appeared from behind a building on their right, and stood facing them, blocking their path to the junction. Horatio estimated there were around twenty in the group. Most were woman but he saw three men; everyone was holding some type of weapon.

"Keep that spear gun in front of you where we can see it," a woman at the front of group said, before adding coldly, "So, what do you want?"

"Why should we want anything?" Sofia answered confidently, but Horatio could tell she was anxious.

"Outsiders are not welcome."

"I'm an outsider, am I?"

"To us you are. Strangers are not welcome."

"So, now I'm a stranger?"

"We followed you from the boat." It was another of the women who spoke, clearly irritated at having to explain anything.

Horatio and Sofia were both livid by that unexpected news. Sofia because she had assumed they would be welcomed; after all, it was her home. Horatio, because he dreaded what might be happening to Defender whilst they were away.

"Go back to where you've come from."

"You have no right to tell me to leave... I..."

Before she could finish, there was the cocking of a gun from within the middle of the group and a male voice butted in.

"Why's that then?"

"Because this is my home," Sofia stated, indignantly.

There was sound of disbelief from the group.

"Is that so?" the man asked sneering, clearly mocking Sofia's claim.

"My house is over there," she said, refusing to be intimidated and pointed as she walked towards some buildings on the other side of the junction.

Those gathered moved closer together and Horatio's first thought was that they were going to attack. Nelson flew off and circled the potential confrontation as Horatio realised they were not only outnumbered, but had guns aimed at them.

"We have lived on Ilhéu de Cima since the sickness came, but I grew up over there. My family have lived here for generations so please tell me why I am not welcome?"

"What's your name?" the question came from the original woman to have spoken.

"Sofia da Silva; my mother was Filomena da Silva, my father was Jorge Carlos da Silva, my grandfather was Jose Maria da..."

"Okay, we get it," the woman said indifferently, and as she walked away said,

"Come with us."

As they began to walk towards the group, one of the men with a gun stopped them. Relieving Horatio of the spear gun and a knife he was wearing in his belt, he said to him,

"You come with us."

Three men, all armed, escorted Horatio the five hundred yards to an isolated house on the edge of the village.

Looking back before entering the front door, Horatio saw no sign of Sofia and although he didn't know it at that time, he would never see or touch her again.

*   *   *

As darkness fell, Horatio stood at the barred window of a room, although it felt more like a cell. This impression was not helped by an excessive number of flies and huge cockroaches which appeared to be sprinting aimlessly across the compacted mud floor.

Although they had taken everything away from him, the one consolation was that with no glass in the window, he could speak to and even stroke Nelson. None of the locals appeared to have taken any notice of the bird and Horatio had to assume they had dismissed him as being of little importance.

Considering the predicament they had faced, Horatio was confident that even though Sofia had stood up to the group, there was no way they would throw her out of her home, or for that matter off the island where she'd grown up.

But then he began to see flaws in that argument. They would never let Sofia stay if they thought either of them were carriers of the virus. The same would apply if they even slightly queried her being born and raised in the village, or, if they distrusted her account of where she'd lived since the virus first struck.

And, crucially, none of those concerns took into consideration what they would do with him.

Once night had fallen, Horatio had his first visitor. A man entered carrying a plate of food and mug of water. He left the meal on a table just inside the door and Horatio noticed he remained at the open door.

"I'm Federico, Sofia's brother," he said in heavily accented English.

Answering in Portuguese, Horatio asked,

"Is your sister okay?"

Also switching to Portuguese, the man answered,

"She's fine but will be kept away from the community until we are certain she is not sick."

Horatio noticed he only spoke of Sofia and wondered what that meant for him, although he did concede that if they intended to kill him they were unlikely to give him food and water.

"Tomorrow morning you will leave."

"With Sofia?"

"No, she stays here."

"So, I can't stay?"

"No."

"And if I don't agree?"

"You will be killed along with my sister. She has been told if she tries to leave, every member of her family will be executed."

"Does that include you?"

"Of course."

"But that's crazy! We have been together for years and have become… um… very close." Horatio suddenly had the feeling it might be unwise to explain exactly how close.

"It's very simple; if you do not go you will die.

"But…"

"No buts. You are lucky that Sofia grew up here and our family are well known. If not, both of you would already be dead. You see, many years ago all those on the island agreed no outsiders would be allowed to land. The risk from the virus for our community was too great.

The only reason we are letting you go, is because Sofia has agreed to stay, but on the condition you can leave safely. She told me to convince you to leave and never, ever return. If you do, not only will you die but so will Sofia and our family.

With that, Federico left, closing and locking the door behind him, leaving Horatio to ask whether it could really be true or just a way of scaring him into going.

*   *   *

They came early the following morning, just as dawn was breaking. Two women and two men. His 'minders', returning him to the boat without any of his belongings.

As they arrived at the beach, with an agitated Nelson flying overhead, Horatio collected the wet swimming costumes they'd buried and asked one of the men to return Sofia's bikini to her.

Telling Horatio to sit at the front, two of the men then rowed the dinghy out into the bay and once alongside Defender, he was ordered aboard. As he climbed up, he heard menacingly,

"If you come back, you will die."

Horatio felt crushed; he would never see Sofia again. Nevertheless, he accepted he had little choice. If he tried to resist, he would not only be committing suicide but signing the death warrant for Sofia and her entire family.

*   *   *

Sailing away from Praia de Sao Tome and the island of Santiago, Horatio was certain he spotted Sofia waving from the beach, but knew it was wishful thinking. She was locked up and probably petrified and would remain there until it was proved she was healthy.

Surrounded by the interminable ocean, for the first time since his boarding school days, Horatio felt truly alone.

Chapter 20

As Defender left Sofia behind, Horatio hated the fact that there was no safe way to get her back. He had lost a truly wonderful friend, a beautiful and tender lover, and someone he had shared some of the most magical and exhilarating moments of his life. He could only hope she would find genuine happiness returning to her village and family.

A desperately dejected Horatio knew that his unpleasant visit to Fogo and short time on Santiago Island had convinced him he must quickly come to terms with the ruthless and cold-hearted extremes individuals and communities would go to protect their own.

Horatio had been left with nothing. They had stolen everything on board including the dinghy, only leaving some of the diesel which hopefully would get him at least as far as the African coast.

On the plus side, the thieves had missed the submerged bag of clothes tied to the anchor chain and the secret cupboard, leaving him with amongst other personal items, the shotgun and cartridges, spear guns and spares, and food.

As crucial as these items were though, they amounted to everything Horatio possessed and he knew that when he reached land, he would be in a race against time to find the means to stay alive.

*   *   *

With no charts of the West African coast to guide him, Horatio knew if he travelled east he would eventually reach land. From there, if he sailed north, he would arrive at the coast of Southern Europe.

For the next couple of hours, Defender made excellent progress. Having eaten a good breakfast which had been provided for him before leaving Sofia's village, Horatio decided to skip lunch to conserve the little food he had left.

As they sailed on, the attentive Nelson intermittently flew off to search the immediate area, whilst Horatio, with pen and paper, detailed the route he hoped to be taking.

He began with the nearest land mass to Ilhéu de Cima; Senegal and its capital Dakar. Although he couldn't be certain, he guessed from the atlas and information he had downloaded onto his tablet, it was approximately seven hundred kilometres as the crow flies.

At a constant fifteen knots per hour, the speed he travelled to conserve fuel, Horatio calculated that he should reach Africa in twenty-five hours.

*   *   *

The following morning, after navigating through the night and even managing a few hours sleep, Horatio felt confident he was nearing the coast of Africa. As a pod of dolphins swam in the opposite direction, he wondered where they might be going and then smiled ironically as he had little clear idea of where Defender was actually headed.

He knew of course that during the hours of darkness, the boat's progress would have been influenced by the ocean currents, but not to what extent, so all-in-all he really had no idea where he was.

A few hours later, with no dry land in sight, Horatio began to think he'd been correct and they had been blown off course. Worse though, he had an irrational fear they were travelling in completely the wrong direction!

With his alarm growing, Horatio sat with the West African section of a world atlas and told himself to keep calm. He was certain that as long as they continued on an

165

easterly bearing, which was not difficult to calculate, then they would definitely arrive in Africa.

However, as dusk began to fall on the second day, Horatio accepted he would have to spend another night at sea, and another ten hours for Defender to be dragged into the unknown by the strong currents.

*   *   *

Lying on the deck, staring out at the sun going down behind him, a flock of what he assumed were migrating birds flew over. Nelson squawked loudly and flapped his wings and as Horatio turned to look at him, he glimpsed a dark outline where seconds earlier there had been just water and sky.

Closing his eyes, squeezing them tight just for a second, he squinted in the same direction. There was no question, he could see land.

Rather than being directly ahead, as he had expected, the coast was on his left and being confident it was Africa, the only explanation for their position, was that they had arrived a good deal further south than Senegal.

Concerned about the fading light, Horatio turned the boat and headed for a beach he could just about make out, hoping to anchor Defender safely for the night.

Quite unnervingly though, as he sailed towards land, the wind strengthened and Horatio saw lightning not far to the north. So rapidly had the conditions changed he had failed to spot the storm until it was practically on top of him.

In rapidly deteriorating weather, Horatio strained to keep the speck of yellow sand in sight, whilst also struggling to manoeuvre the boat. He worried that if the swell got much worse, he would have no chance of reaching the coast and out running the storm.

Just a few minutes later, there was a screeching, piercing, ripping sound. Horatio couldn't believe how loud the noise was and knew they had struck rocks.

Defender came to an abrupt stop. It was as if she had hit a brick wall and Horatio was thrown forwards, violently thwacking his forehead on the safety rail. He knew he had to get the boat to safety or he would lose not only the few things he had left, but quite possibly, his life.

*   *   *

With blood oozing from a nasty gash, Horatio pulled himself up and saw Nelson had gone. If his friend had left the protection of the boat, the situation was certainly dire. Desperate as he was to make sure Nelson was safe, Horatio could see little through the torrential rain and decided he had to discover how bad the damage to Defender was.

After wrapping a cloth around his head to curb the bleeding, he staggered down into the cabin but he saw nothing through the dark; however, as soon as he reached the bottom step he felt water.

Horatio waded through about twenty centimetres of sea water, but far more of a concern was the loud intermittent scraping sound as the boat was rocked violently back and forth by the power of the waves.

Using only touch in the pitch-black, he lifted everything he could find on the floor, up onto the seats and table before checking the contents of the hidden cupboard were above the water level.

Horatio had to assume they were trapped on a reef and decided it was possibly the best place to be until the storm had blown over; remaining wedged on rocks until the sea calmed might be the only way to stop Defender breaking up.

*   *   *

The storm moved on as quickly as it had arrived and Horatio felt the wind die and the sea calm. As the waves stopped battering Defender, he found moving around the boat considerably easier and noticed it had become a beautifully clear, starry night.

Although desperate to see how bad the damage was, Horatio knew swimming at night in unfamiliar waters, could be extremely dangerous, so, using a bucket he attempted to reduce the level of seawater in the cabin.

Convincing himself he was making a difference, when in reality he wasn't, after an hour, exhausted and despondent, he gave up, lay on the deck and finally slept.

*　　　*　　　*

Horatio woke with a start. He'd been dreaming about getting trapped under giant waves and after shaking his head to clear it, remembered the fall and hurting himself. The cut had stopped bleeding so he rewound the cloth tightly, but knew it would need further attention when he had the time.

The crazy night had turned into a glorious day and directly in front of Defender, about a hundred metres away, Horatio saw the beach he had tried to reach. To his right, some way in the distance, there were mountains which he thought might be attached to the rocky cliffs he had spotted as the storm arrived.

Horatio smiled as he noticed he was surrounded by the most dazzling turquoise water, yellow sand and green vegetation; a panorama resembling photos he'd seen as a youngster in magazines advertising exotic holidays. He decided it was just about picture-perfect.

Horatio could see the reef Defender had struck and at any other time he would love to have investigated the coral and sea life, but it was not the time; he had to get the boat to the beach where he could repair her.

Using his father's old binoculars, he then searched for Nelson but saw nothing and just hoped the bird would return when he was ready. What he was fearful of was Nelson encountering something new and unnerving, something that had spooked him causing him to fly blindly away, but there was little Horatio could do to help his feathered friend.

He had no control over Nelson and laughed at the irony; wasn't he just as naïve and inexperienced as the falcon?

*　　*　　*

Wearing only shorts and carrying a loaded spear gun, Horatio lowered himself into the water. He was desperate to assess the damage to Defender.

Finding the water wonderfully warm and crystal clear, he couldn't remember ever having swum in such idyllic conditions. However, his mood darkened when he swam down and immediately found a hole in the side of the boat's hull. Defender was firmly anchored on rocks and he could clearly see the jagged tips pushing into the metre long rip.

Devastated, Horatio understood how serious the damage was; he could never free the boat from the reef and would have to abandon her.

*　　*　　*

With the difficult decision made to leave the boat, Horatio swam to the beach to see where he could make camp. Whilst he had only a few possessions left, they were all he had, so he needed to look after them.

Wading watchfully out of the water onto the warm sand, Horatio had little idea of what to expect. For all he knew he might be walking into a trap, but his initial impression was that the area was deserted. He could see no buildings close by and no animal or human footprints in the sand. There was also just thick vegetation right up to the edge of the beach, which stretched as far as he could see in both directions.

*   *   *

The first night in Africa Horatio camped on the beach. Once he had transferred his belongings from Defender in the last of the evening light, he found something to eat and attempted to dress the gash on his head. Not for the first time, he was grateful for the concealed cupboard as it had kept the medical bag dry.

Horatio then opened the atlas and tried to figure out exactly where he was.

Tracing the journey from Sofia's island with his finger, Horatio decided he had come ashore in the south of Senegal, ideally not too far from Dakar, where he wanted to be. Then studying maps illustrating the whole of West Africa, Horatio saw that Guinea-Bissau was the first country south of Senegal and following the coast, next there was Guinea, then Sierra Leone and Liberia.

Considering the length of time he had been at sea, Horatio tried to be open minded about where he might be. He decided it was highly unlikely he would have sailed as far south as Liberia or Sierra Leone, which left him thinking if he wasn't in Senegal then he was probably in Guinea.

Content at last to have an approximate idea of where he was, Horatio settled down for the night, desperate for Nelson to reappear the next morning.

Chapter 21

After sleeping surprisingly well, as Horatio slowly opened his eyes trying to recall exactly where he was, he was ecstatic to see Nelson perched on the canvas sheet covering his possessions. The falcon was quite obviously waiting for Horatio to wake up because he instantly began squawking loudly, no doubt announcing his return.

Strapping on the arm protector and holding it out, Nelson jumped and landed with a thump, before nestling into Horatio's neck and rubbing the top of his head against his unshaven chin.

The smile on Horatio's face said everything.

Moving Nelson to his shoulder, Horatio made himself some breakfast and, as he ate, began to plan his next step.

*　　　*　　　*

After transferring his belonging into thick vegetation adjacent to the beach, hoping to keep everything safe, he then marked the spot with an odd shaped piece of wood he could identify and went for a swim.

Once washed, with Nelson on his right shoulder, his mother's photos in his pocket, the shotgun at the ready and a bottle of his quickly diminishing supply of drinking water, Horatio headed off to explore.

Having decided he was more than likely in Guinea, he knew if he looked out to sea and then followed the coast to his right, he would be travelling north, the direction he wanted.

*　　　*　　　*

Just a few minutes of walking along the warm, soft and surprisingly pristine sand, he crossed a slow moving fresh water stream flowing into the sea, reinforcing one of Horatio's hopes that finding drinking water might not prove too difficult.

As he paddled in the warm, shallow seawater, he spotted a walkway built out into the Atlantic, with what looked like boats on the far side. Pleased, but also uneasy, he released Nelson to take to the air and moved to the edge of the beach, next to thick vegetation.

The walkway was a wooden footpath jutting out into the water and Horatio assumed it must have been to secure local fishing boats. Disappointingly though, most of the primitive structure had collapsed into the sea and to make matters worse, there were four fishing boats on the far side of the walkway; all half-sunk shells.

Still hidden by the vegetation, Horatio moved cautiously to the opposite side of the walkway and found a path leading inland. Deciding to try it, he'd only covered twenty metres through the undergrowth when he arrived in a small village.

There were ten mud huts with thatched roofs, most of which were burnt out skeletons along with a number of old rusted cars and trucks. Rubbish was strewn throughout the village and Horatio saw his first plastic carrier bag for many years.

Surrounding the huts, he noticed stone walls dividing up land that had once been farmed but was overrun with weeds.

Turning back to the beach, Horatio walked past a thin, scruffy dog which was gnawing on a bone. It took absolutely no notice of him.

*   *   *

A little later, as a dispirited Horatio was wondering if all the missing locals had perished from the sickness, he came to a small river flowing into the sea which was running

172

from a small lake, just inland from the beach. Crossing the stream, he noticed an elongated, tapered piece of wood, about a metre long with a nodule on the end. Trying it for size, Horatio realised by holding the swollen section in one hand, the length would be perfect for a walking stick whilst reversed, it would make more than a useful weapon.

Pushing on he saw a large wreck in the distance, half on the sand, the other half partly hidden in the undergrowth and wondered how it could have been beached so far from the sea. As he approached it, Horatio noticed it was made of iron, not wood like the other boats he'd come across and decided it was for commercial trawling rather than local markets.

A hundred metres further on, he came to a high wall erected on the edge of the sand, and almost opposite, two manmade structures jutting out into the sea.

Mid-point along the wall, there was a large gateway opening directly onto the sea. At one time there had been double gates but Horatio saw that one had been blown off its hinges and lay buckled, ten metres away; of the other, there was no sign.

Wondering what might have caused such damage, he peered through the gap and saw the ruins of what had once been a magnificent house. Picturing a grand home, vibrant, happy and full of life, Horatio was dismayed to find the only remains were breezeblocks and rubble.

Moving on, he noticed a proliferation of large, noisy flies and it occurred to him that he'd not really noticed the pests since landing. As with so many people, Horatio didn't like flies. They were a persistent, relentless irritation and whilst he put their lack of numbers on the beach down to being near to the saltwater, he almost missed a two metre wide hole sunk into the sand adjacent to the wall.

Before he could move, Nelson began squawking loudly and flew directly at Horatio leaving him more than a little confused.

Using the wall as a support, as carefully as he could, he leaned towards the pit and was immediately struck by a grisly, repellent smell. However, when he saw a pile of burnt clothes he wondered what the falcon was making a fuss about.

That though, was before he took a second look. Moving the top layer of rags to one side with his newly acquired walking stick, a horror-struck Horatio understood; the clothes had been concealing hundreds of bones and fragments of skeletons, all of which were blackened having been partially cremated.

His first thought was why? Why were those poor souls left in the pit on the beach rather than being buried in a cemetery? Then he understood, the bones could only be the remains of people who had succumbed to the virus, and in attempting to keep themselves and the neighbourhood safe, locals had incinerated all infected bodies.

*   *   *

Shaken, Horatio walked to the first of the two walkways that jutted out into the sea as Nelson landed on one of the wooden pillars supporting a sign warning people to 'Keep Off – Private Property'. Surprised but heartened, he saw the words were in English.

Looking inland, there was another once prominent house which appeared ramshackled and Horatio thought the first of the walkways had been part of that property. He supposed whoever owned it must have been very wealthy and decided how ironic it was that in the world he now lived, simply being alive had become the most valued commodity. Money, well that counted for nothing.

Moving fifty metres further north, to the second structure, Horatio saw it was noticeably larger and the construction appeared sturdier. There was also a double layer of wood to strengthen it and a roof, although most of that had collapsed.

At the far end of a narrow gangway, which ran forty metres out into the ocean, there was a platform and although initially confused, Horatio brightened as he saw at the midpoint, an old, discoloured sign; 'Pelican Ferry Terminal'.

At last, he had a name.

The ferry walkway was linked by fractured dark wooden planks to a cabin situated on the edge of the beach. Made of sheets of wood with a corrugated red metal roof, it must have been the ticket office.

To his left, painted in ornate letters, Horatio noticed a large, rusting, weather-beaten tin sign; 'Mehera Beach', and a little further on, yet another dirty, faded sign, this time with an arrow pointing to a substantial building in ruins. The 'Mahera Beach Hotel'.

*   *   *

Horatio didn't know whether to be thrilled or disheartened. He had at last found names he hoped he could follow up on, but where were the people? The buildings were abandoned, the cars and trucks damaged almost beyond recognition and there was literally zero sign of life. In reality, only the burnt bodies offered any real evidence of recent human activity.

Pushing on northwards, Horatio wondered gloomily whether he might be the only survivor in the area; a thought that not only dismayed him but left him feeling alone and vulnerable.

With Nelson periodically squawking and swooping down to check on him, they continued along the beach and had to cover a further two kilometres before they came across the next building; a small, dirty white, uninhabited shack.

Just beyond that, there was a large brick structure built on the water's edge and Horatio's spirits again rose as he read an enormous sign; 'Lungi Hovercraft Terminal'.

On the side wall of the building he found a faded but decipherable timetable which told him hovercrafts had once travelled between where he stood and Freetown, capital of Sierra Leone

Map of
Sierra Leone

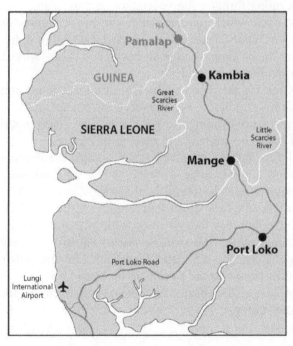

Chapter 22

Attempting to see through the opaque glass of the terminal window, Horatio could just about make out a few pieces of broken furniture and little else except, quite bizarrely, an enormous mound of compressed mud in the middle of the floor. He wondered whether it could have been built by termites.

Continuing along the beach, he paddled through another stream before spotting buildings inland.

Cutting through the vegetation, Horatio came to a red clay track which ran parallel to the beach before turning away at ninety degrees from the sea. Following it, he then came to a main road and beyond, a high wire fence surrounding an airfield.

Crossing the road and the first tarmac he'd encountered since his childhood, as he reached the fence Horatio saw a runway and buildings to his right. With rising optimism that hoped he might at last meet other people.

Following the boundary fence towards the terminal, he noticed a town some distance to the left and squeezed through a hole he found in the wire. Once on the other side, Nelson flew down and landed on the shoulder pad and together they moved towards the airport buildings.

Approaching the main terminal, Horatio realised that being inside the perimeter fence, left him trapped in the security zone and for a moment he considered going back. However, as the entire area looked abandoned, he decided to keep going.

*   *   *

With the runway on the left, he noticed two planes close to a hanger; one had a shattered wing and was lying on its side; the other had its tail section snapped off. There were also two airport buses, the type used to transfer passengers to and from aircraft. They had been set on fire leaving just bare metal frames.

The other side of the runway, further still from the terminal, there was the shell of a helicopter with U.N. Peacekeeper markings on its side and Horatio hoped the airport was important enough to be a base for the United Nations.

Passing a partially collapsed building which resembled the control tower; he then approached the main terminal. On the left of the building was a large grubby, partially destroyed sign which read 'Departures' and, on the right, a virtual mirror image; 'Arrivals'.

Because of the secure border fence Horatio was left with little option but to backtrack or exit via the terminal. Deciding he didn't want to walk back to the hole in the fence, he moved watchfully towards 'Arrivals' where both doors had been ripped off their hinges.

Approaching the entrance, Horatio gently pushed an edgy Nelson from the arm pad and the falcon flew off, screeching irritably.

"I'll see you on the other side," he said, leaving bright sunshine and entering the gloom of the terminal building.

Horatio promptly felt a nauseating feeling that he was in danger and within just a few metres, had to stop to allow his eyes to adjust. With the shotgun ready, he crept warily into a huge, practically empty room.

Everything that could be removed, had been, and Horatio relaxed just a little as there was nowhere left for an attacker to conceal himself. He saw the only remaining pieces of machinery were the baggage collection belts which were bolted down; yet even these had been hammered into grotesque shapes.

Ahead, spread across the arrivals section, Horatio approached a number of booths for passport control all of which lay in ruins and for some reason he suddenly felt threatened. Moving quickly towards the sunshine and praying there were no concealed hazards lying in wait, he was beginning to relax when a shadow shot past from left to right. Before he could aim the shotgun, there was a loud, grinding noise before silence once more enveloped the building.

With his heart pounding, Horatio headed for the door but noticed a large, half-collapsed, 'Duty-Free' sign exactly where the shadow had vanished. Ignoring the opportunity to investigate, he made straight for the exit.

*   *   *

Breathing deeply, Horatio could feel sweat pouring down the back of his shirt so he sat in the warm sunshine to calm himself.

Nelson promptly landed on his shoulder with a thump before nestling into his neck and that's when Horatio cursed himself. Whether he liked it or not, to make it all the way home he needed to man up. He'd be facing many more scary situations, probably some a good deal more nerve-racking than the one he'd just experienced, so he needed to get real about the world he was travelling through.

*   *   *

A few minutes later, as he walked towards the airport's main gate, Horatio was pleased when he turned and saw a large sign high on the terminal which read; 'Freetown Lungi International Airport'. It was a name he could look up in the atlas when he got back to camp.

Leaving the airport behind, a disconcerting feeling unexpectedly came over Horatio. Looking around, he saw no sign of locals, the entire town was deserted and he was completely and utterly alone.

Struggling to counter the dark mood overwhelming him, he petted Nelson for reassurance but couldn't shake off the sense of abandonment and futility. Yet Horatio had always loved his own company, the solitude of walking or exploring on his own and although at that moment he may have been longing for human company, he wasn't at all sure that would be ideal.

Meeting strangers might prove enjoyable, even helpful, but what if they were similar to those on Santiago Island? Then he could lose everything.

*   *   *

Approaching a tarmacked road with the name Airport Ferry Road on a battered sign, Horatio saw a number of buildings on the left, most of which had collapsed or were burnt out. Standing out however, was a modern building with a large lopsided sign high above the main entrance which read; 'First International Bank – Lungi Branch'.

Crossing the main road with Nelson flying overhead, Horatio passed the remnants of a local market. Spread out over a wide area were numerous rusted metal frames, used for propping up stalls and it left him pondering how long it had been since the hustle and bustle of noisy crowds buying food, clothes and the numerous trinkets outdoor markets thrived on.

Deciding not to return to his makeshift camp via the hovercraft terminal, as it would be some distance out of his way, Horatio walked down a tarmac road directly ahead hoping his sense of direction would not desert him.

He entered a residential area where the majority of the houses were set in their own plots, single storey and dirty white with mostly corrugated metal roofs.

Abandoned cars, trucks and various other vehicles littered the area, along with the occasional almost totally consumed animal carcass, although when he considered it, Horatio was surprised there was not more general rubbish lying around. There was though, the usual blight on the landscape; numerous plastic bags trapped by the branches of wild plants, each straining but failing to escape on the warm wind.

To his right, he spotted a painfully thin tabby cat, stalking a bird at least twice its own size. Ever the optimist, Horatio thought and walking on wondered if it had been a family pet in an earlier life.

Passing a large sign on his right for 'Lungi Airport Hotel', Horatio saw a modern three storey building with no doors and most of the windows cracked or shattered.

Overgrown paths and tracks ran from the road in all directions, scarring the land either side of the street and the few trees and bushes still alive, were encircled by unkempt scrub land.

With Nelson flying close by, Horatio approached a 'T' junction with another paved road. The only option apart from the road he was on, ran off to the right and remembering the map, he knew it would take him in the wrong direction.

*   *   *

Within a hundred metres, Horatio approached another crossroads. He saw a large house and walled garden on his right, with a bungalow on his left; both were vacant, matching every other building in the district.

However, as he looked around, something felt different. Horatio stopped, disbelieving. Bizarrely the area was tidy and as hard as it was to accept, he realised someone was keeping the place shipshape.

Choosing to go left, an uneasy Horatio hoped he would soon be back at the beach. Quickening his pace, he saw the houses on both sides of the road came to an abrupt end within a couple of hundred metres and a small river cut across his route. Interestingly he also noticed there were thin strips of land either side of the flowing water that were being farmed.

All things considered, it really did appear that people were still alive and living in the area.

* * *

Ever alert, Horatio closed in on the last building on the left and saw it was a large, two storey construction with outbuildings. On the positive side, the grounds were well maintained and the house looked lived in, but, what sort of welcome might he find if he explored further?

As he arrived at the front garden gate, Horatio called Nelson to his shoulder pad and then stood staring at the rather splendid building. He was in two minds and needed to make a decision. He knew knocking on the door might be risky but, could he really afford to miss the opportunity to finally meet survivors?

Moving Nelson on to his arm protector, Horatio walked the short distance to the gate and then along a paved path towards three wooden steps that led to a raised porch.

"Put your shotgun on the ground and keep your hands where I can see them."

As absurd as it was, the first thought that came to Horatio was how on earth the person could be speaking such impeccable English.

Encouraging Nelson to fly from his arm, the falcon squawked crossly before perching on a branch in a nearby tree where he glared at the man. Horatio then lowered the shotgun to the ground and as he turned, held his hands out to show they were empty.

An elderly man was pointing a rifle at his head and by the dark colour of his skin Horatio presumed he was African, even a local. Curiously though, he was dressed in a suit, shirt, tie and polished shoes and although the clothes may have been creased, he was clearly a man of taste.

"My name is Horatio Mott," Horatio said, sounding a good deal more confident than he felt. "My boat hit rocks near here. I was thrown and both my head and boat are holed." He smiled as he pointed to his damaged forehead, trying to lighten the mood.

When the man remained silent, Horatio's unease increased but he continued in as pleasant a manner as he could muster,

"I'm trying to get home."

The man looked towards Nelson, then back to Horatio before asking,

"Home, eh, and where would that be?"

Horatio struggled to place the accent.

"England."

"England eh. Well, you're a very long way from home.

The man lowered the gun, smiled and said amiably, "You'd better come in and tell me how you managed to end up here."

Chapter 23

As he walked past Horatio, the man picked up the shotgun and led him up the steps onto the wooden porch. He invited him to sit in a wicker chair on the opposite side of a large wooden table from himself; the distance revealing his lack of complete trust in his guest.

Initially, Nelson remained on the branch of the nearby tree, but it was clear he was agitated and studied the man sat opposite Horatio.

"My name is Kadijah Cooper," he finally said as he took his own seat, "and this is where I have lived for the last five years. Now, tell me how you got here?"

"Before I do," Horatio eventually said, "How come your English is so perfect?"

Kadijah laughed.

"You obviously don't know your geography."

Horatio was slightly irked, as he thought he was rather good at the subject.

"We are on the edge of the town of Lungi, approximately twenty eight kilometres from Freetown, the capital of Sierra Leone."

"I had worked that out," Horatio claimed, but then realised he might have sounded rather rude and apologised.

"I like people who speak their minds," Kadijah said, evidently amused. "Anyway, as I was just about to explain, for centuries prior to the virus, the official language of Sierra Leone was English; ninety percent of the population spoke it as their first language, Krio being the main local dialect spoken.

If you look back through our history, for hundreds of years we had very strong ties with the UK. Now, I won't bore you with too many facts but ..." Kadijah looked across to Nelson before describing how British philanthropists founded the capital in 1787 and called it Province of Freedom, renaming it Freetown at a later date.

Undoubtedly the man loved history and quickly went on to explain that the town was originally a British crown colony and within just a few years of its founding, had become home to large numbers of freed slaves; many from Nova Scotia and Jamaica. It was also obvious Kadijah was enormously proud of the part his country had played in the suppression of the slave trade.

"It was men such as William Wilberforce, Thomas Clarkson and Granville Sharp who were leading the fight against the barbaric trade, but we certainly did our bit."

Noticeably warming to his role of private tutor, Kadijah called towards the front door in a language Horatio couldn't place.

A minute later a woman appeared with a jug of water, two glasses and a large bag. Horatio drank thirstily and thanked her. As with Kadijah, she had coal black skin and because of the obvious age difference he assumed she was his daughter. Struggling not to stare, he saw she was also surprisingly tall, he thought about the same height as himself, and she had stunning dark brown eyes, high piercing cheek bones and long hair, tied back with multi-coloured beads.

Horatio thought her beautiful.

Kadijah was evidently amused when he saw the look of surprise on Horatio's face, and again spoke to the woman in a language Horatio didn't recognise.

"She doesn't speak English that well," Kadijah said to Horatio. "But she understands a fair bit."

Then turning to the woman, he added, "Maya, this is Horatio Mott; Horatio this is Maya Bah."

Horatio stood and shook her hand before thanking her again for the water.

Kadijah then spoke in the same dialect to her and Maya began rummaging around the bag. To his surprise she then removed the bandage he had used to protect the deep cut on his forehead and began to clean the injury before smearing the wound with gel and redressing it with a new bandage.

After she left them, Kadijah said,

"Now, where were we?"

But Nelson had other ideas and flew to the hand rail of the porch, perching next to Horatio, still glaring at Kadijah.

"This is Nelson," Horatio said. "He has been with me since he was just a couple of weeks old and is my closest friend." Horatio reached across and petted the Falcon's neck, adding, "He's a Cape Verde Peregrine Falcon."

"Wow!" Kadijah answered, genuinely impressed. "And I suppose he's part of your story, eh? Still… let me finish and then you can tell me all."

Although interested, if he was honest, Horatio would have rather have asked about Maya than continue with the history lesson.

"Over time a British naval base was constructed in Freetown. The frigates would patrol the seas of the Atlantic and any ship discovered with slaves on board was fined one hundred pounds; a huge sum in those days.

In 1833, the British Parliament finally passed the Emancipation Act abolishing slavery, although it took the Americans thirty-two years longer to do likewise."

Horatio tried to stay focused but was having difficulty.

"By 1855, Freetown was home to well over fifty thousand freed slaves and it was why, before the virus, our country was a truly multi-ethnic community. Sadly, that's all gone."

Kadijah sipped his water thoughtfully before saying,

"So, tell me your story."

Horatio produced the family photos his mother had kept in her briefcase and explained who each person was before describing his childhood and finally his plans to travel to England.

By the time he had finished answering the questions, darkness was falling and his host said,

"Will you eat with us, and... stay the night; we have plenty of room,"

"That's kind but can you really spare the food?"

"Young man, we have all the food we can eat, all the fresh water we can drink and we live in this lovely, enormous house. So, yes, we have more than enough of everything we need, except company. Apart from Maya, you are the first person I have actually spoken to in many years, so please stay; it would be such a pleasure."

And Horatio did, for fifteen days, and it proved to be not only one of the most uplifting times of his young life but a great joy.

Sadly though, to his regret, it was only long after he had moved on that Horatio realised how often Kadijah and Maya's guidance and care were to help keep him alive.

* * *

From the first morning, Horatio joined Kadijah on his daily foraging trip, always with a squawking Nelson flying close by. As they left the house, Kadijah gave Horatio a large thick black plastic bag and explained that as often as possible he picked up any rubbish lying around. Once the bags were full he would leave them and collect them on his way home before dumping them in a large pit on the other side of the river.

Wanting to get an understanding of what it must have been like during the virus, Horatio asked where the locals had gone.

Kadijah stopped and sat on a large rock next to the road.

"When it was discovered how deadly the virus was, people panicked and when a town or village became infected, the residents left, hoping to outrun the contagion. Most walked, a few got away in cars or trucks, but there really was nowhere to hide. Millions were on the move, most ending up homeless but still vulnerable to the sickness. As family members died, individuals were left alone and you know, in the end, I suppose most simply gave up running and waited for the virus to kill them."

There was such wretchedness in Kadijah's words.

"The last statement transmitted by the Health Ministry," he went on, "told survivors to burn bodies, protecting themselves as they did. How ridiculous is that! I mean where were people supposed to get protective clothing from?

Anyway, as I moved around, I saw most of the dead were left just where they had fallen and were probably eaten by animals or insects, and you know, part of me felt it was a good thing in helping control the infection.

Once we first got here, there were still a few bodies lying around and we discovered three deep pits on the far side of town all full of burnt skeletons. I suppose a few locals didn't want to run so did their best to stay healthy, but even they must have died."

After a few moments reflective silence, Kadijah added,

"By the way, just out of interest, Lungi's population was more than ten thousand souls; only two of us are still here. So, if that is replicated around the country, or God forbid, across the planet, then more likely than not, the human species has been annihilated."

Trying to change from what was still a difficult subject for Kadijah, Horatio suggested they go to his beach camp.

*   *   *

Defender was still afloat but breaking up piece by piece and Horatio asked Kadijah to swim out to the boat to see if there was anything on board worth salvaging.

After a thorough search, finding little of value, with Nelson perched on the wheel house roof, they sat in the warm sun on the deck.

Out of the blue Kadijah said,

"My wife was one of the early victims of the virus, followed by my three children and every other member of my family."

Horatio was dismayed. He hardly knew Kadijah but had quickly come to like and respect the man and felt genuinely devastated for him.

"Maya faced the same loss," Kadijah continued. "Her husband along with her entire family died. You know, it's impossible to describe the heartache of losing one's family and the constant suffering it inflicts on you. However, for the lucky few; those who meet someone so special, so perfect that together they can rebuild each other's broken hearts and souls."

*   *   *

Horatio adored the morning walks, crisscrossing the local neighbourhood on the hunt for anything new or changed, and it quickly became a habit that Kadijah would point out plants, berries and fruits that were safe to eat from those he should avoid. Horatio always made sure he wrote down the details in one of his mother's notebooks, often making drawings, knowing it was information that could prove crucial to him in the future.

Nevertheless, all was not ideal and Horatio occasionally struggled to appreciate the positives in things he observed. A good example of this were the plentiful privately own gardens they came across. All had reverted to sanctuaries for unwelcome invaders and Horatio could only imagine owners lovingly tending lawns, flowers and vegetable beds.

On one occasion, looking through the open gates of a large abandoned house with extensive walled grounds, Horatio saw a delightful array of colour and looking closer realised all were wildflowers which must have been blown in on the wind.

Just maybe, he thought, after millennia of devastation by humans, Mother Nature was seizing back what had been stolen from her. She had become the planet's dominant power and Horatio wondered whether under her guidance the world would be far healthier and more bountiful.

*   *   *

Probably like so many young, westernised kids, it was only since setting foot in Africa that Horatio realised many of his preconceptions were flawed and he decided to ask Kadijah about one of the more revolting ones.

"Where are all the flies?" he began during one of their morning breaks. "Every picture, photo, in fact anything depicting Africa and the people and animals are covered in disgusting flies."

Kadijah laughed before saying,

"It's simple. What has changed since the virus?"

"There are no people."

"Exactly. Now, don't get me wrong, I don't want to blame humans for all the world's problems, but essentially, flies are a perfect example of humanity's failure. If you travelled around this country before the virus, especially in the towns and cities, flies were endemic and it was almost impossible to escape their attention. What's more, little had ever been done in terms of finding a solution to the problem.

But, you know, for me it really wasn't that complicated. When there is little or poor sanitation, where treatable illnesses are ignored or injuries left to fester, where there are few controlled toilets, where unwanted food is dumped behind the nearest bush or wall and rubbish just discarded, where dead animals in the street are disregarded and left to rot, what are you left with?

Well… one of the less savoury outcomes is flies and they are undoubtedly one of the species not to profit from humankind's demise."

*   *   *

Every day after breakfast, Maya cleaned and bandaged Horatio's ever improving head injury and in return he insisted on helping her with daily chores. Initially it was a little awkward, but with a combination of signs and pigeon English they found little difficulty in understanding each other.

Horatio was also keen to help work the land and although the plots running both sides of the river were narrow, Maya had created a wonderfully productive garden.

On the first occasion he went with her, after she'd explained her work, Maya took Horatio slightly further inland and showed him a walled garden which she had transformed into an orchard with a multitude of fruit trees and berry bushes.

That afternoon he was also in for another surprise when Maya persuaded Kadijah to ask Horatio if he wanted to go fishing with her. He found it strange to be asked by Kadijah but was more than willing to help out.

Watching from the beach, with Nelson on the arm rest, Maya waded out up to her waist and using a small net, repeatedly threw it as far as she could before dragging it back towards herself. Horatio was not impressed and felt it was a time consuming, laborious and probably frustrating method, especially after numerous unsuccessful attempts.

The following day he asked Maya if he might show her an easier way of catching fish. With Kadijah watching, Horatio showed Maya how to load and fire a spear gun, repeating most of what Joshua had originally taught him on Ilhéu de Cima.

Then with mask, flippers and snorkels from Kadijah's seemingly unlimited supply of knick-knacks, a tentative Maya swam alongside Horatio a few hundred metres out from the beach, returning twenty minutes later with two enormous fish.

*   *   *

That evening, eating the fish they'd caught, cooked in a delicious spicy sauce and speaking in English, a more confident Maya giggled as she described in minute detail to Kadijah how simple it had been to catch the fish.

Horatio and Kadijah laughed with her as she tried to explain how she missed the first one but speared the next and they were actually eating it.

"You can have one of the guns," Horatio said. "I'll leave spares and show you how to maintain it."

Although at first Maya refused and Kadijah agreed with her that it was far too much, Horatio told them he had three spear guns and plenty of spares and was struggling to carry them.

"And anyway," he added, "I want you to be able to eat fish like this every day."

*   *   *

Most evenings, Maya cooked on wood fires similar to the barbecues his father had made and whilst they ate on a large table in the back garden, Kadijah would talk about Sierra Leone.

His stories were often colourful, always fascinating and invariably about his homeland before the virus. On one occasion he described how it had always been a country full of rich, healthy foods and that the staple diet of Sierra Leoneans had been rice served with fish, seafood, fruits, potatoes or cassava along with a multitude of different sauces.

After tasting poyo the first evening, Kadijah described how it was a lightly fermented wine made from palm trees and that the locals drank it with almost every meal. He explained that Maya would search for the ingredients locally and then together they would brew sufficient poyo to keep them going.

For Horatio, though, alcohol was a new indulgence. Apart from a couple of occasions when his mother used brandy for medicinal purposes, Horatio had never touched alcohol and on the fifth evening he became decidedly tipsy.

Whilst Maya was clearing up, Kadijah suggested they should have a last drink on the porch before turning in and with Nelson perched contentedly on the back of a chair next to him, Horatio readily agreed.

"It's such a joy having someone to talk with." Kadijah said once they were settled. "Maya is perfect for me, but she will have to leave,"

"What!" Horatio answered shocked, Nelson suddenly becoming watchful. "But, she seems so happy."

Kadijah poured the poyo, leaving Horatio concerned that something was wrong between them. Then after a few seconds, the older man finally said,

"The truth is I can give her most of the things she wants, but I cannot give her something she's desperate for."

"I don't understand."

"I am nearly seventy and not what I was... and, err... I'm not able to... err... Look, this is rather embarrassing but... well... Maya wants children. Rightly or wrongly, she was brought up to believe that having children was everything to a young woman."

Kadijah looked at his feet, rushing the words, which were not getting any easier. "Unfortunately, she has ended up with me, who can't help in that department and there are no other men around."

"But that's absurd. Surely as a couple you both have everything you could possibly want."

"Will you sleep with her?"

Horatio choked on his poyo and as he did, a suddenly fearful Nelson leapt towards him, landing on his shoulder.

"I'm sorry," Kadijah said softly. "That was rather indiscreet, but… well… we've talked about it and Maya has begged me to ask you."

Utterly dumbfounded, Horatio stroked Nelson and remained silent, but his solitary thought revolved around Maya asking Kadijah to ask him; wasn't that just crazy?

Reluctant to admit it, possibly because he had not had sex with Sofia since his mother's death, he was definitely missing what had become an indispensable part of his life and without doubt Maya was captivating.

There was no getting away from his greatest worry though; Kadijah. Five days earlier, the man had been a complete stranger, yet without qualms, he had shown Horatio extraordinary kindness, and he felt a true friendship was emerging.

Of course, the thought of sleeping with Maya was spellbinding. Copious fantasies were derived from far less, but, if it should in any way undermine the way Kadijah or Maya thought of him, Horatio would never go through with it.

"I can see you are torn," Kadijah said with an attempted smile. "Quite understandably by the way, but let me leave you with this. Maya has told me she is desperate to fall pregnant, and we have spoken many times about her leaving me to find a man. Of course, she promises that if she succeeds, she will return, but I know that will not happen. You see, she is not only young and beautiful, but, resourceful and smart and I fear if she runs into the wrong man or men, she will never get away from them."

Horatio immediately thought of the two uninvited 'guests' who had turned up on Ilhéu de Cima and were killed by his mother; it was easy to understand Kadijah's concern.

"Look, I have no idea what is happening elsewhere," Kadijah argued persuasively, "but the one thing I am certain of is that life has been utterly transformed from pre-virus days. Can you imagine a world where the human race has reverted back to the species nature created? Look at chimpanzees, our nearest relations in the animal world. Their lives are built entirely around sex, food and survival, and disturbingly, in their troop they will hunt down and kill other monkeys for both sport and food. Now, of course I'm not suggesting humans will suddenly start eating each other, but my point is, surely it is just a matter of time for our species to revert to behaviour from pre-civilization times."

They both took a sip of poyo before Kadijah continued.

"When I first lost my family, I walked for weeks without seeing a single person, yes, lots of bodies, but no one still alive and in the years the two of us have been here you are the first person we've met. I believe, and I accept I am being pretty cynical, that a world with very few survivors will be run by the most violent and the majority will be controlled and manipulated by that small menacing minority.

Now, if I am right, travelling away from here will be incredibly risky; so if Maya leaves, well... I can't stop thinking about the brutality and violence that is likely to be waiting for her?"

I hope you don't think I am just being selfish, that it's just for me," Kadijah said visibly upset. "Of course, I don't want to be on my own, but tell me, how will Maya survive in a world where everything we've ever known has been replaced by absolute extremes?"

Horatio was uncomfortable with such emotion, especially from a composed, practical person and to give his friend a few moments, excused himself.

Returning from his room he showed Kadijah his mother's notebook and all the material she had collated on measles,

"Not wanting to cause you even more worry," he said gently, "but my mother wrote this before she died. I've taken it as her warning to me."

Watching as his host read through Jessica's notes, Horatio was not surprised when Kadijah finally said,

"God above! If she is right, if this has actually happened… it's a miracle any of us are still here."

Both men sat silently with their thoughts as they finished their drinks. Then, with little more to be said, Horatio rose, called Nelson to his arm, bid Kadijah goodnight and made his way to his room.

*   *   *

Horatio found sleep impossible. He tossed and turned trying to get the thought of Maya and Kadijah's proposal out of his head, but his all-encompassing vision was of her was in a wet swimsuit.

In the end, accepting he would never take advantage of Maya and Kadijah's generosity and kindness, Horatio knew his only option was to move on.

That decided, he fell asleep, but woke almost immediately and with a start. Lying motionless on his side, straining to listen, Horatio heard the door handle turning and saw a shadow creeping across the room. Inconceivably, his mosquito netting began to move sideways and he felt a body stretching out beside him.

Before he could speak, a finger was placed over his lips,

"Shh..."

And Horatio was rolled gently on to his back as warm, delicate lips, softly brushed his.

—Ж—

Chapter 24

Waking late and alone and as he lay in the snug warmth of his bed, Horatio attempted to put some sense into the quite extraordinary night that had just passed.

Maya had been everything he could have dreamed of. Once over the initial shock of her coming to him, they slowly and gently immersed themselves in each other's bodies; Maya revealed the most intimate and sensitive parts of her body, teaching him how to satisfy her. In return, she took him to places he'd never ever been.

*   *   *

Later, whilst Maya prepared breakfast, Horatio sat with Kadijah and what he thought might be the most awkward of situation turned out to be quite the opposite. Kadijah chatted to him about what they could do that day and suggested he show Horatio a tent that might help him stay safe on his journey.

He then went on to describe how he'd been an engineer on the West African Highway.

"For over ten years, as we surveyed land for the projected route, I spent many weeks away from home, often living and sleeping rough. All employees involved were provided with tents as it worked out a lot cheaper than putting us up in hotels, mind you that's assuming there were hotels close to where we were working."

"Look, I'm sorry, but I really can't take it, you and Maya might need it some time," Horatio answered, but as Maya placed a bowl of rice, two different sauces and a plateful of fruit on the table, Kadijah just laughed.

Sitting opposite him, as Maya looked at Horatio and smiled, he knew there would be no guilt or awkwardness about their night together.

*   *   *

Following breakfast and with Nelson on his shoulder, Horatio excused himself and walked to the river where he washed before cleaning his teeth in the fresh flowing water. He then headed for the beach and as he lay in the beautifully warm sea water, he thought about Kadijah and Maya and realised how fate seemed to have been amazingly kind to him.

Horatio didn't like the word blessed, but in some ways that's exactly how he felt. Apart from the terrible loss of his family and missing Sofia, life for him was just about perfect. With Nelson by his side, newly found friends and the fact he was fit and healthy after surviving the virus when billions hadn't, what more could he possibly want?

In truth, God had never really played much part in Horatio's life. As scientists, both his parents had always told the children they did not believe but were still determined to expose them to the teaching of all faiths before they were old enough to make their own choices. They felt at a religious school, such as St Indract's, the three siblings would be introduced to a variety of religious concepts. Of these the most notable were the belief in a definitive presence or God, spiritual awareness, and, the extremes individuals, groups or entire civilisations had always been prepared to go to in their quest for religious supremacy.

All of this knowledge they hoped would aid their three children to make sensible life choices without undue pressure and, for the correct reasons.

As Horatio considered this, he laughed. He had only survived boarding school for a few months, so the chances of him being influenced by anything or anyone at St. Indract's were nigh on impossible.

*   *   *

Arriving back at the house, Horatio found Kadijah waiting in the back garden with an assortment of metal poles and canvas.

"This is what I was telling you about," he said. "Now, let me show you how to put it up."

As Kadijah demonstrated, he told Horatio about his work and career that he had clearly loved and still missed.

"It was just the most remarkable project in all of Africa. Over fifty-six and a half thousand kilometres long, the Trans-African Corridors were supposed to bring all countries on the continent closer together. It would ease the movement of goods and people, and ultimately prove that African leaders could co-operate with one another."

Horatio noticed as Kadijah spoke that he took no notice of a booklet of instruction that was lying on the ground next to him.

"When the virus struck, over sixty percent of the highway had been paved, but there were still many missing links most of which remained mud tracks, more often than not impassable in the rainy season.

My company had the contract to rebuild many of the worst sections on the West African part of the project, but, as with so many initiatives in this part of the world, there was a huge difference between talking and doing.

You see, the original blueprint for a series of continental highways criss-crossing Africa had been discussed for decades and all knew it was so logical for individual countries to get involved. The reality though was arguments and rivalry. From time immemorial, African leaders had always been incapable of working in partnership with each other." As he connected pieces of the frame together, Kadijah repeatedly stood back to study his handiwork.

"Now, that changed when the Chinese signed an agreement with the Economic Community of West African States to build a two thousand kilometre Trans-West African Highway.

This segment would pass through nine West African countries and I was immensely proud my company was selected to be part of the project."

Kadijah stopped screwing two pieces of the frame tighter, had a drink of water, and asked,

"Now why do you think I am telling you this?"

"Is it the road I have to take?"

"Exactly! Well, at least to Dakar, then you'll need a boat. I'll show you on a map."

"You know," Horatio said quietly, "you really are incredibly kind."

Clearly embarrassed, Kadijah shrugged off the comment saying,

"Don't worry, I'll make you suffer appallingly by having to listen to me for hours and hours about any number of subjects which interest me; in the end you won't be able to escape soon enough!"

Both men laughed as the tent was completed and Kadijah then proceeded to dismantle it, suggesting Horatio had a go, which he managed with little difficulty.

"As you can see, it has a built-in groundsheet," Kadijah explained as he watched Horatio work. "It's perfect for keeping away mosquitoes. Also, this is a particularly strong flap which, when fastened, will protect from all sorts of nasties, especially large spiders and snakes."

Kadijah roared with laughter when he saw the look of combined revulsion and trepidation on his new friend's face.

"Also," he then added more seriously, "we have insect repellent. I'm not sure it will still be effective after all these years, but it's certainly worth trying."

When they'd finished packing away the tent for carrying, Kadijah suggested Horatio wait on the porch whilst he collected some things from his study.

*   *   *

When Kadijah rejoined Horatio, he was carrying a number of National Geographical magazines, various books and a large bag that he placed on the floor next to his seat.

"Now, I have some travel books for you; here's A Rough Guide to West Africa, the Lonely Planet of West Africa, which has some excellent maps, and a book of maps from my work, which covers all the places in Africa you'll be going. These are also for you," and Kadijah passed three other books to Horatio. "This one is about the animal life in West Africa, this, local plants and this the natural features of the area."

Yet again Horatio couldn't believe how considerate Kadijah was being and knew the resources he was being offered could be vital in terms of him making it home.

Spreading out a large map on the table, both Horatio and Kadijah smiled as Nelson flew down from a nearby perch and landed on the railing of the porch. It was obvious he also needed to be aware of where they'd be travelling!

"Okay, I recommend you go this way," Kadijah said, pointing to the map and marking it with a pencil. As section by section was explained, Horatio studied the route carefully, especially the trickier segments.

Then, opening the Lonely Planet and Rough Guide books, alongside a couple of the other maps, Kadijah repeated the process, marking each in detail.

"Working on the highway," he said, "gave me a sound knowledge of the roads you'll need but... I'm certain some sections will have deteriorated, possibly considerably, from when I last saw them.

Still… if you take this route," again he pointed, "you should be able to travel almost the whole way to Dakar on pavemented highways."

"You think I should cut inland once I'm in Guinea?" Horatio asked staring at the point Kadijah was highlighting on the larger of the maps.

"I had thought the easiest way would be to stay close to the sea," he continued, "and then I would always know where north is." Horatio thought for a few moments before adding, "I'm nervous about getting lost if I leave the coast."

"Well… you may be right. Certainly your reasons for remaining close to the Atlantic are sound. Unfortunately though, walking or cycling, it will not be long before you encounter sections of your journey that are blocked."

"What do you mean, blocked?" Horatio asked again, perplexed.

"Well… if you hug the coast, on occasions you'll find there are no roads or tracks to follow. A good example of this is just north of here. Follow our beach northwards and it's only a short distance before you reach a peninsular, see, here." Kadijah indicated the exact spot on the map. "Now, if you weren't aware of it, you could waste days following the sea rather than cutting inland on this path, which is the only way to bypass it.

Another problem with remaining close to the coastline is that in Guinea, Guinea-Bissau and Senegal, there are hundreds of bays, river mouths and impenetrable swamplands to negotiate.

Gambia, for example, is a narrow finger of land surrounded by Senegal on three sides. It is no more than fifty kilometres wide and three hundred kilometres long, which sounds fine, except the entire country is split long ways by the Gambia River and there are no bridges spanning it.

Before the virus, the only way across was on ferries and I'm pretty certain none of those will still be running. That means you will have to find a boat, or alternatively, you will have to travel at least three hundred kilometres inland, wasting so much time.

Oh, I know, maybe you could swim… no… that's no good, you might be eaten by crocodiles!"

Kadijah laughed, more so when he saw Horatio was clearly unamused.

"Seriously though, it was the estuaries, bays and wetlands that provided the most serious obstacle to building the highway. Countless bridges were needed and they were horrendously expensive, so governments simply refused to pay up."

Moving on, Kadijah again pointed at the map and one particular region,

"Just here… this area of Guinea is quite high, but I have managed to avoid the worst of the mountains; the rest of the journey though is mostly through low lying regions."

Both men sat quietly with their thoughts before Horatio asked,

"So, I should take these highways regardless of where the sea is?"

"I would."

"And you're saying I shouldn't get lost?"

"Well… I can't guarantee anything. For me though, I feel it's a question of what is the least difficult, because I'm certain much of your journey will be anything but easy."

Horatio stared at the map, clearly troubled by what he was beginning to realise lay ahead.

*   *   *

"Just now you mentioned cycling. What did you mean?" Horatio asked.

"Well, the only alternative to walking is to find a bike. Poorer Africans; those living in villages who worked the land, used them to get around as they were affordable."

"I've seen a few rusted frames lying around, but none that could be used."

"It doesn't mean you won't find one. I'm just saying, if you have the chance, buy it, steal it, do whatever you have to, because it will save you time."

"Okay..." Horatio replied hesitantly.

Kadijah, then left the porch returning with yet another magazine.

"Look, here," he said showing Horatio an article which described how the average speed of the average person on a bike was roughly sixteen kilometres per hour.

"Just imagine if you had a bike, how many days, weeks, months you might save."

"So... I need a bike. Are there any around here?"

"I don't think so, I haven't seen any; the good ones were probably taken by locals trying to escape the sickness."

*   *   *

"Look, would you rather I stopped?" Kadijah said, knowing Horatio was becoming ever more fretful.

"No, please, I really need your advice."

"Okay. But don't say I didn't warn you." This was said with a smile.

"Now, once you get through Senegal, it will be impossible to walk or cycle."

"Why?" Horatio asked, yet again disconcerted.

"Well, the good news is the only passable road going north is a coast road and it runs parallel with the sea most of the way to Morocco, but, you can't use it."

"But why?"

"Because... okay, look here." Again referring to the map Kadijah explained. "Immediately north of Senegal is

205

Mauritania, then Western Sahara and there is no fresh water for the two and a half thousand kilometres from Dakar to where you need to cross the Mediterranean. With no drinking water, you'll die, so at Dakar, or ideally before, you need to find a boat."

"So why don't I find one around here."

"Because in all the time I've been here I've not found a single suitable boat you could use. A few have passed close by, one even pulled up onto the beach and the crew got off and looked around the town. We think they may have spotted us fishing. Anyway, we watched them as they searched a few buildings but they never came near the house. In the end they left taking nothing of importance with them."

"God, I'm really struggling with all this." Horatio muttered, stunned at the unending detail he had to remember.

Eventually he asked,

"So, how far is it from here to Dakar?"

"As the crow flies, eight to nine hundred kilometres."

"And by our route?"

Kadijah noticed the word 'our', before answering.

"One thousand five hundred kilometres."

"Shit!"

Kadijah had never heard Horatio swear and he wasn't sure whether to laugh or not. One of the great strengths of the young man sat opposite him was that he came over as rather old fashioned; he was respectful, courteous and clearly had the ability to relate well to other people. Kadijah decided this was probably the result of growing up on an island, avoiding exposure to the overindulgences of pre- virus youth, but it left him wondering cynically how long it would take for Horatio to be corrupted by the world he was about to enter.

*　　　*　　　*

"Look, I'm sure the further you go, the easier it'll get. You'll learn quickly how to deal with the unexpected, both good and bad, and those experiences will help to keep you going."

Horatio shook his head. He felt incapable of digesting the information being offered to him.

Finally, clearly hoping Kadijah had run out of 'considerations', he asked,

"Is there anything else I need to think through?"

"Sorry… I know I'm probably upsetting you, but it's best to be honest..." Horatio nodded, as Kadijah added, "then, hopefully, you'll be prepared to face whatever comes your way."

Horatio nodded yet again, not at all sure he wanted further pragmatism.

Deciding to ignore the look of frustration on Horatio's face, Kadijah continued,

"Okay, a few other things. Now, we've talked about having to boil water."

"Yea," Horatio answered quietly.

"Okay, so, just as a matter of interest, how are you going to boil it?"

"I'll make a fire…" But before he'd finished, Horatio stopped. He knew where the question was leading and felt pretty idiotic.

"How?" When Horatio had no answer, Kadijah snapped at him,

"Come on, you've got to think about these things'.

"Okay… I really don't know. As usual I hadn't thought it through."

Horatio was seriously irritated, but Kadijah again took no notice and reached into the bag on the floor. Removing three objects he asked,

"Do you recognise these?"

"I don't think so."

"They are old cigarette lighters. Have you come across one before?"

"Joshua, one of the researchers on our island, was the only person I remember smoking." Horatio replied. "He liked cigars and much to my mother's annoyance, my father would occasionally have one with him. I do remember the smell though; it was strong and I liked it." Kadijah flicked open the top of the small, silver, metallic box before spinning a wheel with his thumb, producing a spark, which in turn lit a short length of fabric.

"This," he said, pointing to the burning material, "is the wick, which is soaked in liquid stored in the body of the lighter."

Pointing to two tins with plastic spouts on the top, and a small paper bag.

"These are spare fuel and wicks. With these, the lighters will work for as long as you need. Look after them because they are critical if you want to have fire." Kadijah slid them across the table.

"Also," he said, handing over a thick plastic bag. "Whenever you can, keep this filled with dry grass; it will help to get a fire started."

*   *   *

"Now, if the lighters fail, use this." Kadijah passed over an oval piece of glass and said,

"It's a magnifying glass."

Kadijah stood up and walked down the steps into the front garden where he gathered some dry grass and returning, placed it in a pile on the table. Holding the glass towards the night sky, he turned it at various angles and Horatio noticed a concentrated beam being thrown by the light of the moon.

"Of course, nothing will happen at night," Kadijah explained, "but in the sun the grass will begin to smoulder, then smoke and finally burst into flames."

Horatio was fascinated but wondered how genuinely effective it would prove.

After a few moments, Horatio asked,

"Don't you and Maya need the things you're giving me?"

"Ending up here on our own," Kadijah answered, "meant we could take our time searching local buildings; you know, shops, the airport, hotels, even people's houses. Anything useful we found we took and two of the bedrooms upstairs are crammed full of those things; I have enough lighters and fuel to keep us going for about a hundred years."

*   *   *

"Another thing."

Horatio was gutted!

"Your shot gun will be of little use."

"Why?" Horatio said, piqued but uneasy.

"Well… for a starter you told me you have only a few cartridges."

"Will I need more?" Horatio asked innocently, leaving Kadijah again fearing for the safety of his newly found friend.

"Okay…" he answered candidly, "You do realise you will have to defend yourself because there is no way you will travel thousands of miles, without encountering trouble." Kadijah stood and went inside the house. He returned holding a shotgun with shortened barrels, three boxes and an extremely long and alarming looking knife.

"I have sawn off the barrels."

"But why?"

"Because it's easier to carry, conceal and the shot will cover a wider area. With any luck you won't need to use it, but if you do, this can do serious damage to flesh and bones."

Horatio was speechless. He had never, ever, considered encountering a situation where he would have to shoot someone. Kadijah then stated firmly,

"Look, we agreed I should be honest and that's what I'm trying to be."

Horatio again nodded and after a long pause, he asked,

"What about hunting? If I need to kill animals to eat, surely your gun would not be as effective?"

"Probably not, but you won't need to eat, if you're dead. Survival must be your priority.

You can use the spear gun to hunt, in fact, because it is silent it should be more effective. Just make sure you've had a go with it on dry land."

Horatio again nodded, acknowledging the logic of Kadijah's advice and then asked hesitantly,

"Will people have guns?"

"Before the virus, the world was awash with guns, rockets, weapon of all kinds, and I suppose many will still be around. The question is how quickly will the ammunition have been used up? It's probable you will come across people with guns, but after all these years, I think it is highly unlikely many will still have live ammunition for them."

At least that allowed Horatio to relax, just a smidgeon.

"Now remember," Kadijah advised, "you cannot fire both barrels at the same time, so there must be a split second between pulls, okay?"

Horatio had no idea you couldn't fire both barrels at once.

"Another thing. Very few people will have working guns but everyone will have machetes."

Kadijah picked up the knife, "just like this one," he added.

Horatio saw it was about forty centimetres long with a shaped handle to grip. It had a brutal looking blade that narrowed towards the handle before broadening just before the tip.

"Always keep this sharp and close by; it may well save your life."

Kadijah then passed him a round piece of stone. "Use this every day to keep the blade sharp."

*　　*　　*

"Now, you may come across really bad weather."

"What do you mean bad?"

"Well, luckily it's still November and a month to Christmas."

"Christmas!" Horatio exclaimed having completely forgotten it was only a few weeks away.

"At this time of year, between here and Guinea," Kadijah continued, "the weather varies little from one place to another. Basically, it's muggy and humid. Until April it can be hot and dry, but the rest of the time it's the monsoon season. So… you have five, possibly six months before the rains arrive and when they do, conditions will become extremely tough and unpleasant. Now, I hope you don't mind,"

Horatio dreaded the thought of what was coming next.

"but I've worked out if you're walking, you should try to cover twenty kilometres a day, six days a week. The other day you'll need to rest."

"Twenty kilometres a day, six days a week;" Horatio agreed. "That's one hundred and twenty kilometres. It doesn't sound much compared to how far I have to go."

"No, but at least it gives you a goal."

Continuing to feel utterly overwhelmed, Horatio acknowledged that Kadijah seemed to have worked out just every possible consideration for him as he travelled. A thought then came to him.

"Can I ask something?"

"Of course."

"Now I know the huge distance and endless difficulties and dangers… am I crazy trying to get home?"

Again Kadijah thought how vulnerable Horatio appeared.

"Well… only you can answer that. My opinion is not important. What you must decide is how much do you want to find your family. Once you do that then everything else will fall into place."

Both men sat silently for a considerable time, before Kadijah said,

"I will say though, and please… I'm not trying to influence you. You're welcome to stay with us for as long as you want. We both love having you as part of our family and although it's only been a few days, those days have been truly wonderful."

*　　　*　　　*

Again, both men sat in silence for some time before Kadijah changed the subject by suggesting,

"Now, if walking becomes too difficult, find a boat. You've got experience sailing from Cape Verde, so if you go north hugging the coast, you should be okay. I can't see anyone offering you a seaworthy boat, so you'll have to find a way of seizing one."

After the initial shock of being told, in effect to steal, Horatio said,

"You know, you've really thought about every aspect of my journey haven't you."

"Truthfully?" came the reply, "Well… before we made our lives here, Maya and I talked about moving on. You see, initially we both struggled, you know, stuck on our own, no way of becoming part of a community and helping to build a future. So, I spent many months planning most of the things I'm telling you now, but when it came to the crunch, well… it never happened."

*　　　*　　　*

Leaving weighed heavily on Horatio. His daily routine revolved around Kadijah and Maya whilst his nights were spent drowning in the wonders of Maya's exquisiteness.

On the surface, she clearly adored Horatio; how could she not, considering what they were doing with each other?

Nevertheless, as intimate as they were, Horatio sensed Maya's acceptance that he would eventually move on. She never mentioned the fact, but it was clear her priority was to fall pregnant in the little time they had left. Falling in love… well… that was not a subject to dwell on.

*   *   *

Horatio set himself the task of practising with the spear gun daily and, whenever he had spare time, to read the books and magazine that Kadijah had given to him.

To have any chance of reaching the UK and Berrow, Horatio needed to research everything and anything he could on West Africa, focusing on potential dangers and hazards. It was a region he had not visited so he had virtually no knowledge of snakes, spiders, large cats, insects and other creepy-crawlies. All were at the top of his list of information to read.

*   *   *

During their evenings, usually sat on the porch drinking poyo after their meal, the topic of discussion invariably returned to Horatio's journey.

On one particular occasion, Kadijah asked Horatio if he had been vaccinated.

"As far as I remember, yes… before moving to Ilhéu de Cima my parents made sure we were all inoculated against just about every known disease."

"Good. Don't forget many of the countries you will travel through were beset with some of the worst infections known to man; Ebola, HIV, Malaria, are just a few examples."

Kadijah sat for a few minutes before adding thoughtfully,

"And we had to live through years of the most barbaric civil war."

Horatio was about to ask how such a catastrophe happened, when Kadijah said,

"I've been thinking. If your mother's notes are correct, you do realise how curious it will be to meet women."

"What do you mean, curious?"

"Well… think about it. If there are virtually no females alive and even fewer males, making babies could be… well, awkward." Horatio laughed as he initially assumed Kadijah was joking.

"I'm serious," Kadijah continued when he saw the reaction. "We've talked about it before. The laws of nature state that survival, together with the perpetuation of the species, will dominate behaviour. Look at most animals; they will kill for either or both. So tell me, why should it be any different for the human race?"

Horatio sat in silence, attempting with considerable difficulty, to digest this new angle on survival.

"Let's think this through." Kadijah explained, "Post virus, well… I don't think food will be a problem; there will be plenty enough to go around. So what's the next priority for survivors? Surely it must be the survival of the species.

If your mother's correct and women outnumber men many times over, who will hold the balance of power? Obviously women, and however ludicrous you might think that sounds, they will need fertile men."

"Oh, come on,"

"Why do you doubt it? I mean, look at Maya. She is young and desperate to have children. Now, what makes you think females aren't feeling exactly the same the world over? And you are young, fit and healthy. Oh… and by the way, she thinks you are very handsome." Horatio was shocked as an amused Kadijah continued,

"She did add, mind you, that she wasn't convinced about making love with a bird gawking at her from just a few metres away."

Both men laughed as Kadijah added more seriously. "Look, all I'm saying is you are a young, attractive man, and, that may get you into trouble. Oh, and please don't forget the terrible consequences of HIV. I can guarantee no treatment exists today. If any of those infected are still alive, they could be killing people without even realising it, so be careful, okay."

Horatio was the first to admit, he had little idea about the vagaries of women.

*   *   *

"Be on your guard when you come across survivors, however they appear, and never forget desperate people will go to any lengths to get what they want." Kadijah had clearly moved on to his next concern.

"Unfortunately, history proves that within every group of human beings there's the dishonest, the violent, the selfish, the liars and those who believe that they are far more important than others. These are the people who have always believed they have the God given right to be in control, and I honestly cannot see the world of today being any different, can you?"

Not for the first time, both men sat quietly nursing their drinks before Horatio eventually answered,

"It sounds pretty scary out there," he looked inland, where his journey would begin.

"Doesn't it." Kadijah answered, "However, I could be completely wrong."

Again there was a pause, before Kadijah said,

"You know, when I was young, I read every book and saw every film I could on the apocalypse and the post-apocalyptic world. I was hooked, and, you know, they all painted a world that was dark, uncaring, threatening, austere and utterly cruel. But, just maybe the near obliteration of humans might actually prove to be a good thing. Nature could take back control and survivors would have to treat the planet with respect."

Horatio couldn't believe what he was hearing. It was almost identical to what he had been thinking previously.

"I mean, just look around here," Kadijah was developing the idea, "The extraordinary change in just the last few years. The land now feels alive and okay, I accept it might sound crazy, but perhaps there is a better world ahead."

"I don't think it's crazy," Horatio answered, "I never understood the way people treated each other, or the land. Nature being given the time to repair the planet; how can anyone not be delighted by that?"

Chapter 25

Mid-morning, on a beautiful sunny day, after an enormous breakfast that Maya had insisted on cooking for Horatio, the three set off.

With Nelson on the shoulder pad, Horatio walked with Maya and Kadijah to the Makassa Road. This would lead him to the Port Loko Road, which would take him the seventy-five kilometres to the town of the same name.

When they arrived at the junction, Kadijah pointed the way and no more was said. Horatio quickly hugged them both and, with tears welling, he left them staring after him.

Even though he knew parting would be hard, it proved so much worse and, as he walked away, Horatio was determined not to look back. If he did, he doubted he could keep going.

As Maya and Kadijah also turned away, all three were left with private feelings and sadness; there was however, common ground in that they knew as one, there was no chance of them ever seeing each other again.

*   *   *

The previous afternoon, Horatio had asked Kadijah and Maya to help him sort out what he should take with him and explained that everything would have to fit into one rucksack and a small hand-held holdall.

Kadijah strongly recommended Horatio pack all the valuables, including the jewellery from the fishing boat. He was adamant there would be times when bribing people or bartering would be decisive but warned him that if it became known he was carrying such rich pickings, he would be targeted.

Horatio packed spare clothes including a pair of thick jeans and a woollen jumper for when he arrived in northern Europe, plus a spare pair of solid walking boots. He also carried loose-fitting lightweight trousers, a thin shirt and sweat shirt, spare trainers, hat and sunglasses for the early part of the journey through Africa.

Kadijah told Horatio to pack a sturdy windproof/ waterproof cagoule, which he chose from a number Maya showed him and she explained it would be important if he got caught up in the monsoon rains.

A further couple of items Kadijah suggested, both of which surprised Horatio. One was a long wrap-around scarf for when he encountered sand and dust storms in Senegal, the other was an extremely thin, easy to roll-up plastic cape, for rain in hotter temperatures.

Horatio was then given a waterproof map carrier, and Kadijah showed him how to read a map through the plastic window whilst he was walking. The other maps and travel books would have to be wrapped in plastic bags and packed in the rucksack to keep them dry.

Maya gave Horatio a small washing bag and explained that she had packed his toothbrush, soap, a razor and plenty of blades, a pair of scissors, a few medicines (she explained in great detail what illnesses these were for) and three tubes of insect repellent.

Horatio set aside two of the spear guns, plus bolts and spares which he would tie to the outside of his rucksack, leaving one gun and spares for Maya to go fishing.

He decided, only partly because of Kadijah insistence, that he would always carry the loaded shotgun and had to concede the shortened barrels made it easier. He kept a few cartridges in his trouser pockets, packing the rest of the ammunition in a plastic bag to protect them.

Likewise, one of the three lighters he wrapped in a plastic bag to carry in his pocket, packing the spare wicks and fuel in the rucksack.

That afternoon he charged his mobile and tablet as well as his mother's mobile using the solar chargers, although he doubted he would have need of them.

Maya also gave Horatio a selection of food to carry in the holdall. She included some cooked rice and sauces she had prepared, which he could eat hot or cold, and fruit. She offered him packets of soup, rice and pasta, which although out of date, were still perfectly safe to eat. She explained that all he would have to do was add hot water to the contents, and although not particular tasty, they would at least give him some nutrition.

Lastly, she handed him two small cooking pans, which, with the spear guns and a bottle of water, he would have to tie to the outside of the rucksack.

Late into the night, Horatio ceaselessly rearranged the things he wanted to take. Time and again repacking the two bags until finally, for the very last time, he went to bed with Maya.

*   *   *

Not surprisingly, within no time, Horatio saw that Kadijah had been right; the highway was paved and remained in good condition, hopefully helping him to make decent progress. Having studied the maps, he knew he would walk the seventy-five kilometres from Lungi to Port Loko in an easterly direction, heading inland from the sea and hoped it would take no more than three days.

Initially concerned about the weight of the two bags, especially the rucksack, Horatio accepted it would take a while for him to get accustomed to the load on his back, so ignoring any discomfort and with Nelson flying overhead squawking, Horatio began to feel confident about what lay ahead.

*   *   *

Within a few hundred metres, Horatio came to a long, straight section of the road. There was a broken white line running down the middle of the tarmac and on both sides a deep, overgrown channel. Surprisingly, apart from a few plastic carrier bags and old rusting tins, there was little rubbish to be seen.

Beyond the ditches, Horatio realised there was nothing but jungle; hundreds of thousands of trees, bushes and climbing plants creating an impenetrable wall of deep green vegetation.

As he looked ahead, he could see no buildings; just one abandoned, rusted truck on its side in the left-hand ditch.

Deciding to investigate, for no other reason than it seemed an odd place for a lorry to be dumped, Horatio decided it had crashed attempting to avoid something; probably another car or large animal.

The driver, or rather what was left of him was slumped over the steering wheel; just an assortment of bones held together by tattered clothes. The animals and insects that had stripped him bare of all dignity were long gone, having feasted before moving on to their next banquet.

It was the resting place of an unknown man and Horatio assumed it wouldn't be the last he came across. Death in all its guises was something he was likely to encounter on a regular basis.

*　　　*　　　*

Horatio refused to be downhearted and walking on was determined to accept life as he found it. Looking up at the sun in a cloudless blue sky, he smiled, how could he not, when apart from Nelson periodically shrieking, the only sounds were from the rainforest.

A billion birds singing, insects going about their daily business, monkeys screaming at each other; it was a glorious cacophony of frenzied activities and whatever the future held, absolutely nothing would stop Horatio being captivated by the remarkable world he was entering.

*   *   *

Over the next eight hours, Horatio attempted to move at an even speed. He felt that if he could get a good rhythm to his walking, he would forget the weight on his back and the enormity of the distances he had to travel. There were though, a couple of interesting incidents which tweaked at Horatio's curiosity.

The first of these was when he noticed what appeared to be a long branch spread across the road ahead. It looked as if it had fallen from a nearby tree, although that seemed unlikely as there was nothing growing close to the road.

Initially untroubled, as he walked towards the shape, Nelson suddenly appeared from above screeching noisily. Realising the bird was warning him, Horatio stopped and saw that an enormous snake was slithering unhurriedly across the warm tarmac.

From his reading, Horatio knew he should give them space, never approach or corner them, and never cause them to feel threatened. He therefore remained rooted to the ground and let the snake continue on its slothful way, clearly indifferent to his presence.

Unpacking one of the books on West African wildlife, Horatio found the section on snakes. He had noticed the one he'd seen had a series of rectangular blotches running down the length of its spine, interspersed with dark, yellow-edged hourglass markings and decided it was the common Gaboon Viper.

Reading on he learnt that fully grown it could stretch to well over two metres and assumed the one he'd waited for was an adult. Interestingly, in highlighted red ink, the article stated that if bitten by the ten centimetre fangs, a person would die slowly and in excruciating pain.

Once the snake had slithered through the water ditch and into the cover of the jungle, Horatio relaxed. However, he was left intrigued as to how Nelson had sensed danger. As far as he knew, the falcon had never come across a snake in his life, especially one like that.

*   *   *

The second incident, later in the day, was when he came across a cane rat. Horatio first noticed it in the garden of a derelict, single storey house and looking it up in the book was surprised that it normally lived close to rivers or lakes. It was one of the largest species of rodent, being heavily built and could weigh up to ten kilos.

The added fact that the cane rat formed part of the local diet was a good sign; hopefully meat would be available if and when he needed it.

Walking on, the question of why the cane rat was close to the highway and not near water, intrigued Horatio and he decided that with so many paths leading in and out of the jungle, water was likely to be close by but out of sight.

As if he did not already have enough to carry, Nelson decided he wanted to rest on the arm guard, leaving Horatio struggling, but refusing to deny the falcon his perch.

A question then came to Horatio and he couldn't shake it off. Neither the Gaboon Viper nor the cane rat had scurried away on seeing him. Why? Both had reputations for avoiding contact with humans and Horatio was left with the impression they simply did not fear him.

So, was it a coincidence; both acting in the same disinterested manner, or did it mean neither felt threatened by humans?

Horatio was incredulous. Surely, if that was the case, then, within just a handful of years the most destructive force in the natural world, the supreme hunter with no equal, had become pretty much inconsequential.

*   *   *

Horatio stopped just once and the comfort of removing the rucksack from his back and shoulders was an indescribable relief. He had chosen a village of a dozen houses with rusted, almost illegible signs at either end of the buildings. He'd arrived at Aku Town.

With Nelson keeping watch, perched on a nearby branch, Horatio lay back against a wall and took a well-earned rest.

As he looked about, the houses were more or less identical to many he'd seen around Lungi, single storey, plaster or mud-brick walls, originally painted white, but discoloured and dirty; all with corrugated metal sheets for the roof. Most were adjacent to the highway and interestingly, there were a number of rusted, buckled bicycle frames, a few old cars and trucks; all with deflated tyres, all disintegrating where they had been abandoned.

As the resident ant colony had quickly picked up on him eating, Horatio gathered up his belongings, secured the rucksack on his sore shoulders and moved off. Kadijah had recommended Horatio avoid ants whenever possible, explaining that some species were as organised and venomous as any adversary could get.

He resisted the temptation to look in the houses, the thought of finding decomposed bodies, even if they'd been dead for years was not an appealing one. Horatio admitted he also had a dread of snakes and other 'nasties' lurking in abandoned buildings, finding refuge in walls and roofs. He decided encountering one huge, deadly snake was quite enough for one day.

Starting off, Horatio heard, before he saw, a family of pigs. Four adults and a number of piglets, all grouped closely together, right on the edge of the jungle.

Then, just as he was leaving the village, he came across three painfully thin, bedraggled cows with long, treacherous horns that were grazing on land between the highway and jungle. Horatio wondered whether at one time they had been domesticated animals and was again encouraged, there was plenty of meat available should he need it.

*   *   *

As he left the village behind, Horatio spotted a large hole, just the other side of a rain ditch. The repulsive smell, even after years lying untouched, left Horatio knowing it was yet another memorial to the many unnamed human victims of the virus, burnt to save the world but failing in every possible way.

Such a sad, ignominious end for so many.

*   *   *

Consulting the map, Horatio thought he had already covered about half the distance to his goal for the day and the first of many road junctions that lined his route.

An hour and a half later, having seen little except for tarmac, jungle, the occasional dilapidated building, a couple of abandoned cars, two buckled pushbikes and a good deal of decomposing rubbish, Horatio arrived at Petifu Junction.

Immediately on the left, just after he had passed the roofless Lokomasama Hotel, there was a herd of goats grazing next to the shell of a cottage. He recognised them as West African Dwarf Goats having read an article about them in one of the National Geographical magazines. They were smaller than he would have expected from the photos he'd seen but somehow they were surviving; was nature protecting them in the wild?

Approaching the junction Horatio remembered how adamant Kadijah had been that he should resist the temptation to take any of the alternative roads leading from the main highway, even though some might be running northwards, the direction he preferred to go.

"Never forget roads in this part of Africa can come to a dead end after just a few kilometres; take one and you'll get nowhere except back where you started, having wasted serious amounts of time. Stick to the main routes."

*   *   *

Removing the rucksack from stiff, aching shoulders, Horatio dropped it at the junction and interested in taking a closer look at the Lokomasama Hotel, he called Nelson to him.

As he approached the two storey building, he decided it wouldn't have been a particularly pleasant place to stay before the virus. Looking through a cracked window he saw chunks of the roof had collapsed into the reception area and the few remaining pieces of furniture were broken and filthy.

The rear of the building looked as if it had been destroyed by a serious fire and from the large number of bones, decided a good number of people had been caught up in the blaze.

Making his way back to the junction, Nelson took off and circled overhead as Horatio passed two carcasses, both cows and one only half eaten, swarming with flies. Looking around nervously, for some reason he felt he was being watched and hoped there wasn't a large cat in the area. Only a large predator could have brought down both cows.

As he neared his rucksack, Horatio spotted fruit trees and bushes in the gardens of two houses, some of which he recognised from his 'lessons' with Kadijah and Maya. Although he still had plenty of food and was extremely uneasy about what had killed the cows, he couldn't resist the temptation to pick fresh fruit.

225

Having eaten most of his pickings by the time he retrieved his rucksack, Horatio was determined to walk for at least a couple more hours before making camp. Gathering up his belongings, and with Nelson still circling overhead, he set-off once again.

*　　　*　　　*

Late afternoon, an exhausted Horatio finally decided to stop for the night.

He had arrived at a large petrol station and felt it was probably as safe as anywhere he would find. Erecting the tent behind one of the garages and away from the jungle, Horatio judged that without a fire, he would be hidden from the road.

He ate food Maya had prepared for him and as the sun was setting, Horatio called goodnight to Nelson, who was perched in a nearby tree, and crawled under the canvas.

Chapter 26

Horatio slept surprisingly well and woke to the sound of rain. He dressed under canvas, ate some breakfast and then found the thin plastic cape in the holdall. Wanting to wash and clean his teeth, Horatio knew he shouldn't waste his drinking water, so accepted those luxuries would have to wait until he found a river.

As the rain eased, he finished packing away the still wet tent and other belongings, called Nelson to his shoulder and set off. The newly fallen rain was quickly drying in the warm morning sun and he watched fascinated as a cloud of steam evaporated off the tarmac.

Remaining on the shoulder pad for only a few minutes, Nelson then flew off, circling overhead, clearly keeping an eye on Horatio, who, within just a couple of hundred metres, came to an abrupt stop.

Facing one of the most glorious scenes he'd ever chanced upon; Horatio smiled in delight as two leopard cubs were play fighting right in the middle of the highway.

Remaining perfectly still, captivated by the spectacle before him, he removed the rucksack from his back and then the cape, which he used to sit cross-legged on whilst he watched them at play.

The cubs were undoubtedly relishing the early morning cool air before the day warmed up, although there was probably an appeal to rolling round on warm tarmac.

Surprisingly, an unruffled Nelson continued to circle overhead, but Horatio then heard him call a warning and seconds later an adult leopard sauntered out of the trees. Probably the mother, she gathered up her cubs before retreating into the coolness of the jungle.

*   *   *

Two hours into the day, with the temperature rising, Horatio entered the small town of Lungi Loi.

Kadijah had explained that just past the crossroads, the highway met the railway and the two would run parallel to each other most of the distance to Port Loko.

Lungi Loi was no more than the size of an English village and was made up of a small number of houses all built to the same designs. As Horatio crossed the junction he saw on the map that the road off to the right ran southwards to the coastal town called Pepel.

Passing through Lungi Loi, he had only travelled for a few hundred metres when he saw an extremely old, rusted, single track railway, completely overgrown with weeds.

*   *   *

Tracing his route on the map as he walked, Horatio worked out it was fifteen kilometres to the next junction and if he could maintain a good speed, hoped to make it by midday, allowing him to push on to Port Loko before nightfall.

A short time later, he came to yet another cluster of small houses; again there were no signs of people and Horatio decided it must be a town called Makonto.

The houses were built mostly to the right of the highway, with the railway passing through the centre of the town. As there was no station, Horatio thought it must have been some sort of climb-on, climb-off stop.

Apart from abandoned vehicles, rotting rubbish and the unnerving feeling of walking through a ghost town, he surprisingly encountered a herd of goats, calmly grazing on what would have been the main street. They seemed to be not only surviving but healthy and he wondered why in the absence of people, big cats such as the leopard he'd seen earlier, or even the African Golden Cat were not hunting them.

Leaving the town, as he came to the last of the houses, Horatio saw yet another petrol station ahead on his right and without warning, Nelson flew down and landed on his shoulder.

The large complex comprising a garage/workshop, café, out-buildings and hostel, had been looted and the pumps virtually demolished; people had definitely been there; it was just a case of when.

Feeling slightly less sure of himself and not wanting to waste time, Horatio walked on, but had covered only a short distance when he saw an elderly woman leaving the cover of the jungle on his left. She had a humped back, was limping badly and the all-black clothes she wore were torn and dirty.

When she saw Horatio, she began to call to him in a strange language he didn't recognize but the woman was clearly in trouble and needing assistance.

A suddenly agitated Nelson flew off and instead of circling overhead, he landed in a nearby tree, staring unremittingly at the woman.

When she was only a few metres away, having crossed the storm drain on a plank of rotting wood, the woman raised her hand to her mouth. Horatio understood the universal sign of hunger.

Ignoring Nelson who was squawking annoyingly from his perch, Horatio placed the rucksack and shotgun on the ground and was about to open the holdall to find food when he felt a cold metal edge being pushed firmly against the side of his neck.

Standing warily, whilst raising his arms in the air, Horatio gradually turned but felt the blade follow his movements.

He was facing a young woman, almost as tall as he was, also dressed in black, however, he was left reeling by her hideously disfigured face.

Having little choice but to ignore an extremely animated Nelson, Horatio managed a tender smile; he just couldn't begin to imagine the brutality that had caused her injuries, but it had no effect. The girl increased the pressure of the knife on his neck, before nodding towards the rucksack.

Regardless of his genuine feelings of empathy for the her, he still understood that one wrong move and he would die.

*   *   *

Feeling a trickle of blood running down his chest, out of the corner of his eye, Horatio saw Nelson move to a closer branch, though neither women appeared the least bit concerned.

The girl then spoke in the same language as the older woman had used, and although again Horatio failed to understand the words, her intentions were quite clear. She wanted all his possessions.

Moving sluggishly, endeavouring to delay the inescapable, Horatio noticed the old woman remove a large knife from under her coat. As she approached him; Horatio was unable to resist a rueful smile, there was no sign of a limp or humped back. He then stared as she moved towards his shotgun and knew if he did nothing, he was likely to die.

When the older woman bent down to pick up the gun, Horatio saw the girl look towards her and sensed a miniscule lessening of pressure of the knife on his neck. Without thinking, he swung his left elbow around ninety degrees and struck her forcefully on the side of her head.

The blow lifted the girl clean off her feet and as she hit the ground with a loud thud, the knife she was holding flew out of her hand. Horatio instantly lunged towards the older woman, snatching the gun out of her hands before kicking the knife away.

*   *   *

Horatio could just imagine Kadijah demanding he shoot the two women and that logic was sound. They would have executed him with little or no hesitation or regret, so wasn't he justified in acting in the same manner by killing them?

Horatio was enraged. He had done nothing to threaten or harm them; on the contrary he had tried to help the old woman so he was entitled to payback. The trouble was, when he looked at the young girl's face, he knew he couldn't do it.

It wasn't a question of right or wrong; in the end it was whether anything good could come from their deaths and the answer was no. Horatio knew he would gain absolutely nothing from an act of revenge but, he was left wondering what the hell he should do with them.

With the shotgun pointed at the two women, he gestured for them to move closer together and then called Nelson. As the falcon landed on his shoulders, Horatio said,

"Why hurt me when I wanted to help you?"

They looked at him blankly and he remembered Kadijah telling him that although the majority of people in Sierra Leone spoke English, some only used a local dialect.

*   *   *

Desperate to move on, especially before darkness fell, Horatio began to gather up his belongings but remembered reading that people in Guinea mainly spoke French. As Guinea bordered Sierra Leone, even although he hadn't spoken the language for years, he decided to give it a go.

"Pourquoi m`avez-vous attaqué?" '*Why did you attack me?*' he asked.

The women looked at each other; the older one then nodded and the girl said falteringly,

231

"Nous n'avons plus rien," *We have nothing left*, then before Horatio could reply, she whispered miserably,

"Nous avons été dépouillés de tout alors pourquoi voudrions-nous faire confiance à quelqu'un?" *Everything we had was stolen so why would we trust anyone?*

Horatio asked whether they had food and the young girl translated for the old woman and answered that they ate only what they found whilst travelling.

"So who hurt you?" he asked and again the girl translated, but the older woman became enraged and gesticulated defiantly.

Eventually the young girl told Horatio how they had been attacked in their home and held hostage by three men. Clearly humiliated, she described how for many weeks the men had taken turns in raping her, beating her if she resisted.

With tears flowing she looked at the older woman before adding that when her mother tried to stop them, she was also hurt.

"So how did you get away?" Horatio asked, needing time to think.

"During the days the men tied us up and went out. Often they came back drunk and it was then they attacked me. Once they even raped my mother when she tried to stop them.

A few nights ago, they were really drunk and fell asleep forgetting to tie us up, so we ran."

"Why didn't you kill them; you were ready to kill me?"

"No, please, we would never have done that." The young girl begged Horatio to believe her.

*   *   *

After listening to what they had been through, Horatio was at a loss about what to do. They knew he had weapons and food and if he just let them go, he acknowledged there was a good chance they would follow and kill him before stealing everything he had.

The only answer was to really scare them from following him.

He was more than capable of fighting them off, but if they took him by surprise, he could be in serious trouble. Despite their protestations, Horatio knew he must get as far away as possible, and stated bluntly,

"I'll let you go, but if I see either of you again, I will kill you."

As his words sunk in, it was obvious the woman couldn't believe he was going to release them.

"Merci, merci," the young girl said quietly, as her mother began to cry.

Horatio reached into the holdall and passed them food; then, trying to pretend he was impervious to their problems, he reiterated the warning,

"Do not follow me."

Then pointing west, down the highway from where he had come, Horatio said forcefully,

"Go that way, or… I will kill you. Do you understand?"

"Yes, yes," the young woman said, her relief palpable.

Horatio then told Nelson to fly, picked up the rucksack and holdall, and began to walk away.

"Be careful," the younger of the woman called to him. "The men who raped us, they live where you are going."

"How far?" Horatio asked, attempting to hide his sudden alarm.

"Just before Port Loko, a place called Karina."

Horatio studied the map and saw the village bisected the highway; there was no way of bypassing it.

—Ж—

Chapter 27

It was close to midday when Horatio finally left Makonto and, once underway, he tried jogging to put as much distance between himself and the two women. Twice he stopped, hid and waited, just in case they were following him, but he saw no one.

Horatio had absolutely no regrets about letting the women go. They were prepared to warn him about the three men and if they were being truthful, then both had suffered terribly, especially the daughter. They deserved his compassion and help. If on the other hand they were lying... well... although disappointing, there was nothing he could do about it. He was entirely comfortable with what he had done.

The encounter with the women did however, leave one tricky problem; the three men. If they were still in Karina, he would have to pass worryingly close to them.

Horatio might have believed that people who treated others viciously should be held to account and he might have been incensed about the men's brutality towards the two women, but if he came across them, he would need to act wisely or he could end up dead.

*   *   *

Although shattered from jogging, Horatio was making such excellent progress that he was determined to keep going, whilst Nelson obviously sensing his struggle, repeatedly flew down to check on him.

Ignoring the tiredness, Horatio noticed for the first time since leaving Lungi, parcels of open land adjacent to the highway, which although unkempt, must have been farmed at one time. Further in though, there remained thick impenetrable forest with only a few overgrown trails bisecting the dark, uninviting rainforest.

As he came to a sharp bend in the highway, Horatio heard a loud commotion directly ahead. It sounded like animals fighting and he called Nelson to his shoulder.

Knowing there was no alternative route, Horatio could see the ruins of an isolated farmstead on his right and as he drew closer, spotted a pack of dogs fighting over a large animal; it was still alive and screaming pitilessly as it was being ripped to pieces.

Packs of hungry feral dogs were always going to be a serious threat to human survivors and Horatio had assumed he would encounter them at some stage; however, face to face they were chillingly intimidating.

Keeping the loaded shotgun at the ready, Horatio knew he must keep on walking. Any hesitation on his part would be picked up by the dogs. Drawing level with the pack, he stroked an extremely agitated Nelson and then stared horrified as a huge wolfhound turned its bloodied face and glared at him.

Nelson instantly flew off and began to fly in circles just a few metres above the ground, screeching relentlessly.

Imploring the monster to return to its feast, Horatio winced when two more blood-soaked dogs turned towards him. If they saw him as prey, he could be in grave danger.

Without reducing his speed, he forced himself to remain calm and slowly raised the shotgun. Unblinking, he stared confidently at the gruesome commotion and it was with immense relief when he saw all three dogs return to their feast.

Horatio said a silent prayer. It looked as if the pack had sufficient food to keep them going for a few days, otherwise he felt sure he would have been dessert. It was a chilling warning and one he would not forget.

*   *   *

With the railway remaining close to the highway, Horatio covered the fourteen kilometres to Mabundulia, the town of his third junction, in good time. Nevertheless, due to being delayed by the women and pack of dogs, his hopes of reaching Port Loko that night were dashed.

Mabundulia proved to be no more than a small group of houses, built between the highway and railroad track and as he walked on, a quieter Nelson crisscrossed high over the area.

Although late afternoon, Horatio had no interest in stopping but he understood that the further he went, the closer he got to the three men.

Referring to the map, Horatio saw the village of Karina was only eight kilometres ahead, but he still refused to stop and less than an hour later, as the sun began its daily withdrawal, he was getting extremely close to where the women had been held captive.

An exhausted Horatio struggled to decide what to do. If he carried on the three men might see him, the flipside though was if he kept up his present speed, he could pass through Karina and put some distance between himself and the men before facing the added danger of travelling in the dark.

In the end, Horatio kept going and it proved to be a call that would not only change his view of himself, but also significantly improve the odds on him making it home.

*   *   *

As he approached Karina with Nelson back on his shoulder, Horatio increased his speed to a jog. He wanted to get past the houses as quickly as possible, remaining clear of trouble.

Spotting a battered sign for the start of the village, there was open land on his right followed by a line of houses, with a solitary building opposite. When he was level with what looked like a large residential house on his left, from inside he could hear people disagreeing.

Holding his breath and standing absolutely still, with Nelson becoming ever more fretful, Horatio wavered about what to do next. Reason and self-preservation told him to quickly move on but that didn't take into account an insoluble impasse gnawing away at his conscience.

If he left he would be safe, but in effect that would be condoning the men's savagery. He would be presenting them with a free hand to ruin the lives of God knows how many other people.

Stroking Nelson for reassurance, Horatio decided he could not run away. He could not ignore their actions and knew he had no choice but to face them.

*   *   *

Dropping the holdall and removing the rucksack, an extremely apprehensive, but determined Horatio placed Nelson on a rusted signpost that was sticking out of the ground next to the road and told him to stay there.

He then checked the shotgun was loaded with the safety off and crouching, returned to the house. Closing in on what must have originally been the front door, Horatio ignored it and crept to the side of the building. Spotting light shining through a dirty, cracked window, once again holding his breath, he looked in.

Horatio was immediately struck with how bright the room was. There were dozens of lit candles on all the surfaces. He was also intrigued by the damage; it looked as if there'd been a riot.

In the middle of the room, swaying on his feet, a colossus of a man was holding a long, bloodied machete. A second man was kneeling, he was visibly pleading with the giant who was standing over him, and a third was spread-eagled on the floor, his throat cut.

Horatio was appalled by the gory scene and was about to move when the man standing seized a bottle from the draining board and gulped deeply. Then throwing the empty bottle angrily against a wall shattering it, he screamed at the kneeling man before slashing the blade across his throat.

Horatio struggled to grasp what he was witnessing, nonetheless, he could not tear his eyes away and stared as blood spurted in pulses from the man's neck. Within seconds the body began to convulse and mercifully, collapsed as the wooden floor boards flowed with blood.

Tottering on his feet, the murderer stared at the results of his actions. Two bodies, two slashed throats, a sea of blood and although unsteady he remained standing with his mouth open, disbelieving what he'd done.

Moments later, the man understood, and his absolute disgust and shame was revealed by the look on his face. Falling to his knees it required no translator for Horatio to understand he was begging God to forgive him.

Struggling to grasp how any person, no matter how emotionally crippled, could inflict such awful deaths on what were obviously friends, Horatio asked himself whether the killer truly deserved to wake up in the morning.

*   *   *

Feeling no fear, just loathing, as he stared through the window at the carnage, it was then Horatio knew he could take the life of another human being.

Moving cautiously to the back door with the shotgun raised, he turned the door handle and moved inside, thankful when he found the murderer lying on the floor.

Pushing the door closed behind him, Horatio walked to the man and found him breathing heavily but out for the count. The drink had finally got to him.

Wasting no time, he searched the room and was astonished when he discovered three bikes, all in reasonable condition, leaning up against a wall next to the front door.

Horatio didn't need Kadijah to remind him that if he ever found a bike, he should take it and he had the pick of three.

Continuing to explore the room, he placed all the spare candles he found into an old bag along with three tins of soup, two containers of drinking water and some fresh fruit.

On the floor under the sink, he found two bottles of poyo and decided to keep both and on a shelf above the same sink, he discovered two cycle repair kits.

Horatio actually had no idea if he could even ride a bike. There was a vague recollection of a three wheeler when he was very young and a two wheeler with stabilizers when he was older, but that was it.

He remembered seeing pictures of mountain bikes on the internet and although one was in better shape than the others, all had wide wheels, strong frames and straight handlebars and looked durable.

Becoming concerned about how late it was, he checked on the killer who was still out cold, then removed the front and back tyres, a second bicycle pump and a spare chain.

*　　　*　　　*

Although he felt ending the killer's life was not his duty, Horatio was still determined he should be held to account for his actions. He might have been drunk when he had executed his friends, but what about the violence against the two women? For Horatio it was relatively simple, the man must be punished.

Aiming the loaded shotgun at the killer's head, he knelt down and prodded the man's cheek, there was no reaction. Slapping his face forcefully, there was still no response, so

Horatio pulled at his legs to stretch him out and dropped his arms to his side. He then dragged the nearest body, placing it in an identical position before repeating the task with the third man, but placing it against the opposite side of the killer.

Horatio then ensured all three were lying tight against each other before turning the two dead cronies inwards and lowering their outside arms across their executioner's chest. He did the same with the outside legs, draping them across the killer's thighs and was pleased when both bodies rolled inwards, their cheeks touching. It appeared the three men were kissing.

Finally, using duct tape, probably the same roll the men had used on the women, Horatio secured the murderer's wrists over his midriff and his feet so they were forced together. He then jammed a strip of tape over his mouth.

After stubbing out the candles, all except the one he was holding, Horatio took a last look at the threesome. He was satisfied that when the killer woke he would not only find himself wedged in an immovable, unyielding embrace with the friends he had massacred, but would know he had no chance of escaping them. If that was enough to send him over the edge, then so be it.

The last thing Horatio would feel, even with the murderer's ultimate death, was any regret.

Chapter 28

Having left Karina, within no distance at all, Horatio needed to stop the bike and rearrange the baggage he was carrying, but it helped little, and he continued to sway back and forth across the road. Nearly falling over more than once, at his lowest point he seriously considered dumping the spare parts which were proving so awkward to carry.

Horatio was frustrated with how unsteady he had been to begin with and how difficult he'd found the simple act of cycling. Nevertheless, with a moonlit sky to help him navigate the road ahead, his confidence grew and he began to control his overloaded bike with relative ease.

Unfortunately though, Horatio's speed and stability were not aided by Nelson finding a new, and for him, ideal perch; riding right in the centre of the handlebars.

With only seven kilometres to Port Loko and continuing to make painfully slow progress, a tired and frustrated Horatio had finally had enough.

Rather than make camp though, he lay down in the centre of the road using the rucksack as a pillow, called Nelson to his arm and as the falcon snuggled into his neck, he tried to sleep.

*   *   *

As dawn arrived, whilst Horatio ate, he found one of his mother's notebooks and a pencil and began to recount the horrific ordeal suffered by the two women at the hands of the three men.

With little expectation that they would ever be found, let alone read, Horatio still felt it was important that the world of the future be fully cognizant with the most despicable examples of human behaviour.

*   *   *

With Nelson flying overhead he then set out and quickly felt more confident riding the bike. It seemed that after no time at all, he had left the village of Rosint behind and just a few minutes later approached a battered, 'Welcome to Port Loko' sign.

Approaching the first junction, Horatio saw both roads were tarmac and he remembered Kadijah telling him to take a left turn.

"The Bankasoka River bisects Port Loko," his friend had explained, "so if you need fresh drinking water, you'll have to go into the town centre. Given the choice though, I would avoid it if I could."

Luckily the water Horatio had taken from the house of the three men would keep him going for a few days so he took Kadijah's advice. Cycling on, he saw a dozen derelict single-storey houses on the right and overgrown, open ground on the left. There was a broken goal post lying near the road and a family of goats and four cows calmly grazing, all making the most of what must have been the local sports field.

Horatio decided the area had been mostly residential buildings in its former life and there was the usual motley collection of abandoned, rusting cars; even a few four-by-fours, but no trucks. Surprisingly, there was very little rubbish.

A little further on, Horatio came to a second junction, again with two tarmac roads, and took a left skirting the northern edge of Porto Loko.

He then entered what appeared to have been a large industrial zone and after little time he found the third junction. It was the road that would take him north. Peddling on, Horatio was relieved that, apart from a few

242

weeds that had broken through the surface, the tarmac was still in decent condition.

*   *   *

Horatio realised the northern a suburbs of Port Loko was where the wealthy residents had lived. The houses, mostly with two storeys, had fenced gardens and adjoining land.

He also saw that there appeared to be pockets of buildings all set closely together and wondered whether family groups might have lived in small compounds.

Further out of the town, there were fewer buildings, these being replaced by woodlands and farmland. On his right he came to a large orchard of fruit trees that ran alongside the highway and an old wooden market stall.

Horatio stopped, called Nelson down to his arm and, apart from his shotgun, left all his belongings with the bike in the centre of the tarmac. Trusting it was too early for anyone to be around, he moved toward the stall, but was suddenly confronted by a large dog.

Horatio's first instinct was to raise the gun, thinking it might attack him, but when it bounced up to him with its tail wagging wildly, he relaxed and stroked it.

He noticed there was a group of five houses set in a line and as he reached the stall, heard a door in the nearest house open. A woman appeared, dressed in mud covered dungarees. She looked rather old with streaks of grey in her wiry hair, which was tied back in a ponytail.

Without wavering, she began striding confidently towards Horatio and he saw she was holding a thick pole that would make a very effective weapon.

"We're closed. What is it you want?" She said in heavily accented English.

"Err… nothing, I was just looking around," Horatio answered cagily.

"Where are you going?" she then asked.

243

"To Mange," and he pointed in the direction he was travelling.

"On a bike it should be easy, but be careful, you might find some trouble."

As the woman was being friendly, Horatio pushed Nelson off his arm pad and he flew to the edge of the roof of the stall where he perched, waiting and staring.

"So, how do you stay safe?" Horatio queried.

"There are seven of us who work the farm and people who know us, also know we can take care of ourselves. Those that don't and try it on, well… we deal with them. We are mostly left alone, so we grow food for ourselves and locals."

"How do they pay?" Horatio was intrigued.

"Everyone has something to offer; skills or just hard work. If they want food from us, we want something from them, so we negotiate."

"How many people live around here?"

"Not many. A couple of dozen at the most."

"Men and women?"

"No, mostly woman. It seems we were less effected by the sickness than the men, which certainly makes things interesting," and she smiled as she said it.

Aware he would need more food, Horatio then asked,

"Can I buy food?"

"Of course, but what do we get?"

Horatio walked back to the bike and his belongings, returning with not only the shotgun but the bag of valuables Kadijah had insisted on him packing, plus one of his mother's notebooks.

As he approached, the woman unlocked and lifted the front of the stall to display the produce.

Out of the corner of his eye, Horatio saw the door of the nearest house opening and five women along with a young boy came out.

They appeared to be anything between ten and sixty, the boy no more than a teenager and all held homemade weapons. As far as Horatio was concerned, if they wanted to survive, they had to be able to defend themselves.

*   *   *

"Want a drink?" one of the younger girls said in passable English as she held a carton of water towards him.

"Err… thanks, but no," a thirsty Horatio answered, admitting the water looked tempting.

"Don't you trust us?"

"Of course," he answered, too quickly.

The girl drank from the carton, before again offering it to Horatio,

"With the river nearby, we have all the fresh water we need." It was the woman who'd first approached him speaking, "Please… help yourself."

Sheepishly Horatio smiled, knowing he had been far too quick to question their kindness, though he assumed they would understand his caution. Taking the carton, he drank thirstily before asking about the cost of the fruit and vegetables.

"You tell us what you want and what you have to offer in return; we'll decide if it is okay. If not, we'll come to an arrangement."

And Horatio began to look around the produce.

Although the stall was not large, it was cool and the fruit and vegetables were stored in wooden crates, then placed sloping from the back to the front so that everything was on show.

Opening his notebook containing advice from Kadijah and Maya, Horatio began to select what he needed. He knew if he selected sensibly, the food would stay fresh and keep him going for at least a week.

Pointing out what he wanted, one of the woman took them out of the display and passed them to the younger girl, who placed them on the counter.

Horatio began with fruit, including mangoes, oranges and papaya and chose those that were not quite ripe. He was tempted by other delicious looking fruits such as egusi, a wonderfully juicy local watermelon, but knew it would have been impractical to carry.

In one corner, spotting a crate of small fruits, he asked what they were.

"It's from the niangon tree," the woman answered and Horatio found a reference to it in his notes; small, very sweet and highly nutritious and he asked for some to be added to his order.

Turning his attention to vegetables, he first selected small bright-red jakato which resembled tomatoes. Maya had told him the eggplants were easy to cook or could be eaten raw.

Horatio then picked out pigeon peas which were ripe and ready to eat. He'd read that they were also nutritious and popular with locals, especially the small white seeds which were high in protein.

Once he had selected everything he needed, the question of payment arose and the women suggested they have a drink to work out the total cost.

*   *   *

Collecting his bike and bags, Horatio called Nelson back to his arm and followed as he was led to a large table outside the line of houses.

He was invited to sit on a heavy wooden chair at the end of the table and he transferred Nelson to his shoulder pad and placed the gun next to him, leaning it against the table leg.

The six women and the boy squeezed on to long benches either side of the table, talking in a mixture of English, French and a dialect Horatio had not heard before.

Deciding not to reveal exactly what he was carrying, Horatio said,

"I have some things in here you might be interested in."

He then removed a small, and to him striking bracelet from the bag, having no idea whether it would appeal to the group or not.

One of the younger woman on his left took the bracelet and passed it on and Horatio saw nods of approval until the woman he had originally spoken to, who was sitting on his right, said,

"What use are trinkets to us?"

She was clearly one of the leaders and Horatio answered by saying thoughtfully,

"The world might have changed but does that mean we are no longer allowed to appreciate or want objects of beauty. You know, those small things we would like to wear or that make us feel good?"

There was no answer and for a moment Horatio was not sure whether he had miscalculated. He certainly didn't want to belittle the hardship they faced daily but hoped they could still enjoy special treats.

Finally the women said,

"Of course we still like beautiful objects, but can we afford such things? Our lives are hard and we live sensibly, but… if you have more things in your bag, we might be interested in them from an investment point of view, rather than to wear."

The disappointed look on some of the faces, especially the younger ones, told Horatio everything he needed to know about the dynamics of the group. However, he reached into the bag and this time selected a ring.

"If you want an investment, how about gold?"

Again the ring was passed around and most of the women tried it on.

Nothing was said and an unsure Horatio said frankly,

"This is all I have… so, is it what you want in payment for the food or not?"

"How many other things do you have?" a younger member of the group said from the far end of the table.

"A few, but I have a very long journey ahead of me and I will need to buy other things as I travel."

"Where are you going?" another one asked.

"Further than you can imagine."

"And where's that?"

One of the older woman stood and said,

"I want to hear. Wait till I get back."

*　　　*　　　*

The woman disappeared, returning with glasses, three cartons of drink and a plateful of egusi.

"Help yourself," she said to Horatio. "That one is fresh orange juice." Pointing she added, "that's poyo so be careful, and that's fresh water." Pointing to the plate she then explained, "that you know as watermelon. Now tell us about yourself?"

Horatio asked for orange juice and selected a piece of the succulent watermelon and then prepared for a string of questions said,

"Okay… what is it you want to know?"

The young boy was the first to speak.

"Where are you from?"

"Well… originally I lived in England." He noticed there was a reaction along the table. They obviously knew where his home was.

"So how come you're here?"

"When I was young," he explained, "I moved to an island in Cape Verde to be with my parents. They were scientists studying endangered birds."

"So is that how you got that?" the woman asked pointing at Nelson.

"Yes, I raised him. He was found as a chick and would have died if we had left him on his own."

The questions continued for the next hour and Horatio patiently answered as many as he could.

*   *   *

Moving Nelson from his shoulder to his arm protector, Horatio allowed the youngest to stroke him and the falcon clearly loved being the centre of attention.

Eventually Horatio explained that he needed to get going and what did they want in exchange for the food?

It was the first woman he'd met who answered.

"We want you to take Nanette with you." She put her arm around a young girl on her right.

"Her family come from Forecariah and like you, she's desperate to get back to them. She speaks English and needs someone to look after her, you know… to keep her safe on her journey home."

Horatio remembered from the maps that he had to pass through the town which was located a hundred kilometres away, just across the border with Guinea. Under any other circumstances he probably would have agreed, but answering as honestly as he could, he said,

"I'm sorry, it would be impossible."

"Why?" came the reply.

"Well… firstly I am on a bike and it would slow me down if you were walking." He said this to the young girl, Nanette, "Also, it would be almost impossible to carry the extra food and other things you would want to take. I am already struggling with the things I have."

"What if we can solve the problems?" Asked the older woman, with a confidence that surprised Horatio.

"Can you do that?" he asked.

The woman then spoke French to one of the older members of the group, who was sat further down the table, and she left taking Nanette with her.

"She can take one of our bikes; we have several so it will not be a problem, then…"

Before she could go on, Nanette returned, giggling as she rode on a bike, somewhat erratically and directly towards them. The other woman walked behind her pulling a box on wheels.

Intrigued, Horatio stood, released Nelson who flew off indignantly, and walked towards Nanette. The bike was certainly in good condition, but it was the box on wheels that really interested him.

About seventy-five centimetres square and fifty centimetres deep, set with two pram wheels either side, and a long metal pipe sticking out one end, Horatio realised if he could tie this to the back of his bike, he could pull his belongings, rather than carry them.

He knew it was too good a chance to miss and one he was never likely to be offered again. When the group, as one, agreed to include in his food order, additional fruit, juice, a couple of bottles of poyo, even some fresh chicken, there really was no decision to make.

Nanette needed little time to sort out her few possessions whilst a delighted Horatio attached the bar to the rear of his saddle before packing the cart.

Chapter 29

As they set off, Horatio was still fascinated by the group who he thought were simply remarkable survivors. He defined his short time with them as absorbing but bordering on the surreal, and not for the first time struggled to come to terms with his good fortune.

Initially it took Nanette some time to relax when pedalling, whilst Horatio needed to get to grips with pulling a weighty cart behind him. Nelson though quickly realised the potential for yet another new perch, on the its various edges.

*   *   *

It took little time for Horatio to regret packing so much in the cart, controlling his bike was difficult enough without the added weight and instability from behind. Nevertheless, they made surprisingly good progress and by mid-afternoon had arrived at a handful of buildings and the next junction.

Calling a stop to have a drink, Horatio checked the map and confirmed they were on the right road to Mange and only twenty kilometres away.

When Nanette realised where they were headed next, she told Horatio in excellent English about visiting Mange with her parents and described how the town had always had an excellent market; one which her mother had loved.

*   *   *

Taking a left onto the new highway, Horatio kept half an eye on Nelson who was alternating between perching on the handlebars and the edge of the cart and found himself smiling as he watched Nanette become more confident and daring on the bike. At one point she was actually zigzagging from side to side, giggling the entire time and Horatio decided it was time to build up their speed.

He remembered the article that described how an average cyclist covered fifteen kilometres an hour and knew if they could get anywhere near that, they could reduce the journey time to Nanette's home significantly.

*   *   *

As they rode on, Horatio saw the countryside had changed. Gone was the intimidatingly impenetrable jungle and overgrown storm ditches, to be replaced by open land that had once been used for farming. Like so much however, the world around him was reverting to wild savannah.

Less than an hour later, the highway took a sharp turn to the left and wide swathes of flat land appeared on both sides of the road.

When Horatio came to a stop, Nanette pulled up alongside him.

"What's wrong?" she asked, worry in her voice.

"Listen," Horatio answered excitedly. "Water!"

Nanette laughed at Horatio's delight and said,

"Locals know it as the Kaba River, but it's actually The Little Scarcies River."

Referring to the map, Horatio saw they were close to a small village called Bantoro and he climbed off the bike and began pushing it over some rough ground to an overgrown red clay track.

A couple of a hundred metres further on they came to the river and with an astonished Nanette's looking on Horatio immediately stripped down to his pants before wading in. Ducking his head and gulping mouthfuls of fresh water, every time he surfaced Horatio laughed. Then, remaining close to the bank, where the river was only about half a metre deep, he sat on a submerged stone and allowed the flowing water to pour over him. Rarely had he felt so wonderfully invigorated.

*   *   *

Sitting on the bank in the warming afternoon sun, Horatio waited for Nanette to finish washing in the river before telling her he did not want to arrive in Mange late in the evening.

Nanette was more than happy to make an overnight stop, so they searched the immediate area finding a small patch of ground, surrounded by tall trees.

After carrying their belongings and pushing the bikes to the campsite, Horatio then erected the tent. He had already decided that Nanette should use it, especially as he preferred to sleep out in the open and although she initially refused, she finally agreed when Horatio told her he would not take no for an answer.

He then collected wood, lit the fire and with Nelson settled on a branch overlooking the campsite, they ate food the group had given them, including the fresh chicken and fruit juice.

As sundown arrived, Horatio headed back to the river to sit on the same submerged stone where he swilled the plates, cups and knives. He then shaved with the blade and soap Maya had given him, cleaned his teeth and finally washed himself and his filthy, sweat ridden clothes knowing they would dry overnight.

By the light of the fire, Horatio hung the wet clothes between two branches and with Nelson back on the same perch, he sat down next to Nanette.

Offering her insect repellent which she declined, as he sprayed himself, Horatio asked,

"How old are you?"

"Fifteen."

"So how come you speak such good English?"

"I was sent to a missionary convent run by nuns and all lessons were in English. The school was near my home and although my family spoke French, my parents believed that to be successful I needed to speak English."

Horatio looked at Nanette, seeing the same dark mahogany skin and striking features of Maya. She was rounder in the face and although young, her body was well developed. There was no doubt she was a striking looking young lady, but, he also saw innocence. If she ended up on her own, without anyone to look after her, she could definitely end up with serious problems.

"Who do you expect to find at home?" he then asked,

"Well... not my mother. She died from the virus. We were together staying in Port Loko with her sister, my aunt, and her family... they all died. I was left on my own and tried so many times to get home before those at the farm took me in. They were wonderful and kind, but I couldn't forget my family and needed to get back to them."

"What happens if your family are not there?"

"I don't know. I'll decide if it happens."

Nanette sat staring at the fire and Horatio thought she looked anxious. Hardly surprising when there was a real possibility she would find none of her family had survived the virus.

A few minutes later, she rose and said goodnight to both Horatio and Nelson, who was up in the nearby tree. However, as she was about to zip up the tent flap, she stuck out her head and said, mischievously,

"Anyway, if the worst happens, I'll stay with you and Nelson."

*   *   *

The following morning, after damping down the fire, taking down the tent and packing the cart, they had fruit and some chicken for breakfast. Then, making sure all the containers were full of fresh water from the river, they mounted their bikes and with Nelson already in the air, they set off. Horatio told Nanette it would take them an hour to reach Mange.

"From there, if we do well, we might even make Forecariah and your home before dark."

*   *   *

The first part of the journey was as straightforward as Horatio had hoped it would be. The highway remained in reasonable condition and importantly, flat. Nelson was also content having found his new perch on the narrow edge of the cart.

Much to Nanette's delight, the falcon shrieked noisily whenever Horatio hit a bump or crack in the tarmac and she decided it was just like the boss reprimanding his personal chauffeur.

Keeping the Little Scarcies on their right, they cycled for ten kilometres before seeing a large iron bridge up ahead.

With tall buttresses at either end, spanning what had become a wide, fast flowing river and the town of Mange on the far side, Horatio found the view unexpectedly impressive.

*   *   *

As they approached the bridge, Horatio was both surprised and frustrated to see a barricade mid-point over the water. It appeared to be a solid wall created from junk, including various vehicles on their sides, large pieces of furniture and slabs of masonry.

Staring at the Little Scarcies before referring to the map, Horatio realised the only alternative to crossing the bridge would entail them backtracking to find another crossing point. However, as far as he could tell there were no other bridges, so they would have to travel some distance away from their highway before finding a shallow ford, and even then they may not be safe.

*   *   *

Accepting the only practical route to Nanette's farm was to negotiate the impenetrable looking gate, erected in the centre of the barricade which he knew would be heavily guarded. The question was how dangerous the people controlling it were and what did they want in return for their safe passage?

Horatio stopped and told Nanette to remain where she was. Then calling Nelson to his shoulder, he dropped everything except the loaded shotgun and approached the barrier.

When he was twenty metres from the fortification of junk, two women appeared, both holding machetes. They were directly above him, probably on a platform and high enough to stop him reaching them.

Horatio stood still and one of the woman began to speak in a local dialect he could not understand. When the second woman realised, she asked if he understood English and when he nodded she said in an oddly cultured voice,

"If you want to cross, you have to pay."

"Pay what?" he answered.

"And there are two of you, so that will be extra."

"Extra what?"

"Food, tools, weapons, anything you've got, but you will pay."

"What gives you the right to charge us?" Horatio asked, exasperated by the time they were wasting.

"It's our bridge because we control it. River crossings have always been fought over and this one is no different."

Horatio was struggling to contain his frustration as she continued,

"We're creating our own community and we will succeed if we control the crossing, so you have to pay."

"Okay, you've made your point." Horatio thought for a moment, assessing the risks before adding, "How do we know you won't attack us once we go through the gate?"

"You don't."

"So how do you expect us to accept?"

"Because you have no choice."

"We can go further upriver. Find another crossing." "You can, but be warned; if you think we're unreasonable, inland they'll kill you and negotiate afterwards." The women laughed, however the point was made and Horatio knew he had little option but to agree.

Returning to Nanette he explained the situation and both agreed it was the simplest and probably safest way to cross the river, nonetheless they also knew it was risky.

Horatio pushed Nelson off his arm pad and as he took to the air, told him to keep an eye on what was happening.

"Does he really understand?" Nanette asked doubtfully.

"I have no idea, but there's been a couple of times he's kept me out of trouble. I sometimes think he has a greater awareness of what is going on, than I do."

*   *   *

Pushing their bikes, they approached the barrier as the same two women appeared on the platform above them.

"You want to come through?"

"Yes… please," Horatio replied as pleasantly as he could.

The gate immediately began to slide sluggishly sideways and Horatio saw the two women were inside waiting for them.

With the shotgun at the ready, Horatio told Nanette to remain where she was and still pushing his bike, he walked towards the women

"What about your friend?" the English speaker asked. "Making sure we'll keep our word are you?"

"Well… I certainly want to make sure she stays safe," Horatio answered, determined not to reveal how anxious he felt.

"Important, is she?"

"I only met her yesterday, but I have promised to get her home and that's what I will do."

The first woman he had spoken to then called towards Nanette in the language Horatio had originally failed to understand.

"She's asked where my home is," Nanette said, translating for Horatio. "Shall I tell her?"

When he nodded, she spoke confidently and he caught the word Forecariah.

The woman then turned and a third woman appeared. She was younger than the other two, and for some reason, appeared uneasy.

Nanette told Horatio she was to move alongside him and again he nodded his agreement.

The younger girl then stared directly at Nanette, before speaking in yet another dialect Horatio had never encountered. He watched as Nanette replied confidently in the same dialect and a short exchange between the two followed before the oldest of the women said to Horatio,

"It's your lucky day, but only because your friend lives nearby."

With Horatio feeling only partly relieved and still uncertain they could be trusted, he asked,

"So, if she didn't, what would you have done to us?"

"That, you'll never know," came back the answer, along with a wicked smile.

*   *   *

The first gate closed promptly behind them as they entered an area with a rickety looking shelter made mostly of similar junk to the barricade. Directly ahead, in the centre of the bridge, there was a second, almost identical barrier and gate.

Grudgingly, Horatio saw it was an ingenious design. It allowed those inside to charge travellers from both directions and once they had them through the gate, they could then hold them between the two barricades.

Horatio heard Nelson squawking from high up on the wall and although he appeared relatively calm, it didn't help ease the possible threat they faced.

Two dogs on leads entered the enclosure and although neither looked restless, Horatio knew they could turn in a second.

"As you are not local, we'd normally charge you more, but as your friend is from around here, we'll be fair. So… what do you have?"

It was Nanette who answered and in English.

"A little food and jewellery."

"Let's see."

Horatio, reached in to the cart and produced two bottles.

"Orange juice and poyo," he said, hoping the bottle of poyo would do the trick.

"Poyo… how did you get that?"

"It came from the group who were looking after me," Nanette answered.

"Okay, we'll take both. Now the jewellery."

Horatio reached into the cart but was determined not to reveal the bag or the other bottle of Poyo, so withdrew the same ring and bracelet, he had been resigned to losing to Nanette's group.

"The oldest woman grabbed at the ring and tried it on and Horatio saw it fitted perfectly. The second woman studied the bracelet before saying,

"So what else do you have?"

"You mean that's not enough?" Horatio answered, his annoyance obvious.

"Just answer," she demanded, smiling smugly.

"That's all," he lied, determined not to let them gain the upper hand.

"Perhaps you're lying."

"Look, just take the stuff and let us go."

"Maybe we want more."

Horatio saw there were five women, all armed with machetes, but no guns and the two dogs. He needed a resolution and swiftly.

"Right," he said, moving Nanette to a position directly behind him. "This is where we're at. There are five of you, all armed. Then there is me with a loaded gun, plus Nelson." Horatio deliberately ignored the dogs, hoping they were pets rather than trained to attack.

"Who's Nelson?" One of the group asked.

"He is," Horatio answered, pointing towards the falcon.

"And what's that going to do?"

"Do you really want to find out?"

The two closest women looked at each other as Horatio called to Nelson, who squawked, took-off and flew in a circle overhead. The young woman nearest to Nanette began to snigger, however, a fraction of a second later she screamed as Nelson dived, talons outstretched, avoiding her eyes by a hairsbreadth. He landed on Horatio's arm protector and stared menacingly at the group.

"Don't forget, I have this." He raised the shotgun and aimed it at the nearest of the women.

"How do we know it's loaded?"

"That, you'll never know," he answered, smiling as he mimicked the earlier exchange, then added bluntly,

"Let us go or you will get hurt." Looking around, he then added candidly,

"You might believe you can win, and maybe you can, but how many of you are prepared to die trying?"

Horatio told Nanette to stay back and repositioned the shotgun to fire at the women who had been negotiating with him.

"You three are dead…" he nodded at the two women from his arrival and the young girl who had joined them, "firing only one barrel which leaves me a second shot, so who else wants to die?" He said this staring at those on the periphery.

I will also guarantee, if the falcon sees me being hurt, he will strike back which means he will more than likely rip out the eyes of at least one of you. So ask yourself, do you really want to upset him."

Horatio again, deliberately glared at each of the group.

"So, decide, because I'm finished playing your games."

"Well said!" It was the nearest and oldest of the women who clapped as she spoke. There was genuine endorsement in her voice.

"I mean it," Horatio stated definitely.

"Oh, I'm sure you do. Right… we'll have the juice, poyo, ring and bracelet. Are we agreed?"

Chapter 30

"How did we get out of that?" Nanette asked. It was midday, the sun was in a clear blue sky and they had begun the next part of their journey, the thirty kilometres from Mange to Kambia.

"You know, they really frightened me. I was certain they were going to kill us."

"There was a possibility they would have," Horatio replied, "but remember, people are doing things they would never have done before the sickness. Everyone is desperate and trying to stay alive and if it helps them survive, they'll justify hurting, even killing people."

As they cycled on, Horatio asked himself whether he was any different. Just months before he would never have considered standing up to those women; it was not part of who he had been, but no longer. He would do whatever had to be done to keep them both safe; that was all there was to it. But was it, was it really?

He then remembered Kadijah saying that the longer his journey lasted, the easier it would be for him to deal with the unexpected, no matter how disturbing and as usual his friend had been right.

In the four days, just four days, since leaving Lungi, Horatio had encountered human behaviour he would never have believed possible. Yet he knew it was just the start; just the beginning of having to deal with the unfamiliar, no matter how forbidding, brutal or intimidating.

There was the positive though, Horatio was learning to channel his anger. It had flared up, but he had coped, he had controlled his reactions and calmed flashpoints before they had erupted into serious violence.

Mind you, he did question whether he actually liked the new version of himself.

"You know, you were so brave," Nanette suddenly interrupted his thoughts. "Weren't you even a little bit afraid?"

"Afraid!" he answered laughing, "I was absolutely terrified."

*   *   *

Two hours later they arrived at a collection of derelict buildings and a broken, rusted sign naming the hamlet, Gbonkomakent. They had seen little except a few grazing animals and two large, jam-packed holes in the ground for burning the dead. He had steered Nanette away from them. There had also been a small groups of mud houses but they didn't warrant a mention on the map.

*   *   *

With Nelson hovering serenely overhead, they cycled through Gbonkomakent and then built up speed. Horatio saw that unlike the surrounding area from Mange, most of which had reverted to forests, the land appeared fertile on both sides and interestingly, some looked as if had recently been cultivated.

Nanette pulled alongside Horatio and told him moringa was growing in the fields. Slowing down, she called across to him,

"It's one of the most important crops we have because every part of the plant is used. The fruit, seeds, flowers, bark and leaves; nothing is wasted. Even the roots help to make medicines."

She then came to a stop and pointed to a field of lush green leaves, fifty metres in from the highway and said,

"My grandmother used to say you could treat just about any illness with moringa. She swore by it, claiming it boosts the immune system and is even used for cancer. Oh… and it is supposed to improve your sex drive."

Nanette giggled as she said this and Horatio laughed with her.

As they moved on again, she added,

"My grandmother was what you would call a witch doctor. I remember her treating people in the villages around our farm and everyone trusted her."

*   *   *

The longer they were together the more Horatio realised that, for her age, Nanette was extremely knowledgeable. She appeared to be in possession of countless snippets of information which could be useful and he felt that wherever she ended up, she would prove to be a real asset.

Just a few kilometres on, they came across a hamlet where the houses looked lived-in. As with the fields of moringa, Horatio could see the land was being farmed and Nanette suggested they stop to find food.

"I'd rather not," Horatio answered warily. "This village is pretty isolated and if the locals don't like visitors, we could be in trouble."

"But surely not everyone wants to hurt us?" Nanette asked, despondently.

"Hopefully not, but we can't be too careful," Horatio answered with a good deal more cynicism than he intended.

*   *   *

They reached the outskirts of a large town twenty minutes later. Curiously though, Horatio could find no mention of it on the map and even Nanette couldn't help.

With Nelson flying overhead, they first entered a residential zone with a large number of single storey houses on their right and Horatio told Nanette to stay behind him and match whatever speed he was doing. On the left was open ground and a small orchard.

Increasing his speed, he noted with interest that there had been a huge fire which had engulfed both sides of the highway. Buildings, vehicles, plants and trees; all just charcoal remnants.

Pushing on he realised much of the town had been overwhelmed in the firestorm and must have been abandoned years earlier.

*   *   *

As they rode on, moving quickly along what must have once been a bustling high street, Horatio noticed some of the buildings were undamaged by the fire. He even thought some might still be occupied and again increased his speed, with Nanette alongside him, he decided it would be better not to run into any locals.

As they peddled through the town centre, they came to a junction where their highway crossed three other roads, one of which was tarmacked and Horatio finally identified the exact point on the map.

A few minutes later, as they were leaving the built up area, an old man appeared on the porch of a ramshackle hut, quite unbelievably he was smoking a pipe.

As he saw the bikes approaching, he limped into the centre of the road and held up his hand.

With a craggy face, burnt sienna skin and snowy white, wiry hair and beard, there was something almost noble about him. Horatio slowed to a stop and reached behind him for the shotgun.

"You'll not be needing that," the wizened old man said in French.

Nelson then landed on a broken, rusting television aerial on the roof of a nearby house and Horatio, not sure what to do next, asked about the fire.

"Four years ago," the man explained. "Terrible it was. Happened in the middle of the night and most of the hundred or so who had survived the virus died in their

265

sleep from the smoke. If there is such a thing as a God, please tell me why he would allow that to happen on top of everything else we've suffered?"

He then spat on the ground in disgust.

"That's awful," Nanette said and it was the first time Horatio had heard her use French; he was impressed.

"Aye, it was, but you have to carry on. Now there are seven of us and I'm the only man."

"Where are the others?" Horatio asked surprised.

"Working in the fields. Because I'm old, they let me rest. I am very lucky because they look after me. Mind, I still have my manly duties to perform." And he grinned cheekily.

Ignoring the glib remark, Nanette asked,

"Do you have enough food?"

"Aye, we make do; they even grow and dry tobacco for me. What more can I hope for at my age?"

The man was thoughtful for a moment before saying,

"Do you want a drink?"

"That's very kind, thank you, but I must get my friend back to her family."

"Where's that then?"

Nanette explained that she lived just outside Forecariah.

"Forecariah aye."

"Yes, is the road safe?"

"I don't really know. We see no one. Mind you that's hardly surprising. This country was a disaster even before the virus; civil war, starvation, all manner of incurable diseases, and then the virus. We really must have upset someone upstairs." He pointed to the sky.

Horatio was about to move on when the man said thoughtfully,

"You know, come to think of it, we did have one family come through here, but it was years ago. They were trying to get from near Conakry, to their village and had walked about a hundred kilometres and seen no one."

"How many were there?" Horatio asked.

"Oh… two woman, one older man, two girls and a young lad."

The answer was further confirmation of Jessica's prediction; a world where it was rare to meet people, and those that you did were mostly women.

Horatio leant back and reached into the cart, removing his last bottle of poyo. He offered it to the man, who smiled and thanked him for his kindness.

It was only as they cycled away, Horatio understood what the man had meant when he'd revealed 'his manly duties'; and he couldn't stop himself laughing.

However, the more he thought about it, the more Kadijah's opinions on the relationship between men and women in their 'brave new world', were reinforced.

*　　*　　*

Fifteen minutes after they had left the town limits, Horatio stopped, referred to the map and said to Nanette,

"It's eight kilometres to Kambia, where we cross the Great Scarcies River, so we have two choices; we make camp here, wait until dawn when hopefully most people should be asleep and try to cross then, or we keep going and see what happens."

"What do you want to do?" Nanette asked. "I think we should keep going."

Nanette agreed.

"I remember crossing the bridge at Kambia. If it's the same as at Mange, can't we find another way?"

"No, it's the same problem. The only alternative is to go inland, but I have no idea what we might encounter and it could be far riskier."

After passing groups of farm buildings and the abandoned village of Kabaranka, late in the afternoon they spotted the outskirts of Kambia and Horatio again called a stop.

"If we get through the town easily," he said, "we should reach the Guinea border tonight and then we can make camp, which is all good unless we hit problems. I really don't like the thought of being stuck in a large town after dark."

"So, let's make camp, here," Nanette suggested, even though she knew her family were getting ever closer and she was frantic to get back to them.

Horatio saw they had stopped close to a large abandoned farm and, after looking around the area, it was agreed they make camp at the rear of the main house.

*   *   *

Nelson flew off to hunt as Horatio realised the sky was full of heavy black clouds and assuming there was a storm on the way, quickly erected the tent.

He considered lighting a fire, but as they still had cold food to eat and it was a warm evening, he decided not to take the chance of being seen.

When the rain began, Nelson returned with his dinner and found a sheltered perch under the eaves of a nearby barn, whilst Nanette, who had been clearing away their meal, suddenly dashed for the tent, shouting at Horatio to join her.

By seconds, they both made it, scrambling over each other before the heavens opened and Nanette, wiping away the rain from her face, began to giggle.

Horatio, who struggled to see the funny side of nearly getting soaked, also ended up laughing. Nanette's infectious joy at something as simple as rain was wonderful, although, he was quickly brought back to earth when she suggested they should sleep together in the tent.

Horatio's initial reaction was one of surprise, not just because she was so young, but because the next day he would be dropping her off with her family and they would never see each other again.

He did admit to himself that the thought of sex with Nanette had crossed his mind; what man would be any different, but he knew he would be taking advantage of her.

As the rain went from heavy to torrential, Nanette took hold of Horatio's hand and literally dragged him further into the tent.

"We don't have to do anything," she said shyly, "but I don't want you out there in the rain. In here you can stay dry."

And that is what happened. They slept back to back, but only after talking for hours about their families, and their lives before and during the virus.

*　　*　　*

When Horatio woke, Nanette was fast asleep in his arms, with her hand on his chest and he closed his eyes and relaxed. It may have only been a few days since leaving Maya, but he already missed being touched, whilst touching in return. Although there were only a couple of thin coats thrown over them, Horatio was warm and snug and really didn't want to get up.

Eventually Nanette woke and she was mortified to see the position she was in and how they'd spent the night. As she was desperately trying to apologise Horatio laughed and simply said, 'good morning', adding that he couldn't remember the last time he'd had such a good night's sleep.

—Ж—

Chapter 31

As they cycled towards the centre of Kambia, on a lovely warm and sunny morning, with Nelson perched on the handlebars, the thing that struck Horatio was the number of houses that looked lived-in and it left him wondering whether at long last they were somewhere which was supporting a sizeable community.

Peddling at a leisurely pace, on the right he saw uninterrupted rows of single storey houses and on their left, open land interspersed with groves of cultivated trees and bushes.

Further on, they came across a number of commercial and industrial outlets which unlike the earlier houses, appeared abandoned; most were mere skeletons of their moneymaking days.

Entering an area of residential houses, Horatio saw many of the gardens had trees, bushes and brightly coloured flowers and interestingly, the many red clay paths and roads leading away from the highway, appeared to have been in recent use.

He was convinced they would come across survivors and hoped they were friendly and welcoming.

*   *   *

Moving towards the bridge, which could be seen from some distance away, Horatio and Nanette came to a tarmacked road on the right and, to their disbelief, directly ahead there was a market being set up in a large carpark.

Coming to a halt, Nelson immediately flew from the handlebars onto the shoulder pad and they stared at the simple but delightful scene unfolding before them. Stallholders busy preparing for the day ahead, people milling around talking and laughing with no one seemingly armed or anxious.

Bearing in mind how early it was in the morning, Horatio was amazed when he spotted a small bar on the edge of the square full of customers. In the far corner, opposite the bar, a man resembling a preacher was delivering a sermon to a small crowd; in any other age, the scene would have been that of an ordinary market day in an ordinary town.

*   *   *

As Horatio and Nanette were discussing their next move, a small girl walked up to them and keeping her eyes firmly fixed on Nelson, said in a quiet but confident voice,

"Hello."

Nanette translated as again Horatio was unable to understand.

Still struggling to take her eyes away from the falcon, the girl then asked,

"Where have you come from?"

When Nanette explained that she lived not far away, the girl skipped on and spoke to some women who were chatting at the nearest stall. Together the group turned and Horatio wasn't at all sure by the look on their faces that they would be welcomed.

Two of the women walked towards them, both unarmed so Horatio lowered the shotgun. The older one spoke to Nanette in the same dialect as the girl and it quickly became apparent they were friendly, especially when both switched to using English.

When Nanette explained that she had grown-up on a farm close to Forecariah, both smiled and the younger one took hold of Nanette's hand and led her through the stalls; Horatio was obviously expected to tag along behind whilst struggling with both bikes and the cart.

*   *   *

When their arrival became known, people gathered around leaving Horatio feeling exposed. However, he accepted there was little he could do without creating a scene and that might prove dangerous.

Approaching the bar, the young women indicated they should sit at one of the outside tables and with Nelson relatively calm on the shoulder pad, Horatio nodded. He positioned the bikes against a wall, making sure he could reach the shotgun, before sitting next to Nanette.

Nelson immediately flew off, landing on a nearby roof ledge, staring as a young man appeared at the table with three glasses and a large bottle of water.

Horatio and Nanette drank thirstily, amazed to find the water contained both lemon and ice and as they were thanking the two woman who had joined them at the table, the waiter returned with a selection of food on three plates.

For some probably unsound reason, Horatio became troubled by their generosity and told the women they couldn't pay. Instantly, the group that had built up around the table laughed whilst the woman explained they were guests and were not required to pay.

Horatio looked at a crowd of about twenty, all of whom were unarmed and saw only three were men; two more mature, one in his twenties. There were also two young boys, both under ten on the fringe of the group; the rest were made up of women and girls of all generations.

"Where are you from?" the older woman sat with them asked Horatio.

"England," he replied speaking for the first time.

"How are you so far from home?" It was a woman from the back of the group who asked in reasonable English.

Slightly taken aback, although he knew he shouldn't be, he replied,

"When the virus struck, I was living on the Cape Verde Islands."

"How come you're with her then?" the eldest of the men asked, undoubtedly querying Horatio's answer.

Nanette, seeing where the questioning was going, began to answer in the local dialect, but Horatio interrupted and said,

"Recently my mother died and I left the island; I'm now trying to get back to the rest of my family. Three days ago I met some people who asked me to help Nanette reach her home. As it was on my way... of course I agreed."

"So, where are you going?" came another question from somewhere in the crowd, the person asking in French

"As I already said, England... to find the rest of my family." Horatio also answered in French much to the disbelief of those gathered around.

The younger of the women sat at the table, reverting to English, then said,

"Impossible. You'll never make it."

Noticing Nelson was perched calmly preening himself and seeing nothing in the faces of the crowd to worry him, Horatio said,

"You're probably right but... well... I'll do my best. Some of my family may still be alive so I must try to find them."

That seemed to calm the doubters and a few of the crowd dragged chairs to sit with the strangers.

*   *   *

Horatio called Nelson down to his shoulder and as had become the norm, the falcon promptly became the centre of attention, especially with the children who all wanted to stroke him.

As they ate the delicious food, whilst answering a multitude of questions, Nanette, in turn, asked about the area around Forecariah and her home.

"There are survivors still there and they are doing well. Some bring their produce to the market and we get to hear about how they are getting on," answered the younger man.

Nelson had obviously become bored and he flew off as Horatio asked,

"So how safe are you?"

"Well… we're over eighty people." It was the same young man who answered. "If any of us are attacked, we all go to help and so far, we seem to have the numbers and weapons to scare troublemakers away." When the man pointed, Horatio saw a large stack of weapons, mostly machetes and they were ready to use.

Horatio was definitely impressed with their self-sufficiency and hoped that such a welcoming and generous community would get stronger and grow. Taking another drink, he then asked about the ice.

"We have solar panels," answered the older woman sat at their table. "Luckily they were installed before the sickness came so unless the system breaks down, we have a limited amount of electricity."

Horatio was intrigued. The town was well organised and working together; they had food, security, even electricity; just maybe it was a model for the future, a hands-on solution to the survival of the human race.

*   *   *

As they had lost most of the morning, albeit in a truly fascinating town, Horatio apologised and explained they wanted to reach Nanette's farm before nightfall.

He thanked them all as he finished the water, and leaving Nanette to say her goodbyes, called to Nelson and went to the bikes.

As the falcon landed on Horatio's shoulder, two young women and the younger of the men approached him.

"We didn't want to say anything in front of your friend, but there are serious problems north of here." It was the man that spoke. "So far we have been safe, but people coming from Forecariah describe how a man and a woman are raiding farms. They are extremely dangerous and no one can stop them."

"But, why?" Horatio asked, rightly concerned.

"We've heard they have vicious dogs and if anyone gets in their way, well... the dogs are used. It seems they usually locate a farm around Forecariah, remove the owners or worse, then live in the farmhouse for a few weeks before stealing what they want, and moving on.

One story going around is that they slaughtered a family for not doing what they were told to do, but... honestly, we don't know how true it all is. If you are interested though, there are three farming families in town who lost everything to the couple and came here to escape them. Their homes are north of here, on the way to Forecariah and they have said they will only go back when the couple have moved on or been dealt with."

Horatio thought about what he was hearing and then asked,

"The highway; is it safe?"

"We think so, but because of the rumours none of us leave town more than we have to and we travel no further than we really need to."

*   *   *

With Nelson still perched on his shoulder pad, Horatio pushed the bikes towards Nanette and as they set off, riding side-by-side, with Nelson circling overhead, Nanette said, "Do you know they told me if I can't find my family, there would always be a place for me here. How lovely is that?"

Horatio nodded but was hardly listening. His mind was focused on the rumours and whether he should tell

Nanette. The last thing he wanted was to scare her, but he was uneasy about keeping the truth from her; especially if her farm had been targeted.

In the end Horatio felt he should wait. At least that way, if nothing had happened then he would then save her unnecessary distress.

*   *   *

Leaving Kambia, they crossed the Great Scarcies River and began the eight kilometre journey to the border town of Pamalap.

Either side of the highway there was a mixture of woods, shrub land and farm buildings, although, not all together surprisingly, the area was deserted.

A short time later they arrived at Ta-Iri, a small village with few buildings and a wide red clay street, leading off to the right. On the map Horatio saw the road ran parallel to the Great Scarcies River before simply petering out after a few kilometres.

Map of
Guinea

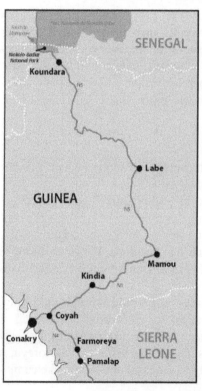

Chapter 32

"That's the border." Nanette said pointing.

Nelson immediately flew down and perched on the handlebars studying where they were headed and buildings began to appear on the right hand side. Just a few moments later, a large parking area split down the middle by a large square concrete structure appeared on the left, Horatio assumed it was the border control between Sierra Leone and Guinea.

The layout was simple but effective, allowing each country to have its own customs area and Horatio was interested to see three abandoned army vehicles close by. He wondered why such indestructible vehicles would have been left behind when they could inflict serious devastation on survivors.

*   *   *

Cycling on, they entered Pamalap which was confirmed by various rusted signs.

"I'm back in my country," Nanette called across to Horatio smiling.

"So, how far to your farm?" he asked.

"In distance I'm not sure. We often came here for the market but always in Dad's truck because it was too far to walk."

Again, Horatio consulted the map and judged it to be thirty kilometres to Forecariah. Knowing they were unlikely to reach Nanette's farm before dark, he suggested they cycle as far as the town of Farmoreya, which was about half way to the farm and then make camp.

*   *   *

As they negotiated Pamalap, there were three large signs, signifying they were on the N.4 highway and Horatio recalled Kadijah telling him that major roads in Guinea were numbered and the N.4 would take them north through the southern part of the country towards the capital Conakry.

With Nelson once again in the air, Horatio felt a disappointing change in the road surface; much of it was crumbling, as copious weeds and other plants breached the tarmac in search of sunlight.

The land adjacent to the highway had also changed; wild scrubland and resilient trees dominating what had probably once been fields; and there was no sign of the impenetrable jungle of earlier.

*   *   *

Much to his relief, the journey to Farmoreya proved uneventful, however, because of the state of the road they arrived later than Horatio would have liked. Approaching the outskirts, they found the town split by a small bridge over a short inlet which was part of a wide river. This ran parallel to the centre of the town with the majority of buildings on the far side of the crossing.

"As it's getting dark and there's fresh water, I think we should stay around here for the night," he suggested.

Nanette readily agreed and with Nelson circling above, they crossed the bridge.

Moving slowly, searching for a safe place to stay, Horatio became confused when he heard Nelson screeching loudly before swooping directly towards them.

Coming to a stop, in the silence of the abandoned town, Horatio was dismayed to hear dogs.

Scanning the area, ahead on the right there was a modern two storey concrete building which had been built on a junction between their highway and another wide red clay road which ran off to the right. With little time to think, he pedalled towards the main door, calling to Nanette to keep up and again heard the sound of dogs. They were definitely getting closer.

*   *   *

Entering the reception area of what he thought might have been a bank or government offices, Horatio slammed the door behind them. Straight ahead there was a bare concrete staircase and with Nanette following, he sprinted with his bike and the cart into a downstairs side room before grabbing the shotgun, cartridges and spear guns.

Taking hold of Nanette's hand Horatio then ran up the stairs and found a room at the front of the building. Shutting the door behind them he knelt, staring through the large square hole in the brickwork that must have once been a window.

Desperate to call Nelson to him, Horatio knew he could not without drawing attention to themselves; Nelson would have to cope on his own.

*   *   *

Sauntering down the highway, from the direction of Forecariah, Horatio spotted a woman and man, both looked to be in their twenties. They had machetes tied to large rucksacks on their backs and were having difficulty reining in two huge hounds on long leads.

Horatio found it baffling. If this was the murderous pair from the rumours, they appeared oblivious to their whereabouts being exposed. In fact, they were not only laughing loudly whilst sharing a half full bottle but were taking no notice of the commotion their dogs were making.

The couple seemed completely indifferent to potential danger, and to Horatio, blasé about encountering other people. He decided they must either have no fear of death or were convinced they would survive whoever or whatever they came across.

As the couple drew level with the junction their hole-in-the-wall overlooked, Horatio pleaded for them to turn left onto the red, clay road, that would avoid any possibility of the couple passing their hiding place and the dogs sensing their presence.

Not taking his eyes off the hounds for a second, Horatio was devastated as the largest of the monsters began to yank violently at its leash in an attempt to drag the man towards their building. A fraction later the other brute joined in, snarling as it pulled the woman towards their safe haven.

*   *   *

Horatio understood the French being used as the man yelled at his dog to quieten down and the woman asked whether they should check out the buildings.

Then, without warning, Nelson flew into view and Horatio's immediate reaction was to scream at him to get away. More so when from a great height the falcon began to dive at an astonishing speed.

Levelling out just above the ground, Nelson caught the larger of the dogs in the rump with his lethal talons, ripping open the skin and both dogs leapt into the air as one, mouths snarling, endeavouring to seize their attacker before it flew off.

An already nervous Horatio began to truly panic when a clearly undeterred Nelson again flew at the group. He was clearly making a second pass, and in doing so, gave the impression he was driving the couple towards the clay road and away from Horatio and Nanette.

When the woman spotted the second attack, she cowered behind a collapsed wall. However, the man was so incensed, he stood tall, gripping a long wooden pole and whilst struggling to restrain the dog, he waited to swing the baton at Nelson as he passed.

Horatio had to close his eyes fearing the worst, but within the blink of an eye, Nelson had again ripped open the rump of the second dog with his sharp pincers and shrieked in celebration as he flew away.

*   *   *

It was only later, once the couple and their hounds had followed the red clay road out of town that Horatio asked Nanette how she was.

"Okay, I think. You know, I'm sure Nelson kept them away from us. Am I crazy to think he deliberately pushed them away from us? He was so brave."

Horatio couldn't agree more. Nanette merely confirmed what he knew Nelson was trying to do, and yet again he understood how blessed he was to have such a loyal friend.

Chapter 33

Having spent a sleepless night on the concrete floor of their room in Farmoreya, Horatio and Nanette set out early next morning and by mid-afternoon, just before reaching the outskirts of Forecariah, they reached the road they needed.

Turning left onto the potholed and rarely if ever used narrow track, within a kilometre they arrived at a junction with three other roads, all overgrown and surrounded by scrubland, interspersed with trees and bushes.

Nanette stopped, dismounted her bike and whilst pushing it, walked directly into a wall of dense undergrowth at the side of the road.

Telling Horatio to stay close, she quickened her pace down a narrow, completely overgrown track and clearly thrilled to be home and desperate to find her family, it was hardly surprising she left Horatio some distance behind.

Struggling to control his bike with the wide cart, and, of course, Nelson perching precariously on the handlebars, he eventually caught up to find himself in a large open space with a well-maintained house, outbuildings and chickens, wandering freely.

*   *   *

Nanette had waited nervously and after leaving their bikes she took hold of Horatio's hand and walked towards the house.

With Nelson having returned to his shoulder, Horatio kept hold of the loaded shotgun with the safety catch off.

"The Lord be praised! Is that really you?" Speaking French, the voice came from their left and when they turned, they were faced with an older woman and young boy.

Nanette raced towards the pair screaming in delight.

"Aunt Jeanette!" and the three hugged each other, crying and laughing.

And that began five delightful days for Horatio.

*   *   *

During the afternoon Horatio was introduced to all the members of Nanette's family and given a tour of the farm and section of the Forecariah River that they fished.

Horatio was told that Aunt Jeanette ran the house and did most of the cooking, whilst three cousins, an older uncle and Nanette's sister and brother fished, worked the fields and maintained the orchard.

Before joining the family for their evening meal Horatio swam in the river and washed himself and his clothes. He never seemed to tire of the delights of sitting, semi-submerged in cool, fresh water and letting the river flow over him.

*   *   *

Unusually for Guinea, Nanette's family were Christians who still practised their faith. They spoke French as their first language and apart from Uncle Mamadou, all spoke rudimentary English.

Horatio offered the family his last bottle of poyo at the evening meal and after grace, he enjoyed a boisterous, but charming family reunion. Sitting outside around a large wooden table the chatter was endless. The family were desperate to know how Nanette had survived, and of course, the sadness on hearing about the loss of her mother.

Aunt Jeanette explained how the virus had taken Nanette's father and two older brothers, but all agreed it

284

was a blessing that her younger sister and brother had survived. She of course, was still heartbroken.

Horatio was also very much involved, especially with Nelson perched on a tree close by, and answered endless questions about his home and his time on Ilhéu de Cima.

The mood changed when a cousin named Joan, who was sat on Horatio's right, described how all the family got together as soon as they realised how deadly the virus was.

"After some discussion, we chose this farm as our base because it had fresh water, fish in the river and good fertile earth to work and, for well over five years, we've worked hard and looked after each other."

Aunt Jeanette then said,

"We agreed the family would always come first and because of that, and with the help of the Lord Jesus Christ, we've made a good life for ourselves."

As the family crossed themselves, Aunt Jeanette added that there were frustrations; mainly due to the fact they were Christians in a Muslim country and found it difficult to mix with other survivors.

Cousin George, went on to explain that a few of their friends had survived, but lived far away, so only rarely did they get together.

Uncle Mamadou, using Jacob, Nanette's brother to translate, then spoke in a local patois which was completely lost on Horatio.

"The Church, so important to all of us, has closed. Before the sickness, every Sunday evening we'd meet friends and other Christians and all join together in prayer, but that's gone. Now there's no church and no priest to take services." He was understandably upset and Horatio noticed unhappy nods of agreement from around the table.

*　　　*　　　*

As he lay on a straw bed in one of the outbuildings that night, Horatio was struck by what a joyful and positive haven the family had created. He found it inspiring that they genuinely believed all of their many achievements were from God allowing them to live, and as a result, were unwavering in their determination to make the most of every single day.

He was left considering once again about whether having something to believe in, to underpin one's life, could actually create people with a tougher, more resolute attitude to life. It certainly seemed to be the case with Nanette's family.

Removing his mother's notebook and pencil from his holdall and by the startlingly bright light of the moon streaming in through a small window, Horatio followed his first entry with 'Nanette's Story'.

*   *   *

Over the next four days, Horatio ate, slept, swam, reread the books Kadijah had given to him and worked with the others, although they would only let him do less demanding jobs which included sitting by the river, fishing.

Having to use French most of the time, was also a bonus as Horatio knew if he managed to get as far as France, being proficient in the language may prove decisive; and that future was something Nanette talked to him about repeatedly.

Horatio sensed she wanted to remain with him, and although they had only been together a few days, admittedly quite extraordinary days, a strong bond had grown between them. Moreover, as reluctant as he was to admit it, Horatio had a growing affection for Nanette which was hardly surprising; she was vivacious, attractive and resourceful.

Yes, she was young but without doubt special and of course he would love them to be together, but he knew it would not only be impractical but selfish.

Horatio could not remain on the farm indefinitely; he had a commitment to search for his family which was non-negotiable. At the same time, he would not dream of persuading Nanette to leave her family; she had only just found them after years apart.

In the end Horatio's hand was forced by Aunt Jeanette when she insisted he stay and celebrate Christmas on the farm.

She explained that every year since the sickness, the family had invited the few Christians in the area to join them for three days of celebration, and they were desperate for Horatio to be part of the festivities.

And Horatio was sorely tempted. He knew being with Nanette's family and friends over Christmas would give him wonderful memories to take with him on the long road ahead; but... and it was a huge but, without his own family, he knew he would struggle to fully embrace the occasion.

*   *   *

On the fourth day at the farm, as Horatio was fishing, Nanette joined him and began talking about Christmas.

"What date is it today?" he asked, recalling that just a couple of days before leaving Lungi, Kadijah had told him it was a month until December 25th.

"I asked my Aunt the same question," she answered, "and she told me I needed to remember the sickness had scrambled everyone's lives, therefore no one could be certain what day it was. Apparently, when they moved here, she started a calendar based on what people could remember and they're still using it today; she did admit though that she had no idea how accurate it is.

So, birthdays, religious events, even days of the weeks, they're all guesstimates. Then when I asked if it really mattered, she wept and said that without a true calendar, our culture, values, history and beliefs will be eroded until they are lost forever."

*   *   *

When Nanette left him to help Aunt Jeanette in the kitchen, Horatio swam and after calling Nelson to him, lay on the bank staring at the clear blue sky. It was then, he knew what he had to do.

If he were to fulfil his promise to find his family, he must move on from the past and that included his mother, Sofia, Kadijah, Maya, and now Nanette, to focus on the future.

Before their evening meal, Horatio told firstly Nanette and then her family that he would be leaving after breakfast the following morning.

*   *   *

That night Nanette came to him. She was confused and couldn't understand why he was going. As they lay in each other's arms talking, Horatio could feel himself weakening. Nanette was offering him not only a new family, but herself, and if he succumbed to such a glorious temptation, he knew there would be no turning back.

Try as she may, and Nanette tried just about everything she could think off including sex, when Horatio declined, she grudgingly accepted it was the end and they fell asleep wrapped around each other.

*   *   *

The following morning, with his things packed and having said his goodbyes, Horatio was about to walk with Nanette to the highway when Nelson flew towards him screeching. Horatio and Nanette reacted together; both knew it meant danger.

Nanette shouted for her family to get in to the house when from close by came the terrifying sound of hounds.

"Please God, no!" Nanette screamed.

As her family were asking what was happening, Horatio grabbed his shotgun, checking the safety catch was off.

Moments later, the couple they had encountered at Farmoreya, with machetes in one hand and the two dogs tearing at their leashes in the other, marched into the open area outside of the farmhouse.

An extremely agitated Nelson landed on the edge of the farmhouse roof as Horatio moved the gun to behind his back. Their only chance was to catch the couple by surprise.

Confident beyond belief, the pair walked to within just five metres of Horatio, who held out his free arm, moving the family and Nanette behind him.

The man, straining to control the larger of the two animals, mocked him in French,

"How heroic, shielding loved ones? We'll see how truly brave you are." Looking around, the man added,

"At last we've found you. We knew there was a family near here, living the good life, eh… and now it's ours."

The woman spotted Nelson and said to Horatio,

"Your bird is it? We'll be feeding him to the dogs."

Man and woman both giggled hysterically.

"This will make a great base," he then said thoughtfully. "From here we can control the entire area. You know, we might stay here forever." And again they both laughed.

Turning to the family, who stood quivering behind Horatio, the woman stated harshly,

"You have five minutes to leave."

The dogs, desperate for blood, sensed it was their time and began to howl.

Then, from behind Horatio, Uncle Mamadou spoke loudly, fearlessly and Horatio could only guess at what he said, but the implication was obvious; they were going nowhere.

A second later, as he released the dogs, the man roared, "Go get them!"

*　　*　　*

Horatio raised the shotgun, pulled one, followed immediately by the second trigger, and stood paralysed as he saw Nelson fly into his peripheral vision; he had no idea whether the falcon had been caught in the blaze of gunshot or not.

Seconds later, the area resembled a war zone. The two dogs had taken the shot full on, from no more than a couple of metres and momentum had carried the lead animal right up to Horatio's feet, but the brute was dead before it landed. The other monster was whimpering in distress, lying on its side, blood pouring from countless hits.

Although the man and woman had been critically injured, they had been partially shielded by the dogs, leaving only the upper part of their bodies exposed to the shot. The woman was still upright, staggering, utterly disorientated; her face had been hit so many times and by the state of her eyes, she was blind.

The man was on the ground, thrashing incessantly, whilst clutching at his face; blood was gushing from a myriad of deep wounds and Horatio watched mercilessly as life drained from his young body.

*　　*　　*

Horatio was desperate to escape. It had been three hours since the bloodbath but he was still suffering, more than likely in deep shock.

Both dogs were dead, one having had its throat cut to put it out of its misery, whilst the man had died, in the end quietly but not peacefully. The woman was so bloodied she was beyond recognition. Nevertheless, with little regard for her injuries, Uncle Mamadou had bound her wrists and ankles and tied her to a tree, stating that she should be executed without delay.

Aunt Jeanette had overruled him. She argued that everything they had achieved would be worth nothing if humankind merely reverted back to the random violence of pre-virus days. Agreeing the woman should be punished and harshly, Aunt Jeanette acknowledged that death might be a fair penalty but stressed the decision would not be theirs. If justice was to be done and be seen to be done, then the injured woman should be taken to Forecariah where the whole community could decide on her punishment.

*   *   *

Ignoring the family's pleas to remain, Horatio whispered inadequate goodbyes and pushed his bike and cart towards the highway. He had asked a tearful Nanette that he be allowed to leave on his own and with Nelson snuggled into his neck on the shoulder pad, he headed out.

Desperate to walk at least to the highway with Horatio, Nanette couldn't understand why he insisted on setting off alone.

"Look, I know you're struggling with what you did, but if you hadn't, my family would have lost everything including their lives. They would've probably been killed by those repulsive creatures."

An ever-more tearful Nanette told him repeatedly that if he just walked away, her family could never thank him properly for saving them and they wouldn't forgive her for letting him go. The only answer Horatio had was that he had to get away.

Chapter 34

Horatio was completely oblivious to his surroundings.

He was so angry, shouting at himself as he tried to escape the scene of his first killing; and that is how he regarded it, a killing. Therefore, he was a killer.

Unlike the earlier murderer of the two men by their friend; at Nanette's farm there was no leaving the outcome to chance, it was solely down to Horatio. He had pulled the trigger and therefore been responsible for the death of another human being.

*   *   *

Sometime later, and he had no understanding of how long, Horatio began to reduce his speed. Stroking Nelson's head he told himself to calm down.

"Okay, think this through." He said out loud. "Uncle Mamadou's comment triggered the attack, but I knew before then what the couple were likely to do and it was inevitable I would fire the gun. If I hadn't, Nanette's family would have been slaughtered. Therefore... am I justified in killing another person?"

Cycling on much more slowly, Horatio knew it wasn't just the death of the man; he deserved no mercy, and frustratingly, once again Kadijah had been right. He'd said there would be times when Horatio would have to act instinctively which could result in injury even death, and that's exactly what had happened. So why hadn't he been better prepared for the emotional destruction that accompanied slaying another human being?

As he was dissecting his limited ability to handle the consequences of his actions, Horatio came to a sudden stop, got off his bike, sent Nelson into the air, and lay down in the middle of the tarmac looking up at a stunning, clear blue sky.

Not wanting to move, to remain forever in the warm sunshine, Horatio argued that although he was being overly sensitive, there were good reasons to feel the way he did. His father leaving for example, or his mother dying, maybe the twins not being around when his world collapsed, even losing Sofia and Nanette; and it was then that Horatio understood.

He was far too immature and emotionally unprepared for the world he had become part of since leaving the island. There had been highs, amongst them meeting Kadijah, Maya, Nanette and so many other good people, but coming face to face with the very worst of human depravity and wickedness was eating away at him.

Having set out to find his family, not an unreasonable ambition in his mind, it was time for him to adjust his thinking. He needed to come to terms, and very quickly, with the extraordinary physical and mental demands on him or they were likely to destroy him.

*   *   *

With Nelson having returned to the handlebars, Horatio cycled north along the N.4 at a speed he was unlikely to be able to sustain. Forecariah was just a blur, as was the bridge he crossed but he paid little attention to either the landscape around him or the condition of the tarmac.

Nelson was clearly irritated by being thrown around by the uneven surface and eventually flew off, circling overhead and squawking his displeasure.

Still speeding through the villages of Félinya, Koulèté, Dandaya, and Tambaâdi, Horatio ignored a fresh water river near the hamlet of Fandie. Only as he approached the town of Maferenya did he slow, knowing he needed to find a safe place to camp for the night.

Even then however, he faltered. Stopping meant sleep and Horatio knew if he closed his eyes the terrifying blood-soaked images of that morning's attack, would haunt him.

*   *   *

Maferenya was a sizable town, yet still Horatio saw little. The map had indicated the buildings continued for over three kilometres but if it had been inhabited, he saw no one.

Leaving the built up area, with darkness falling, he again increased his speed and almost immediately hit a deep pothole. Horatio couldn't believe it as he was thrown, landing awkwardly.

Initially he thought both the front wheel of the bike and his left wrist, on which he had fallen, were broken and as he tentatively pushed himself up from the tarmac, Nelson flew down noisily to see if he was hurt.

By the light of the moon, Horatio inspected his wrist, which was throbbing and painful, but he was more worried about the cart and front wheel. Attempting to ignore any discomfort, he saw the cart was upright and in one piece, the front tyre was punctured, but the bike and wheel frame seemed undamaged.

Knowing there was little he could do until morning, Horatio ate, applied the mosquito repellent liberally, spread his coat on the tarmac and attempted to sleep.

*   *   *

Hours later, still wide awake, with vivid images of the bloody attack in his mind, Horatio finally accepted he did the only logical thing. If he hadn't fired, everyone, himself included, would have been torn to shreds by the dogs and if by some miracle anyone had survived, the couple would have had no qualms about executing them.

They were animals, just like their dogs and neither would have cared about what they saw as acceptable collateral damage. If it helped achieve their goals, killing was simply a means to an end and guilt, compassion, remorse, would never have entered their thinking, they were needless emotional burdens.

Understanding the couple's mind-set finally allowed Horatio to stop punishing himself and he quickly fell asleep.

*   *   *

At first light, ignoring the pain in his arm, Horatio changed the inner tube and was relieved there appeared to be no damage to the wheel frame. Whatever though, because of his stupidity he would need to use one of only two spares he had.

Nelson flew off to hunt, whilst Horatio ate, packed his belongings and then together they set off with Horatio in a far more positive frame of mind.

After the disaster of the previous night, he rode far more circumspectly and succeeded in negotiating the unending potholes and cracks with little difficulty.

*   *   *

Guinea was mostly open land with an abundance of trees, bushes, shrubs and a stunning array of multi-coloured flowers. Horatio intermittently spotted wildlife; some grazing with little or no fear, some just a fleeting glimpse of an image scurrying past and he would never tire of the ever-present cacophony of sounds from birds, insects and other mysterious creatures.

That morning was warm and sunny and as had become the norm, the houses, farms and industrial outlets he passed, were abandoned.

Arriving at Kendoumaya, Horatio still saw no signs of human life, just the familiar cluster of dirty-white single storey houses. At the village of Toguiron, he crossed an unnamed river on a rickety bridge and by tracing it on the map decided it formed part of a series of tributaries that ran to the coast, creating a wide estuary before joining the sea. Kadijah had told him the region was low lying and at risk of flooding, but for Horatio it was wonderfully green and fertile. It looked perfect for farming, but, where were the people?

*   *   *

Having negotiated the crossing, Horatio stopped and manoeuvred his bike and the cart down a sharp drop to the water's edge. It was late morning and he wanted to take a break from cycling.

He swam, washed clothes and his injured arm in the fresh water of the river, before eating a light lunch, aware the food he had would not last him for more than a couple of days.

From the scenery, Horatio felt he would have little difficulty in gathering fruit and vegetables but was mindful of Maya telling him that with the demands of travelling long distances every day, he must eat healthily and that included meat.

He had regularly seen animals he could hunt down, it was just that; even having speared fish and fed fresh bird meat to Nelson when he was a chick, Horatio struggled with the notion of killing for his individual needs.

*   *   *

Leaving the cool, invigorating water behind, Horatio saw on the map that his next goal was Coyah and remembered Kadijah telling him it was not a single town but a number

297

of large built up areas all linked together. These included Conkary, the capital of Guinea.

He also warned that Coyah not only had a pre-virus population of well over eighty thousand but that there was no way of avoiding its town centre and the next highway he would need to take.

*   *   *

Fifteen minutes later Horatio began entering an urban area and reading the map, he saw it was the outskirts of Lefourédaka, the first of the towns connected to Coyah and Conkary.

Calling Nelson down, the falcon reclaimed his perch on the handlebars and Horatio checked that the shotgun and one of the spear guns were loaded. He then cycled, unhurriedly through the suburbs.

Horatio saw a stream on the left and a collection of small terraced fields running down to the waters' edge and was certain they were being cultivated. Just possibly he would come across people working on the land.

Pushing on, he passed mostly residential properties, however the further he cycled into Lefourédaka, the more commercial structures dominated the scene.

Coming to what appeared to be an overgrown football ground, again on the left, Horatio saw a dark brown mass of clay and weeds with no markings, the only giveaway were the two broken sets of goalposts lying neglected at either end.

Then, as he approached yet another expanse of open land he saw three women working in a field.

Horatio was so astonished, he slowed to a stop to confirm what he'd seen. Drawing closer, he thought they may have been three generations of the same family; one was older, one middle-aged, whilst the third was younger.

When they saw him, all three stopped work and stared. The oldest was covered in a traditional Islamic black abaya, the other two in jeans and loose blouses and they were dripping with sweat, their clothes and hands covered in soil.

Horatio was seriously impressed. The plot might have been small, but the women had planted neat rows of seedlings and saplings and created a productive fruit and vegetable garden.

Remaining on his saddle, Horatio watched as the middle-aged woman approached him. She was gripping a two-pronged fork; a formidable weapon if required.

"Where are you going?" she asked in heavily accented French.

With the shotgun resting on his lap and machete in the cart immediately behind him, Horatio replied simply,

"North."

"So where have you come from?"

Horatio pointed to the highway behind him and said,

"There."

The woman, clearly not sure what to make of the new arrival, stared defiantly at him; Horatio, because of what had occurred at the farm, was determined not to get too close and he was guarded as the other two women approached.

"What's that then?" the older woman, said pointing at Nelson perched on the handlebars.

"A friend," Horatio replied also in French.

The youngest then walked confidently to the bike and asked whether she could touch the falcon. When Horatio said she could but to be gentle, the girl began stroking Nelson down the length of his back.

Seeing no threat, the other two women moved toward the bike and looked in the cart. When the oldest picked up the bag with his valuables in an irritated Horatio said,

"Put it back. Don't touch my things."

Snatching her hand away, she mumbled an apology as he asked,

"Are you the only people here?"

"No," the youngest replied, still stroking Nelson.

"There are other women but the men are in Conkary."

"Where's that?" Horatio asked. Even though he knew the direction of the capital, he wanted to keep the women talking.

Holding the shotgun at the ready, he slid off the saddle, but he remained close to the bike as the middle-age women pointed along the highway and said,

"Keep going; when you come to the next junction, turn left."

"So how many people are here?" Horatio inquired.

"Not many and all women. We work the fields and run our homes."

"And the men are in Conkary?"

"That's right. Apart from the three leaders, most fish or do other work during the day, then they drink at night. When they feel like it, they come to our homes." It was the middle-aged women answering and by her tone Horatio realised there were issues between the sexes.

"So, families don't live together?" he asked.

"There are no families. All that ended with the sickness. Now, we try to survive and make the best of what we have."

"So the men don't help?" Horatio asked, wanting to understand if it was safe to enter Conkary or not.

"We don't really see them, only when they want... you know." Again it was the middle-aged woman who spoke and it was clear what she was referring to.

"I don't understand. Why would they want to stay in town and not here with their families?"

"It was chaos after the virus. No one knew who was alive and who wasn't. People were scared and shut themselves away or some moved away. Then things became clearer and we saw that everything we had ever known had been taken from us."

That familiar picture was emerging: panic, death, ruin, survival. Once again Horatio heard the same story.

"After a while," the woman continued. "As the horror of catching the virus faded and we saw people were no longer becoming infected, a group of us got together and it was then that we realised virtually all the men had died.

If we were to have any chance of surviving then everyone had to work together but the men didn't want that. A few saw the chance to be in control and although there weren't many left, they were... are, physically stronger so they took over. When we argued, they attacked us, raped even the youngest girls, and then forced the boys and older men to leave their homes to work for them. My youngest son is with them.

They live in the centre of Conkary and come here and take whatever they want, and yes, we give anything and everything to them otherwise we would be dead."

The older woman then spoke,

"It was not only the men; some of the girls joined them, mostly the idlest and some have become nastier than the men."

"So you're made to give them whatever they want?"

"That's about it," the middle-aged woman replied.

"You can't fight back?"

"We've tried, but whenever we resist, one of us is killed as a punishment. There are so many more women than men; what does one less matter to them?"

"That's appalling."

"Well... that's how it is. We accept it or die. I suppose we could leave but where would we go that would be better?"

"How many men are there?"

"We're not sure but there are three leaders; one man and two women. The rest, we think about fifteen of them; they fish, find food, steal, make poyo, and do what they're told to do. They're treated worse than slaves."

Horatio was dumbstruck which the oldest woman took as a sign he didn't believe them and said indignantly,

"If any of the men stands up to them, one of his family from before the sickness is taken, tortured and executed. Always in front of him. Now... you tell me... how would you fight that?

Chapter 35

Even though he was genuinely concerned for the women, as he pedalled away Horatio told himself the men in the capital were not his problem and he should avoid getting involved.

Using the map, he quickly worked out the shortest route to the N.1 highway avoiding Conkary, but as he cycled on Horatio felt more and more shamefaced about deliberately disregarding the struggle of not only the women, but a good number of their men.

*　　　*　　　*

With Nelson circling overhead, Horatio was startled when the silence of the mostly deserted town was shattered by the ringing of a bell.

To him it sounded like the hand-held sort which matched the one which had perpetually punctuated the school day and been ingrained into his life at St Indract's.

As Nelson returned to the handlebars, clearly agitated, Horatio stopped, listened and wondered if it was some type of signal, a system that had been set up to warn of strangers arriving. If that proved the case, it was unlikely to be good news.

Accepting he had little option but to carry on, he loaded one of the spear guns and checked the shotgun was also loaded with the safety switch off.

*　　　*　　　*

With a feeling of impending disaster, Horatio noticed the few tracks of open land had given way to an endless stream of abandoned houses and compacted clay paths and streets; but still there were no residents to be seen.

The entire vista was of derelict, dilapidated buildings and he was deep in thought as he entered Soumaya district.

Constantly searching for anyone spying on him, Horatio saw that the heavily built up district was interspersed with rivers, streams and lakes. There were even flooded areas which must have become far more problematic to residents during the monsoon.

As he turned a corner, he was thankful when just a few hundred metres ahead, the junction with the N.1 came into view. Maybe the bell had nothing to do with his arrival.

*   *   *

Approaching the intersection, unlike Horatio's current road, the N.1 looked remarkably well preserved with the tarmac unbroken.

Slowing as he reached the junction, to his left he saw a barricade of wrecked cars and burnt out trucks on the Conkary road, and ominously, guards.

Hoping he hadn't been spotted, he took a right turn and headed inland.

*   *   *

Again, building up his speed, Horatio was dismayed when almost immediately he spotted a group of people spread across the road, directly in his path. The five were lean, exceptionally dark skinned and looked to be in their late teens or early twenties. They all held a weapon, mostly machetes except for a woman in the centre, who was gripping a handgun. She was powerfully built and it was clear she was in charge.

Assuming doubling back would solve nothing, Horatio initially considered building up speed to outpace them, but if the girl with the gun was only a semi-proficient shot, he would probably die. His only option was to stop and see what would happen.

Ensuring the shotgun was directly behind him in the cart, out of sight, Horatio moved a restless Nelson from the handlebars to the shoulder pad. Then, using his uninjured right hand and hoping not to be seen, he laid the spear gun flat on the handlebars with the bolt pointing directly at the woman in the centre of the group.

*　　*　　*

Regardless of the damage he could inflict with a single bolt, Horatio knew he would need the shotgun to take out the other four. The problem was he'd have little time to grab it and fire, before being overpowered.

As they approached him, the two men and three women moved into a 'v' shape, the female with the gun in the centre, slightly ahead of the others. Quite bizarrely, however, the thing that caught Horatio's attention was not the fact they were laughing and joking, but the faded, dull white line running down the centre of the highway. He thought if he focused on that inconsequential detail, it would help him to stay calm.

As the group moved ever closer, Horatio sent Nelson into the air and watched as his friend flew directly towards the group before turning away. All five hesitated, just for a moment, but it was enough to expose their nervousness.

Ten paces from the bike, the leader held up a hand and the group stopped, as did Horatio. He then looked at the group with clearly contrived surprise before asking in French,

"Is there a problem?" This was however, said with a good deal more confidence then he felt.

Initially there was only silence; the five stared at him unblinking in a blatant attempt to intimidate him which confirmed that Horatio had to strike first.

"Only you; you're on our property." It was the older of the men who replied, unhurried menace in his voice.

Then, out of the corner of his eye Horatio saw movement; people had appeared on his left and he realised he would quickly be surrounded.

*   *   *

Trapped, Horatio squeezed the trigger of the spear gun.

There was an immediate and penetrating blast of an object airborne, before with astonishing power, the bolt struck the woman holding the gun. The metal shaft buried itself in the centre of her chest, practically passing through her upper body. As she shrieked in disbelief, the other four turned towards their leader and that fraction of a second was all Horatio needed.

He seized the shotgun and fired a single barrel at the two figures on the leader's right leaving two attackers standing. Turning the gun on them, they instantly dropped their weapons, raised their hands in the air and knelt down.

Again there movement to Horatio's left, but before he could react the youngest of the three women he'd met earlier ran towards him. Following on behind were the other two who were leading a further twenty people. Most of the group were woman but there was also a handful of very young boys and old men, who immediately tied up the two survivors.

*   *   *

Under no circumstances did Horatio want to get delayed. He saw the two survivors were secured and for a second time in just two days, was desperate to escape a blood-spattered scene of death.

Before setting off, Horatio told the group it was time to take back control but they needed to move quickly against the guards patrolling the highway. If they could show them their leader plus two others were dead, whilst two others were seized, they would likely back down.

"Whatever," he said plainly, "do not give those at the barricade or in Conkary time to reorganise themselves. If you do, the cost to you will be ruthless."

Pleading with him to stay, all three women he'd spoken to earlier thanked him, stating time and again that he had given them a chance to start anew and they were determined not to waste the opportunity.

Finally, Horatio asked to see the dead leader's gun and as he suspected, not only had the weapon not been fired for many years, there was no ammunition in the chamber. It was yet another salient lesson Horatio needed to learn if he was to survive.

With that, he called Nelson down to the handlebars and set off along the N.1.

Chapter 36

Pedalling away from Coyah, Horatio's thoughts focused on the two killings he'd been involved in. Of course he felt remorseful; who wouldn't? But he was determined to move on and not allow guilt or those deaths to prevent him from facing the future with optimism.

He had come to understand that life was not just about surviving the virus, although that in itself was a blessing, no… it was about discovering a bearable way to go on living. If survivors could emerge from the darkest of times with a belief in working conscientiously and conducting themselves correctly, with an ability to build self-worth and dignity, and the confidence that their lives would eventually improve, then just maybe the human race of the future would recover and grow into something quite outstanding.

However, without these powerful traits, those left alive would never escape the unremitting downwards spiral into immorality and lawlessness; taking with it any hope humanity could endure.

*   *   *

Horatio was under no illusion that poverty, hunger, anger, even loneliness could never be a justification for malicious or criminal behaviour, especially for those on the receiving end who struggled to fight back. But he also wasn't naïve enough to believe that humankind's baser instincts could always be held in check. Nevertheless, for an inexperienced and essentially decent person, as Horatio was, it certainly helped put perspective into his ability to withstand the 'new' world he'd entered and was rapidly adopting.

*   *   *

From almost the moment he left Coyah, with Nelson in the air but always close by, as Kadijah had predicted, Horatio found the going increasingly difficult. The highway was no longer flat but undulating, whilst always climbing, his next objective, Mamou, was over two hundred kilometres further ahead.

The positive though, was the scenery. It was stunning. Even allowing for the fact that the land closest to the highway had mostly been stripped of vegetation to make way for development, stretching as far as the eye could see, there were deep and variant greens of the rain forest interspersed with tall, forbidding rock formations jutting out of the earth, stretching up to the gods.

*   *   *

During the seven days it took him to reach Mamou, Horatio cycled through an assortment of abandoned villages including Kouriya, where the map showed a rusting, overgrown railway track ran parallel to the highway.

He was then dismayed to notice, on his left near the village of Mambiya, kilometre after kilometre of barren landscape. Years after being abandoned, extensive quarrying had resulted in the entire area remaining devoid of anything alive.

He found the contrast between the environmental destruction alongside the magnificence of the vibrant rainforest dominating his right, both depressing and inexcusable.

Incensed by the government's blindness to the unholy mess it had sanctioned, part of him was pleased the local population had disappeared. There would be no more quarrying and Mother Nature would be given time to make good the appalling damage inflicted.

*   *   *

With Nelson alternating between taking to the air and perching on the cart or handlebars, Horatio briefly stopped at an unnamed river just after the small hamlet of Wondikhoure where he swam and filled his water containers.

It was just a short time later, after cycling through the villages of Nyinaya and Kantoukhoure, that Horatio came across a small band comprising mainly women travelling in the opposite direction. Calling Nelson to the shoulder pad and with the shotgun ready, but out of sight, he slowly approached the group. He counted nine women, of mixed generations, three men, two of whom were fairly young, two babies who were being carried and three children. Interestingly the eldest of the men was a priest.

Moving closer, Horatio called out to them in English, "Where are you going?"

When the priest indicated with a shrug that he didn't understand, Horatio repeated the question in French. Ignoring the query, the priest said,

"We were about to stop for refreshments, would you like to join us?"

*   *   *

Horatio was asked to join the priest and two younger men on a thick blanket in the middle of the road. As he moved Nelson to his arm pad, all three men looked uneasy.

"Don't worry," Horatio said, "he's friendly, unless upset or he sees me in trouble."

He then saw three of the women unpacking some of their bags. One lit a fire and two others produced cups and a tin kettle.

Horatio again asked where they were headed.

"First we go to Abidjan in Cote d'Ivoire where we leave Paulo and his family," the priest said looking at the young man next to him. "Then on to Libreville in Gabon, our home."

"You have a very long journey ahead of you," Horatio said sympathetically.

"Not as far as we've already come."

"What do you mean?"

"We started out at Lourdes."

"What! Lourdes in France?"

The priest nodded, leaving Horatio stunned. However, he recognised he could gain a real insight into his own journey as they had followed the same route he needed to take, but in reverse.

"And you?" the priest asked.

"My home is in England. I'm going to find my family."

*   *   *

Horatio not only stayed for the hot drink, a strange concoction similar to the tea his mother used to brew, but readily accepted an invitation to share their evening meal.

Adding most of his remaining food to their meagre supplies, he was eager to talk to as many of the party as possible about their journey and with the agreement of the priest, Father Benjamin, he took notes.

Sat around the fire, with the light was fading, Horatio had to smile because, as normal, Nelson had quickly become the centre of attention and he willingly told the story of how their relationship had grown into something quite unique.

In return, he listened carefully as members of the group described the problems they had encountered and the risks he was likely to face.

*   *   *

Simon, the youngest of the men, began by describing how they had grown up as Catholics and when Father Benjamin had offered a once-in-a-lifetime pilgrimage to Lourdes, they had willingly signed up.

"The trip was wonderful until the virus arrived, then, within days we witnessed France literally imploding. As people became ill and started to die, panic quickly set in and the emergency services, police and military lost control.

We then heard the Government had abandoned Paris, but within no time, rumours were rife that the President along with the whole of his administration were dead. With nobody in charge, France was rudderless and everything we had ever known began to disintegrate around us."

Father Benjamin then took over by explaining that flying home was not an option.

"Our incredible coach driver agreed to take us to Marseille where we might be able to hire a boat. The trouble is once we got there, no crew was willing to take us. In the end we accepted the only way of getting home would be to travel on foot through Spain and from there trying to cross the Mediterranean to Morocco."

One of the younger women, June, butted in and stated with irritation,

"We were supposed to be home in just a few weeks but look at us; we've been on the move for years and of the fifty-two who started out, only seventeen of us are left."

Simon, clearly disappointed with her, replied adamantly,

"Come on, it's been no one's fault."

Horatio realised that all the time spent trying to get home, always having to rely on each other, must have created divisions and disagreement, even resentment within the group members, and he listened carefully as Simon continued.

"You know very well that each time there was a major decision to make, we all talked it through and only went ahead when agreement was reached. No one's been to blame for the awful things that have happened. Just accept God has chosen the path we must tread."

Before the younger woman could reply, one of the older women tearfully whispered,

"We lost two women, five men and seven boys all within the first few weeks. Some were to the sickness, but most were fighting off attackers. You see, none of us had any idea that being African and black would be such a serious problem. It didn't take us long to realise our few personal belongings, food or water were irrelevant to the gangs; all they were interested in were our young girls."

*   *   *

Horatio noticed that Father Benjamin appeared to be taking a back seat to let the others speak. However, as the group fell silent, he described how as they attempted to leave France for Spain, they had found roads frequently blocked by violent groups. Because of the babies, young children and elderly in the party, they had become an easy target.

"We managed to stop the many attacks. Every one of us who could, fought valiantly, but there were so many injuries, even deaths that our numbers declined. On top of that, sickness was a constant problem, and not just from the virus. We had to stop for over a month when our eldest member fell seriously ill and then died." He crossed himself before adding quietly, "as did a beautiful new born girl."

Horatio noticed tears around the group and began to understand the anguish they must have suffered. How ironic he decided, that devoted Christians, who believed God's kindness and love would see them all safely home to their loved ones, had ended up with so much sadness and bitterness in their lives.

*   *   *

One of the younger girls, Estelle, then spoke so maturely that the group sat intrigued.

"But not everything was bad," she said with a most appealing smile. "Remember all the babies born, the help and kindness from so many strangers, and then the most incredible gift from a farmer and his wife."

To her obvious annoyance, Ruth, an older woman, interrupted her.

"That was just before Perpignan. We were desperate for water and stopped at a farm and the farmer's wife was so welcoming. Not only did she give us as much water as we wanted but told us that if we helped in the fields, we could stay in one of their barns. We were all so exhausted and many of us in poor health, so of course we accepted."

*   *   *

Father Benjamin then continued the story by explaining that for months on end, the couple had fed them and provided a safe haven, wanting little in return. He then added,

"We knew we could never repay the compassion and generosity they had shown but it did reinforce our belief that God was still watching over us." He then looked around the group and smiled humbly.

"Once back on the road though, our progress was again painfully slow. It took us many months to arrive at the town of Tarifa, a port in southern Spain. We thought naively our troubles were nearly over."

The youngest of the boys then joyfully described,

"And on clear days if we stood on the harbour wall, we could see Morocco."

The rest of the group laughed with him.

*　　*　　*

Paulo then spoke for the first time,

"Anyway, we had found ourselves in the most beautiful of places with stunning beaches, but we were trapped. We were at the mercy of a community who ignored us and refused to allow us to live in the town, even though most of the buildings were empty and habitable. So... we ended up scavenging for food and fresh water,"

Another lady who was clearly agitated stated harshly,

"Shelters we had to make out of rubbish, that's what we lived in."

Father Benjamin, obviously sensing growing anger amongst some of the group, took up the story in a more forgiving manner.

"Little by little, the locals realised we were honest and just wanted to get home. Finally, after months of living hand to mouth, two of our younger girls were offered a job. They worked in the harbour gutting and sorting fish as they were landed. Both proved so willing that three more of us were offered work in the fields. Two then picked up jobs in the bakery and then one in the brewery; but still no boat would take us the fifteen kilometres across the Straits of Gibraltar to Morocco.

Two things then changed everything. The first was when winter arrived and four town houses were offered to us. Although some distance from the harbour and town centre, compared to where we had been living, they were perfect.

The second, was I learnt that no crew would take us because of pirates. Local fishing boats were regularly attacked along the coasts of the Mediterranean and Atlantic and they took no prisoners."

*　　*　　*

Life for the group might have improved but they were still determined to one day make it home. Virtually every evening they would talk about their families and seeing them again, but in the back of everyone's mind was whether any of them would have survived the virus.

Finally, according to Father Benjamin's estimation, a year later the same fisherman who had employed the two girls, agreed to take them across the Straits.

"The skipper's name was Jorge. His wife was Nanina and it was their son Phillipe who had persuaded his father to make the trip. He had fallen for Viviane, the elder of the two girls.

Jorge had originally decided he would go as far as a nature reserve west of Tangiers and to start with things went well. That was until we reached the Moroccan coast and as we passed Tangiers, in the night sky, we saw fires burning across the city. It was like a huge fireball."

Father Benjamin then described how there followed a lengthy, and at times bitter, debate. This was mainly because some people, including Viviane, felt the boat should turn around and return to Tarifa. They argued that their life in Spain had improved so much they could make a permanent home there.

"In the end, Jorge was persuaded to sail south along the Moroccan coast, to escape the dangers of Tangiers. He also agreed that anyone who wanted to, could return with him to Tarifa."

*　　*　　*

"Next morning was a beautiful sunny day with fresh winds and Jorge began the search for a place to drop anchor. Making excellent headway, members of the crew, especially Phillipe, pointed out landmarks that we sailed past including the old town of Larache and its harbour."

Simon then laughed as he told Horatio that although Jorge was desperate to find a safe place to drop us off, his son was not so keen. Because they were making such good progress, Viviane had not decided whether she would stay with the group or return to Tarifa. She still wanted to know about her family, whilst he wanted time to persuade her to stay with him.

Phillipe was so desperate to remain with his young lady for as long as possible that Jorge agreed to keep sailing south."

*   *   *

Picking up the commentary, whilst she wrapped a shawl around her shoulders as if it were a cold winter's night, a calmer June explained,

"For two days we sailed non-stop. We passed Rabat and Casablanca and even saw the Canary Islands far out in the ocean. Then the crew suddenly began shouting at us to get below and we were told us they had seen another boat."

The priest took over saying that he had been standing next to Jorge and Phillipe in the wheelhouse when they had seen a large ship in the distance. Both thought it was pirates.

"They told me not to worry though because it was a schooner and they couldn't follow us because they needed much deeper water. Jorge immediately changed course, to hug the shallow coastline. They'd heard the pirates were not skilled sailors, but when they did manage to capture a boat, all the men were killed and the women taken away."

*   *   *

"One of the most serious problems we faced," Father Benjamin continued, "was the land we were passing. Hour after hour, all we saw was sand and rocks; there was nowhere to drop us off.

317

Phillipe explained that he had friends who had sailed south of Morocco. They had told him that travelling through countries bordering the Sahara was almost impossible; there were no rivers or drinking water to be found and the day time temperatures were deadly.

Of course, I was worried Jorge would turn back but quite incredibly, he told me after what we had been through, they were not prepared to force us to go back to Tarifa. He had decided with his crew, to keep going south until they finally found somewhere safe to drop us off." The priest looked around the group and said,

"Again we were so fortunate, but there was a further consideration in that neither Jorge nor Phillipe knew the waters and that meant we had to look after what was left of our food and drinking water.

Phillipe told me I would be responsible for rationing and astonishingly, the whole crew would be included. We knew we could supplement our food by fishing, but water, general hygiene and boredom were issues we all had to deal with."

*   *   *

Whilst those around the fire listened, Father Benjamin continued and Horatio was in awe of the group and the many who had helped it survive. He promised himself that he would try in the future to focus on the positive rather than his habit of over analysing the violent or cruel acts he had encountered.

"Jorge explained how according to the charts, a peninsula we had passed was the border between Western Sahara and Mauritania and I felt we might just make land in a place that gave us a chance. Phillipe suggested a good spot to drop anchor might be the Parc National Du Banc D'Arguin, but all we saw was more of the same; rocks, sand and an unforgiving landscape.

It took two further days in ideal conditions to sail from Mauritania to Senegal, then, having passed Nouakchott the capital of Mauritania, we arrived at the mouth of the Senegal River and the city of St. Louis where Jorge spotted fishing boats.

Incredibly, the first skipper we spoke to invited everyone ashore, explaining that they lived in the old city and rarely saw anyone from the outside. With a few misgivings we all stepped onto dry land and what followed bordered on the unbelievable.

That evening, in the company of the most hospitable people possible, we all enjoyed the most wonderful evening and as it came to an end, the locals insisted we stayed in town.

It was a week before Jorge and his refreshed crew set sail for Tarifa and with Father Benjamin's blessing, Phillipe had asked Viviane to return with him. She needed little persuading.

As we watched the small fishing boat fade into the distance, I marvelled at Jorge and Phillippe; their compassion and kindness were incomparable and I prayed for their safe arrival home."

*   *   *

Paulo then took on the narrative saying that after a long rest in St. Louis, a local fisherman offered to take them south.

"He told us he needed to visit a friend and that he would take us to Mbour, just south of Dakar. From there we needed to take the N.1 to Kaolack to cross the Saloum River and then the N.4 south. The man said he had originally come from near Kaolack, but when the sickness arrived he had run away and ended up in St. Louis. He was only making the trip to persuade an old friend and his family to join him.

319

We arrived in Mbour after a long and tiring trip but one without problems. We then followed the fisherman's instructions and found the crossing for the Saloum River, again without difficulty. From there we took the N.4 south and made steady progress to the town of Farafenni in Gambia, but found the road was blocked by the Gambia River.

We were told all the boats were moored at Banjul the old capital, over a hundred kilometres downstream. It left us no option but to travel inland to cross the River at the Senegal, Gambia border. Once there we then picked up this highway where we met you."

Chapter 37

Hardly surprisingly, they talked well in to the night and Horatio ended up sleeping on the tarmac, alongside the priest, with Nelson perched on the handlebars watching over him.

Next morning as he cycled away to fading shouts of goodbye and good luck, Horatio felt quite downhearted. He would love to be part of a group for the arduous journey that lay ahead of him, not just for security but companionship; and strangely enough, laughter; something in short supply since he left Kadijah and Maya.

The group may have suffered terribly but there was still joy and friendship in their lives. Of course there were issues between members, but surely that was just a microcosm of human nature. The crucial thing was they were still together, still working hard for each other, still putting their own lives on the line to protect the majority, and like him, still determined to find their families.

*   *   *

Pedalling doggedly up a steep incline and making disappointingly slow progress, Horatio thoughtabout the many stories he heard and was left extremely concerned about what lay ahead. Then much to Nelson's consternation, he came to a sudden halt.

Finding a comfortable place to sit, Horatio removed his mother's notebook and a pencil from the rucksack and began to write up, 'Father Benjamin's Story'.

Recounting their words provided him with much vital information, but it also raised difficult questions; the most imperative being should he just give up on the idea of going home?

Unlike Father Benjamin's group, he was on his own, well... except for Nelson and had no real understanding of where he was headed. It may have been many weeks into his journey but he still had thousands upon thousands of kilometres to go and everything considered, it felt like an impossible duty.

Just maybe, Horatio thought, he should take stock and consider returning to Kadijah and Maya to build a new life for himself.

Telling himself to stop being so self-centred, he wrapped the notebooks in plastic bags to protect them from damage and was determined to focus on all the wonderful people he'd already met and extraordinary places he'd passed through. Crucially, he would also be excited by the spectacular experiences that still awaited him.

*   *   *

On the move once again, with Nelson airborne, Horatio realised that yet again Kadijah had been correct. He had stressed that Horatio should not attempt to walk or cycle north of Dakar and certainly not through Mauritania, Western Sahara or the southern part of Morocco. He needed to find a boat, something emphasised by Father Benjamin's journey.

Kadijah had also been right when he told Horatio to avoid rivers, swamplands and lakes. Father Benjamin had ended up wasting considerable time rerouting inland because they could not find a way to cross the River Gambia.

All this information had left Horatio determined to travel inland before crossing the great river in Senegal and only then buying, commandeering or stealing a boat.

*   *   *

Having decided to stop only briefly for something to eat at midday, Horatio was thankful when he arrived at a junction just before the town of Koliagbe. According to the map the lane to the left should lead him to a large lake.

With the undulating nature of the highway, he had found cycling gruelling and Kadijah had suggested the area could be ideal for a few days' rest.

Before turning onto the red clay track though, Horatio saw a large building on the opposite side of the road and decided to explore. He left his bike on the highway, called Nelson down to the shoulder pad, and walked to what he assumed was a shopping mall.

In the shape of an inverted 'U', metal shutters covered in graffiti protected most of the shop fronts, those left unprotected had been stripped bare.

An overgrown carpark was the graveyard of three vehicles; a burnt out truck and two rusted shells that looked as if they might have been saloon cars in an earlier life. There was considerable rubbish strewn throughout the mall and for some reason Horatio was left with the feeling that survivors were still around.

As he was about to return to the bike, Horatio spotted the remnants of a large fire behind one end of the building and the stripped, grilled bones of good-sized animals were lying in heaps. Strangely, it reminded him of family barbeques in their Berrow garden.

After releasing Nelson to fly, Horatio cycled down the uneven mud lane with derelict single storey houses on both sides of the road, followed by an ever-widening stream on his right. Two hundred metres further on, he saw where the river was fed by a lake.

Leaving the track and with some difficulty, Horatio pushed the bike and cart. Remaining close to the water's edge he was interested as the lake widened to about fifty metres across and he realised he was walking along a relatively narrow channel, towards a seriously large body of water.

Two islands appeared in front of him, the smaller one closer to land, the larger further out and on the opposite shore there was a landing stage for boats.

Much of the land surrounding the lake looked to have been worked, and although wild and overgrown, signs of fruit and other crops having been cultivated remained.

Further on, an amazed Horatio spotted a huge dam with a few well-kept houses; just maybe friendly locals might be close by.

*   *   *

The largest of the buildings, probably once used as offices for the maintenance and operation of the dam, was mostly in ruins. With only one wall remaining intact, the rest of the original construction was scattered over a wide area.

Re-joining the clay lane to approach the buildings, Horatio spotted smoke coming from a house on the edge of the lake, directly in his path.

Checking the shotgun was loaded, as he drew nearer he saw no signs of life. However, just then, a woman came out of a door and began talking to a man sat on a rocking chair overlooking the water.

Both looked elderly, easing Horatio's apprehension and he decided there could be no harm in speaking to them. When he was just a few metres away they still hadn't seen him, he coughed and waited. The pair turned towards him and smiled.

"Bonjour. Ça va?" both said in French and in unison, whilst staring at Nelson.

*   *   *

The couple offered him a drink which he readily accepted, and as they were talking he saw a crowd of people crossing the dam, from the far side.

It turned out that three families lived next door, the others had made homes around the lake and dam, but most evenings everyone ate together, sat around a large open fire.

Surreally, Horatio realised he had again stumbled across a most remarkable community.

Seventy-five survivors, along with fifteen children born since the illness, were living in harmony, working hard, creating a comfortable, sustainable life.

All had arrived at the lake in the aftermath of the contagion, all struggling to outrun death, and for some unfathomable reason, only three had subsequently died.

*   *   *

Horatio was invited to join that evening's meal and he was left speechless by a menu of roasted goat, freshly caught baked Tilapia, a fish pulled from the lake, home grown vegetables, and fruit. Seemingly just a normal meal following a hard day's labour.

With Nelson perching close by and as always, the centre of attention for the children, Horatio enjoyed every moment of the evening.

Not everyone understood French but all spoke Susu and Horatio recalled hearing it on his travels. He was told that it was widely used throughout Sierra Leone and the coastal areas of Guinea.

*   *   *

Horatio erected his tent close to the water's edge and that night he slept soundly for the first time since arriving at Nanette's farm.

The following morning he swam, washed himself and his clothes, shaved and cleaned his teeth before simply relaxing in the warm sun. He decided he had found a sort of paradise.

The elderly couple, Ibrahim and Alioune, came to see him and suggested they went for a walk; Horatio willingly accepted.

They set off and followed a small, fast flowing river and arrived at yet another dam. Much larger and holding back an enormous lake, Alioune told him it was twelve kilometres long and eight wide and it helped feed their own lake.

"That over there, is Mount Gangan, beautiful, isn't it?" Ibrahim said pointing and Horatio had to agree; the district around the two dams was stunning, although Horatio felt the term mountain was rather misleading; to him it resembled a wide plateau and was not very high.

"But it is a reminder," Alioune said,

"Of what?" Horatio asked.

"Graves! Graves were discovered at the bottom of the mountain." Alioune and Ibrahim starred disconsolately towards Mount Gangan. "Hundreds of dead bodies, including soldiers were found and from then onwards there were rumours, people were executed and then buried in mass graves during the night of 7th July 1985. Decades ago maybe, but…"

For Horatio it was another stark reminder of the barbaric nature of human behaviour before the virus.

"It was before our time in Kindia," Ibrahim said unhappily, "but even now people still talk about it. It is said landmines were laid surrounding the mass grave, deterring anyone from going near. Before the sickness, government soldiers followed up on the rumours and confirmed what had happened. They also defused the mines but I don't think it will ever be forgotten."

*   *   *

As they walked to see a system of channels the community had built to syphon water from the lakes to irrigate crops, Horatio was told there were three other communities of

326

survivors living around the two lakes. Two were Muslim, one Christian and they all kept very much to themselves. However, several times a year, celebrations were held with all being invited. Horatio also loved the fact that there had never been any serious disagreements between the various communities and on the rare occasion there was a difference of opinion, the two groups concerned sat together and talked. From what he could tell, they always ended up agreeing the same thing; arguments achieved little, and no one should ever forget how blessed they were to still be alive.

As idealistic as it all sounded, Horatio felt it was another example of survivors rejecting out of hand the pre-virus world of violence, money, intolerance, corruption and selfishness.

He just hoped that in the future such a grateful and generous attitude towards one's neighbour would not become diluted by that inescapable human flaw; craving for the things they didn't have.

*   *   *

Horatio had reluctantly decided to move on a couple of days later but not before he had seriously considered staying and even building a new life for himself next to the lake. He knew the locals would welcome him but was again unable to make what might prove to be an irreversible decision.

Ibrahim had recommended he cycle through Kindia as early in the day as practical.

"It's about ten kilometres from here to the outskirts of the town and at that time the road will be empty."

"Was Kindia important?" Horatio asked.

"Before the virus it was very important and the fourth largest town in Guinea. I'm not sure it was true but, it was claimed two hundred thousand people lived there, including the military headquarters of the Guinean Armed

Forces. There used to be soldiers everywhere, which was good for the town's economy but they also caused some serious problems."

Ibrahim told Horatio that Alioune had run a book shop in the centre of town and he had worked part-time as a clerk for the army and he couldn't believe what had happened when the sickness arrived. Tens of tens of thousands had died and all sorts of weapons were just left lying around.

"Military equipment everywhere and if you knew where to look you could find a complete arsenal; it made a few people extremely powerful.

I suppose the only positive was that the rival gangs ended up not only slaughtering each other but using up all the ammunition. I think the guns are probably useless now.

We hear there are still problems in the town, fewer than before, but it can still be a dangerous place. If you're interested, I know a short cut to avoid the centre."

Chapter 38

Leaving before dawn, Horatio turned left when he reached the junction with the derelict shopping centre and with Nelson circling overhead, found the highway deserted so picked up his speed.

Approaching Kindia's outskirts he looked for a petrol station on his right which Ibrahim had told him led to the short cut around the south of the town.

Slightly concerned about leaving the highway and ending up lost, Horatio decided it was worth the gamble.

Spotting the petrol station ahead, he needed to find a road on the right with the strangest of names; Cor1.

Finding the turning without difficulty, Horatio called Nelson to the handlebars and was pleasantly surprised to see the new road was tarmac and in excellent condition.

As dawn broke over the eastern horizon, he passed a derelict bar and restaurant, then two further kilometres on, a hotel. All these confirmed he was on the right road and it was only a short time before he rejoined the highway. Turning right, he then passed a group of small shops, all in ruins, followed by a large ransacked supermarket and whispered his thanks to Ibrahim.

*　　*　　*

Leaving Kindia behind, the highway continued to be undulating, with some difficult climbs, but nothing Horatio felt he couldn't tackle. He hoped he could cover most of the one hundred and thirty kilometres to Mamou, before he made camp that night.

With a noticeably relaxed Nelson flying high overhead and picking up his speed in ideal conditions; thirty degrees, no wind, low humidity and glorious sunshine, Horatio reached Kolente in excellent time.

And of course, Kadijah had been right when he told Horatio that the highway through the interior of Guinea was surrounded by spectacular scenery. As far as the eye could see, it was a mix of deep, lush green forests interspersed with ragged, stark peaks extending out of earth.

Horatio saw little or no sign of human impact on the countryside.

*   *   *

Arriving in Kolente and the Great Scarcies River mid-morning, Horatio found it strange to be crossing the river for a second time. The first had been at Kambia and he was reminded of the local market and wonderful welcome he and Nanette had received.

It was no surprise that the wide, fast flowing river from Kambia had shrunk to a narrower, more placid, inland tributary; nevertheless, with no bridge, it still needed crossing.

Not wanting to be delayed, Horatio pushed the bike and cart through a shallow ford he'd found by following a mud track that lead straight down to the water's edge.

*   *   *

Just over an hour later, with Nelson returning to his perch on the cart, Horatio moved slowly through the small town of Souguéta with its Mosque, supermarket, garage and shops. As he had come to expect however, all were derelict and there was no sign of people.

Just after exiting the town, Horatio was surprised to see what he would have described as a traditional African village. The buildings were small and round, with thatched, cone shaped roofs. All were built of clay, painted white and appeared reasonable well maintained.

There was rubbish scattered around and a few goats and cattle, which tellingly were tethered. If the village was still in use, Horatio was left asking why anyone would live in mud huts when just down the road there must have been hundreds of brick built houses lying empty.

Horatio then peddled past what had become a familiar, yet awful sight. A large hole had been dug close to the highway, and it was almost full of burnt skeletons.

*   *   *

Cycling on from the village, Horatio remained confused, and wondered whether the survivors living in the mud huts were trying to return to a traditional way of life; just maybe they were relearning skills their grandparents and great grandparents had used.

With Nelson staring at him from the handlebars, Horatio stroked him as he answered his own question. In the new world, people would have to find a way to live without modern equipment, comforts or other conveniences. Survival would require having the ability to adapt to rigors and difficulties rarely experienced before the virus. Having said that though, Horatio conceded he was primarily referring to highly advanced nations, rather than those in West Africa. Some of the locals where he was travelling had lived for generations with poverty, killer diseases, civil war and other conflicts, and they may well adapt effectively to a simple, non-digital driven way of life.

*   *   *

Still determined to cover the twenty kilometres to reach Kolenten before stopping to eat, Horatio remembered that Kadijah had told him, that section of the highway would

331

take him from the coast to the highest elevation he would face.

Mamou, the next major town he would visit, was eight hundred metres above sea level and from there he would have to continue to climb to well over a thousand metres.

The scenery continued to be a mix of rainforests and savanna, sporadically interrupted by tall rocky peaks, but overall the land appeared bleak and unproductive.

Peddling by the occasional isolated hamlet, he was left wondering what work the locals would have been involved in.

*   *   *

One of Horatio's concerns from the beginning of the journey was that Nelson would struggle. He wondered whether the constant change in landscapes and differing ecological variations, might cause the falcon problems in searching out food to kill on the wing. However, he was adapting effortlessly and overall appeared relaxed and content.

As expected the highway proved demanding, but Horatio never felt unable to cope. That was until the front tyre suddenly deflated but considering the distance he had cycled it was hardly surprising that from time to time he would need to repair a puncture.

*   *   *

Making Kolenten in good time, even allowing for the puncture, Horatio negotiated the town, crossed an unstable bridge over a fresh water river, where he decided to stop, eat and rest.

As he filled his water containers, he couldn't resist the temptation to swim and although he wanted to get on, he washed himself and some of his clothes, shaved and cleaned his teeth.

Setting off once again, this time soaking wet, he knew that with the temperature and warm sun, within just a couple minutes he would again be oozing sweat.

*   *   *

Mid-afternoon, well on the way to Mamou, Horatio unexpectedly met another person.

Having sped through the hamlet of Ouâkâ, as he turned a sharp bend in the highway, there was smoke ahead. He saw a fire had been lit right next to a dilapidated single storey, brick building and on its porch there was an old lady sweeping with a broom made from twigs.

Wanting to keep moving, he decided not to stop, but as soon as the woman spotted him she called out and three others, all younger and holding machetes, joined her on the porch.

Horatio moved Nelson to the handlebars and checked that the shotgun, spear gun and machete were within easy reach. It was not that he felt threatened, just that he needed to be prepared for anything.

Coming to a stop in the middle of the highway, twenty metres from the house, and hoping they would understand him, Horatio said in French,

"Bon après-midi," 'good afternoon'.

The four women stood still and stared at him, waiting; for what he had no idea, so Horatio cycled on.

As he drew level with the porch, the old woman said,

"You don't belong here."

"What do you mean?"

"We haven't seen anyone for weeks, then you turn up, and you're white." She was becoming more hostile as she spoke. "So, why would a white person be around here?"

Before Horatio could answer, she continued pointing at Nelson.

"And what's that?"

"Just a friend."

333

One of the younger women, clearly trying to placate him, then said more agreeably,

"Where are you from?"

Horatio was in two minds about answering; part of him wanted to keep going, but he accepted whenever he had spoken to locals, he had always gained valuable information. "I'm heading for Mamou," he answered, revealing as little as possible.

"There's nothing there," the youngest of the four said. "No one lives around here, just us."

"Where have they gone?" Horatio asked.

"Those who survived the sickness moved to Conkary. They said it would be safer and they would find food."

"So why didn't you go?"

"At the time, our father wouldn't let us. He said we could farm what we needed. Then he became ill and died and by then everyone we knew had left. We've only ever lived here, so didn't know how to get to Conkary."

Wanting to know about the road to Mamou, Horatio asked,

"Are there any problems around here?"

"What do you mean?" It was still the youngest talking.

"Is it safe to travel?"

"I suppose so, well except for the lions."

"The what?" Horatio thought he might have misheard.

"Lions," she repeated.

All the reading and research Horatio had done previously told him that apart from a handful protected in the wild and zoos, there were no lions in West Africa.

"Around here?" he asked.

"We've heard them." It was the older women, in a more conciliatory voice. "And I saw one, a few years ago."

"So did I," the last of the women to speak claimed.

Big cats living locally! Horatio was pleased to have spoken to the women. He felt confident though that the lack of current sightings meant he would encounter no problems; a view that was reinforced when one woman said she could never remember a lion attacking a person.

Believing he would learn nothing more, Horatio decided he needed to push on. However, as he was about to thank them for their help, the older woman asked if he would like to share food with them.

Tempted as he was, something really didn't feel right about the group, especially the older women's creepy manner. One minute she was hostile, the next overly welcoming and generous, leaving Horatio uncertain of their intentions towards him.

With a nervous Nelson eyeballing the women, he called his thanks and cycled on.

Chapter 39

Horatio sensed the weather was changing. From an almost perfect day, dark clouds were building and soon after, the rain began falling. Horatio stopped, covered the cart and his belongings with a plastic sheet and cycled on.

The rain was warm and he actually found it refreshing; even Nelson appeared to be enjoying getting a wash as he circled calmly above. That was however, until an ear-piercing clap of thunder, quickly followed by a ferocious lightning bolt which illuminated the entire area, sent the falcon to his arm protector.

Increasing his speed, Horatio needed to find shelter. If the lightning intensified there was no way he wanted them to be out in the open.

Through the worsening visibility he saw a building ahead and what looked like an ancient bus and hoped he could find somewhere to wait out the storm. As he frantically pedalled, the rain strengthened, becoming torrential and Horatio headed straight for the bus.

Practically throwing the bike, cart and Nelson up the steps through the open door, he laughed as he realised how close he'd been to getting completely drenched. Forcing the door shut behind him, he was thankful that he'd manged to prevent his possessions from getting soaked and Nelson from taking flight into what was becoming a violent storm.

Looking around, Horatio saw the old vehicle had been in a serious collision. It was half on the tarmac, half on the grass and the driver's side had caved in. The man's door had taken the bulk of the substantial impact, but his broken skeleton, for that is all that remained, was still in his seat with the seatbelt fastened.

Inside there appeared to be little damage and importantly the roof was intact, keeping them dry. Most of the windows were smashed or cracked and the six tyres were all flat, but the seats were fine.

*　　*　　*

Drying his hair with an old cloth whilst Nelson scanned the inside of the vehicle, Horatio sat on the front seat behind the driver's partition, ignoring the body. Realising he wouldn't be able to light a fire, he began unpacking his food to see what he could eat cold or raw.

For no reason, Nelson suddenly shrieked and from the back of the bus came a rustling sound, immediately followed by a whispered 'shush'.

Grabbing the shotgun, making sure the safety catch was off, Horatio rose and stared at the far end of the bus where he could just about see behind the last pair of seats. Directly in front of the back row, there was a woman and child cowering.

Moving unthreateningly down the length of the bus, he asked in French whether they were alright.

A face, with two large, fearful eyes then appeared above the back of the seats and nodded. Horatio said gently,

"Come out; you are in no danger."

Slowly, the woman stood, keeping the girl behind her and Horatio saw she was African with very dark skin, high cheek bones, deep brown eyes and a tall lithe body. He thought she was slightly older than Maya, but in some ways looked similar.

His food may have been dwindling fast, but Horatio still couldn't stop himself from asking if they were hungry.

When the woman nodded, he walked back to the front of the vehicle and with the rain falling in torrents, probably heavier than Horatio had ever experienced, he called his fellow passengers to join him.

Moving Nelson onto the metal handrail on the back of the other front seat, the girl stared in fascination at the bird and reached out to stroke him.

Horatio smiled, took her hand and guided it down the length of Nelson's head and back; both bird and girl were clearly thrilled.

As they ate, the girl, whose name was Sylvia, spent the entire time stroking Nelson and talking to him in a dialect Horatio couldn't decipher.

*   *   *

It turned out the woman, Domani Binta, was not Sylvia's mother and they were trying to get back to her farm and family who lived just outside Mamou.

A little later with Sylvia bedded down for the night on the double seats at the rear, having insisted that Nelson perch on the handrail above her, Domani Binta began her story.

*   *   *

When the virus struck, Domani had been hundreds of kilometres from her husband, Yakubu and her three children, Anjuwa, who was ten, Alex who was nine and Eunice, the youngest who was seven. They were all on their family farm just outside Mamou whereas she was far away having just finished a contract as a metallurgist.

Domani had trained in England and had worked in many different countries before marrying her childhood sweetheart and settling down. However, finding permanent work for her qualifications, skills and experience was extremely difficult. As a result, whenever and wherever work was offered, she dropped everything and travelled as required.

Working part-time was extremely well paid, especially by local standards, allowing her family to live comfortably.

338

Before the virus Domani had built a reputation which led to regular work in what had once been the largest producer of aluminium ore in the world.

The difficulty though was the mine was six-hundred kilometres from her farm and the transport links were non-existent.

Most of her contracts were between two and five weeks and she always stayed in the same lodgings on the outskirts of Boke.

*   *   *

Domani had been in high spirits. She had just completed a one month's contract at the mine and her earnings plus a bonus would take the pressure off her husband and keep them afloat for months. He was working all hours, with no help other than from the children, yet the farm was losing money and she knew he was at his wits end; her latest pay packet would help considerably.

Then, the following morning at breakfast with Mariama her landlady, Domani was about to leave when the television had a 'Breaking News' headline.

She said she'd been aware of a sickness in S. E. Asia, but assumed there was nothing to worry about, that was until the reporter described how quickly it was spreading and more ominously, that it was killing people. A second report containing footage of riots throughout the most affected countries then appeared and she knew she had to get home and quickly.

*   *   *

As Domani unlocked her car, parked opposite her lodgings, she was hit on the back of the neck and collapsed. Confused and in pain, she tried unsuccessfully to get to her feet and could only watch as a complete stranger picked up the car keys she'd dropped. The woman, with a man in the passenger seat, then drove away in Domani's car.

Initially furious about being mugged, the difficulties that lay ahead quickly became clear.

Without a car, how would she get home? There might have been buses, even trains, but she had never used them and didn't even know where to find a timetable.

Stunned as well as being extremely afraid, Domani still understood that waiting for the local police was not a realistic option. They might pretend to investigate, but they'd do nothing; in fact they were probably in on the robbery!

*   *   *

Her car was gone and that was that; she needed to get home.

Over the years she had worked at the mine, Mariama had become a good friend so Domani returned to her lodgings to try and sort out what to do.

From the house phone she tried to contact her husband but no one answered and with no mobile signal at the farm she was left helpless.

Again, trying to ignore her frustration and with Mariama's help, Domani went into Boke for buses or trains to the capital Conkary. All they found were shut ticket offices with posters that read: 'Until further notice all rail and bus services have been cancelled'.

That evening, Domani discovered that whilst they had been out all local and international landlines had been cut-off. With no means of contacting her family and worried sick, she was at a complete loss as to what to do next.

*   *   *

Spending the following day in town, again with Mariama, she searched for a means to begin her journey home, even offering to pay a man with a truck to take her to Conkary. She found no one willing to help.

Left petrified her family might be exposed to the virus and not survive, that evening Domani told Mariama that if necessary she would walk home.

After receiving the expected reaction, she explained that her family was her life and she would do absolutely anything to get back to them. If that required her to walk the whole five-hundred and sixty-seven kilometres, then so be it.

* * *

True to her word as dawn broke the next morning, Domani began her journey home with a few personal belongings, food and water; plus an old road map Mariama had insisted on giving her. Worryingly, she was also carrying her last wage packet, far more money than was safe, but it was cash she might be able to use to get help.

* * *

Horatio was left speechless as she described the early months of her trek home. He'd been on the move for only a few weeks and been severely tested but listening to Domani he quickly understood how relatively fortunate he'd been.

She described being attacked, robbed of her wages and raped on so many occasions she couldn't even remember the faces of the men who had forced themselves on her. She also told Horatio that she truly believed the world had gone mad; that the devil had won the battle between good and evil.

"One incident though, one single moment of compassion changed everything." She told him, "I'd been left for dead by three men who had raped me, witnessed, by the way, by two women who looked on seemingly

341

indifferent to my humiliation. You know, it was at that time my faith in a compassionate God ended, as did my desire to go on living.

The attack had happened just outside the town of Kolaboui and whilst the men were taking turns, I closed my eyes to shut out the pain. I forced myself to focus on the truly meaningful thing left; my family.

When the men had finally had enough which felt like hours later, they dumped me by the edge of the road. Bloodied, bruised and in absolute agony, I truly wanted to die. I wanted God to take me to a safer, kinder, more joyful place where I could wait in peace for my children and husband."

Domani told Horatio that she sobbed as she thought of her family; she had come to believe she would never see them again, never hug or kiss them goodnight. She was near death, already lost to them and it felt like such a waste; such a tragic loss.

Unable to move, loathing the cruel heat of the noontime sun on her raw, bloodied body; she felt something on her lips. It was manna from heaven, nectar, a life-saving tonic; cool, thirst-quenching, water!

Was it a miracle? Was it the sort of godly act she'd lost faith in; the sort of kindness she assumed had become extinct in their post-apocalyptic world. She had no idea, but however it was defined, her faith in the goodness of people had been rekindled.

*   *   *

It was months later, that Domani found out that an elderly couple, Louis and Esperanza had witnessed the attack, taken pity on her and literally dragged her back to their home.

They had cared for her, fed her, cleaned up after her and tried to make good her appalling injuries and it was Esperanza who told her she had lost the baby.

342

At the time Domani had been unconscious, not even aware she was pregnant. If she had known, there was no way she would have wanted to give birth to the child of a rapist.

Nevertheless, all the kindness, all the genuine love they had shown for a stranger, could not heal the inner turmoil and emotional havoc that still lurked in the deepest parts of her mind.

*   *   *

Domani described to Horatio how she had struggled with the simplest of tasks and found even looking after herself impossibly challenging. She was impatient to succeed and became quickly frustrated and angry with herself over the smallest failure. No matter how grateful she was to the wonderful Louis and Esperanza, getting home dominated Domani's every thought.

During the months of relearning how to manage routines and simple chores, she never gave up hope of returning home; for without home, she had nothing and was nothing.

*   *   *

Impatient to get on with her journey, Domani decided to talk to Louis and Esperanza, but that never happened because Louis died.

It began with a painful fall and as the cuts and bruises quickly healed Louis felt in good spirits. However, within just a few days he worsened and took to his bed. Less than twenty-four hours later he came down with a punishing fever and what had appeared an innocuous mishap, killed him inside two weeks.

For Domani, when she saw the shattering effect Louis's death had on his wife, any thought of leaving disappeared. She had been a complete stranger and one close to death when they had taken her in and for months had nursed her night and day back to reasonable health. Without them she accepted she would have died and could never thank Louis and Esperanza enough. There was no way she would walk out on Esperanza when she was needed the most.

*   *   *

The following day, as Louis was buried, Domani realised he had been a Muslim and it left her puzzled. In all the time she had lived with them, neither Louis nor Esperanza had mentioned religion and she wondered whether they had worked out she was a Christian and so steered clear of any possible conflict.

Domani remembered instilling an open and constructive attitude towards diversity, be it colour, belief, gender or nationality into her own children; to her it was just being practical. However, since the virus her only thoughts on religion tended to be critical and self-destructive.

Sat on her own at the back during the funeral service, Domani had come to the conclusion that the 'new' world she lived in would be far safer and gentler if the historic misuse of absolute power by religous leaders, was rejected by survivors.

It may have been clutching at straws but she knew her own survival from the horrific attack was proof that strangers from differing religious backgrounds could share their lives lovingly and peacefully.

So, if this was the case, didn't it follow that if outsiders were welcomed into communities, sharing would become the norm and learning from each other would automatically follow. Crucially, each person's strengths and weaknesses would be accepted, appreciated, even respected and not used to justify persecution grounded on prejudice and intolerance.

It may even result in launching a principle to underpin civilised societies; that it's okay to be different.

*　　*　　*

For the next few weeks, day and night Esperanza sat on the old sofa on the porch, only occasionally taking herself to the bathroom. She was withdrawn, remained silent and in a world of her own, so Domani willingly took over the daily household duties.

The garden though was a different matter; she was even unsure about what to pick for their meals. Fortunately, the neighbours introduced themselves and told her they were very fond of Louis and they were always around if anything was needed.

So with their help, Domani cooked the meals, which Esperanza hardly touched, kept the house tidy and tried to work the garden to ensure they had a constant supply of food.

Once a week, a local woman delivered meat she had killed and prepared, wanting nothing in return. It was through her Domani discovered that before the virus Louis and Esperanza had been integral to the local community. She was told they were always the givers, never the takers and that was clearly reflected in the attitude of locals to his passing. It also reinforced Domani's promise to remain with Esperanza for as long as needed.

Heartbreakingly though, it was only for a few more days. Esperanza never recovered from losing her beloved husband, blaming herself for not doing more and it consumed her. Initially she refused food, then water, until even her closest of friends found it impossible to help her leaving Domani at a loss as to what more she could do.

She was desperate to comfort Esperanza, to care for her as she had been cared for, but nothing she tried made the slightest difference. In the end, along with her friends, Domani reluctantly accepted it was Esperanza's right to choose her own end. As her will to go on weakened, so did her health and within just a few days she passed away peacefully.

At her funeral the following day, the community supported Domani, insisting there was nothing more she could have done. Nonetheless, she had lost the two special friends who had quite literally saved her life as well as giving her a reason to live.

That night, as she lay alone in the house that had become her home, Domani experienced an unnerving feeling of being alone and unable to cope.

*   *   *

Crawling out of bed in the dead of night, Domani needed to move on, to get away from the reminders that lurked in every corner of the house and more than ever, she wanted to be back with her family.

Packing the few things she might need, as dawn was breaking she set off from Kolaboui.

Attempting to get her bearings after so long, she studied a map and saw she needed to take the highway to Conkary. From there, it was the N.1 to Mamou and all the way to her farm.

*   *   *

"Am I am going on too much?" Domani asked Horatio.

"No, honestly, please don't stop. Describe everything you can remember."

"You know you're the first person I've really spoken to since I left Louis and Esperanza."

And she then told Horatio that it had taken fifteen days to cover the distance to Boffa and to her relief, she came across no other people.

Horatio smiled as he told her, he felt the opposite. One of the things he struggled with was the lack of people, especially in larger towns where he assumed there would be survivors.

"My mother thought only a small percentage of the world's population would have survived the virus and when I read her notes I thought it was crazy, but now, well… she was right."

Horatio went through his mother's sums and after being initially unconvinced, Domani realised it all made sense and that troubled her. Getting home might be a reality but who would she find alive when she got there?

*　　*　　*

Horatio asked her to continue, so she explained that her elation at arriving in Boffa was crushed by the River Pongo; there was no way of getting across.

She talked to an old woman she had met in the town and was told that there had been no ferries since the fuel ran out so that left swimming the half a kilometre or travelling in land to the bridge at Fatala. Domani may have been a competent swimmer when she was younger but tackling the crossing would have bordered on the suicidal.

A day later she found the bridge, followed by a village called Soumbouyadi. She remembered the name because there was an orchard full of ripe fruit and as she filled a bag with various berries and fruits she heard a noise behind her. Turning she saw three women, all carrying weapons and on horseback.

"Where are you going?" one of them asked pleasantly enough and Domani told her she was headed for Conkary and then on to her home near Mamou.

"Why don't you come with us? Join us for something to eat; I think tonight we're having roasted goat."

Domani said to Horatio that although she wanted to carry on, and was aware of the possible dangers, the thought of a hot, cooked meal was too tempting to ignore so she accepted.

347

*   *   *

The leader of the group, Kadiatou, offered Domani a ride and she climbed up behind her. From a very young age, she had always ridden horses and was a fine horsewoman and as they set off she was looking forward to the ride and seeing their camp.

Surprisingly, she noticed they trotted away from Soumbouyadi in the direction she'd just walked, except they didn't cross the bridge but carried straight on.

A few minutes later, after wading through a shallow stream, they came to an assortment of abandoned buildings, one of which Domani realised had been the local medical centre. For some distance they then followed a wide river and Kadiatou called to her that it was called the Fatala River.

Domani then told Horatio she suddenly became fearful. She realised she had no idea where she was, in which direction they were moving or how she would return to the highway.

*   *   *

After what seemed like hours, whilst their path mirrored the meandering river, they came to a hamlet and Domani saw three single storey buildings, squeezed into a narrow strip of land between the river and jungle. She was intrigued when she noticed a cluster of islands. The four largest had wooden buildings but there were no bridges connecting them to the bank.

Approaching the settlement, a group of children ran out to greet them and after dismounting, the three horses were led away by two young girls.

Domani was then taken to the nearest building and they entered a large room with a group of chairs set around a low, oblong table. She was invited to sit next to Kadiatou, then an old, extremely 'weathered' looking woman approached with glasses of water and a plate of small snacks on a tray.

"If Mamou is home, why were you coming from the other side of the bridge?" Kadiatou asked.

Domani realised they must have been watching her for some time but still answered,

"I had been working near Boke when the sickness came. My car was stolen so I had to walk." She then described being attacked, rescued by Louis and Esperanza, how both had died and that once again she was trying to get home to her family.

The snack having been eaten, Domani was taken to a second building, slightly further away from the river, bordering the jungle. Kadiatou showed her a room where she could rest until the evening meal and also suggested she could stay there that night. Within seconds she'd crawled under the mosquito net into a clean sheet and was sound asleep.

*   *   *

Domani woke with a start and remembering where she was, she got up and grabbing a change of clothes, headed for the river.

The first person she met was a young girl and when she asked about a safe place to swim, the girl pointed and said,

"Just follow that path."

Within just a few hundred metres, Domani found a section of the bank that had collapsed and after undressing, she waded safely into the river. The water was wonderfully cool, fresh enough to drink and she washed her body and swilled her clothes.

"Stay close to the bank."

Domani saw the same three women on horseback and assumed they were making sure she was safe, but something didn't feel right.

Quickly drying herself, she dressed in her dry clothes and returned to her room. Having hung up her wet things to dry overnight, she then went out again.

*   *   *

Standing on the river bank, opposite the cluster of islands, she saw the river was noticeably wider; up to a hundred metres across and the flowing water was swirling and churning through narrow rock strewn channels. As well as the four she had seen earlier, Domani counted half a dozen smaller deserted islands; whether inhabited or not, with no bridges they all looked to be completely cut-off by the strong currents.

As she was about to walk away, she noticed buildings on the far bank and remarkably, what appeared to be about twenty people walking in lines of twos towards the river. Even in the fading light she could see the whole area was enclosed by thick rain forest and unnervingly, she suddenly felt trapped.

Returning to her room, Domani was afraid. The community had obviously been built in the middle of nowhere, set apart from the rest of the world and she had to assume that was the point of its location.

*   *   *

With darkness falling, she was collected by Kadiatou, who strangely asked what her married name had been. As they walked back to the building where refreshment had been taken earlier, she replied Binta.

Apart from three women at one table and the two horse riders from the afternoon at another, the room was empty. Domani was invited to sit opposite Kadiatou.

The women from earlier were introduced as Odete and Awa and when they said hello, it was the first time she had heard either speak.

When the meal arrived served by another old woman, oil lamps were being lit and a bewildered Domani couldn't understand where they could get large quantities of oil from.

As they ate, with the three women on the other table noticeably attentive, Kadiatou enquired about where Domani had lived, worked, about her family and strangely, she kept returning to her qualifications; her school exam results, university degrees and other diplomas and certificates.

Odete and Awa spoke little but Domani was aware they were listening to every word and she realised that whenever she asked a question of them, Kadiatou turned it back into another question for her.

At times it certainly felt like she was being interrogated, however, the meal was delicious and filling so Domani decided she'd been right to accept their invitation.

*   *   *

"So what are your plans?" Kadiatou asked as the plates were being cleared.

"Well… tomorrow I will continue my journey home."

"You could stay here for a few days to rest up, if you want to."

"Thank you, but I can't. I haven't seen my family for… oh, many years, so I must get home."

"With your talents you could make a real difference to what we are trying to do here."

"Well… that's kind of you, but, I must see my family again."

The three women on the other table then rose and left; they had said nothing to Domani or amongst themselves for the entire meal.

Following a short awkward silence, Kadiatou said,

"You said your farm was just outside Mamou?"

351

"Yes, north of the town. Our land runs alongside the N.5., highway. My husband runs the farm whilst I work whenever I can to help with the bills."

"So you won't reconsider staying for a few days."

"I can't, I'm sorry."

"Fair enough, well… Let's have a night cap before we turn in."

Awa stood up and went to the back of the room, returning with four drinks in old clay mugs.

"Here's to you," Kadiatou said and they all clinked their mugs together.

Domani thought the sweet taste of the thick liquid delicious and decided it must be some sort of homemade fruit liqueur, but that was the last thing she remembered.

Chapter 40

Domani told Horatio that she woke to the sound of rushing water in a small, bare room. It was a different room and her head hurt, her throat was parched and her body felt as if it had taken a beating.

As she lay on the bed thinking, Domani realised the only logical explanation was she had been drugged and it was probably that last drink together. She also remembered it was just after she had repeated her determination to leave the next morning.

Standing unsteadily, she first went to the window and saw she was in a hut on an island; one without a bridge linking it to the river bank.

By the position of the sun, she thought it must be late afternoon, so wondered how long she had been asleep and she accepted she was going nowhere.

Moving to the door Domani found it locked, so returned to the window to discover it had been nailed firmly down; why was she being held hostage?

Looking around the room, on a small table against the wall there was a tray with food and a jug of water. Deciding she needed energy, she ate everything and drank most of the water, then with nothing else to do, she climbed back in to bed and fell asleep.

* * *

Hearing a noise outside, then the unlocking of her door, Domani saw someone entering.

"How are you feeling?" Kadiatou asked. She was clearly on her own.

"What do you care?" Domani answered, knowing she was being rude.

"I'm sorry but you left Pati am no alternative."

Domani had no idea what or who Pati am was and really didn't care.

"Will you come with me please?" Kadiatou said moving back to the door.

Domani got up knowing she had little option, drank the remainder of the water and followed.

It was a warm, beautifully clear night as they walked the short distance to a small dinghy in which were two women; both armed with machetes and holding oars.

The trip to the bank opposite to the one Domani had been standing on the previous afternoon, took just a few minutes, but it was bumpy and the women struggled to control the boat's course in the strong currents.

Landing close to the buildings she had seen, Domani confirmed they were surrounded by dense impenetrable jungle.

She was led to another building and as they entered a large room, she saw it was lit by dozens of oil lamps. There were rows of trestle tables, each with twelve people sat on benches.

With all eyes on her, she was escorted to a table near the front where she was invited to sit between Odete and Awa, whilst Kadiatou again sat opposite her.

And so began a bizarre yet enchanting evening.

*   *   *

As the room sat in silence, a haunting melody sung by a woman playing an old but tuneful piano came from the back of the room and Domani couldn't remember ever hearing such a soulful song. When the last note was played, the silence continued; the profound effect on those gathered was visibly moving.

An older woman at the front then rose from the centre chair of five and Domani assumed it was some sort of top table; clearly they were the leaders of the community.

"For the benefit of our guest," the woman looked directly at Domani, "that was written and sung by Jaaja Aida; our most accomplished musician and teacher."

After grace said by another of the leaders, the food arrived and Domani was impressed by the quality; there were no choices but absolutely nothing was left on any plate.

Whilst eating little was said, but after the community had filed out one table at a time, the five leaders asked Domani and Kadiatou to join them. Standing as one, they turned and moved towards the far end of the room before entering a small, intimate room. She saw comfortable chairs around a low, oval table and oil lamps burning brightly.

*   *   *

"Are you sure I'm not talking too much?" Domani asked again, and Horatio smiled and repeated that he was absolutely certain.

Taking a deep breath, she went on to explain that the five were introduced to her as Pati am Aminata, or Grandmother Aminata. Pati am was Grandmother in Fulu and Pular, both local languages; she was head of the community. The other four were Yumma Mary, Viviane, Fatoumata and Camara; Yumma being mother.

As a warm, sweet drink was served in beautifully crafted, ceramic cups, Domani was again asked about her school and university, followed by her degrees and other qualifications.

Even though she was being held against her will and the questions were identical to those asked earlier by Kadiatou, Domani remained calm, answering everything truthfully.

Next she was asked about her career choices, work experiences and finally her family.

Pati am Aminata then thanked her before saying,

"We began nearly six years ago, when we realised the high death rate of the virus and that most survivors were female. With almost all males dying, we understood something innovative had to be done and quickly or the human race would simply end."

Pati am Aminata described how within a few days of the global catastrophe unfolding, through a dream, God had revealed to her the way forward.

Although Domani had once had faith, Pati am's assertion that God had spoken to her through a dream, really didn't impress her at all.

"Of course, at first I didn't believe any of it," the leader continued, "so I remained with my family waiting for the virus to take us, and it did: they all died, but for some inexplicable reason, I lived and it was just one of the many signs given to me by God.

And then God be praised, my closest friend," she looked towards Yumma Mary, "had also survived. Was it yet another sign?"

For the first time, Yumma Mary spoke.

"As we searched in vain for a base, God reminded me of my uncle and told us to come here to his farm, but we arrived to find his entire family dead. As saddened as I was personally, we couldn't escape the fact it was meant to be. God had brought us here, somewhere safe to build our new lives and begin moulding our future.

Pati am Aminata and I travelled to search for likeminded survivors, people who would commit to the beliefs that would ultimately underpin our mission to build a new order. God be praised, we found Yumma Viviane, Fatoumata and Camara.

Together, with my uncle's machinery, animals and buildings, we worked his land and have been here ever since."

"But..." Pati Aminata said, "six years on we still need educated adults to teach our young."

"So, what is the project?" Domani asked, not at all sure why she was showing any interest.

"It's simple; God has shown us how to preserve the human race. Our life's work is to restock earth with young people whose talents, education and morals will empower them to go forth to reclaim the land. They will be the 'new' explorers; pioneers with courage and resolve to establish new communities, all in God's name."

Trying to take it all in, Domani was incredulous, yet in awe. If the human race was on the edge of extinction, the likes of Pati Aminata and the Yummas, no matter how implausible, may well be the last chance saloon for human survival.

"Will you join us?" Pati Aminata said unequivocally.

"What?"

"I asked if you will join us. You are intelligent, educated, have distinctive experiences, including raising a family. We know our young would benefit enormously from your teaching and influence."

"I must find my family. I'm sorry, but getting home is what matters to me most."

The seven around the table fell into an uncomfortable silence before Domani noticed Pati am nod towards Yumma Mary who said,

"In the five days that you have been here."

"Five days! What the hell do you mean five days?" Domani was seething. She couldn't believe they had incarcerated her for nearly a week and she hadn't been aware of it.

"We apologise."

"Apologise! You cannot just say sorry and move on. You talk of God's work, God's signs, yet you act like feudal tyrants." Domani stared at the women, never blinking; she was furious.

"I was about to say, whilst you slept we sent three of our people to your home. They found it with little difficulty, especially knowing your surname was Binta, and… well I'm truly sorry, but the farm was abandoned; there was no sign of life anywhere in the area."

At that moment, Domani's world died.

*　　　*　　　*

A tearful Domani told Horatio that it took her many days before she could accept her beloved husband and beautiful children were gone.

During those darkest hours she rarely left her room, lying on the bed remembering. Food was brought by Kadiatou, but even with her encouragement, she scarcely ate a thing.

On the sixth day, Domani discovered Kadiatou had not been one of the party to visit her home, and feeling relieved, from then on they spent many hours talking. Initially she was suspicious but slowly felt more comfortable with a bond, even a friendship, developing between them.

On the following day, quite out of the blue, Yumma Mary visited Domani but she refused to talk. However, she returned every afternoon, sitting patiently waiting for her to talk about her loss and eventually on the tenth day, as she was leaving, Domani thanked her.

Yumma Mary smiled and said,

"That's better, isn't it?"

*　　　*　　　*

Over the next week, Domani made a few momentous decisions. The first and most significant was conceding that being part of the community would help her get over the loss of her family; she didn't need or want to be alone at that time without the support of friends.

She began going out, walking around the town, and within a month Yumma Mary showed her where the youngest were taught and the classroom was waiting for her. Everyone she met was welcoming and friendly, none more so than Kadiatou, although Domani always had the feeling she was being watched, and wondered whether that was Kadiatou's role in the community?

*   *   *

"Within just a couple of months, I felt valued for the first time since leaving Boke. I felt useful and realised that in the eyes of others I was important."

Domani told Horatio that the weeks became months, and months years, although time was immaterial. She loved her work, forming constructive relationships with all the children, most of whom had also lost their families to the sickness.

"But, you know, I was never able to shake off the feeling that something was wrong, that things were not what they seemed. I began to believe the leaders were concealing parts of their work, especially concerning some of the youngsters.

On the whole, my thirteen and fourteen year old girls were lovely and a pleasure to teach, and I became fond of the group. However, over an eight week period, two of the seven left and I didn't see them again. The next month another left and within six months they'd all gone.

"Each time, I spoke to Kadiatou or Yumma Mary who oversaw the education of the girls I always received the same answer, 'It was time for them to live up to their calling'.

I was immediately allocated another group of girls; the same age and again, loved working with them, so erroneously I blanked out my concerns. But, I know I let them down badly."

*   *   *

Domani went on to describe how she became very close to Sylvia, one of the new girls. She had been found wandering alone near Mamou, so they had things in common.

"She's the girl asleep at the back," and Domani smiled as she explained.

At the beginning she wouldn't talk to anyone; she was desperately unhappy and reminded me of myself when I had first arrived so I persevered. She finally confided in me after two of the girls from the group left. I found her crying behind the classroom and when I asked her what was wrong, she looked at me coldly and said, 'You don't know?'

I told her I had no idea what she was talking about; that I had only been informed the girls left because they were ready to move on. Sylvia stared at me as if I had gone mad.

"You can't really believe that?"

I promised her that I had no idea of what was going on, that I'd been told it was their calling.

"Calling! Since when was being fucked, or more likely raped by a boy who you've never met, been defined as one's calling?"

I was shocked, absolutely stunned, and told her to stop being ridiculous, that the leaders were godly people and would never permit such a thing. But then I saw her tears and knew she was telling the truth.

*   *   *

Domani went straight to Pati am Aminata, by-passing Kadiatou and the Yummas, something she had never done before and trying to remain calm, asked for details of the project.

At the start, the leader was irritated about being questioned, and asked Domani why she wanted to know.

Explaining that of the first group she taught, all the girls had left and never returned, and that the same thing was happening with her current students. She added that the only explanation she'd ever received was that it was their destiny, and that wasn't good enough; she needed to know what was happening to them.

Pati am told Domani to sit and said,

"When we first met, I explained that through a number of signs we had been summoned by God to help save the human race. Do you remember?" When Domani nodded, she carried on.

"I also told you, we were creating a new generation of people to send out into the world to carry God's word?"

Again Domani nodded.

"Well, that is what we are doing. Nothing more, nothing less."

"But how?" Domani asked bluntly.

"Because you have made such a difference to our children, I will explain."

Pati am told her that they had created two strands to their project. The first, to build a new town to help survivors adjust to the world as it had become and that was the part she saw; people coming and going, some remaining here permanently, others moving on. But we also use the town as a staging post for the young, those who God has brought to us for his will to be done.

"Tell me, which God?" Domani asked. "Because I'm confused. No God I've ever heard of would want the young and innocent to be forced to fall pregnant, and by a complete stranger."

Domani saw a flash of irritation on Pati am's face, before she quickly regained her composure.

"Well, let's start with our God, shall we? The God we serve is not an old God. Our God is of no religion, for we believe the old religions were instrumental in forcing thousands of years of untold misery on generations of people across the whole planet.

Our God has no hidden motives, does not demand to be put on show or worshipped in buildings full of gold by servants dressed in the most stunning fineries ever made.

Our God has shown us the way to move on from the old domineering religions, those based on control, guilt and the terror of our ultimate death. As you have witnessed, we believe in the positive, peaceful, caring and innate love humans have for each other and we have incorporated these into our daily lives.

But, make no mistake Domani, our God would never have been acknowledged by the fanatical, bigoted, self-indulgent, control obsessed religious leaders of the past."

*   *   *

Domani told Horatio she was left speechless, but had to admit Pati am had summed up, in a few words, one of the most complex and destructive essentials of human behaviour; the need to believe in something, and it had been a curse on all people since the beginning of time.

However, she hadn't answered her question, but before she could remind her, Pati am said,

"Now, to go on, and please, let me stress, what I am about to tell you is not known within the town. There are rumours and gossip, but the facts are only known to a handful of people in the community and I ask you to respect that confidentiality."

Domani nodded for the umpteenth time, beginning to realise how important she had become to them.

"The second strand of our mission concerns the restocking of the world."

Pati am Aminata stopped for a second; it was as if she was weighing-up how much detail to go into. Then without hesitating she continued,

"Early on we made a decision not to put a low age limit on sexual activity likely to result in pregnancy. After all, that is a major component of our mission. However, we were extremely conscious of not wanting to frighten young girls with sex or childbirth, if that happened it might set us back years, something we couldn't afford.

Some distance from here, we located another farm, ideal for what was needed and all the boys and young men were taken there.

Please believe it is a joyous place. All those involved have chosen to accept what God requires of them and they are housed in comfort and well fed. We have nurses, two doctors and two mid-wives; all experienced and every birth takes place in a specialist medical centre. When I say specialist, of course, that is relative to the situation we face. Nevertheless, I doubt any women currently has such expert attention when she gives birth. And please believe me, they have a choice."

"So what happens if they don't want to take part?" Domani asked, thinking of Sylvia.

"Well, if we feel they could be valuable here in town, we return them and give them specific jobs on the farm or in the fields; we do need to provide a large amount of food for both communities. By the way, Kadiatou is one of our returnees."

Domani was surprised, however, the more she thought about it, the more obvious it was and she asked,

"And if they are not sufficiently valuable to the project without producing babies, what happens to them then?"

"I'm sorry to say, they become a casualty of survival."

"Okay, but what happens to them?" Domani repeated.

"We do all we can for them. We take them far away, but they are provided with food, clothes and other essentials, but then left to their own devices."

"How many of my girls have not chosen to be part of the project."

"From your first class, only one and of the two that have recently moved on, both have agreed to participate."

"And what happens to those who agree?"

363

"Well, you are a mother." For a second Domani thought Pati am was about to smile, but changed her mind. "Simply put… we pair them up with a male, attempting to find the best match and then, well… not wanting to be coarse, we let them get on with it."

"So how many babies have been born since you established the farm?"

"Initially, we had difficulties with girls conceiving. We never did discover why but the doctors felt it was most likely psychological not physical. However, those problems seem to have disappeared and I am delighted to say that over the last five years, one hundred and eighty-seven babies have been born healthy. The oldest is coming up to six and the progress being made is wonderful to witness. These are the children of the future, and it is them who will ensure the survival of the human race. "

"Boys and girls?"

"Of course."

"Then why are there no boys or come to that, men, here in town?"

Pati am Aminata did smile this time. It was as if she knew she was not going to get away with any detail of the project before the inquisition came to an end.

"I repeat, I only tell you this because you are extremely valuable to the community, it is our hope that very soon you will be willing to move to the third part of the project, again, that's for your ears only."

Domani nodded her agreement, rather than answering with a probable lie.

"Strange as it might sound, at the same time as I had a most revealing dream, so did Yumma Mary. Neither of us realised this until we began discussing the role of males in the project. When I explained what God had instructed me to do, Yumma Mary said she'd had an almost identical dream. We took this not as just a sign from God, but an indisputable command.

Experiences had taught us that by their very nature males are stronger, more violent and less forgiving than their female counterparts. You see, both of us had suffered terribly at the hands of angry, xenophobic, brutal men and therefore, for us, God's word was above reproach."

*   *   *

Domani's incredulity erupted. How come she'd been married to the most wonderful human being for over fifteen years, and he was quite definitely a man? And furthermore, was she to believe her beloved son was some sort of monster, waiting for his manhood to arrive so he could abuse, molest or rape every female who crossed his path? How dare this narrow-minded woman suggest that all men were made the same, how dare she impose an edict keeping men and women apart, preventing them from forming loving and lasting relationships.

Before Domani could react, and in hindsight it proved a blessing, Pati am said with no hint of sarcasm,

"Always remember, the last five years have proved beyond doubt that women can do all things men can do, and, a good deal more competently and effectively. Until we can raise to adulthood sufficient numbers of boys in our image; in other words the complete opposite to traditional man, then we only need the male of the species to make babies."

*   *   *

Back in her room, Domani knew she had only just made it before saying or doing something that she would have regretted. As she lay on the bed breathing deeply to calm herself, she accepted her future was in the balance. Any negative reaction from her and she would never leave, and after what she had just heard that was the only thing that really mattered.

Nevertheless, as much as Domani hated to admit it, part of her agreed with some of what she had heard. She found Pati am Aminata's opinions on the 'old' religions credible and thought provoking, in many ways matching her own and felt their leader had a clear insight into the perils of omnipotence within any set of beliefs.

Pati am Aminata understood that evil would use exploitation to seize religious power and wickedness to grab absolute control through the manipulation and indoctrination of the less educated. These would then be secured by the crafting of an absolute reliance through superstition, underpinned by the weakness of people's innate fear of death.

In some ways, quite brilliantly, the project was built on a system of beliefs that was not based on any established religion, but every religion. It was so clever in its concept, the problem was in its practical interpretation.

Ultimately, there was no possible way Domani could or would accept any belief structure that forced sex on the innocent and upheld the compulsory segregation of the sexes.

*   *   *

The next day, after class, as Domani left the building Sylvia was waiting.

"We've been told," she whispered, "we'll be going away and I really don't want to."

"Are you sure?" Domani asked.

"What... of course I am."

"Okay, tell me as soon as you know when you're going."

And Domani walked away. She accepted that after her chat with Pati am she was probably being watched, but she still needed to find a means of leaving and taking Sylvia with her.

The following day, after class again Sylvia asked to speak with Domani.

This time, alone in the classroom, the young girl said angrily,

"Last night three of us were given our talk and I couldn't believe it when my closest friend walked in. I haven't seen her for months as she was taken from your first class. Her name was Juliette and she really liked you."

Domani remembered her as a delightful girl who was sorely missed.

"Well... she talked about how wonderful moving on would be and how privileged we were to be selected to do God's work. Then, when it was over and she was being led out by Yumma Mary, she hugged me and pushed this into my hand.

Sylvia passed a note to Domani but as she was about to open it Kadiatou walked in.

Domani instantly said harshly,

"Now, find the others and make up before the evening meal."

"What was that about?" Kadiatou asked once Sylvia had gone.

"Oh, silly really; just teenage girls being teenage girls."

"Did she tell you they were leaving soon?"

"She mentioned it, but I don't think that's the problem. She's being teased and I told her to sort it out before it becomes serious."

*   *   *

Domani went straight to her room and read the note.

'Whatever they say, do not believe them,' it said in spidery handwriting. 'It's too late for me, but not for you. Do not come here. I talked today because I'm the only one not pregnant. The boys; I've had three so far, are okay, but I feel sorry for them. They are fed, clothed and exercised,

367

but always locked up. They might have everything, even sex, but no freedom.

Please tell Miss Domani one of the girls overheard a nurse talking to a friend about her and she's coming to work with the original babies born here. The girl also said the people who went to Miss Domani's farm didn't actually go. They lied to her.'

*   *   *

Domani missed the evening meal claiming she was feeling under the weather; in reality she was trembling with rage and unable to think clearly.

Was it possible they had lied to her? If that was the case, they were more deceitful, more callous than any leader of the old religions, whom Pati am had judged so readily.

She had no idea how long she'd lived in the community; it really didn't matter. What did matter was that by lying, Domani had lost precious time when she could have been looking for her family.

*   *   *

"You know," Domani whispered to Horatio just after she'd checked on Sylvia who had called out in her sleep.

"I really thought the project could be incredible, an undertaking that would benefit the human race, but I realise they were just selfish, only interested in themselves, not a greater calling."

"How did you get away?" Horatio asked.

"The day after I skipped the evening meal, Sylvia spoke to me and said they were being taken the following afternoon so we had to go that night or not at all.

I told Sylvia to wear as many clothes as she could and only carry one easy to manage bag, and we'd meet behind the stables once everyone was asleep.

To get away, we needed a horse."

*   *   *

As she left the house, Domani thanked God it was a cloudy night, with rain in the air and although it would make travelling slower, rain would make tracking them more challenging.

She found Sylvia waiting and together they moved into the stable.

Although having only ridden twice since arriving in the community, both times with Kadiatou, Domani's familiarity with horses from a young age, meant she could saddle a horse and ride it with little difficulty.

Halfway along the stables she spotted a horse she recognised and deciding that was the one, they moved slowly toward it. As she quietly slid back the stable door bolt, from behind a dark corner Kadiatou emerged.

*   *   *

As Sylvia squealed and grabbed Domani's hand, Kadiatou said solemnly,

"I know what you're doing."

"So, what happens now?" she asked, moving Sylvia behind her.

"Is this what you really want?" Kadiatou probed.

"What would you do if you had been lied to about your family being alive?"

"Who told you?"

"It doesn't matter, what matters is the lie, and you must have known."

"I didn't, not until two days ago. You have my word on that. Now we must go,"

"We!"

Domani couldn't believe it but didn't care; they might actually get away. Kadiatou then led them outside into

369

heavy rain where two horses were already saddled up and ready to go.

*   *   *

They had been riding at speed for at least an hour with Kadiatou leading, Domani and Sylvia on the same mount, when Kadiatou pulled up and dismounted.

"We must give the horses a break," she said.

As they led their horses, walking side by side, all three drenched from the heavy rain, Domani turned and hoping Sylvia would not hear, asked,

"You really expect me to believe you knew nothing?"

"Yes, because it's the truth. I admit I was told to watch you so they would never have told me the truth just in case we ended up as friends. You see, that's how the leaders think."

They walked in silence for a while before Kadiatou said with a tired smile,

"And I do."

"Do what?" Domani asked, puzzled.

"Like you."

*   *   *

With the rain easing they remounted and kept riding until they saw the first sign of dawn breaking, then Kadiatou stopped and suggested they have something to eat.

Guiltily, Domani realised she'd had no time to think about food and again it was Kadiatou who appeared to have planned for every eventuality.

They ate cold but nourishing food and rested the horses before continuing, but within just a few minutes Domani's horse slipped on a steep incline covered in treacherous mud.

Domani and Kadiatou knew immediately the horse was lame.

They faced two serious difficulties: how to destroy the poor animal in front of Sylvia and how to carry on with just one horse.

The solution to both was obvious but Domani initially refused to accept it. In the end, Kadiatou said tersely,

"Enough talk. Both of you get on my horse and leave. Go now. Let me do what has to be done and I'll continue on foot."

As she walked towards the lame horse, she handed a machete over to Domani,

"You may need this," she said, and it was not until that moment that Domani realised how much Kadiatou had been a part of her life. From the time the three horsewomen found her walking alone, they had hardly missed a day when they did not see each other and Domani would never forget the help, care and company Kadiatou had given her. Yes, there had been issues, especially when the trust between them was being sorely tested, but Domani would never forget the huge debt she owed her friend.

"Anyway," she said to Horatio, "within just a few hours of leaving Kadiatou I was completely disorientated and had absolutely no idea of the direction we were heading. Then, totally by chance we came across the N.24 highway, a road I knew quite well. We were further north than I wanted to be so we walked south until we found the N.1 and met you.

—Ж—

Chapter 41

As dawn arrived Sylvia woke and began to play with Nelson. As tired as Domani and Horatio were after just a couple of hours sleep, neither wanted to put an end to Sylvia's laughter and as it was still raining he began to prepare some food.

"But you've already shared so much with us," Domani said, visibly uncomfortable with Horatio's generosity.

Paying no attention to her, he unpacked the last of his food, called Sylvia to join them, and they ate breakfast with Nelson perched behind his new friend, periodically shrieking at her. Horatio could have sworn he knew damned well it would make her laugh.

*   *   *

When the rain eventually stopped, Domani told Sylvia she could go outside so she ran out calling Nelson to follow her.

"What happened to your horse?" Horatio asked as he packed his things, wanting to get on.

"Nothing. He's over there, under that large tree chewing his breakfast." Domani giggled and Horatio couldn't believe after everything she'd been through, she still had a sense of humour.

Knowing Domani had the horse, Horatio suggested that if she wanted, they could travel to Mamou together. In the past he had tried not to be held back by people on foot, but with a horse, it would probably be him slowing them down.

Domani was clearly delighted to be continuing with a man and, in this case, his falcon.

"You know," she said cheerfully, "I would never have guessed I would end up spending a night in a bus with a complete stranger. I know it's dreadful to say but... I assumed you would rape me or God forbid Sylvia."

"What!" Horatio replied horrified.

"Sorry, that was unfair."

Domani looked dejectedly to where a laughing Sylvia was playing with a screeching Nelson.

"But, as I told you, I've been attacked so often, lost count of the number men who've raped me." She then smiled and said, "But you... you are so different and special. Thank you."

And she gave Horatio a hug.

*   *   *

A few minutes later they set off, Domani and Sylvia on the horse, Horatio pedalling next to them whilst Nelson flew low overhead.

It was a warm, still, sunny morning and he was relaxed and enjoying the ride. Steam was rising from the tarmac like a thick sea mist, and the smell of a fresh new day following torrential rain so reminded him of home.

Water ditches they saw had filled with rain water, some even overflowing onto the surrounding land and Horatio swore the plants and trees had perked up before his very eyes.

However, the one burial pit they came across brought reality back with a thump. It was full of water with burnt out human remains, some weirdly floating to the surface and Domani told Sylvia not to look.

*   *   *

Making surprisingly good progress, they arrived in the outskirts of Mamou mid-morning.

"Do you know of any short-cuts around the town?"

Domani explained there were none that she knew off, and that they needed to enter the town's centre to find their next road, the N.5.

"You had better lead me," Horatio suggested and as they travelled through what must have been a sizeable town, Domani excitedly pointed out various crumbling buildings; a car showroom, shopping mall, bank and high school.

Horatio watched for signs of residents, moved the shotgun to within easy reach and to Sylvia's delight, called to Nelson who landed with a thump before settling on the handlebars.

He then asked Domani what the population of the town had been before the virus and she told him she thought about eighty thousand, again leaving him mystified by the lack of people.

"Don't you find it bizarre that the place is empty?" he asked.

"Bizarre no," Domani answered, looking around. "Sad, scary, cruel; the definitions are endless. I can't believe what had been a dynamic, welcoming town… is now… well, dead."

They stopped at the junction with the N.1 and as they turned left onto the N.5, a somewhat subdued Horatio grasped that he had been on the N.1 for over two hundred and fifty kilometres. The problem was he still had just under the same distance to go to get to Labe, followed by the same, yet again, to get to Koundara.

All his efforts were just a drop in the ocean compared to the total distance he had to cover to get home and Horatio felt like he was treading water.

*   *   *

Within a few minutes of joining the N.5, they left Mamou not having seen a soul and Horatio noticed, since the initial excitement of arriving in town, Domani had said nothing.

Of course he understood; how could he not? They had seen no survivors out of a population of eighty thousand, what hope was there that her family were still alive?

Feeling Domani's trepidation at what lay ahead, Horatio suggested that if it would help, once they were at her farm he would stay with her to make sure it was safe.

*   *   *

As they moved ever closer to the farm, Horatio noted how fertile the land had become. Both sides of the highway were covered by extensive woods, unkempt fields or orchards with trees planted in formation. They passed a few abandoned buildings, probably farm houses, most having become sad ruins of what they had once been. None of their previous occupants appeared to be still living off the land.

*   *   *

"There it is," Domani called to him, and pointed to her left where Horatio saw the tops of buildings seemingly encircled by tall trees.

She immediately pulled off the road onto an overgrown track, nearly throwing Sylvia in her excitement and galloped through trees towards a group of seven buildings about fifty metres in from the highway.

Horatio was left well behind, but even in his haste to catch up, he saw that at one time the land must have been an idyllic place to set up home.

As he reached the largest of the buildings, he saw Domani had dismounted and was helping Sylvia down from the horse.

Grabbing the shotgun before leaving the bike and cart, Horatio called Nelson on to the arm protector and moved towards Domani. However, she immediately held up a closed fist as a warning to stop. With a long-handled machete in one hand and visibly tense, she whispered,

"Somebody's here."

"Are you sure?"

"I saw a head, in one of the upstairs rooms."

"Okay, stay here with Sylvia. I'll go."

"We go together."

"No… for Sylvia."

Domani hesitated but accepting Horatio was right, told him to go to the rear of the farm house where a door led into the kitchen.

As Horatio crouched and moved away, an agitated Nelson flew off and circled overhead.

*　　*　　*

Opening the door noiselessly, Horatio found the kitchen was a large family space, but as he walked into the room, there was a noise from above. Someone was moving around.

Taking a deep breath, with the shotgun raised Horatio moved hesitantly towards a flight of stairs straight ahead.

Entering a small hall running from the front door, absurdly, all he could hear was the pounding of his heart and ticking of a wind-up kitchen clock.

Dismissing the distraction, Horatio turned to climb the stairs, looked up and came face to face with a young woman. She was glaring at him menacingly, whilst holding a long wicked looking knife aimed at his midriff.

"The gun is loaded," he said, slowly and in French.

The woman looked at the shotgun, then her knife, smiled and replied also in French,

"That settles that," and she lowered the knife and handed it to Horatio handle first.

As he reached for the knife, Horatio heard someone crossing the kitchen and a shout,

"Horatio, no! It's Kadiatou." And he saw for the first time the daring woman who had played such an important part in Domani and Sylvia's escape from the community.

*   *   *

Once the confusion had calmed and introductions had been made, Kadiatou explained that she felt the farm was still being used and suggested they search the immediate area.

With Domani she began with three outbuildings located to one side of the farm house, whilst Horatio, Sylvia and Nelson were asked to look at another three just behind the house.

Having searched two of the buildings which Horatio thought were more like large sheds or barns, as Sylvia was asking about Nelson and how he had raised him, there was the sound of a baby crying coming from inside the final building.

"Go find the others," he instructed Sylvia. "Tell them to come at once."

Releasing Nelson who headed for a nearby tree, Horatio approached the only door. Sliding it open, he was immediately hit by the most appalling stench coming from piles of putrefied vegetables towards the back wall of the large room. Trying to ignore the foul smell, Horatio stood still and waited, eventually hearing the faintest of noises. He said quietly in French,

"Don't be afraid."

There was another rustling sound from a different direction.

"Please come out. I'll not hurt you."

Horatio heard a frantic 'shush', followed by the piercing cry of a baby.

"Please… let me help you," he called out again.

Then, at last, he saw a movement from behind the piles of rotten crops and a young girl slowly emerged holding a small bundle.

As he was about to approach her, Domani, Kadiatou and Sylvia ran into the shed, coming to an immediate halt.

The girl with the baby stared at Domani. Domani stared at the girl.

"Anjuwa! My God, is it you?"

"Mama!"

*   *   *

Carrying the baby, arm in arm with her daughter, Domani led the way back to the house.

Sat around the large kitchen table, with Nelson perched on Horatio's shoulder cooing as Sylvia stroked him, they drank the refreshingly cool water Kadiatou had poured for everyone.

"Daddy died when the virus was at its worst, "Anjuwa said tearfully, "and when people heard, they came to take his body away. They told us they were burning all the dead and we had to give them his body but we refused. Anyway, we had already buried him in the woods and refused to tell them where he was."

There was a short pause; Anjuwa was clearly struggling.

"Mummy, just a few days later, little Alex died."

A shocked silence fell over the room as Domani hugged her daughter; both were in floods of tears and as the others looked on, how could they not be overwhelmed?

"One day he was fine, the next he was ill, the next… he was dead."

More tears, more despair.

"I buried him next to Pappy so they could be together."

"Eunice didn't understand what was happening and I was so afraid but I did all I could for her. I tried my best and… waited for you to come back."

Anjuwa took her mother's hand and said coldly,

"You didn't come."

Domani's guilt was palpable, but what could she say? No one who knew her would ever have blamed Domani for not being home when her family needed her the most but...

"A couple of months later," Anjuwa continued unemotionally. "Eunice became sick and I was so angry. The sickness was supposed to have finished, but my little sister, the last of my family, died."

There were more tears, they were all, including Horatio, at breaking point.

"No one was there. Everyone I knew had gone, and I had to watch Eunice die. I was eleven, how was I expected to bury my entire family?"

The room was heavy with anguish, guilt and a million other emotions, but Anjuwa was not about to stop.

"Where were you?" she asked, staring at her mother; the accusation was heart breaking, "Where were you when I needed you, tell me... please... why weren't you here for me?"

*　　　*　　　*

How could there be an answer? How could the actions and/or reactions of those caught up in the apocalypse be rationalised or defended? Survival might have been arbitrary, but the desire to live, the resolve to carry on... that was so much more personal.

Domani had spoken about how there had been so many occasions when she wanted to give up, when she was desperate to end it all, yet she had never given in to such insanity whilst she still had family to live for. But, even so, how could she ever justify her absence to her only surviving child?

As Horatio sat listening to the appalling wretchedness brought on by the death of loved ones, he saw it as one more catastrophic illustration of how the virus had crushed so many lives, slaughtered so many communities and shredded so many families.

And he acknowledged there would never be a plausible reason behind it, because to arrive at that level of understanding there would have to be a rational explanation as to how a common, well-understood illness managed to rip the heart out of the entire human race; and it was far, far too late for that.

Chapter 42

Horatio was taken aback by Anjuwa's reaction to Domani. However, during the late afternoon he overheard them talking in one of the bedrooms, and as they were sat around the kitchen table eating a delicious meal Anjuwa had prepared from ingredients she'd grown, mother and daughter sat together, repeatedly hugging and holding hands.

When the discussion turned to Kadiatou arriving at the farm, she explained she had been searching the house when everybody arrived.

Domani then asked how she had managed to get away from the search party on foot and Kadiatou described what had happened.

"About an hour after you left me, I spotted a group on horseback and recognised the riders. It was clear they were searching for us, so for the next couple of hours I led them in the opposite direction to the one you'd taken."

This was said modestly, but all listening knew that without Kadiatou, Domani and Sylvia would have been caught and taken back to the community.

"At one time I thought about stealing a horse," she continued, "but I decided it wasn't worth the risk and knowing, with all the rain, I had little chance of picking up your trail, I walked until I found the N.1 just north of Mambiya.

I kept to the highway, getting soaked in that horrendous storm, until I came across this really odd family, just outside the village of Ouâkâ."

"An old woman with three... I suppose, daughters?" Horatio asked remembering his encounter with the family.

"Yea. Anyway, as soon as I approached the house, they were all over me, offering me dry clothing, food and a bed for the night. I thought they just wanted information on what was happening in the outside world, but as I wanted to get here, I told them I couldn't stop." She looked at Domani before adding," and thank goodness I did."

"I don't understand?" Sylvia said.

Horatio was intrigued by the strange family as Kadiatou explained.

"Well… a little further on I came across what had been a large shop, probably a supermarket and there was a local girl heading in the opposite direction. We talked and she asked whether I had passed the four women. When I said I had, she told me they were well known for delaying passers-by and then stealing from them. She told me there was even talk about them murdering some of those who resisted and before we parted she asked me to warn others I came across."

Horatio was shocked and not for the first time. He realised how close he'd come to a serious problem and said,

"I was stopped by them and must admit, the offer of food was tempting, but… I don't know, they were weird, especially the old woman, so I carried on."

"Looks like we were both lucky then," Kadiatou said.

*   *   *

The next day, Horatio, with Nelson on the shoulder pad, discovered a dam about five hundred metres from the farm and a good distance in from the highway. He thought it must be where Kadiatou had found the drinking water but also understood how such a sizeable lake could help the family make working the farm a worthwhile venture.

Over breakfast, when Anjuwa was still in her bedroom getting the baby ready for the day, Domani told them that the baby's father was called Uche, short for Uchecchukwa. He had been told farm machinery and equipment was still lying around, left by local farmers when they tried to escape the sickness. Four days earlier he had left in search of things they could use.

Anjuwa had told her mother they found each other about a year after Eugene had died. She described how it was at a time when they were both as lonely and desperate as each other and in need of someone to trust. Initially the situation they found themselves in might have thrown them together but they quickly became good friends, then lovers and finally parents.

*   *   *

For the next few days, early each morning, Horatio worked the fields which were all adjacent to the lake, helping prepare the soil for planting. Then after a mid-morning snack, he went hunting with Kadiatou.

It was her suggestion that he join her, and Horatio was quick to recognise how foolish he'd have been to turn down the opportunity to hunt with someone who knew exactly what they were doing. Within a couple of hours, it was evident to him that Kadiatou was a superb hunter and as he studied her locating, trapping, killing and then skinning prey, he realised how utterly lacking he was in the skills required to be successful.

On what became their daily outings, she taught him how to identify tracks and hunt down targets. She then explained in detail how to build effective traps and how to kill, skin and prepare an animal for the 'pot'.

On the third day together, Horatio mentioned the spear guns and Kadiatou was genuinely intrigued by the weapon, never having come across one before. After some discussion she wanted to experiment to see if it was possible to hunt with it and spent the following day working on various methods of using it within a trap. Come evening, Horatio had three very different but practical designs to try out.

*   *   *

On one occasion when they were out, Kadiatou found a herd of white, large-horned cattle and rounded them up before driving them to the farm and securing them in pens. She told Horatio that historically the cows had been domesticated, but generations of being free following the virus, had left them running wild, unprotected and vulnerable. She explained that she wanted to establish a healthy herd to leave for Domani when she finally moved on.

*   *   *

As a result of their hunting, although Horatio accepted it had very little to do with him, the evening meals were not only delicious but wholesome and even he had to admit that within a couple of days he felt healthier. By ignoring Maya's advice, he had been eating a pretty unhealthy diet but was determined to improve it once he moved on from the farm.

Predictably many of their mealtime discussions were about the riverside community and as Kadiatou had been in a position of trust, the questions were usually directed at her.

On one occasion Domani said,

"Pati am told me that the males were locked away because they couldn't be trusted."

"That's what we were told. Because they're stronger, you know, more physical, and, well... more comfortable using violence." She looked at Horatio before adding with a smile, "Not all men, of course, but the leaders had a point. They believed it was inevitable that if the men were free, they would challenge their leadership and the right of women to decide the future of the community."

As the only man around the table, Horatio decided it might be wise to just sit quietly.

"Undoubtedly some of the men would," Domani offered.

"True, but the strategy is flawed," Kadiatou proposed. "Firstly, you can't have babies without men making the girls pregnant, and secondly, the girls need to agree. I know for a fact that many of the women on the register to be paired up, were adamant they would not go with men if they didn't want to. Equally, I spoke to men who were so angry about being used, they were going to refuse to have sex with the girls; something the leaders had never considered. To them men were all the same and would never turn down sex with any female."

Unexpectedly, it was Sylvia who then spoke.

"I suppose if you keep wild animals locked up, you know, controlling their every move, eventually they will fight back. Isn't it just the same for those poor boys?"

"Absolutely," Domani answered, "but remember, defying your government or leaders is hardly new and often provokes extremely violent responses. Pre-virus there were endless conflicts originating from serious dissatisfaction such as terrorism, the murder rate in The States; the wars being fought."

Kadiatou nodded and said,

"Isn't it interesting though that over the last… say fifty years, women have become just as brutal as any man. For me, it's as if they're saying 'we are better and far more effective than men, whatever we're doing, and if that includes the use of violence, so be it."

"Horatio?" Domani asked looking at him,

"Well… for me…" he began quite perceptively for someone of his age, "it's not so much what women want, but what they are capable of. Each sex has its assets and its flaws, and accepting this, might be a sensible starting point in the world in which we now find ourselves. But…" he continued solemnly, "there is a much greater problem facing us all. Surely, it doesn't take a genius to see that from time immemorial, there have always been liars, thieves, those who live only to control others, even killers, and for all these people, the cost of their actions in terms of human misery is irrelevant.

In this new world, as in the old, there will be a minority of men and women who are vicious and domineering. They are the people who crave power and control over those incapable of resisting them. A few will be crazy, deranged, mad; use any words you want, but let's not fool ourselves, people like this are even now seizing what's left of the human race for their own selfish needs. Like it or not, it is up to the silent majority, those who are peaceful, compassionate, self-sacrificing, committed to others… to squash the ambitions of the destructive minority."

Those around the table sat staring at Horatio were left speechless.

*   *   *

On Horatio's eighth day at the farm, Uche returned and as soon as they met, Horatio knew the family would be in safe hands. Even allowing for Kadiatou and her skills, without a man to fight for them, Horatio had been reluctant to leave the family on their own.

However, Uche seemed honest, friendly and most importantly, devoted to Anjuwa.

This left Horatio to plan his departure and that same afternoon he oiled and overhauled the bike, cart, shotgun and spear guns and following their meal, he told the group he would be leaving the next morning. He then left the table and went to his room to pack.

As he was tidying up, there was a knock on the door and Kadiatou asked if she could have a word. Horatio invited her in and as they sat together on the bed, she asked about his plans.

He explained he was heading for Gambia and from there, would try to find a boat to sail to his home and family in England.

"Well, you never know," Kadiatou said standing, "we might meet again in the future," and she gave him a hug and a kiss on the cheek.

Lying in bed thinking, Horatio realised how much he adored his short time on the farm. Being outside most of the day, working the fields and then hunting; it was a routine he could quite happily adopt, but sadly, it was never as simple as that.

He continued to miss his family desperately, the heartache of the loss never leaving him and as wonderful as it was to witness Domani and Anjuwa's joyous reunion, it deepened his own feeling of helplessness. Horatio was desperate for the love of those who were once irreplaceable to him.

*　　*　　*

An early breakfast the next day was a subdued affair. No one wanted Horatio to leave but all understood his reasons for going. Domani especially, knew it had only been her determination to see her family again that had kept her alive, and she absolutely understood Horatio's decision. As sad as she was to see him go, she made sure he had everything he needed including as much food and fresh water as he could carry.

Chapter 43

Horatio remembered Kadijah telling him that once he left Mamou, he would face the most demanding part of his journey. He would have some steep climbs to negotiate before traversing the Fouta Djallon region; a total of a hundred and thirty kilometres.

Not for the first time, a revitalised Horatio realised how fortunate he'd been to meet Domani and decided if there really was a God, he would ask that Sylvia, Kadiatou, Uche, Domani and her family were kept safe and out of harm's way.

He needed no convincing that if they were free to go about their lives without unwelcome attention, they would work all hours to build a beautiful home and productive farm.

His one concern was Kadiatou. He would miss her and their hunting trips, but worried that by working hard to help make the farm a success, she was repaying a debt.

Horatio knew she regretted her work with the community and the way she had treated those held there against their will. His worry was that she should never forget she had her own life to live, beholden to no one. As with all survivors, Kadiatou owed nobody a single thing; regardless of the unpleasant duties she may have undertaken on behalf of the leaders. She had walked away and wiped her slate clean, it was time for her to live the way she wanted.

Didn't every living person have regrets, guilt or remorse about unbearable, yet avoidable decisions they had made during the sickness? Wasn't the ability to make those decisions the crux of survival?

*   *   *

With Nelson perched on the cart and pedalling unhurriedly in an attempt to conserve energy, Horatio climbed ever higher. The map told him that fifty kilometres ahead was Dalaba, at just under two thousand metres above sea level, the highest town in Guinea, and he just hoped from then onwards, his journey would become easier.

He remembered talking with Domani after breakfast the previous day, when she had explained that he would only begin to descend once he was well past Labe, the largest town in the region. She also told him that because they were so high it might be difficult to find fresh drinking water so should conserve what he had.

"That doesn't mean there's no fresh water; it's just that you might have to leave the highway to find it; something I know you would rather avoid."

Horatio knew from reading the books that the average height of the Fouta Djallon was nine hundred metres and was thankful he would avoid Mount Loure, the highest point at over a thousand five hundred metres. He also knew he would feel a drop in the temperature and that on average it should be thirty degrees centigrade during the day, falling to fifteen at night.

*   *   *

The formidable landscape he travelled through consisted primarily of spectacular views across grasslands, interspersed with inhospitable granite rock jutting up towards the heavens and Horatio supposed the plateaus, jungle canyons and valleys dominating the vista had been shaped by erosion from rain and rivers over millions of years.

Arriving at Bouliwel at midday and pushing straight on, it was with relief that a weary Horatio finally entered the town of Dalaba.

He spotted the once majestic mosque which Kadijah said he should look out for and Domani had said he should try to visit. Disappointingly though, as Horatio moved closer, he could see only two of the four minarets of the original building still standing, and even those were crumbling, so he decided to just keep going.

He also read that a few of the original colonial buildings in the town still stood, but there was no sign of them. Built by the French, who were attracted to the region by the spring-like climate, the magnificent views of the lowlands and the stunning walks, Domani had described Dalaba as the most enchanting town in the entire country; although in truth he found it impossible to agree. To him, like so many of the 'old world' towns he'd come across, it was an empty, abandoned, lifeless pile of bricks and mortar, reflecting little of any illustrious past.

Although he noticed a lake to his right, Horatio decided not to stop. He still had most of the water he'd taken from the farm and was hoping he could reach as far as Bomboli before making camp.

*   *   *

Pedalling through the abandoned village of Mitty, Horatio covered the fifteen kilometres to the village of Bomboli in surprisingly good time. Exiting the village, he saw woodlands on both sides so pulled off the highway and almost immediately found an ideal spot to make camp. It was a small, flattened piece of land surrounded by trees and hidden from the main road.

In the remaining daylight, with Nelson perched on a low branch in a nearby tree, Horatio erected his tent and lit a fire; the night time temperature was proving significantly colder than he was used to.

Deciding to follow up on his promise to eat more healthily, he left the camp to hunt for his evening meal. However, returning empty handed some considerable time later, having failed to see any prey let alone kill it, Horatio had to make do with the cold food that had been packed for him by Domani.

Finally, by the light of the flames, he completed his journal and read up on the region he was travelling through. He found one article particularly thought-provoking as it described how farmers in Guinea were struggling to grow crops due to poor quality soil and was left wondering whether this would affect availability of the fruits and vegetables he regularly collected. Ultimately, he may have no option but to hunt for a good deal of his food.

*　　*　　*

Horatio slept well that night and put this down to cooler temperatures and sleeping under canvas; something he had rarely done since originally setting out on his journey.

Feeling upbeat about the day ahead, once he had eaten and packed his things, with Nelson on the handlebars, Horatio set off just after sunrise.

In almost perfect weather, he hoped to make the ten kilometres to Pita without difficulty, but Nelson was not his normal self and Horatio wondered whether he was ill or maybe missing Sylvia.

*　　*　　*

As always when arriving in a built up area, Horatio checked the shotgun and spear gun were loaded and within easy reach. He moved Nelson onto his shoulder and was pleased to see he was in better spirits.

Entering the outskirts of Pita, Horatio saw little to inspire him. The town, once home to over fifteen thousand people, was clearly abandoned and felt void of any recent human influence.

Following the N.5 at a measured speed, he saw shops in various states of collapse, a couple of petrol stations and what looked like a variety of commercial buildings and assumed he'd arrived in the central district of the city.

Ignoring the E ring road, a further sign Pita must have had a congested centre in its former life, he noticed a mosque on his right and as Horatio drew level with the less than impressive religious building, the highway took a sharp turn to the left. Negotiating the bend, not really taking that much interest and going much faster than he should, Horatio couldn't believe it when directly ahead, there was a line of people crossing the road. Nelson, realising there was a problem, flew off the shoulder pad and left Horatio to control the bike.

Hoping his rarely used brakes would slow him down, Horatio thought there must be at least twenty people, all of whom scattered when they saw him bearing down on them.

He then watched disbelievingly as the woman who'd been at the front of the line moved to the middle of the highway and held up her hand. With a pounding heart, Horatio screeched to a halt merely a metre away from her.

"I am so sorry," a breathless Horatio said in French, hoping she would understand.

Realising he was embarrassed by his reckless riding, she laughed and said kindly,

"It is unusual to meet anybody these days, let alone a cyclist on the Tour de France."

Feeling mortified that he had created such mayhem, but realising she was teasing him, Horatio also laughed and apologised again.

The woman then turned and called the others in a language he did not understand, and he watched as they regrouped in their original line.

"We are going to the mosque;" she then said. "If you wait, we would like to invite you to share food with us."

Yet again Horatio was taken aback by the generosity of survivors. They had no idea who he was, he'd just come very close to running them over, yet they wanted him to join them for a meal. For all they knew he could be a mad man running wild.

"Thank you, that is so kind, but I need to get on," he answered genuinely touched.

"Where are you going?"

Horatio laughed and said,

"Would you believe England?"

"No, I wouldn't, but there again, I stopped trying to work out the way of people in this crazy, mixed up world, a long time ago. We are still here though and blessed to have been favoured with life, so we must work hard for each other, follow our faith, and be generous to all. So… good luck and may your God go with you."

*　　*　　*

Horatio waited as the group moved towards the mosque, disappointed he couldn't take up their offer, but if he kept going he could cover the thirty kilometres to Labé before nightfall. Horatio had no idea what to expect at Labé; he had read that before the sickness, it had been the principal city and administrative capital of the Fouta Djallon region and Guinea's second largest city with a population of well over two-hundred thousand people.

It had also been second only to the capital Conakry in terms of economic importance; leaving Horatio to assume survivors would be there. The question though was whether they would be welcoming or dangerous.

On the plus side, he had spotted a short cut on the map which would allow him to avoid the city centre. He would need to cycle through the outskirts, which were mostly residential and then negotiate an unmade road northwards, rejoining the N.5 as it exited Labé.

Horatio distinctly remembered Kadijah's warning about leaving the highway, but avoiding the city centre was important, especially if there were survivors and they proved difficult.

*　　*　　*

Just before entering Labé, Horatio stopped at a river to fill his water bottles and wash and wondered whether it might be one of the numerous tributaries of the River Gambia, one of the great waterways in Africa. Setting off again, fortified after a bath in the chilly mountain water, with Nelson circling overhead, Horatio arrived in the suburbs and was promptly fascinated by the road system.

On both sides of the highway, plots of land were divided by mud tracks, each a hundred metres square with one or more houses and gardens, many with mature trees and bushes. All were overgrown and overrun with weeds which led Horatio to think there were no people around.

Referring to the map, as he arrived at the fourth junction, he saw a derelict restaurant on his left and a homeware store on his right. It was the turn off he needed.

Calling Nelson to him, Horatio turned left and cycled along a dusty, red clay track, quickly deciding it would probably be easier to walk and push the bike and cart.

The map informed him that he needed to cross twelve junctions before rejoining the N.5 and as he passed the third junction, he saw a substantial single storey house on the right, with land on the far side. The garden was well kept and the glass in the windowpanes unbroken; something he'd rarely ever come across.

Drawing level with the front door which was ajar, he noticed the inside looked lived in. Horatio let Nelson take to the wing, before checking his weapons were at hand and walking on guardedly. He found an old man sitting in a threadbare armchair with a small stall next to him. As Horatio approached he asked,

"Do you want food for Christmas Day?" Speaking in French, he must have decided Horatio was neither Muslim nor local.

394

As Nelson landed on the branch of a nearby tree, Horatio left the bike and cart and walked towards the stall where various fruits and vegetables were on display.

"Christmas Day?" he asked, confused.

"You're a Christian aren't you, and you don't know?" The man chuckled, teasing his visitor.

"I'm not really sure of anything anymore," Horatio said.

"That's hardly surprising. So, where are you from?"

"England. I'm trying to get home."

"Then you've a very long way to go." Again the man smiled.

"How do you know it's the twenty-fifth of December, are you a Christian?"

"No, I'm a Muslim. Before the sickness Fouta Djallon was one of the most important areas for Islam, not only in Guinea but the whole of this part of Africa."

Horatio sensed the old man was quite well-educated; probably an old hand at dealing with life's ability to shock and confuse and he was immediately reminded of Kadijah.

"Anyway, once things had settled down, a woman at the mosque decided to draw up calendars for the future. It was ingenious as without them we'd never know what day, week or month it was and crucially, when to celebrate important Islamic dates."

Horatio decided that along with recording the experiences of the people he came across, he would start his own calendar on that very day: December 25th.

"So, do you want food?"

Horatio still had ample provisions from Domani, nonetheless, whatever was in some half-litre bottles looked tempting but he wanted to keep his valuables for something he really needed.

"It's home-made ginger beer. Do you like it?" the man asked,

"I've never had it."

The man passed a dented metal cup towards Horatio,

"Try it and don't worry; none of my drinks are alcoholic."

Horatio took a sip and instantly adored the sweet taste. "Well?"

"It's really good," Horatio said as the man stood and picked up three bottles from the shelf.

He then handed them to Horatio.

"Thank you, but… well, look, I'm sorry but..."

"Who's asking for anything?" the man interrupted laughing loudly,

As he retook his seat he said, "Tonight people will come here to buy food and my beer, so I need nothing from you. Accept it as my gift on Christmas Day to a fellow human being."

As a genuinely touched but embarrassed Horatio packed the bottles in the cart, he asked,

"How many people live around here?"

"Nowadays, with all the children being born, we have a couple of hundred."

"In all the places I've been, very few men survived the sickness."

"Same here. A handful of men and a few boys survived, but now there are probably fifty men and a couple of dozen boys."

A fascinated Horatio just had to ask the obvious.

"So… how does it work; hundreds of women and only a few men?"

The man smiled and said cheerfully,

"At first it was a bit awkward. The men were prepared to be flexible, you know, who they slept with, but that caused problems, especially for the couples where both survived. So now there are plenty of boys and girls being born and things look good."

To the surprise of the old gentleman, who evidently hadn't noticed the falcon, Horatio called Nelson back to his shoulder pad, thanked him again and headed for the N.5.

—Ж—

Chapter 44

As he departed Labé, Horatio had to agree with Kadijah's description that the landscape of high peaks and deep bottle green forests, interspersed with open plains of untouched splendour, were just simply stunning.

It was an image he'd never forget and each evening he documented the experience of travelling through the beautiful, yet relatively unknown Fouta Djallon in his log.

The first night, after speaking to the old man, he also began his calendar. It was the twenty-fifth of December, Christmas Day, perfect for making a start. However, no matter how hard he tried, he couldn't be exact about the year, although he was confident he was eighteen years of age.

As always, once he'd finished writing, Horatio made sure the notebooks were wrapped in plastic bags to protect them from rain, the humidity and any damage.

*   *   *

Twelve days later, having negotiated some extremely steep and severe bends on the way down from the heights, the terrain became far easier to negotiate. The high peaks flattened out, the entire region was just seventy metres above sea level, whilst the scenery turned to a mixture of barren scrubland, broken up by dark exposed rocks with the occasional wooded area. The impressive highlands may have remained on his right, but the immediate area surrounding him was most uninviting.

*   *   *

Horatio knew from the books that it would get hotter as he dropped down from the Fouta Djallon, nonetheless, the return to the daytime heat still took him by surprise. Daytime temperatures would rise up to the mid-thirties whilst at night they would fall to fifteen degrees. The other factor was that there was unlikely to be rain, and Horatio remembered Kadijah telling him that in December the rivers would dry to solid mud, and he should always safeguard what water he had.

*　　　*　　　*

What had been an uneventful journey once he had descended from the highlands, changed on the evening of the twelfth night out from Labé.

Nelson was perched on the handlebars, having spent most of the day circling overhead, and as it was getting late, Horatio slowed to find somewhere to camp.

Suddenly, from the trees on his right, there was a booming, threatening growl and Horatio knew it had to be a large cat, probably a lion.

Nelson took off screeching and began circling high over the trees, whilst Horatio increased his speed, desperate to put as much distance between himself and whatever it was.

Moments later as he turned to look for Nelson, he caught a fleeting glance of him about half a kilometre away and worryingly, he was shrieking noisily as he dive-bombed the ground.

Understanding he shouldn't draw attention to himself, every emotion in Horatio's body was ordering him to go back, but what the hell could he do to help?

Terrified or not, he would not desert his friend and he slowed the bike, turned around, grabbed the loaded shotgun and headed back in the direction he'd just come from.

A few seconds later, as he was building speed, Nelson landed on his shoulder pad and immediately began to… well… Horatio was not sure how to describe it, but for the next twenty minutes his agitated friend cawed endlessly at him.

*   *   *

Cycling until it was almost dark, Horatio hoped they were a safe distance from the big cat.

Finding a suitable camp site, he put up the tent, gathered wood and lit a fire as a further deterrent. After eating a cold meal, washed down with ginger beer from the rather odd, but incredibly kind man in Labé, he completed his calendar and journal.

Thinking through what had happened, Horatio wondered if he'd become complacent, too relaxed, and decided he needed to take more care and to be a good deal more vigilant. He knew he had no experience of dealing with most of the wildlife he would encounter, some of which could be extremely dangerous.

Calling goodnight to Nelson who was perched on a nearby tree branch, Horatio slept under canvas, something he had decided to do every night, just in case.

*   *   *

It took a further five days to reach Koundara and the journey proved disappointing. He arrived at the junction with the N.23 and a small, derelict group of houses, but still saw no human activity. There were sightings of various animals, but the cacophony of magical sounds that had engulfed him during so much of his travels had mostly died out, whilst the countryside was uninspiring and tedious.

Even Nelson appeared indifferent.

Horatio arrived at Koundara early in the morning after a dawn start. He'd read that the town had a pre-virus population of over thirty thousand while the local area had over one hundred and thirty thousand. Kadijah had described it as having been an important commercial hub and chief trading centre for cattle, chicken, rice, peanuts, millet and corn.

There was a hospital, airport and the meeting place of the N.5 and N.9, a highway running west into Guinea-Bissau and east to the town of Youkounkoun; also an important trading centre in its own right.

Horatio wondered whether because of the size of Koundara, there might be survivors, but after initially seeing houses mostly set well apart, interspersed with a few fields that had once been cultivated, he noticed only ramshackled, abandoned buildings. All were in ruins or collapsed. It looked to Horatio as if it had once been an extremely poor district.

Pedalling towards the centre of town, he saw a few commercial premises that had survived mostly intact, but no people, just a motley assortment of grubby looking cats and a few mongrel dogs, none of which paid him any attention.

Just a few hundred metres further on from the junction of the highways, Horatio was pleasantly surprised when he noticed the remnants of public gardens with literally dozens of well-established trees and the occasional bench. Although overgrown, he decided it must have been an idyllic sanctuary away from the hustle and bustle of a hectic town centre.

*   *   *

The northern outskirts of Koundara continued for about a kilometre and then buildings gave way to deserted fields overrun with wild plants and bushes.

As the tarmac remained in a reasonable condition, Horatio increased his speed, hoping to cover the forty kilometres to the border with Senegal by mid-day.

An hour later, with Nelson remaining overhead, he came to a ninety degree left turn in the road and slowing, heard a mélange of magical sounds: animals, birds, insects, all going about their daily lives. Their songs were so memorable from earlier, Horatio knew he was once more entering the tropical rainforest.

Shortly after, he decided to stop for a break and with Nelson perched on the low branch of a huge tree, he ate a cold snack and read about the local district. He discovered he was entering what had been defined as a critical region for conservation, the 'Badiar National Park' and was pleasantly surprised when he found an article explaining that in a world which had been committing environmental suicide for millennia, areas such as the one he was sat in had been established to offer a respite for endangered wildlife.

The Badiar National Park was attached to the much larger Niokolo-Koba National Park in Senegal and Horatio was thrilled when he realised he would have to cycle through both.

*   *   *

They had been established in ninety eighty-five, primarily to prevent man's plundering of endangered wildlife. Decades of uncontrolled poaching, had caused immeasurable environmental damage, bringing countless species to the edge of extinction.

Another of the articles described how the main landscape was principally wooded savanna and open forests with the Koulountou and Mitji being the main rivers. The Koulountou was one of the two main tributaries of the Gambia River and both were important during extremely high rain fall.

Horatio would not be travelling near to either river but would cross many other smaller tributaries, giving him access to a constant supply of fresh water.

He read one piece which described how the parks were home to many threatened species such as African elephants, monkeys including the western red colobus, baboons and the roan antelope, but Horatio frowned as he decided he wasn't quite so enthusiastic about other local species including various types of python, spotted hyenas and leopards; admitting though that it was their home and he was the intruder.

*   *   *

Judging he had just over twenty kilometres to the border between Guinea and Senegal, Horatio set off with Nelson in the air and crossed two small rivers, stopping at the second to fill his water containers and wash.

Map of
Senegal

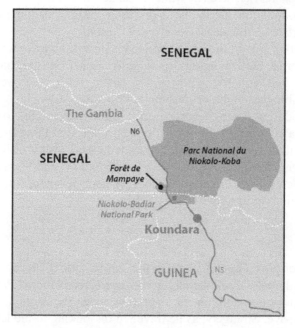

Chapter 45

With Nelson switching from perching on the cart or handlebars to flying overhead, Horatio avoided an ugly quarry, saw a dam with a substantial lake behind it, the occasional commercial property and a number of rivers. As mid-day approached he then came to a number of official looking buildings, some houses and shops, and numerous red clay tracks running in all directions from the highway.

Horatio assumed he'd arrived at the border post and this was confirmed when he cycled under a raised but damaged wooden barrier, a dirty white container with an extension built on the top, and a rusty sign stating in obvious order of importance, Alfândega, Douane and Customs.

Either side of the hand-operated, splintered barrier were two brick built buildings set slightly back from the road. Both had collapsed, corrugated metal roofs and were probably part of the official customs post.

Peddling on, there was an open shelter close to the road with a sign hanging from a roof beam, the first three lines of which were rusted and indecipherable. The fourth line though, identified the shack as 'Immigration' and Horatio wondered how effective the border controls would have been housed in a small, lean-to shed.

*   *   *

As soon as Horatio crossed the border into Senegal he knew he would see the larger Niokolo-Koba National Park on the right and on the opposite side, the Forest de Mampaye. Strangely, as he travelled on looking to the left, he could see very few trees, just river beds slicing through open savanna, intermixed with sparse scrubland; there was no sign of a forest.

Ahead there was a built up area on the left and Horatio decided it had been a Senegalese border town. In reality though, it was just a handful of dilapidated buildings, a derelict petrol station and large car park overrun with weeds and wild plants. It was another example of nature reclaiming yet another of man's once all conquering settlements.

Not wanting to stop, Horatio built up speed on the well preserved tarmac and with Nelson on the handlebars, the warm wind blowing his feathers against the grain, the pair gave the impression they were thoroughly enjoying life.

*   *   *

Horatio couldn't stop himself smiling when he saw the first signs they were entering what one article had called the riparian forest of the park. Kadijah had also used the term explaining that it defined a forested area next to a river, lake, marsh or estuary, adding that the Niokolo-Koba National Park had an abundance of waterways running through it.

However, inexplicably and shockingly, dozens of what must have been cultivated fields appeared on the left, where Horatio thought the Forest de Mampaye should have been. The fields were set back from the highway and cut into rectangles with buildings sitting in the centre of the huge expanses of deforestation.

Deciding it was a good time to eat, he found the magnificent sounds resonating from the forest on his right, were overshadowed by the extraordinary damage to his left. He could only suppose the government of the time had authorised locals to strip bare the neighbourhood, giving no thought to the long term harm being inflicted.

Why? Horatio asked himself, had it been so necessary to deforest regions critical to endangered species, rather than farming less ecologically important districts? The vista on his left merely emphasised the selfishness of the people prior to the sickness, and not for the first time, he had no answers.

*   *   *

After packing up, with Nelson back in the air, Horatio set off, and to his relief within a few hundred metres the vast farmlands on his left disappeared from sight, being replaced by a wall of forest.

Both sides of the highway were thick with trees and he adored the feeling of being wrapped up; virtually sealed off by Mother Nature. However, just a kilometre or so on, he spotted an overgrown track on his left and was quickly brought back down to earth; behind the narrow strip of forest, open farmland was again dominant; it truly was an eyesore.

Horatio sped up, pleased to be only a short distance from the next town, Kalifourou which he wanted to get through before making camp that night.

*   *   *

Nothing he'd read had given Horatio any information about Kalifourou and the only thing he could recall Kadijah telling him was about the upgrading of the thirty kilometres track to Medina Gonasse; it was the government's final project before the sickness arrived.

With forest continuing on his right, Horatio entered the built up area and saw a few buildings still standing and none intact. In fact, the only thing of note was that in the centre he crossed a junction with a second upgraded highway.

*   *   *

Almost immediately after Horatio exited Kalifourou, with Nelson perching on the cart, he picked up speed, wanting to keep moving for a few more hours before setting up camp.

Much to his delight, within no time forest again appeared on both sides of the highway. Unfortunately though, once again this was short lived as the trees on his left were replaced by overgrown fields which encroached to the very edge of the road.

Cycling at a decent speed, he was startled when for no reason Nelson suddenly squawked and left the cart, flying high into the air.

Knowing something must have spooked him, Horatio slowed to look for the falcon but could only make out a group of large birds circling just above the ground about fifty metres in from the highway.

Coming to a halt, he saw Nelson soaring high over the airborne scavengers and finding it impossible to ignore, decided to investigate. Finding his book on birds Horatio walked towards the commotion, identifying most of the birds as vultures.

Comparing their features and colouring with photographs in the book, he saw they were a mix of hooded vultures and Ruppell's griffons. He then noticed one he'd not seen before which the book named as a brown snake eagle; a bird of prey and one on the very edge of extinction.

Sat on a large stone, reading that at the time the book had gone to print, all three species he'd identified were in rapid decline due to poachers, farmers and especially shepherds. In Horatio's mind, no matter how justified, it again proved how much the human race had to answer for.

*   *   *

Nelson remained in the air, screeching, while Horatio moved closer, accepting he needed to be extremely careful. A few of the giant birds had landed on a carcass and it was clear they would protect their meal, if they felt threatened.

Inching slowly forwards, he stopped short of an unidentifiable, bloodied mass of skin and bones. However, before he could react, he heard and saw dozens of birds that had gathered near farm buildings. Intrigued, Horatio was frustrated that his view was blocked by bushes, so he crept towards the gathering, and realised something had been ensnared.

Arriving just a few metres from a large number of giant, agitated birds, an uneasy Horatio watched fascinated as they jostled each other in a weird kind of dance. He then noticed a few individuals, clearly the more audacious, move towards the rear wall of what looked like a farm outbuilding, however on every occasion as they managed to close in, they instantly leapt backwards or took flight.

Horatio's first thoughts were that it resembled a comical dance from a pantomime, but in reality it was anything but amusing. A huge mass of scavengers were after their next meal, and whatever the poor thing was, it was trapped and condemned.

Extremely conscious of the size and number of vultures but wanting to find out exactly what was being threatened, Horatio returned to the bike and collected the loaded shotgun.

*   *   *

As he made his way back towards the carcass, Nelson landed on the shoulder pad and as he closed in, he saw it was not one but three almost entirely devoured bodies; a female lion and her two cubs. Saddened by such magnificent beasts being torn to shreds, Horatio was also confused. All the reading he'd done described how lions in West Africa were on the verge of extinction, with only a handful still wandering in the wild.

He had heard the male a few days earlier, and the old woman and her daughters had told him there were a few lions still in the area, but even so, the chances of coming across a mother and cubs, even if dead, must have been extremely remote.

Turning away from the carcasses towards the abandoned farm buildings, Horatio raised the shotgun and walked slowly towards the frenzied gathering. Moving closer he saw the birds were focused on a small rectangular outbuilding with no roof and three undamaged walls. Quite evidently their next meal was inside the enclosure, and, with the predators waiting to strike, there was no chance of escape.

Not sure what he should do next, Horatio's instincts agreed with Kadijah's advice,

'Emotions aside, it is usually better to walk away and let nature take its course.'

But… and it was a huge but, what if the trapped prey was a third lion cub?

*   *   *

Deciding he could not walk away, Horatio guardedly advanced on the assembled flock but when Nelson took flight leaving him alone and surrounded, he promptly regretted his rashness.

Attempting to ignore the frightful racket Nelson was making from above, Horatio wavered when he saw that as one, the entire gathering of huge birds had turned and were glaring at him. Were they really warning him to keep away?

Struggling to contain his growing apprehension, Horatio couldn't quite believe it when, apart from Nelson's piercing shrieks, an unnerving silence fell over the gathering. Without any doubt, close up vultures were the most terrifying creatures he'd ever crossed and if he needed confirmation of the rapid collapse of the invincibility of humans and their supremacy over all of nature, these birds were it. They were in no way daunted or intimidated by his presence; on the contrary, they were setting the rules and the principal one was, do not go near our next meal.

*   *   *

In the end, Horatio reluctantly accepted he should walk away. The alternative was that he might have to shoot vultures, a species close to extinction and that was something he was not prepared to do.

As he was about to leave and in the silence of the moment whilst bird and man took stock, Horatio heard the faintest and most pitiful of cries. Never had he encountered a more pathetic, strangled whine. He had no idea what could have made it, except that it was a youngster.

He then heard Nelson squawk loudly from overhead and saw him diving before landing on top of the furthest of the three walls. He was perched directly over the vultures' quarry and Horatio was anxious the falcon could be torn to shreds if he got in the bird's way. He called to him but it had absolutely no effect, Nelson was going nowhere.

*   *   *

Horatio could wait no longer; he needed to act and so he fired into the air watching as the scavengers and hangers on took flight with a shrieking uproar. Dust and dirt showered the area and Horatio saw his chance, creeping into the windowless, three-sided pen.

Crossing the mud floor, in the far corner he spotted a clump of light brown, woolly fur and watched mesmerised as a tiny head with wide, black eyes appeared from within the bundle.

Horatio froze, but that was not all; the first face was followed by a second, and to his utter astonishment, a third; Horatio couldn't stop himself giggling like a demented fool.

"Oh, my word, lion cubs!" he said, completely captivated.

In unison the three orphans gawked at Horatio and began to hiss and screech in the same pathetic squeal he'd heard just moments before. Then, clearly panicked, they jostled to scramble up the vertical wall towards where Nelson was still perched over them.

Thinking they might hurt themselves, Horatio backed away.

*   *   *

Deciding to give them space to calm down, he sat at the entrance to the three-sided enclosure, leaned against the nearest wall and felt a mixture of awe and unease.

Watching Nelson, who hadn't moved an inch, Horatio accepted he faced a stark choice and one that he needed to make without delay. How on earth though, could he be detached when faced with not one, but three lion cubs with zero chance of survival without their mother?

All resolve to let events take their natural course vanished into thin air.

*   *   *

Ultimately, Horatio knew the decision was only as tough as he chose to make it.

If he left the cubs and continued his travels, they would suffer a quick, probably distressing death. If he attempted to take them with him, as feral lion cubs they would reject him and any help to the bitter end. Neither was a viable option.

And, there was Nelson. Quite evidently the falcon was ignoring Horatio and taking it upon himself to protect the orphaned cubs.

Initially, Horatio was shocked by this train of thought, yet the more he thought about it, the more he knew that it was not impossible for Nelson to act in such an unselfish manner.

—Ж—

Chapter 46

The first night after discovering the cubs, Nelson remained stubbornly perched over them, not even flying off to find food. His presence seemed to be keeping the vultures away and other predators, much to Horatio's relief.

After setting up camp at the open end of the three-walled enclosure and lighting a fire on the other side of the tent from the cubs, he poured fresh water into the billycan Maya had given him. He was certain without their mother's milk the cubs must be desperate for liquid and he crept as close as he dared before placing the pot on the ground.

Backing away, Horatio saw three faces staring at him from the bundle of fur, so he whispered to them in the same way he had with Nelson when he was a tiny chick.

Curiously, from above, Nelson began cooing and Horatio had to laugh; could he really have been joining in?

*   *   *

At the end of a quite remarkable day, Horatio ate a little food and settled down by the fire to sort out what he was going to do; but what exactly can you do with three defenceless feral lion cubs?

As had become his night time routine, Horatio wrote up his journal, unsurprisingly a rather lengthy entry and filled in his calendar for the day. He then first checked the area close by the tent and fire, made sure Nelson was comfortable before creeping close to the cubs, always whispering gently.

*   *   *

Early the following morning, Horatio read everything he could find about lions, which unfortunately amounted to very little in practical terms.

It did appear that the three orphans were more than likely Senegalese Lions, also known as West African Lions, and at the time the book went to print, there were only thought to be fifty left in Senegal.

He learnt that the weaning of lion cubs usually began at ten weeks, finishing by ten months, that they should be fully grown by three to four years old and by two years should be able to successfully hunt.

Of course, none of this helped Horatio with the actual age of the cubs. They were the size of a small family dog and as far as he could make out, that suggested they were between two and four months old.

Interestingly though, unlike domesticated cats, lions could not purr, which left him wondering how he would know they were relaxed and happy. This made Horatio laugh out loud as he knew he was being crazily anthropomorphic, exactly how he'd always been with Nelson.

He also discovered lions could live up to seventeen or eighteen years of age and realised the three orphans may not live past the next couple of weeks let alone nearly twenty years.

Having digested all the information he was still left unsure; he had little understanding of how to care for lion cubs and no idea of their basic needs.

Even the food they should have was a mystery, or, come to that, if they actually ate anything other than their mother's milk and it was the lack of information on food that worried him the most. If they were still at the suckling stage, Horatio knew there was little he could do to save them, and rather than letting them starve he would put them out of their misery himself.

*   *   *

413

Mid-morning on the first full day in camp, after his reading, Horatio was delighted when he searched the area the other side of the farm buildings and found a fresh water stream. A constant supply of drinking water was essential if he wanted to remain where he was.

Being anything but serious, Horatio then told Nelson to stay behind whilst he went in search of food. However, as he walked away, to his incredulity the falcon appeared to understand and instead of flying to his arm as usual, Nelson remained steadfastly perched on the wall watching over the sleeping cubs.

Horatio carried the loaded shotgun for his own protection, but following Kadiatou's advice, would kill his quarry using the spear gun. Unfortunately though, after setting out feeling optimistic, it proved to be one of the most maddening days he could remember.

When he first entered the forest, Horatio had immediately seen and heard an abundance of both birds and animals making the prospects of success realistic, but, he quickly learnt spotting and catching prey were entirely different things. He was actually quite hopeless.

*   *   *

In the end, more by good fortune than skill, he came across the carcass of a dead warthog on the edge of a road. The large beast was surrounded by vultures and other hangers on, but as soon as he approached, they reluctantly scattered.

Much to his relief, the almost complete body smelt fresh, so Horatio assumed it had only just died and using his machete, he removed both hind legs plus a meaty section around the shoulders.

*   *   *

Returning to camp, when Horatio was about fifty metres from the tent, he began calling out,

"Come little ones. I'm home, come to me."

Nelson squawked in reply, definitely answering the homecoming call, whilst the only effect it had on the cubs was to make them hurry back to their corner and curl up as one.

Sat by the fire, Horatio again tested the meat and decided it was definitely fresh. He selected a thigh for cooking on the fire, then cut into the flesh covering the rest of the leg and shoulder to make it easier for the cubs to get at the meat.

Feeling surprisingly anxious, chatting endlessly to no one, he crept towards the furry bundles and placed the food next to the water bowl, before retiring and retaking his seat against the far wall. He then watched enthralled as within just a few minutes a woolly, spotted bundle of fur crept towards dinner, followed a few moments later by a second and finally, a third. It was clear that not only had they been weaned, but they were starving.

A decidedly relieved Horatio laughed as he heard huffing, mewing and the strangest of noises whilst the three little ones gorged on the meat.

Later, after cooking and eating the hog meat which he found rich and delicious, he wrote up his journal and completed his calendar. He then checked on Nelson and the three orphans, who were back in an indistinguishable bundle of fur, completely crashed out, with every morsel of food having disappeared.

*   *   *

Once established, Horatio's daily routine changed little. After breakfast he waited for Nelson to return from hunting. Usually he would be carrying his catch, obviously intending to eat this perched on the wall, whilst he kept an eye on the cubs.

Horatio then sorted out the campsite, filled his water carriers from the stream, freshened up the cub's water bowl and remove all the stripped bones from the cubs' previous meal.

He would then walk about two hundred metres away from the tent and throw the leftovers into a ditch. Finally he would collect wood for the fire, to make torches.

Since his encounter with the lion near Labé, Horatio felt much safer moving around at night holding a flame, so he devised a way of binding thick sticks to long reeds, large leaves, brushwood and twigs. When lit it made a passable torch.

Once the jobs were finished, Horatio would take time out to sit as close to the cubs as possible without alarming them and would hold out one hand, encouraging them to approach. He also chatted endlessly, deciding it had worked with Nelson as a chick, so why not the cubs, although in all honesty, he could never imagine forming similar bonds with the orphans.

Then, on the third day there was limited success when one of the cubs crept up to him, sniffed his hand before scurrying back to its siblings. Horatio was ecstatic.

*   *   *

The daily search for meat typically followed an early, light lunch. Horatio would set out for the woods, occasionally going via overgrown fields to check if there was any prey close by.

From the first attempt, he'd tried to copy Kadiatou's example when hunting or setting snares and he remembered when she first saw the spear gun at Domani's farm. Seriously impressed she had experimented with it, telling him he should never waste cartridges to kill, adding that guns were loud and might alert people that you were close by.

The problem for Horatio though, was that no matter how hard he tried to implement her methods, he was on his own and when things didn't go well, he struggled to understand why.

As giving up was not an option, he began making snares and after hours of testing and retesting the design Kadiatou had recommended, he finally narrowed the problem down to an issue with the trigger's automatic release. Through trial and error, he found a way of using a strong but flexible twig to make the set-up simpler yet more reliable.

In essence, by skewering pieces of the previous day's kill onto the tip of the bolt and forcing the spear gun horizontally between the branches of a tree a metre off the ground, he could conceal it with brushwood and leaves.

Even with his change of design, Horatio's first six attempts proved a fiasco. Either the spear gun fell to the ground as it was not jammed effectively between the branches, the trigger did not release the bolt at the optimum moment, the meat was taken but the gun failed to discharge, or the prey was spooked and vanished into the trees.

However, on the seventh occasion, sat just twenty metres away patiently waiting, Horatio watched as a Spotted Hyena entered the clearing. Kadiatou had told him it was critical he was not too close to the snare, or the quarry would pick up his scent.

Sitting still whilst holding his breath was almost unbearable but Horatio was fascinated as the hyena moved cautiously smelling the air, circling the trap numerous times before eventually skulking towards the bait.

Finally Horatio's patience was rewarded when the hyena moved towards the meat and opened its mouth to devour its find. At that exact instant, there was a loud whoosh of air followed by the bolt flying at an inconceivable speed straight through the back of the animal's mouth and into its brain.

As he sat staring at the dying hyena convulsing in the last throws of life, Horatio had mixed emotions. He wasn't at all sure how he felt.

*   *   *

Whether it was tracking an animal or catching it before shooting it, each success made the process a little easier and although initially saddened by the slaughter, he came to accept it was as nature had intended. Many of the animals he hunted were carnivores themselves and he decided that if you lived by the sword, you deserved to die by the sword.

Most of his kills were hyenas and warthogs; possibly because they were some of the most effective scavengers, and as he became more competent at tracking and shooting prey, he also managed to kill African stripped weasels, the occasional green or patas monkey, Guinea baboons and a variety of mongoose; on occasions he even caught a small common Duikers antelope which the rapidly growing cubs adored tearing to pieces.

*   *   *

Horatio would regularly encourage Nelson to have a break from his duties and take flight as he set about cleaning and dividing the kill. Late in the afternoon as he delivered their food, he called the cubs, making certain they knew who had supplied their meat, and he would sit down, leaning against one of the side walls and talk endlessly.

Never bored as he watched them, whether it was at play or demolishing food, Horatio was truly enchanted. He would smile, laugh and giggle uncontrollably as he witnessed them squabbling over a simple plaything or a juicy chunk of meat. Day in and day out he witnessed them growing and gaining weight and he began to believe they might survive.

*   *   *

Initially, Horatio worried that so much of his time was taken up looking after the cubs' every need, he was left with little time for Nelson. However, in reality, it proved quite the opposite.

From his high perch, Nelson watched over the orphans day and night, clearly taking on the role of irreplaceable companion, exactly as Horatio had when he had been a chick. Was the falcon really replicating that role, believing he could have the same positive effect on the lion cubs that Horatio had had on him?

*   *   *

It was not long before Horatio discovered all three cubs were female, something he felt was probably a good thing. Having a male within the group would only complicate things and he really needed to keep their upbringing as simple as possible.

Not surprisingly, he also saw that they had entirely different personalities. The first to approach him, and the one who seemed least nervous, had a nick in her right ear and black spot close to her nose. She was by far the most adventurous and he named her Faith, as she had the most confidence in him.

Of the other two, one was the largest by some way but also the most fretful, never relaxing if Horatio was close by. She was a darker colour than the other two and always waited for Faith to take the lead then, when she saw everything was safe, would frequently takeover bullying the other two to get at something she wanted. He named her Hope, in the hope she would eventually come around to trusting him.

The third was the smallest and cutest; probably the runt of the litter, but with plenty of spirit and huge bravado. She had a lazy eye and lighter colouring than her sisters and Horatio loved the fact that although she was physically inferior and would let Faith take the lead, she was never far behind. She was willing to get stuck into whatever they were doing and refused to be bullied by Hope. Horatio named her Charity because in bodily terms, she might be the poor relation, but she would also always be there to back-up her siblings.

*   *   *

Faith, Hope and Charity; names Horatio had been captivated by as a young boy. After reading the inspirational story of the three timeworn aeroplanes that had taken on the Italian air force to defend the island of Malta in the Second World War, he had always been in awe of the exploits and courage of the pilots.

Three Gloster Sea Gladiators, part of a consignment of eighteen had arrived in Malta in March nineteen forty, originally bound for HMS Glorious. However, although many were shipped out to join various war efforts, some remained and they became the Malta Fighter Flight. It was these that stood against a vast armada of Italian fighters and bombers based under a hundred kilometres away in Sicily.

For nearly a fortnight they flew in twos or threes to thwart attacks and became known as 'Faith, Hope and Charity'.

Horatio still treasured the memories and could even recall the final citation in an article he'd read as a small boy; 'Outnumbered and out of date, these little aircraft and the fearless resistance they mounted on behalf of the Maltese people, have already become a legend almost without equal. Over time, the names Faith, Hope and Charity will become synonymous with courage and selflessness in the face of impossible odds and prove the perfect example to us all. They will assume a much loved and valued place in the mind-set of popular historical storytelling.'

* * *

Over the following two weeks, Horatio saw a marked change in the cubs. They grew physically stronger, their movements were becoming more controlled and coordinated, and their ever-increasing boldness was plain to see.

Fascinated by all that lay beyond the enclosure, they gingerly worked their way towards the tent and fire to discover what was out there. Then, one day after returning from his daily hunt Horatio could not find the cubs. Initially alarmed, he began to search for them, finally seeing Nelson about three hundred metres away flying low over the ground.

Calling out as he walked to the spot, he found the three cubs play fighting over a small rodent, one he later identified as a Senegal galago or bushbaby and incredibly, Nelson was keeping an eye on them.

Pleased they had succeeded in catching prey even it was extremely small, at least it was a start.

Regrettably though, Horatio saw the poor mite was still alive and the cubs were clearly not hungry, they just wanted some fun.

As he moved closer, Faith and Charity stepped back and he reached down to pick up the appallingly battered victim, intending to put it out of its misery. Hope, on the other hand, with a paw on the belly of the almost dead, galago, began to growl; she was standing her ground.

Horatio was delighted. He had been presented with the perfect opportunity to establish who was in charge. Forcibly, he pushed Hope to one side.

The cub's instant reaction was to leap straight back, before attempting to nip Horatio's hand. Seeing her coming, he made sure she missed, then grabbed her by the scruff of the neck, picked her up, smacked her hard on the nose and in no uncertain terms, tossed her away from the galago.

Hope was utterly stunned. She shook her head, clearly bewildered by what had just happened and for a few seconds stared defiantly at Horatio before coming to her senses and cowering as she skulked back to her sisters.

For Horatio, the point had been made. He was the boss.

After putting the galago out of its misery, and not wanting the cubs to think they had done wrong, Horatio threw the carcass towards them so they could carry on with their game.

He then noticed Nelson perched on a nearby tree. He'd obviously been scrutinising the incident as it played out. Calling him over, the falcon immediately landed on the arm protector and snuggled into Horatio's neck; he definitely approved of the lesson Hope had just received.

*   *   *

It may have taken time, but Horatio was overjoyed when the cubs began to accept him as leader of their small pride.

Although, that said, he also realised the closer they became, the more problematic any future parting of the ways would be.

Faith was the first to accept Horatio. After creeping up and sniffing him following their meal, unexpectedly she began to follow him as soon he entered their enclosure. She had obviously put two and two together and realised it was Horatio who provided their food and could therefore be trusted.

Charity was the next, mimicking her sister in appearing entirely untroubled being around Horatio, and she also began to follow him.

Sadly Hope continued to reject all his attempts to get close to her; her trust issues were obviously deep set and Horatio was not at all sure how to deal with them.

*   *   *

It was after a couple of colder nights that things began to change quite significantly.

After his earlier encounter with the lion, Horatio had decided to sleep under canvas. However, from the first night in the camp, he wanted to keep an eye on the cubs so he slept under the stars between the tent and the fire.

Towards the end of the third week he was woken by a very peculiar noise, and one that was worryingly close to him. Tentatively he felt around, only to discover a warm, furry cub under his blanket, curled up against him.

Remaining on his back, looking up at a beautifully clear starry sky, he assumed it was Faith.

From that night onwards, after initially being wrapped up with Charity and Hope in the corner of the enclosure, she would move in with Horatio and just a couple of nights later he found a second cub lying next to him; it was Charity.

Finally, to his disbelief, Hope must have been waking lone and cold and joined her sisters in their warm, comfortable bed.

Horatio found it interesting however, that Hope never lay alongside him, always keeping her distance, and that none of the cubs showed any fear of the fire.

Even Nelson, who was never far from the youngsters, moved his perch to a part of the wall overlooking the tent and fire. Although he no longer needed to stay awake to watch over them, his duties were far from over.

*   *   *

With the cubs growing and developing so rapidly and with Nelson appearing far more at ease, Horatio began to think about delaying their departure. Remaining where they were for even a few extra months, although disappointing in terms of him getting home, could prove crucial for the cubs' survival and although he was loathed to admit it, he was captivated by the three orphans and didn't want to disrupt the unexpected progress they were making.

Faith, like Nelson, was becoming an absolute joy in his life; she even began to demand Horatio play games with her; something he loved to do.

Charity, although initially more hesitant, learned to trust Horatio and spent more and more time with him, always wanting attention. And finally Hope, well… Hope was Hope and it was unlikely she would ever truly relax around him. Nonetheless, there were positives and Horatio could see that she was becoming calmer and less panicked by things going on around her, even when he was involved.

In reality though, he had little idea what the future held in terms of his bond with the cubs and came to the conclusion that no matter how long it took, he would not move on until all three were ready to face the world.

Chapter 47

Much to Horatio's dismay, the exuberant mood in the camp came to an abrupt end as darkness arrived on his thirtieth day with the cubs.

Following many hours of heavy rain, Horatio had fed the cubs and was raking through the fire, keeping it alight and burning strongly, when Nelson flew off. The falcon rarely ever left the three orphans, especially after dark, so clearly something had spooked him.

Without warning, there was a deafening roar and in the gloom Horatio could just about make out Nelson, high in the sky shrieking repeated warnings.

There followed a second growl, this time louder and closer still to the camp, and Horatio knew it was a lion heading in their direction.

His most pressing concern though was not for either himself or the cubs, but Nelson. The falcon was behaving in exactly the same manner as the previous time they had encountered a lion on the road from Labé; revealing no alarm, just repeatedly dive bombing the animal in a clear attempt to turn it away from the camp and cubs.

*　　　*　　　*

Despite his concern for Nelson, Horatio knew he should focus on the cubs. Time was critical as he remembered reading how male lions commonly killed cubs, especially if not their own. He had to get them to safety.

Initially he considered the farm buildings, but quickly rejected the idea. From searching them earlier, Horatio knew none would provide them with a safe haven strong enough to keep a lion out, especially if it was an adult male.

Suddenly there was a thunderous, third roar, nearer still, and in the ever-deteriorating light, Horatio heard Nelson's screeches change. He was becoming more and more agitated, but there was nothing he could do to help his dearest friend.

More growls followed and Horatio wondered if Nelson was having an effect. It certainly sounded as if the lion was incensed and he wondered if it was because he was being provoked by a bird.

Horatio ran to the enclosure and cubs, ignoring the fact that he would scare the living daylights out of them. He found them quaking, squeezed tightly together in their corner.

Without thinking, he grabbed the two nearest cubs by the scruff of their necks and with great difficulty due to how much they'd grown, ran back to the tent before literally hurling them through the open flap. He then returned for the third cub and realised because of her size, it was Hope. As he seized her neck, she instinctively slashed him across the face with her sharp claws, opening a large gash. Then, quite unbelievably she seized him around the neck hugging him with both her front paws, determined to hang on regardless.

As he entered the tent and deposited Hope with her sisters, Horatio heard Nelson creating mayhem; it gave him just enough time to zip up the flap.

*   *   *

Shotgun in hand, struggling to tie a rag to his cheek to stop the bleeding, Horatio faced the entrance to the tent and realised he could no longer hear Nelson.

Faith had a tight grasp on his leg, whilst Charity had moved as close as she could to him. It was only Hope who remained slightly behind, but even she was creeping ever closer to join her siblings.

Just seconds later, in the light from the fire, Horatio saw the shadow of a huge beast through the side panel of the tent. It was an adult male; its mane, the striking centrepiece of the silhouette passing by.

All three cubs moved as close to him as possible and stuck their heads under his blanket. All Horatio could do was stroke them and pray the canvas would protect them.

*   *   *

Avoiding the fire, the giant shadow ambled past the tent towards the three-walled enclosure. Holding his breath, Horatio detected little of the previous menace in the beast's demeanour and wondered where Nelson was.

There followed a noise of snuffling and chomping and it was evident the lion was eating the miniscule leftovers from the cub's meal.

Horatio looked at the cubs and even in their grim situation, he had to smile; the three were squeezed tightly together, their heads still stuck under his blanket, with their rear ends inelegantly exposed.

Moments later there was the most ear-piercing sound; the lion, who was just a metre away, roared as it sauntered towards the tent. Horatio then heard slurping before the entire side of the canvas began to shake and collapse inwards.

Clutching the shotgun he thought the monster was trying to bring down the tent, but then, with utter relief, he understood the lion was licking the sloping canvas to drink the residue from the earlier heavy rain.

*   *   *

Finally, Horatio watched as the shadow moved on, first bypassing the fire before delivering yet another resounding growl and vanishing into the night.

Waiting for what seemed like a lifetime, he used the time talking to the cubs, encouraging them to come out from under the blanket, but in truth he was solely focused on Nelson. All he could do was pray the bird was unharmed and had returned to the wall whilst waiting for them to leave the protection of the tent.

Once he felt the threat had passed, Horatio retied the bandage around the gash on his face then warily unfastened the flap of the tent and watchfully crawled out.

Faith followed, with Charity just a few seconds behind. Predictably, Hope stayed put, trusting only in the safety of the blanket.

Looking towards his latest perch on the wall of the enclosure, Nelson was nowhere to be seen and even though Horatio was nervous about drawing attention to themselves, he called out.

*   *   *

Although it was a beautifully clear, star-studded night, he still struggled to see the area close to the tent, let alone further afield.

Mindful of not wanting to scare Faith or Charity with a flame, he talked calmly to both as he lit a couple of torches and to his surprise neither backed away. Then, moving in circles, Horatio scoured the camp before widening the search area, finally arriving at the ditch with the discarded scraps. There was still no sign of Nelson.

Uncertain about what to do next, Horatio was about to turn back when he heard a strange noise close by. Assuming the cubs had found leftovers worth eating, he called them, but was ignored.

Holding the torches to the side, keeping the flames away from the sound, he closed in and saw Charity standing next to her sister. Faith's nose was almost touching the ground and she was whimpering, whilst frantically licking at a dark, indeterminate shape.

428

Horatio leant down and stroked her before moving her to one side. Faith had found Nelson.

*   *   *

With the falcon in his arms and tears in his eyes, Horatio carried Nelson back to the tent as the two cubs scampered beside him jumping up to see what was going on.

Horatio had little or no experience of injured birds; in all their time together, Nelson might have been fearless, even reckless, but he'd never appeared hurt, just indestructible.

Desperate for anything that might offer him just a smidgeon of hope, Horatio vaguely recalled when studying on the dining room table in the Berrow house, there had been a loud crash. When he investigated he found a bird had flown into his parent's patio doors and it looked as if the impact had killed it.

Horatio decided by its black and grey colouring, and size, it was a Jackdaw and as he had stroked the still warm feathery body, hoped it might be stunned rather than dead. He had placed the lifeless bird on a towel and left it in the garden shed and an hour later, when he went back to check on it, he found the bird perched upright. Horatio remembered being overjoyed when it flew off seemingly unharmed.

*   *   *

Throughout that night, sitting in the tent with a lifeless Nelson on a blanket in his arms, all three cubs settled down alongside Horatio, as close to their battered feathered friend and minder as possible.

As shadows from the flickering flames of the fire threw images across the tent, Horatio was touched by the loyalty of the cubs. Without doubt, for some unfathomable reason, three lion cubs and a falcon had formed an incredible, yet inimitable bond and Nelson's pain was their pain.

Horatio's day had been both physically and emotionally gruelling and although he'd pledged to stay awake, he couldn't make it through the night, eventually falling into a deep asleep.

*　　*　　*

But he had the perfect wakeup call.

Three cubs, bouncing, leaping and chasing each other around the tent whilst making the strangest of sounds, with Nelson perched on the shaft of the spear gun, flapping his wings and shrieking.

It was absolute mayhem and an overjoyed Horatio burst into laughter. Nelson then jumped onto his bare arm, oblivious to the pain his talons would inflict, before snuggling his head into his soulmate's neck, cooing softly.

Chapter 48

Horatio knew they had little choice but to move on. They were camped in the lion's territory and there was a good chance of him returning, so to remain where they were would put the cubs in serious danger.

He was also desperate to avoid Nelson coming into contact with the lion again. By his perilous tactics, the falcon had revealed how far he was prepared to go to protect the cubs and Horatio was desperate to avoid any repeat of his heroics.

It was much sooner than he would have liked, but Horatio decided moving on was not the end of the world. The cubs had survived thirty days in the camp, developing and growing by the day and Horatio felt all three, even Hope, had become sufficiently resilient and mature to handle the unfamiliar and alarming trials they'd face every day in the future.

*   *   *

Hoping if the lion returned it would be at a similar time in the evening, Horatio felt if they moved on without delay, by nightfall they should be relatively safe.

Unfortunately, he failed to include in his plans the small matter of how he would persuade three orphaned lion cubs to leave the only sanctuary they had ever known and follow him.

As soon as dawn broke, Horatio fixed his battered face with antiseptic cream and plasters from Myra's medical tin; the last thing he needed was an infection in the deep gash. He then packed his belongings before leaving the tent.

However, it was clear Nelson and the cubs had other ideas, remaining under canvas to continue their games. Horatio called them, wanting to pack away their canvas home and was ignored, so he began loosening the guy ropes, deciding when they realised what was happening they would join him outside.

As the side of the canvas began to collapse in on itself, the first out was a squawking Nelson followed swiftly by Faith and Charity. Hope of course, refused to budge; that was until the entire tent collapsed around her and she scrambled out. After seeing her sisters, she bounded over to them, immediately demanding to be licked and nose-butted by both her siblings.

As Horatio worked, Nelson remained perched on the wall checking on the cubs. They, in turn, were glaring at Horatio, clearly fretful and confused about what was going on.

After a quick snack and a final tidy of the camp site, Horatio stamped on the fire killing all the flames, to ensure there were no problems after they'd left.

Then, with the cart loaded, he took a last look around the campsite before calling the cubs and Nelson and pushing the bike towards the highway.

*   *   *

The old mud track that ran from the farm to the main road was overgrown and rutted, making it difficult to follow and this wasn't helped by the fact Horatio had to keep turning around to check on the cubs.

When he finally reached the tarmac, much to his irritation, only Faith and Charity were with him and there was no sign of Hope or Nelson.

Feeling a touch uneasy after the events of the previous night, Horatio reluctantly decided he would have to leave the bike and cart and walk back to the enclosure.

Not wanting to waste any time, he removed the shotgun and spear gun from the cart and although loathe to admit it, actually considered leaving Hope behind. She continued to struggle with anything new and he worried her frequent episodes of panic would hold them back. Horatio felt he really needed to get them to a safe campsite by nightfall.

He tried to convince himself that even though the last thing he wanted was for anything to happen to the cubs, if he had to choose between losing all three or saving two and losing one, no matter how painful, he would do it.

Suddenly shaken by his pathetic attempt to justify leaving Hope alone, Horatio shook his head to clear it and set off down the track. Almost immediately he noticed Nelson repeatedly swooping low to the ground and quite literally nipping Hope's hind quarters with his razor-sharp beak, as he flew by.

Laughing as he watched every pass the falcon made, and Hope spitting and squealing as she ran to escape the next bite, Horatio realised that quite incredibly, she was heading straight towards the road and her siblings.

Did Nelson really know what he was doing?

*   *   *

In almost perfect weather, Horatio worried that their progress was excruciatingly slow.

As he rode the bike down the centre of the highway he constantly called to the three little ones to keep up but the world surrounding them was far too thrilling and tempting.

Repeatedly stalking a movement or chasing a sound was so much more exciting than responding to Horatio, and even when he did finally succeed in getting them back to the tarmac, invariably they'd pounce on each other in mock battles.

Whether the distance they had travelled was sufficient to keep them safe, Horatio had no idea. If he was honest, he was so captivated by the three bundles of fun and their never-ending fascination with the strange world around them, he just let them get on with it.

*   *   *

As he listened to the cacophony of sounds from the forest and with fleeting glimpses of animals, birds and insects, nothing, not even his isolation from other people could dampen Horatio's love of life.

He was surrounded by Mother Nature, in the company of Nelson and three lion cubs, and apart from desperately missing his father and the twins, what more could he possibly want?

To be continued.

Acknowledgements

This first volume of 'The Second Coming of Eve', has only been possible with the help and advice of many friends.

Daniel, David and Sam at New Generation Publishing have, as always, been on the end of a phone or e-mail, happy to help in any way possible. Their continued support had been invaluable.

Sue Mead, Peter Brown, Ellis Davis, Ann Poole, Steph Lewis and my wife Gail have all been willing to give up considerable time to ensure the final manuscript is as error free as possible and my heartfelt thanks go to them.

Finally, Nick Roberts has worked closely with me on the covers and maps and I am extremely grateful for his creativity and expertise.

Lightning Source UK Ltd.
Milton Keynes UK
UKHW04f0243091018
330193UK00002B/51/P

9 781789 552683